A Log Across the Road

Part II: A State of Emergency

It is 1952, the height of the Malayan emergency. As ten men travel through the terrorist-infested jungle, one of them asks the question: 'What were *you* doing ten years ago?' This story answers that question.

Against a backdrop of the Second World War and the uneasy peace that followed, the pattern of their lives emerges. One man has known and loved the wives of two of his companions; one has fought with the terrorists he now pursues. After years of bitterness and hardship, another is about to find some happiness; a fourth can only face the past through a haze of alcohol.

But across those ten years their lives have touched. Gradually they are drawn together in a brilliantly complex pattern up to the day of their fateful journey through the jungle.

The first part of *A Log Across the Road*
Wars Within Wars
is also available in Fontana

SHEILA ROSS

A Log Across the Road

Part II: A State of Emergency

Every stream must join a river
before it can flow to the sea
MALAY PROVERB

Collins
FONTANA BOOKS

First published by Wm. Collins 1971
First issued in Fontana Books 1973

Printed in Great Britain
Collins Clear-Type Press
London and Glasgow

For all those who lost their lives during the Malayan Emergency, 1948-1960. And to those who were left behind.

This is wholly a work of fiction, but much of the story is based on fact. Kuala Jelang is an imaginary district and Perangor an imaginary state; so are all places mentioned in Malaya other than real state capitals and well-known resorts. All characters are fictitious and any resemblance to persons living or dead is purely coincidental.

My thanks are due to Group Captain Paul Gomez, CBE, RAF, for his help and advice and to his wife, Jean, for plodding through my original script with such patience and care. They are also due to my husband and daughter, without whose co-operation this book could not have been written.

CONTENTS

Book 1

IN WHICH THE STREAMS LEAVE THE WATERSHED

Section Two

Book 2

IN WHICH THE STREAMS JOIN THE RIVER

'A State of Emergency has been declared'

Book 3

IN WHICH THE RIVER FLOWS DOWN TO THE SEA

Kuala Jelang

'. . . Communist Terrorists attacked a vehicle carrying a number of civilians and members of the Security Forces in the Ulu Kuala Jelang are a yesterday. Altogether ten persons are missing. Security Forces are following up . . .'

Typical Malayan Press report, circa 1952

THE TEN

James Weatherby District Officer, Kuala Jelang

Philip Morrison Officer-in-Charge, Police District, Kuala Jelang

Stanislaus Olshewski Medical Officer, Kuala Jelang

Donald Thom Forestry Officer, Kuala Jelang

Sharif Ahmat Senior Inspector, Malayan Police

Jogindar Singh Sergeant-major, Malayan Police

Vincent Lee Chee Min Detective-sergeant, Malayan Police

Omar Corporal, Malayan Police

Abdul Karim Constable, Malayan Police

Ramakrishnan Clerk, Bukit Merah Estate, Kuala Jelang

BOOK I

IN WHICH
THE STREAMS LEAVE THE WATERSHED

Section Two

51. PEACE COMES TO TANJONG MAS

Omar

We had grumbled enough about having to work for the Japanese, but it was better than starvation. At least while we were working there was always a small ration of rice at the end of the day. But one day the lorries did not arrive to take us to work and that evening there was no rice at all. The ration that I received, enough for one person, did not go very far with my large family, but at least it was better than no rice at all. Adohi! What is there worse to hear than the cry of a hungry child?

They did not come the next day, nor the next, and, in fact, we never saw another Japanese.

We thought at first that the lorries had broken down and then perhaps that there was no more work for us for a few days; but a few days grew into weeks and then months and we knew that work was ended. I never dreamed that the day would come when I would wake every morning *hoping* to hear the Japanese, but that is how it was.

Rumours were rife, but where they came from I do not know. We waited and waited and nothing happened.

Perhaps, if we had been in better condition, we might have ventured forth to find out for ourselves. But it is difficult to use either your brain or your limbs when you have fallen into the state of lethargy that long-term hunger produces.

I did not move away from my own house very much, and if I did it was only to see that every other house was the same. People lolling on their steps or verandahs, too tired to take an interest in anything. Nothing moved. Not a cat or dog scraped among the sand, but only the occasional human being.

And so we waited, hoping that something would happen. Anything. We knew that nothing could be worse than seeing the little children dying of starvation and being powerless to prevent it.

When a lorry-load of soldiers did arrive we were almost beyond caring and it did not register with us immediately that they were white instead of yellow. We just stood and looked and I doubt if any of us had any thoughts in our heads at all.

There were two officers with the trucks and about a dozen

soldiers. After watching them for some minutes I think what struck me first was not their colour but that they were unarmed. We had grown so used to the sight of Japanese soldiers and their generous use of the rifle butt and bayonet that it seemed strange to see soldiers without any rifles at all.

One of the officers spoke Malay and carried a loudspeaker. Through this he addressed the kampong, telling us first that the war was over and that there was nothing more to fear and, secondly, that the other officer was a doctor who would examine all members of the kampong and issue medicine where necessary.

Many of my people are still not used to Western medicine and as soon as they heard this most of the women and children began to creep away. Remembering how often I had wished that there had been a doctor for Zaitun, I called to the women not to be so foolish.

Quite suddenly the terrible apathy fell away from me and the years of discipline and training came to my aid. I remembered who I was.

I would like to say that I marched smartly up to the officer and saluted, but that would not be true. It is difficult to look smart in a threadbare pair of shorts, patched with pieces from many sarongs and flour-bags, and it had been many months since I had owned any kind of shirt or shoes. I could not have saluted, as I no longer had a songkok or any head covering, and it is quite impossible to march at all when your legs are as swollen with beri-beri as mine were, let alone come to attention. I suppose I waddled over and stood as straight as I could, and at least my voice was still strong.

'428 Corporal Omar reporting, sir.'

There were several other police who had evaded the oath, or were deserters like myself, but I was the senior. It was my duty to take charge.

'Ah, good. Well, Corporal, will you explain that we are only here to help and try and get these people into some sort of line.'

He seemed quite unperturbed by my garb and, to be treated as an NCO again, made me feel I was still a man after all.

My colleagues were quick to follow my example and in no time we had an orderly queue of women, children and old men lined up before the doctor.

He was a very young man, and when I took Zaitun before him I felt too modest to explain what had been the cause of her affliction, especially when the other officer had to interpret. But I think he understood. He shook his head and I felt him to be sympathetic, but the other officer told me that, although a consultation with another doctor would be arranged, he doubted if anything could be done.

The soldiers meanwhile had off-loaded the truck and were busy doling out rice, salt, dried and tinned fish, milk, vitamin tablets, and, most blessed boon of all, cigarettes. When you have smoked grass, palm leaf, and even seaweed for three years, there is nothing more wonderful than that first inhalation of real tobacco.

The lorry came every day for a week, and after the second day the children would wait for it to turn off the main road and follow it, shouting and laughing and catching the bars of chocolate and fruit which the soldiers threw to them. What sound can give more pleasure than the happy laughter of little children?

On the third day a European woman came with the lorry. She wore a grey dress with a red cross on her arm. She was a nurse, but she gave us all clothes; shirts and shorts, sarongs and blankets. The children tore round the kampong, posturing and gesturing and dressing-up, as children love to do. It was like Hari Raya!

At the end of the week the Malay-speaking officer came again and told all of us, police and soldiers, that the next day a truck would collect us, to take us to the Central Police Station, where one of our own officers would interview us.

We were like children returning from the town.

The officer had been in army uniform, but with the police badge in his cap, and was as thin and undernourished as the rest of us. After he had taken down the particulars of each man and we had been photographed, fingerprinted and issued with the rudiments of uniform, we had all met in the police canteen for glasses of coffee.

Men had been brought in from villages all over the state; Malays, Sikhs, Punjabis, and a few Chinese. Wah! So much news to impart, so many stories to listen to. The officer, the only European there, had been a prisoner of war in Singapore and, as he was a bachelor, had volunteered to work for a few weeks before going on leave.

'You'll have to find a wife to feed you up, Tuan,' we told him – we were very bold!

'Your wives don't seem to have done much for you!' he retorted.

Rank and station were put aside. We were sorry when a sergeant came to tell us that we had all been granted fourteen days' leave with pay and now we would be transported back to our kampongs and must report for duty in a fortnight's time.

Wah! Was my wife impressed by the real money I laid on the table. But she laughed at my uniform, hanging on me like one of the dummies we used to place in the padi fields to scare off the birds.

All the children laughed and danced round me – they had energy to spare again these days, Tuan Allah be praised. Only little Zaitun, nearly fifteen now, sat smiling into space while she played with the petals of a moonflower.

52. RETURN TO DAUN CHEMPAKA

Sharif Ahmat

It was the end of the year before we reached our kampong.

We had all suffered from the anticlimax immediately following the surrender. Being keyed up for the invasion for so long, trained and retrained to take part in the fighting and prepared to meet the British and partner them when they arrived, to help them harry the Japs from the peninsula, it was frustrating just to sit and wait. One by one the guerillas quietly faded away. We presumed that they were making for Pahang and Perak, where their colleagues had virtually taken over certain areas and declared their own government. It was an exasperating time all right, those few months between the surrender of the Japs and the British return.

I went down to Singapore with Hassan and the European officers after Lord Mountbatten had accepted the surrender. It was the first time I had been there and I felt a real country bumpkin, marvelling at the city, with its tall buildings and magnificent harbour.

After that we reported to our own headquarters in Kuala Lumpur; then for a long leave.

I cannot, even now, tell you what that homecoming was like without getting a lump in my throat and gooseflesh on my arms. Already there were animals again, cropping the grass that spread below the grove of chempaka trees for which the village is named. The scent wafted towards us and the breeze blew the white flowers down to form a fragrant carpet on the sward. It was beautiful.

But what is there more beautiful, more tender, than a mother's love? I had not seen my mother since that fateful day nearly three years ago and was shocked by her appearance. Always small, she seemed to have shrunk to doll size; the skin hung loosely on a body of skeletal thinness and her hair was streaked with grey.

But her eyes, those huge eyes, which I have seen filled with stern pride, laughter and sorrow. Those eyes, when she perceived her eldest son – he whom she had thought lost for the past five years, he who had been her first-born pride and joy, he who had always treated her with love more than respect – they seemed like great pools of soft brown velvet. Shining with a light of such rare happiness that everyone who had come forward when they saw Hassan and me approaching, turned their own eyes to her and smiled in sympathy.

Gone was my mother's dignified restraint. With a cry like a young girl, she dropped whatever it was she had been holding and flew to Hassan like a homing bird.

My brother is tall, taller than me, and he lifted her like a child; patting and hugging her as one does a child. I saw her tears overflow and wet the shoulder of his shirt and watched as he pulled a handkerchief from his pocket and wiped those tears away.

Women went flying in every direction to prepare a meal; men pressed forward to ask question after question, and the children stood and gaped, fingers to mouths and eyes wide.

The terrible reprisals of 1943 had been accepted as part of the fortunes, or evils, of war, and my sister's wedding day became just one of the many occupation memories, to be talked of, put aside and resurrected as the conversation ebbed and flowed in its endless circle.

Hassan was to march in the Victory Parade in London and he now became not only my mother's pride, but that of the entire kampong.

They were happy months, those of early 1946. For my mother, the first happiness after three years of sorrow, and for us, her ambitious sons, a new beginning.

53. BETTER LATE THAN NEVER

Jogindar Singh

I waited until the end of the year in Singapore. Long enough to terminate my employment with the prison and to be on the spot for news of my family. But when, after three months, no one had contacted my uncle, I set off for Kuala Lumpur.

I had never been to the Police Depot before, although I had often heard my father speak of it. It seemed that where-ever one looked there were barrack blocks, offices, parade grounds, MT yards, games fields and officers' quarters. It was huge. People were everywhere and I felt that there must be someone here who would at least have known my father at one time, if not the present whereabouts of his dependants.

During the course of the day, I spoke to a Sikh officer, ASP Ram Singh, who had, I had been told, spent most of the war as an inspector in Batu Rimau, which was where my mother's family had lived. He could not help me as far as my father were concerned, but he did suggest that, if I intended enlisting, I should do so without delay, and certainly before I went north to make further inquiries.

'When so many men are enlisting or returning to the Force,' he advised, 'even a few weeks may make a great deal of difference to your seniority in the long run.'

I took his advice and, to my surprise, when I returned the next morning with my completed application forms, I was told that the Adjutant wanted to see me.

I was even more surprised when he shook hands and told me to sit down.

The Adjutant was a European ASP who had spent the war in the army and had only recently returned to Malaya – he told me this during the course of our conversation, but mostly it was about myself.

'We've been expecting you to appear,' he told me, 'and I gave orders that you were to be sent in to me when you did.'

I was not kept waiting long for an explanation. He pulled open a drawer and extracted a file of letters and soon had one smoothed out in front of him. It was one of those blue air mail sheets and I could see that it had an English stamp on it.

By this time I already had out my own letters – the ones that had been given to me in prison more than a year before. I put them on the desk tentatively and the Adjutant looked up.

'What are those?' he asked.

I explained.

'Ah,' he leafed through them until he came to a name, Boswell, then he tapped the letter before him. 'One of the Assistant Commissioners, Mr Boswell, whom you knew in internment, had hoped to be back by this time, but he's not fit yet – if he ever will be – so he's written out a list, both black and white, of personalities with police connections with whom he came into contact during the war. I'm afraid that on the whole your compatriots did not show up too well, but there is a short list of praise-earners. I am pleased to say that your name is on it.'

We talked for a little longer while the Adjutant read through my testimonials; then he handed them back and got up.

'The Force is proud of men like your father and yourself,' he said. 'I wish you the best of luck in your future career.'

He shook hands again and I was soon back with ASP Ram Singh, completing formalities. My next move was northwards to Perak, and I spent several weeks going from place to place, following rumours and advice, in search of my family. But I never did discover what had happened to them, and now I suppose I never shall.

It was pointless to delay my training any longer, and when the next intake was admitted to the Depot, I was with them. I should have been a recruit five years ago; still, as my uncle says, better late than never.

54. AN IDYLL REPAIRED

James Weatherby

It was a wonderful day when James was finally able to leave the hospital. Wonderful for the staff too, I should think – it had been difficult enough for me, visiting him, but how they kept their tempers I shall never know. The Matron informed me that in all her years of nursing, she had never come across such an impossible man – she said it in front of him though and with a twinkle in her eyes, so I felt there was hope.

We were married very quietly early in the new year, just a year after his last flight. But I didn't marry an Air Commodore. James was bitter, and it was no use explaining to him that his prang had had nothing to do with it, it was just the end of the war. He didn't want to believe anything good at that time, and when Substantive Wing Commander, War Substantive Group Captain, Acting Air Commodore Weatherby left the hospital as plain Wing Commander, he could hardly bear to put on his uniform.

I suppose you can guess where we spent our wedding night? Yes, we went to the pub where we'd had that silly row. At first I had not been keen, afraid that it would fall flat, but I was wrong, thank God.

I'm not sure that the receptionist recognised him until he signed his name – and even that looked different now, signed with the other hand – but when she looked up he was waving our marriage certificate under her nose and there, for the first time in a year, was that old, wonderful, white grin.

'Married at last,' he told all and sundry, 'and if I still had two arms I'd carry her over the threshold – lump though she may be!'

I found it difficult not to cry. All the emotion that had been pent up for so long threatened to overflow. I said nothing; just looked at him, and I saw the old James shining through and knew that it would be all right. I took his arm and led him towards the stairs.

I wore the same dress too, but it was a shock, looking in the mirror, to see how much I had aged in only a year. I was only twenty-eight and James was under thirty still, but we both had grey in our hair. I had to fasten my own pearls this time and I saw him frown and bite his lip, but I did my best to pass it off.

I did not take a bag down to dinner that night.

I had met James's parents on several occasions, and knowing how they would love to have him at home for a time, I had suggested that we spent his leave there. A honeymoon could come later, I thought, and so did he.

We spent two days at our pub, then travelled down to Devon by train. Poor lamb; I watched him as he slept, head jolting with the motion of the carriage. I would have to forgive his tempers, I knew. It wasn't only losing his eye and his arm. He did not regret losing his wife, but he had also lost his son – Elsie claimed custody of the child and he did not contest it – but I knew he loved the little boy. It would be up to me to make up for some of the unhappiness he had had, to ease his loss and help him in his still so longed-for career.

It was six years since I had first taken Elsie home as my wife and four since I had first met Helen. We had been over storm-tossed seas. But when I looked at my adored wife, helping my adored mother, and as happy in the company of Nannie and my father as they were with her, for the first time in my adult life I didn't care a damn if I never saw the air force again.

We had three months with my parents and when, at the end of the second month, Helen felt sick one morning and told me she was pregnant, I slid down the banisters and shouted the glad tidings for all to hear.

'You'll come and look after us, won't you, Nannie?' I sang, and waltzed her round the kitchen, frying pan in hand. She pushed me away and carried on cooking the breakfast.

'She hasn't had it yet,' she said dryly, but I could see she was as pleased as I.

I groaned when my posting came through though. Air Ministry. Oh well, I suppose I could expect pen-pushing from now on. But AM, oh Gawd.

'Ever hear of a General who hadn't done a spell in War Office?' Helen asked me, and my father backed her up. 'Well, be thankful they haven't thrown you out.'

She could be tart, my spouse.

Once our destination was known, Helen went off to London – which she knew far better than I – to house-hunt. She had luck too and rang me up the next evening with her news. She'd found a flat in Richmond – I nearly had a heart attack when I heard the rent, but I told her to take it just the same. A year of incarceration had not been hard on my bank balance and, after all, we weren't too badly off.

She came back, tired and hungry and full of plans. She talked while the three of us sat and listened, and my mother put an arm round her and told me that it would be worth losing both arms to gain a wife like her, but not both eyes. I agreed.

Taken by and large, I was, for the first time in many years, a very happy man.

Our daughter, Angela, was born in the winter of that year, 1946. Poor Helen, it was the coldest winter in our memory and I fretted the whole way to the hospital, terrified that we would be stopped by snow.

I was glad it, she, was a girl. I had no desire ever to see Elsie again, but I did miss my son. But for all Elsie's faults, she had been a good mum, and it didn't seem right to upset the boy, so I made no attempt to see him.

I wanted another son, one day, but for the present I was glad to be able to love the tiny thing without feeling that I abandoned Toby. And Helen? Helen wanted what I wanted. It was not selfishness on my part, we just wanted the same things. Helen is a wonderful wife.

55. WEALTHY AND NOTABLE LOVER GENTLEMAN

Ramakrishnan

It is for long time that I am lying low after re-entry of most hated British. I am glad when Bengali police chief is having transfer to more salubrious post, for who knows what this prideful fellow might pass on in way of informations, false or true?

Truly I am most disillusioned man; disappointed in behaviour of would-be Nipponese saviours and fellow-countrymen both. Everybody is welcoming back British pigs and forgetting state of slavery endured hithertofore. Mr Ramasamy, no relation, is forever rubbing fat hands and pronouncing satisfaction at future prospects when all white peoples are returning, gentlemen and ladies both, to do deals with him in silk store, and already new stocks are being received from countries far and near.

It is eleven months precisely that I am working for Mr Ramasamy, no relation, when said gentleman indicates ripe daughter Devi and again makes mention of fact that loyal workers can be expecting rewards.

When before I am holding trumping card, I am thinking it is because husbands of Tamil race are between few and far in district. But in new Colonial era this is no longer so. Many Indians of diverse races and dialects are travelling country length and breadth, so I am knowing that there is other reason afoot.

Aha! I am saying to myself one day after much careful watching and observation both. 'Mister,' I am saying, 'I am after knowing full well why it is that husband is required for Miss Devi. For it is very plain that she is big in belly.'

At that, said gentleman goes most ashen colour and wrings hands in supplication most humble, denying all such happenings and maintaining that Miss Devi is virgin most pure and unsoiled.

I am waiting for two weeks over when Mr Boss Ramasamy, no relation, is relating at last truthful and sordid facts regarding daughters.

'It is true,' he is telling me, 'that Devi is with child, and second daughter also. It is most shaming thing to happen to daughters who have become, alas, overripe. I will raise wages of you and Devan both if you will marry my daughters before their time.'

Devan is assistant next senior to self.

'I will be clerk,' I say.

'Very well, man. Clerk it is.'

For new status I am demanding three pairs each white drill trousers, three shirts of silk, and socks of various colourings. Also desk in back but prominent part of store, with pile of ledgers and trays for innings and outings.

'I have fulfilled my part of the bargain,' Mr Ramasamy, not yet relation, is saying after one more month, 'you are now clerk, with desk and ledgers and much face. What more do you want before marriage takes place?'

For reply I am asking, 'And what colour will child be, man?' Yellow, I am thinking.

'Oh no,' said gentleman is wringing hands, 'Nipponese had already left before. Child is black, man. Of that there is no doubt.'

And when I am not believing that such opinions can be proven, Mr Ramasamy, not yet relation, is telling me story most long-winded and specious.

'Father is married man,' he is saying, 'most distinguished and wealthy notable of our own race. Only I am not having daughter taken as second wife or concubine. For that reason only I am wishing husbands for daughters both.'

If he is wealthy man, I am thinking, I can demand funds whatever, and am putting said proposition before Mr Ramasamy, boss.

He is wringing hands again and rolling eyes every which ways.

'He must not know that I have told you,' he says, 'he is most proud and haughty fellow. But I will raise wages by further five dollars *per mensum* and will recoup from this gentleman in due course.'

'Twenty dollars.'

'My God, man. Are you for bleeding me dry?'

'If he is wealthy man, you can ask favours for allowing fornication with said daughters,' I am saying.

'All right. Twenty dollars. But he will be angry, mind. And now will you give a date?'

'I am thinking about it,' I say.

Truly I am holding trumping card.

But that is now more than four months back and I am rich man now. How I am becoming rich man I will relate as follows:

I have been clerk for one month when door of most inglorious happenings is opened to me.

Every afternoon for as long as I have been undertaking lowly employment in silk store, I am seeing Devi or other of ripe daughters entering shed at far ending of orchard field.

Aha! I am thinking, this is where they are trysting with wealthy and notable lover gentleman. If I am recognising him, fifty dollars, or even one hundred and fifty, will not be too much rising in wages.

Also, sometimes I am seeing Mr Ramasamy, no relation, entering same hut and I am betting that he is receiving fat payments from wealthy lover gentleman. Truly he is man of many diverse leanings, silk store owner, cattle man, market gardener, and pimp both.

I am watching for several afternoons between two and four o'clock precisely from behind cattle shed. I am seeing Miss Devi and two sisters approach orchard shed and also Mr Ramasamy, no relation, but no lover gentleman. All are going higgledy-piggledy, at different times, towards shed and verily my head is being buzzed and muddling by all these comings and goings.

Next morning I am approaching said shed myself.

It is only small shed with sleeping platform taking up half of space, with bolsters and mats. Over high window above platform is pulled old faded sarong on strand of wire.

On instant I am having most clarified idea. I am standing on platform and drawing curtain to give inch of view to one side. Window is next to tree and concealment in foliage therefore is easy task. I can be peeping tom and, once recognition of wealthy lover gentleman has taken place, blackmail is forever possible.

Next afternoon I am already hiding in tree when Devi is coming to shed. Without ados she is taking off all garments and prostrating herself on sleeping mat. Truly I am finding it hard to remain in tree.

Miss Devi is of rounded proportions most goodly and of skin lighter in colour than Muriani, who was field worker and not spoilt daughter of most bountiful father and plaything of wealthy and notable lover gentleman.

I am still enjoying view of future bride when door is opening to admit white garbed gentleman, and Miss Devi is already rolling eyes, wriggling and giggling. Man, it is being difficult exceeding to remain in tree under such circumstances.

Gentleman is remaining with back turned – and why for should he look at wall or window when there is spectacle on sleeping mat most goodly to behold? I can see from motionings that he is lifting dhoti, then he too is prostrating himself and lifts head for me to see face first time.

Good gracious me! This is moment I am waiting for and indeed shock is being so great that I am tumbling topsy-turvy, upside down, and hugger-mugger from leafy bower and hitting head with most uncomfortable knock against roots of tree. Truly this Mr Ramasamy is of personality most wily and vexatious.

It is not taking me long to reach conclusion that only with observance most patient and catching of Mr. Ramasamy in position of undeniable guilt can blackmail be maintained to fullest extent. And so I must be biding time for ripe moment.

I am taking up position on following afternoon in foliage most luxurious and concealing. But this time I am carrying notebook in which to record all details for future confrontation of Mr Ramasamy, no relation.

This afternoon, performance is with second daughter and I am pleased to note that shape and skin are of lesser quality than that of Miss Devi, having less shine and showing bony structures, which are not made for comfort and joy both.

Every afternoon I am peeping. Verily Mr Ramasamy's actions with Miss Devi are filling me with disgust most horrible and vile. I am hardly able to watch ; and so I am going again to see next day and next.

After six days my notebook is nearly full of revolting details and at moment of conclusion I am breaking glass of window, shouting rightful abuse and waving notebook at Mr Ramasamy, no relation.

'Oh, perpetrator of most dastardly crime,' I am shouting,

'pimp most incestuously inclined and filthy swine both. I have seen and recorded every vile act of impurification. I am telling you, Mister, you are tossing on troublesome seas forthwith.'

Aha! Indeed I have caught rogue most red-handed and he is turning colour of greenish grey, like shed skin of grass snake or old cattle manure both. He is blubbering and wailing so that I cannot make out actual words.

'You had better see me in office, Mister,' I shout, and leave him in state of botheration most extreme.

When he is arriving at store, Mr Ramasamy is not being so flustered, but still very agitated man. There is no need to mention terms, because said future father-in-law is mentioning them for me.

'I can get you good job as estate clerk on Tanah Kuning Estate, where Chief Clerk is friend and brother,' he says, 'and I will pay you so much *per mensum* for the rest of my life if you will marry Devi now and take her away from here.'

'And what sum will you be paying each month?' I ask, striking the hot iron.

'Fifty dollars.'

'One hundred.'

'Seventy-five.'

'One hundred.'

'Eighty.'

'One hundred dollars,' I say, 'and that is final, Mister. One hundred dollars *per mensum*, each and all properties to be bequeathed in will and testament at time of death.'

Mr Ramasamy, future father-in-law, groans and is saying I am hard man and I am telling him that he is incestuous bastard and reminding that at present time only future son-in-law has knowledge of such acts.

So it is coming to pass that I am taking Miss Devi, daughter of Ramasamy, to wife and am taking up abode and most congenial position as clerk on Tanah Kuning Estate. With father-in-law Ramasamy's cash arriving each month on dot and wage more dignified than hitherto received, yours truly is beginning to find world less disillusioned place.

My wife is giving birth one month precisely after marriage. But child is of sickly disposition and within three months is succumbing to enteritis, with much vomiting and purging. I am not minding and have already made sure that wife's belly is large once more. No more chances are being taken and making sure that belly is full always is most efficacious method of preventing bastards arising therefrom. Also Devi is most rounded and goodly to look upon when pregnant, and it is therefore all round most congenial proceeding.

56. THE REUNION

Abdul Karim

It was several weeks after the war ended that the news seeped through to Pasir Perak. We had seen very little of the Japs, so it made little difference to us at first.

Then one day Inche Yacob, our headmaster, made the announcement to the whole school and declared a holiday. 'Not that your parents will bless me,' he said. He was always saying things like that!

Of course, the first thing my father did was to uncover his boat from where it had been hidden under the passion vine for so long. Wah! What a state it was in. But we soon got to work and it wasn't long before he was off to sea again and we had as much fish to eat as we wanted for, of course, the seas were teeming, not having been fished for so long.

But it's August 1946 now and that was nearly a year ago. Nothing much happened in the kampong, except, of course, that there was food in the shops again, and cloth and tools. As far as I was concerned I still went to school every day and played with my friends or helped Pak in the afternoons. But the day I want to tell you about was when I was on holiday and he had agreed to take me, with Rokiah and Noraini and Musah – my classmate, whom I disliked, but my father thought smart – on a turtle-egg collecting expedition. We do this sometimes during the holidays and usually stay out all night.

Pak was in a very good mood on that occasion and made jokes about Noraini's white face showing up in the moonlight and how we would have to blacken it first with the embers from the fire!

Noraini can be quite cheeky and told my father that, if he wanted his meal, he would have to be nice to her – imagine a real Malay girl saying that! Mak says there are some things which are in the blood and can never be changed and I'm beginning to think she's right.

We all collected driftwood for the fire, then the two girls prepared the meal, fresh fish which we had caught with our casting nets in the shallow water.

Every so often we would walk along the beach to see how the turtles were getting on, but you can't hurry a turtle, so we were able to enjoy our meal with plenty of time.

What better food is there than that caught fresh and eaten fresh from your own fire on the beach on a cool night? I hoped everything would go well and Pak would take us out again. It was more fun when we had the girls to cook for us than when we went out on our own.

Our turtles are protected. That means that they cannot be killed for meat, and during the mating season certain parts of the beach are reserved and no one is allowed to disturb them. Several of the turtles we watched that evening were over five feet long and nearly as wide. Wah! I'm sure that's where the idea of tanks came from!

They crawl slowly, slowly out of the sea, the tide touching them less and less each time, until they are on the sand, then they stop and rest for a while – it always seems ages to me.

Then comes the long passage up the beach. Adohi! They move so slowly that I would like to give one a good kick, but Pak says I would only break my toes. They groan and grunt as they heave their lumbering great bodies up the beach, leaving two tracks behind them, exactly like those I've seen in pictures of where tanks have been – you see, I was right. I don't know how much they weigh, but it must be a great effort to heave all that armour plating across the sand.

At last the turtle reaches what she considers a good spot to lay her eggs, then we're in for another long wait. Eventually she begins to dig – and you should see the sand fly when those flippers get to work. This is when we must start watching carefully, because one she's finished laying she will cover her eggs up and we may not be able to find them again.

There is a deep, deep hole, four feet or more, before the turtle is satisfied, then she places herself over it and begins to lay. Plop, pause, plop, pause. The eggs that look so like ping-pong balls fall into the hole.

We spread out and took one turtle each to watch. I must admit I grew a little bored – keeping still for so long is not much fun and Pak would have been furious if we had disturbed them.

When my turtle had finished laying and covered up her eggs, I marked the spot with a cairn of coconut husks and went back to the fire.

Noraini was already there, wide-eyed and bubbling with excitement. It was the first time she had seen the giant turtles so close to.

'When I grow up, I'm going to marry a turtle fisherman,' she announced, 'then I'll make him take me with him every time. I'd never get bored.'

'I would. I'm not going to be a turtle fisherman. It's all right going with Pak, for fun.'

The first green streaks of dawn were appearing in the sky and I was cold.

'Let us fetch more wood,' I suggested, 'and remake the fire.'

By the time it was really light, all the turtles had returned to the sea and it was easy to go back to the marked spots and dig up the eggs. The law only allowed us to take a certain number of eggs – the rest have to be allowed to hatch out – so when we had taken our lot, we covered each hole over again and smoothed the sand.

We had come some way from the kampong, so into the boat went the sacks of eggs, followed by us. Pak started up the outboard and we chugged home, tired and pleased with ourselves.

But our adventures were not over for the day.

Pak had counted the eggs, put some aside for sale and a number to keep ourselves, then the rest he had divided into two smaller sacks for Che Fatimah.

As we entered her garden, Pak and I, each with a sack over our shoulders, and Rokiah and Noraini walking just ahead, a voice called out, 'Hold it,' and there was the click of a camera.

We were all so surprised that none of us moved until Rokiah's mother and aunt came forward to greet us.

Two smiling, young Chinese came forward as well, both in white drill slacks and long-sleeved shirts and ties – I'd never seen anyone wearing a tie in our kampong before.

Both men wore gold wrist watches and pulled out packets of cigarettes, which they offered to my father. One of them had a camera slung round his neck from a leather strap and the other carried an open notebook and several propelling pencils of different colours in his shirt pocket.

'And what's your name, little girl?' The one with the notebook asked Noraini in English.

She just shook her head and giggled behind her hand.

After that they stuck to Malay, asking both Noraini and Che Fatimah question after question.

Che Fatimah repeated the story we had heard so often, then they asked Noraini how she liked school and a lot of other things which did not seem to have anything to do with having a white skin and freckles. Then they asked Rokiah and me some questions too.

They took some more photographs then; not of Pak and me, but of Che Fatimah and the two girls. My deadly hatred, Musah, had arrived and in the last picture he was standing between Rokiah and Noraini, holding a hand of each. He spoke to the reporters in their own dialect and looked so superior that I dug my nails into my palms with rage.

Just then four Europeans walked into the garden; three men and a woman. Two of the men, one of whom was a police officer, I had seen before, but the others were strangers. The woman had coppery-coloured hair, streaked with grey, and she walked slowly, with a funny look on her face, happy and worried at the same time, sort of excited, but scared.

I looked at Noraini then and my mouth fell open. I wished I had been listening, but I had heard Che Fatimah's story so many times that my mind had wandered. Pak told me afterwards that the Europeans – Noraini's parents, of course – had arrived much earlier and had gone for a walk while they were waiting.

By this time quite a crowd had gathered. Someone motioned the reporters to step aside and the woman advanced towards Noraini. No one else moved and the only sound was the surf frothing on the beach and the clack-clack of the palm fronds in the breeze. She went down on one knee before Noraini and put her arms round her waist. Noraini just stared. Then her mother leaned her forehead against her daughter's – she was a tall woman and Noraini is very small – and I saw tears falling on the sand between them. The heads matched.

A sigh went up from the crowd and Che Fatimah began to cry. Then the woman's husband lifted her up and stood with an arm around each pair of shoulders. The camera clicked again.

Poor Che Fatimah. Noraini has gone. Not at once; her parents visited her every day for a few days, to let her get used to them, then they took her away. Che Fatimah has a big sum of money now and a handsome coffee service, but she says it is not the same. I think Rokiah is lonely too.

Che Fatimah had not been too happy about the interviews with the reporters – whose paper was taking much of the credit for finding Noraini – but when she received a complimentary copy of the Malay edition of the newspaper, she swelled with pride.

Rokiah came running to our house with the paper for Pak to read. There we were, right on the front page, Pak and I looking like a couple of surprised monkeys, with our shoulders bent under the sacks, and the two girls, hand-in-hand, and all of us gaping wide mouthed.

'Wah!' said my father, 'it certainly looks as though Che Fatimah has a couple of village idiots for friends!'

'HUNT ENDS IN REMOTE EAST COAST KAMPONG' were the headlines.

Underneath, in slightly smaller letters: 'Malay woman defends European child against Japs.'

And below that: 'Thou good and faithful servant, well done.'

And then in ordinary print, first how the parents had spent a year trying to trace their daughter, then Che Fatimah's story – only it didn't sound quite the same as when she told it. Noraini seemed to have gone through a far more adventurous time once she had reached Pasir Perak than we had realised.

'Wah!' exclaimed my mother, listening as Pak read the article aloud, 'I didn't know that the Japanese had been here, and in and out of our houses, so often. And fancy never suspecting that Noraini had spent all those hours hidden up trees and under the floorboards!'

Of course Mak believes everything that is printed and my father got quite cross with her, calling her a stupid, ignorant woman, who could be taken in by fairy-tales, just like the rest of them.

The whole article painted the courage and loyalty of Che Fatimah in such glowing terms that she was too pleased to deny some of the silly things that were said.

57. STRANGERS IN UNIFORM

Philip Morrison

Have you ever been afraid to meet your wife? It was ridiculous. I had moved heaven and earth to get myself posted home or to get Sally out and, now that the train was actually stopping and a porter was walking down the platform, calling, 'Victoria, Victoria,' I was terrified.

Of course, I had been stupid to stay on in Italy in the first place. When the Germans finally had capitulated and we had walked out to meet our own troops, I could have gone. But like a mug I had volunteered to stay on – mainly because I wanted to make sure that the Scum were not badly done by and to follow up on the notes I had left with the various people who had helped me escape. And then, of course, I was caught.

I had nothing to prove that I was married, and Sally – who can be extremely obstinate – would not send the certificate. She still has that bee in her bonnet that it will pay us in the long run to keep our marriage quiet until it suits us. You can't argue with her. She couldn't have got a posting to Italy anyway, because she's dug in in some Far East intelligence job, and she couldn't join me as my wife because she wouldn't admit to being one.

But that was past history now. I had left, and all the way through Europe on the MEDLOC train I had been filled with alternate waves of excitement at the thought of seeing her again and a terrible hope that perhaps she had not been able to get leave. And here we were.

Standing on the boat-train platform, waiting for Philip, I shivered. Partly because of the draught which always whistles round one's legs on railway stations and partly with apprehension. It was so long – more than eighteen months.

The train was late and I searched vainly for him as the carriages disgorged their load of khaki, and dark and light blue. Boots and gaiters swung past, kit-bags at ear level, subalterns and red hats, some scruffy erks, a couple of ATS.

And suddenly we were facing each other, puzzled, nervous and ill at ease. For an awful instant I panicked. Was this stranger the man I was married to? This madly good-looking creature in tartan trews and glengarry, peering down at me? 'Philip?' I asked.

And then his arms were round me and my cap went flying and I started to cry. Great dry sobs that I couldn't control. It was all so silly. I was cross with myself and cross with him for surprising me so. And yet it was all wonderful and he was here. With me. In the flesh.

I took his arm and hugged it, 'I'll never let you go,' I said.

I hadn't recognized her at first. And then, of course, it occurred to me that, although I knew she would be in uniform, I had visualised her in battledress, trousers tucked into boots and hatless – as she had been when I had seen her for the first time. I wasn't expecting the small figure in neat SD.

Poor little thing. She looked like a rabbit transfixed by a stoat. Was I that bad? I had travelled in battledress, keeping my best jacket and trews and Sam Browne to change into when we reached Dover, but perhaps it would have been better if I had changed into a pullover and a pair of old corduroys. I bent down and wrapped her in my arms.

We spent a wonderful evening – eating at an Italian restaurant, naturally. I shouldn't think the food was much good, but the waiters made a great fuss of us. Having commented on our good Italian, they asked us where we learned it, and when they heard – well! Dinner was on the house and out came bottles of wine vastly superior to those being imbibed by our neighbours. It was all great fun.

I had nothing very much to tell Philip – life had been intensely dull – but I was avid for his news. He had been to Gianna Maria's wedding and Tom had been there – he had been accepted back into his own army after all and was doing a liaison job with the British in Trieste – but there was no news of the Scum. Dougal had left the army apparently and just disappeared. Still, that is what we would both have expected of him.

We were the last to leave the restaurant, bowed off the premises with great éclat and promises to return. And so to bed.

Quite suddenly the months of separation and frustration slid away and we were back on the pine-needles, looking at the stars. Marrying as we had done could have been so wrong, such a tragedy – but for us it was going to be right and we both knew it. It was wonderful to enjoy a man so much and to know that he belonged to me, wonderful to know that we had made no mistake. Perhaps, because we both knew that under different circumstances we might have been different people, with little in common, but tied, and, as things had worked out, found ourselves happy to be tied, our union was that much stronger than it would have been had we met and married in a more normal way.

It seemed no time before the telephone rang and a voice reminded us that we had asked for an early call. Philip stretched and held out his arms and I went into them for a last five minutes' warmth, and lying there, looking at the light in his eyes, I knew that I was as much to him as he was to me. So much luck, so much happiness, seemed too fragile to hold.

My reception at the Depot was much as I had expected. The second battalion was about to go into suspended animation, I was told by the Adj, and I would be posted to the first. It was going to be hard, unlearning all that I had learned during the past few years and starting from scratch again. I said as much as he handed me my ration card and railway warrant. But he merely shrugged, 'You're not the only one – chaps like you coming in every day.'

With two weekends conveniently placed, Sally had managed to get twenty-one days' leave.

We spent a few days in Inverness and a few days farther north, idling in the glory of the autumn gold. I remember once in Italy, on a really beautiful day in the mountains, that I said I would not exchange it for the Highlands in the autumn and I had been right. It was cold, but, as we ate a picnic lunch, sitting on a rug spread on the grass of a meadow on the Black Isle and gazed over the deep blue inlet, with the purple heather and bracken on the turn stretching as far as the eye could see, it was the nearest we had been to our days with the group.

Then west to my home. I had had no qualms as far as taking Sally to meet my mother was concerned, because I was pretty sure that they would like each other. In fact, they had a lot in common and I soon realised that, in my mother's eyes, Sally could do no wrong. They talked about the East and the war, and Mama was genuinely upset when I told her that Sally wouldn't come to her when she heard that her father had died. Bravery was, in her opinion, the greatest virtue, and when I recounted a little of Sally's past, I could see the admiration positively shining from her eyes.

But our leave went fast and soon it was time for me to put Sally on the southbound train. I wanted to ask permission and then get married again, but she has a stubborn streak – as I already knew, only too well – and flatly refused to bow down to service etiquette.

'If your colonel would really hold our marriage against you – and I doubt if he would – then, frankly, I think you'd be better out of the battalion. Out of the army for that matter.' And that was all she would say.

If only she had not had that fixation about staying in the air force and following me around, I could have come clean in the first place and no complications would have existed. I felt it was her fault and that the least she could do was to stop being so bloody-minded and let me do it my way. Would it really upset her pride so much to ask permission to get married? Pig-headed little so-and-so. It was the cause of our first row – but not the last.

Eventually we agreed to compromise. If we were to remain at the Depot for long, Sally would try and get a posting north and, when I thought the time was ripe, I would announce the fact that I was a married man and produce my wife. Meanwhile we would let things slide; she had already been promised Christmas leave and it was not so far off.

'Coldest winter for more than a hundred years,' the headline of the newspaper on the seat beside me told us. But I didn't need to see it in print. We dawdled north on the so-called *Flying Scot* and never had I been so frozen in my life.

I tried to knit, but spent more time sitting on my hands than using them to hold the needles. It was nearly Christmas and I was in a hurry to get it done. I finished the baby's vest and started on a boot and an old lady sitting opposite smiled knowingly. I smiled back, but it wasn't my baby that I was knitting for, but Gianna Maria's due at any time.

Philip was to meet me at Edinburgh, where we were to have a couple of days on our own before going north to spend Christmas with his mother. I looked forward to a shopping spree because, besides other things, I was desperately short of clothes and, if we were to stay in hotels and I was going to continue knitting Gianna's baby clothes, I really thought it time I had a wedding ring. Uniform had become second nature, but the war was over now and I couldn't live in slacks and jerseys – the only things I had needed on the only leave I had taken before Philip's return. I had gone to Ireland then to stay with Mary O'Connell – a widow for three years now – who lived on the outskirts of Dublin with her father and small son. Thinking of her made me realise once again how lucky we were.

Waverley Station arrived at last and there was Philip, pacing up and down the platform in kilt and SD jacket, not even a greatcoat. Scotland might be cold, he informed me, but nothing to three winters in the mountains of Piemonte – as if I didn't know.

He took my arm and hustled me out of the station, and I could sense at once that he was bubbling over with excitement. We were hardly out of the place before he enlightened me.

'Sally, I take it all back, all the things I said when we had that row last leave. You wrote once, when I was still in Naples, to say that you could get yourself posted to Hong Kong or Singapore, but not to Italy – does that still hold good?'

'I suppose so,' I said. 'I haven't tried.' He had caught me completely unawares. 'Why?'

'Because rumours are rife that the battalion will soon be on the move and everything points to it being the Far East. At the beginning, at any rate, we gather there will be no wives. If you could get anywhere out there it would be better than here.'

'I'll see when I get back,' I said, 'but now I'm on leave. And there's something you haven't noticed.' I jerked my shoulder with its stiff epaulette against him – we were sitting in a taxi by then.

'Good God. Same rank as me – I can't allow that!'

I had recently been promoted to Flight Officer, but kept it as a surprise.

'You're still too young to draw marriage allowance,' I pointed out, 'if we're living out, somewhere in the East, you'll be glad of the extra pay.' At that moment I had no idea what a profound truth I had just uttered.

Mrs Morrison was sweet. It was no hardship for me to spend Christmas with my mother-in-law. Just one more stroke of luck. There was a tiny parcel for me at the top of the Christmas tree and I knew it was from her by the way she watched me undo it, although the donor was not named. I could see her pleasure in my pleasure.

It was an old-fashioned ring, an emerald, square-cut, and surrounded with tiny diamonds.

I just kissed her. I couldn't put my thanks into words. Not only for the ring, but for the way she had accepted me, the clandestine wife of her only remaining son. Philip had told me of the tragedy of his family, how she had lost them, one by one, and although he said she moaned, she had not moaned with me.

I suppose that things do even out and that after all the frustrations while Philip was still in Italy, we did deserve our luck.

'What chance of a posting to the Far East?' I asked the Wing Commander on my return from leave.

'Good, I should think,' he said. 'There's nearly always a man who doesn't want to go and both units are short-staffed just now. Why? Do you want one?'

'I'm not sure yet,' I told him. But not for long. Within forty-eight hours Philip was on the phone.

'Sally,' he yelled, and I could only just hear him over the dreadful line, 'get cracking on that posting. Singapore. We're being sent to Malaya. I'll write.'

I sent a wire to him the next day and went off to buy my tropical kit.

58. THE WAR IS OVER

Sharif Ahmat

Assembling for the Inspectors' Training Course was not unlike being a recruit again. We all arrived at the Depot the evening before the course was due to commence and were allocated beds in a long, concrete barrack block.

There were already half a dozen or so candidates unpacking when I arrived, and imagine my chagrin and surprise when I found one of them to be Hasbullah.

I had not given him a thought since the night I evaded the Japs and joined Hassan.

A feeling, which I can only describe as a mixture of disgust and frustration, swept over me. To think that, Jap toady and collaborator as he had been, he still held the same potential future in the Force as I.

It was the same old Hasbullah. If I hadn't known him so

well I might have been taken in by that wide smile and outstretched hand.

'Well, Mat. I haven't seen you for ages. How did things go after you left us so suddenly?'

I ignored the hand. My thoughts flew to my mother and how her face reflected the suffering she had endured. So many dead and maimed. What was the point of fighting, if people like Hasbullah were still to be on top at the end of it all?

I fingered the puckered scar above my elbow and looked him straight in the eye.

'This was caused by a Jap bullet and is the very least of the wounds my family has to show.'

Well. I had to hand it to him. He didn't blink an eyelid, but smiled the smile of a tolerant schoolteacher when one of his dimmer pupils is being fractious.

'As you say, it was a Jap bullet.'

'But the Japs were led by a Malay.'

'Oh, come off it, Mat. I was on duty that night; I couldn't avoid taking them round.'

'And yet you led them to me.'

Hasbullah sighed, a sigh of patience nearly exhausted, but I could see the smile muscles were becoming taut – and I was glad.

'Is it my fault that, just because the door opens, you leap from your bed and scramble through the window like a mad thing? Be reasonable. You can't really blame the Japs for shooting – talk about behaving in a suspicious manner. . . .'

'And if I had stayed quietly in bed?'

'They'd have carried on to the next hut. It was purely a routine inspection.'

'A likely story.'

'Come on, Mat. The war's over. If I ever gave you cause to doubt my integrity, I'm sorry. Shake hands, man. You know I hated the yellow bellies as much as you did.'

I said nothing, because I was finding it difficult to control my temper. But I pointedly put myself into the at-ease position and clasped my hands firmly behind my back.

Hasbullah's smile faded at the slight and I was aware of one of those moments when time seems suspended. He still stood with outstretched hand, I stood with hands behind my back, my expression as wooden as I could make it, and the other occupants of the room stood and watched us. The silence was intense.

'Best to shake.'

I swung round at the sound of a familiar voice.

It was Inspector Ram Singh – ASP Ram Singh now. He stood just inside the door and I wondered how much he had heard.

We all sprang to attention as he moved forward and signified with a wave of the hand that we could relax.

'Sharif Ahmat, isn't it?' He held out his own hand.

'Tuan.' I did shake *his* hand. He had been a good inspector when I served under him and decent enough to me.

'Hasbullah is right. The war is over. It is better to shake hands and forget.'

Still I did not move.

Ram Singh gave a very slight shrug and walked along the line of men, introducing himself and announcing that he would be the chief instructor for our course. Then he went back to the door and paused, looking straight at me.

'Some of you have not been long in the Force and others I know only from your records. But Ahmat I know well. It was I who advised you to sign the oath of allegiance to the Japs, was it not?'

I came to attention to indicate the affirmative. 'Tuan.'

'And I advised you rightly. Not that it helped your family much. Oh yes, I know all about the tragedy of your father and your brothers. Your eldest brother and I were gazetted at the same time and we attended the Police Training College together at Hendon. I hear he is now on a fingerprint course?'

'Tuan.'

'Three times in Britain already. Soon he will be turning white!' A polite titter passed over the room. He was deliberately softening the atmosphere. 'We often talked about the war years and many is the time I told him that it was all very well for a young bachelor to run off to the hills, but the older men like myself – ' he indicated a few grey streaks in his beard ' – had our wives and children to think of. Many is the time I have undertaken duties which I did not relish, so perhaps I too should be called a collaborator.'

There was dead silence throughout the room. Ram Singh stood like a rock, only his eyes moving to each of us in turn. He was a tall, handsome man, with ramrod military bearing. He had always been known as a hard disciplinarian, but just. His face had become very stern.

'I want no feuds on this course. And no talk of collaboration. The war is over. Is that clearly understood?'

There was a chorus of 'Tuan,' and the senior man present called the rest of us to attention.

After that we got on with our unpacking in silence, until unaffected, new arrivals began to stream in and the normal chatter of a barrack-room took over again.

I wrote to Hassan that evening and to my surprise, when I received his reply, he wrote:

'Ram Singh is right. There are so many Hasbullahs, they are not worth worrying about. The war *is* over. My advice to you is to forget it and concentrate on the future.'

He went on to tell me about the course he was attending and how he expected to be posted to CID Headquarters on his return.

I took the proffered advice and concentrated on the course and I'm pleased to say I passed out top – this was a fillip to my pride, as it is difficult for us to compete against the Chinese and Indians, who are usually far better educated. I never did shake hands with Hasbullah, but we were polite to each other and as far as possible kept out of each other's way.

To my delight, on completion of the course, I myself was posted to the CID HQ in Kuala Lumpur, and when Hassan returned from England we found ourselves working in the same building.

It was wonderful to renew the comradeship that we had found during the occupation, but I did not feel it could last for long, and I was right. The years in the jungle had taken their toll and it was not many months before he was admitted to the TB hospital.

Attention and care were unstinted, but every time I visited him he seemed more wan, more finely-drawn, until one day the surgeon took me aside and told me there was no hope.

I cannot say it came as a real surprise. And yet, when I looked at him and thought of my father dying in madness, my brothers killed and Mahmood becoming a fly-by-night playboy with heady ideas, it seemed so unfair that Hassan, so young still and with such a future before him, should die.

After a battle with the medical authorities and the police, and assurances from our mother that she would be the only person with whom Hassan would come in contact, they eventually allowed him to be removed to Daun Chempaka so that Mak could nurse him during his last days.

He came by ambulance as soon as I was able to get leave to accompany him, and we made him comfortable on a specially-acquired hospital bed. This we set on the verandah – on the very spot, although he did not know it, where my brother Ghazali had fallen under my father's maddened thrust – from where he could watch the changing faces of the mountain which he loved, and which had been partly responsible for the early termination of his life.

He lived for nearly a year and I believe that in those last months he was able to assuage much of my mother's loneliness. The bed on which he lay is still there, inhabited now by the little cat that kept him company until the end, and beneath a yellow song bird which still trills in its wicker cage.

We buried him near his brothers. I do not believe it will be long before my mother joins them. She is alone again now. My sisters married and far away, Mahmood disinterested, my father an unhappy ghost. She is still a proud woman, but life has not been kind.

59. HOGMANAY

Donald Thom

Everyone was drinking and quite a few people were already way into the wind – and I guess I was one of them. Well, what the hell? It was Hogmanay, wasn't it? Judas Priest, if a good Scot can't get drunk at Hogmanay, when the hell can he get drunk?

I'm not sure which year it was, is. 1946, I guess. I mean was. 1947 is. Who cares? Well, I do. At least, I care about it being the 1st of January – I don't care which year. I only know it's the wrong one. My mind sure travels back on 1st January – guess it always will. I tried looking at my watch, but there's something wrong with my eyes – won't focus. Not that I'm drunk, mind you – Thom never gets drunk, only drinks. Good chap, Thom.

'Wha's time?' The guy I asked was sitting bolt upright on the stairs beside me.

'Four o'clock.'

'How you know it's four o'clock? You din' look at your watch. I'm not drunk.'

'I don't know, but I know it's four o'clock.'

I was about to argue, but then I remembered, never argue

with a drunk. I got away from that guy, because it looked to me as though he might be going to puke, and who wants to be spewed over? So I moved to a chair and had myself a good think.

Yeah, I know what we were doing at four o'clock. We were just getting up. We'd made love for the last time and then she'd gone. Why did she go back? If she hadn't, she'd be here now – Mrs Thom. Mrs Marijke Thom.

Mrs Thom – the other Mrs Thom, Mrs Monica Thom, well, she was Mrs something else now. She'd been keen on hurrying the divorce through on account of she was having a baby. Baby by that Frog. Well, she'd got her divorce – I wasn't going to hang on to any woman who didn't want me – and I'd agreed to her having custody of the child, my child. I had no idea where she was now – didn't care – Canada, or France maybe.

I hadn't returned to Canada myself, not at all. We hung around Europe for a year or so. I got out of going back to Holland, but I rejoined the battalion when they moved over to the Rhine Army. Once the war was over, I applied to get out, go back to university, but I didn't want to go back to Canada – too many memories of that college – it wasn't so easy being accepted for a British university, too many limeys, I guess. Anyways, here I am. Edinburgh. Good old Bonny Scotland, land of my ancestors. I always told Monica my name would be a help one day – but she didn't want to keep it – rather be called by the name of that Frog.

I still have a couple of years to do – didn't have to do the full course, on account of my having done a year plus in Canada before I joined up. It's not a bad joint here – I'm not sure where I am, but I know the people who own it are friends of mine. Quite a party. Glad I stayed in Edinburgh for the winter vac.

Two more years. 'Yipppppeeeeeeeee!' Heh, heh! That sure put all those old world Highlanders to shame.

They think they're doing the Eightsome Reel over there. Do you know, I think I'm getting a little high? Too many people leaping and yelling; I wonder where they get their energy from? What'm I saying? Energy? I'll show 'em!

60. A TEMPORARY HOME

Stanislaus Olshewski

Would you believe it, I had to carry that hulking great Canadian all the way back to his digs? It was just about the other side of the city, the building where he lodged, and not a taxi in sight. Bloody cold too.

It was just as I was telling all and sundry that the Eightsome Reel was a Polish dance and the Scots had copied it, that this great hunk came hurtling into the circle, yelling as though all the demons of hell were after him. He sent both my partner and me flying and then someone felled him, screeching, 'Damned Yankee,' as he did so! Of course it was the wrong moment to tell the Scots that they couldn't drink either and, to cut a long story short, it ended up with one 'damned Yankee' and one 'damned foreigner' in a heap in one corner.

I can't remember much about the party actually. I was down from St Andrews with some of the other med. students who'd stayed behind, and how we became involved I don't know. Some people called Wallace asked us, I think. Better find out. Oh well, it seems that I have a temporary home for a few days. I don't even know this character's name, but when he emerged for a short while just now, he suggested I cook some breakfast and stay on. There're two beds, so why not? He's the first Canadian I've come across since leaving prison camp and it makes a change.

As you will have gathered by the date, I've finished my first year and, taken by and large, things aren't going too badly. Not that it's going to be all that easy from now on. Although I've spoken, and written, English for so long, I'm still apt to worry about putting down the wrong thing. But I wasn't wrong about one thing; I do have a vocation. Of course I have a lot of people to thank; most of all Colonel MacArthur, for getting me started on the right track – if it hadn't been for him I wonder if I would ever have got this far. Doing the first exam in camp put me a leap ahead straight away, and at my age that's something to be thankful for. So many other people were decent, helpful and encouraging, and, in a nebulous way, I have that little WAAF to thank too – it was her nightmares that first made me want to practise medicine. Sally – wonder what's happened to her?

Sooner or later I shall have to think about the future. Haven't given it much thought yet, but if I want to get my British nationality I shall have to stay in Britain for a while after I qualify, or go to a British colony.

Right at the moment I think I could do with some breakfast myself. Wonder where that chap said the bacon was?

61. THE FIRST FEATHERY ISLANDS

Philip Morrison

As soon as the battalion was disembarked and we were settled in to our new home in Singapore, I realised that life, as far as my personal problems were concerned, was not going to be plain sailing.

Only the CO and one senior major had their wives booked to follow them, and it was made perfectly clear that those were the only wives who could be expected out for some time. The colonel didn't care for wives at the best of times – rumour had it that his own was a bitch and he would have done without her as well. I hadn't met her, she'd been away the whole time I was at the Depot, but if his own home life was not happy, he was unlikely to be sympathetic towards one of his juniors whose wife came out under her own steam. And no hope of quarters, even if he should prove amenable in time. Quarters were few and far between and for another couple of months I wasn't even eligible to put my name on the waiting list, nor draw marriage allowance.

In the circumstances, I waited for news of the arrival of Sally's ship with mixed feelings. Oh, blast the colonel and his narrow-minded, dogmatic principles. Was it my fault that I was sent to the second battalion? The colonel had no time for any battalion but his own. Or that I'd fought an unorthodox war? I suppose he would have thought better of me if I had stayed meekly behind wire and made no attempt to escape. Stodgy old sod.

Oh well. The only consolation to date was that Sally was bound to be stationed at Changi, which was the only RAF Station with WAAF on it, and our barracks were only a stone's throw away. We'd manage somehow.

I sat silent amid the chattering group of naval and army officers in the main lounge of the Grand Oriental Hotel.

Outside, sounds of traffic – horns, brakes, and the cawing crows as they flew in from the harbour to make one of their furious assaults on some speck of garbage left lying in the street – were muffled.

Inside, the gentle whirring of long-stemmed fans, flowering from high-domed ceilings, and the soft-soled slap of the Sinhalese waiters as they padded between the tables and bar, took me back to my childhood. Tall, dignified and stately, these quiet-voiced old men with their tiny knots of hair and crescent-shaped tortoiseshell combs, had always spelt out homecoming for me. As the commuter in UK starts putting away the crossword and looks at his watch when the train draws into the penultimate station, so, for me, Colombo has always been the end of Europe and the beginning of the East. Next stop home.

I had had little enough to do on board – beyond repelling the advances of the Ship's Adj – but dream. And dream I did, all along the familiar route: Port Said, Aden, Bombay, Colombo. And soon it would be Singapore. I had been ashore at every port, listening with one ear to the amused or incredulous remarks of my companions – 'Oh, do look at that heavenly hat!' 'What *is* that chap wearing – looks like a winding-sheet!' 'What an extraordinary vehicle!' 'Oh, do listen – isn't it priceless?' – and with the other ear hearing all the dear, familiar sounds that meant home. I was happy, saying little and smiling a lot – I must have been a very dull companion.

But we were soon on board again, adding our ebony and ivory elephants to the pouffes from Port Said, the cameras and make-up from Aden, and the silk bought in Bombay.

After that it seemed no time before we were sailing through the Straits, Malaya so close on the port side that the urge to jump overboard and swim for it was almost uncontrollable. I had missed lunch, refused to go inside for tea, remaining glued to the rail in case there was some familiar landmark that I might miss.

It is impossible to convey the emotion which came over me as Singapore harbour came in sight. The excitement which had been surging through me ever since boarding the troopship at Liverpool reached fever pitch as we passed slowly, slowly, between the first feathery islands. The sea changed colour from deep ocean blue to the turquoise and eau-de-Nil of sheltered reefs. Sand and palm tree, coral and kelong. The very air smelt different. Home. It was almost home.

A vessel sailing through tropic seas has a sound all its own. How can I describe it? A gentle sound, windblown but serene, a lazy, swishing sound that you never hear in northern waters. I listened and felt and revelled in the familiar, homecoming melody of the warm sea.

Soon it would be evening. The engines slowed as the pilot manœuvred us through the myriad stationary vessels, to drop anchor in the inner roads. Multicoloured specks, seen leaving the shore, had not materialised into the launches they inevitably were. The rattling anchor chain had ceased; we were still, alone, at peace.

And then the most almighty explosion rent the air and for a terrible, shivering moment I was back five years. I closed my eyes, hearing the rattle and report, but knowing also that soon would come the crescendo, climax and, at last, silence. I opened them to meet the amused gaze of the first officer, at whose table I sat in the dining saloon.

'Chinese New Year,' he said, 'it's only the second time they've been able to let off fire crackers since the war. Noisy blighters, but you can't blame them – after all, we have Guy Fawkes's night.'

I laughed and he moved on down the deck.

The launches were now all around us, nipping in and out and buzzing like inquisitive bees. Medical, customs, immigration, police. But before the first occupant of the little boats had set foot on the gangway, the Tannoy crackled and the voice of the OC Troops announced that, owing to a holiday on shore, due to start the following day, we would not be disembarking for forty-eight hours.

There must have been many people with mixed emotions in that ship. Wives disappointed at further separation; wives glad to have a brief reprieve; men who groaned at having to spend two more days on the troopdeck, and old sweats who told them that things on shore would be even worse.

For myself, I didn't really mind. I was sure that Philip would have enough initiative to wangle himself on board somehow, and I was so entranced with the sights and sounds of Singapore harbour at last that I was happy just to watch it for a spell.

As the sun went down and the sky reddened all around us, I could have cried at its beauty – and the memory of that other glow that had bathed this harbour five years ago. For, coincidentally, this was again February the thirteenth, Friday the thirteenth too, five years to the day since I had left these waters, under such very different circumstances.

The dinner gong sounded and I tore myself away from the evening sky. There would be to-morrow and, before that, the night.

'Friday the thirteenth,' grumbled my neighbour in the saloon, as he surveyed the menu with a jaundiced eye, 'I take it that "prawn cocktail à la Penang" is the same as "Mediterranean prawn cocktail, prawn cocktail à la Barren Rocks, and prawn cocktail Indienne"? Oh well, nothing else to do but eat. Fat chance of seeing anything of Singapore.'

'It's my lucky day,' I said.

All the diners looked at me in surprise.

'You're a queer girl,' one said, 'coming to meet your husband – you couldn't get here fast enough a couple of days ago and, now that you're held up for another forty-eight hours, you say it's your lucky day!'

I just smiled. I didn't feel at that moment like recounting the events of half a decade ago.

And then I looked up and saw Philip entering the saloon. He hadn't changed and was still in daytime togs, khaki shirt with rolled-up sleeves, kilt and webbing belt. He looked healthy and alive, skin darkened by the sun and lighter streaks in his hair. I had the same feeling that I had had on Victoria Station on his return from Italy – was I really married to this madly attractive man?

I watched him pick his way between the stewards and tables, but did not get up to meet him; there was a vacant place at our table for eight, I wanted to have him here, to show him off.

'Look,' I prodded my neighbour, 'you see, it *is* my lucky day.'

I got up then and Philip was beside me. We smiled into each other's eyes, then I introduced him, and the first officer suggested that he should join us – as I had hoped he would – and soon he was munching away while being bombarded with questions by those who had reached their journey's end.

'You see,' I said later, as we stood by the railing and looked over the harbour lights, 'my hunch did prove right.'

But while he was gone, getting our drinks from the bar, I thought that after all this subterfuge had gone on long enough. I had made no secret of being a married woman on board – why should I? I knew the job I was to do ; once dug in I thought it unlikely that the air force would care whether I was married or not ; unlikely that they would post me home. And now, almost his first words when we had been alone, were to the effect that the colonel would have a fit if he knew that he was meeting his wife. Oh, bugger the colonel, I thought, this was something we must tackle soon. I knew I had been pig-headed, but why the hell should Philip ask for permission to marry at this stage, and go through all that nonsense? I wanted him to stand up for himself, to stop being so damned lily-livered with this man, who could not possibly be the ogre that he was made out to be I was sure. But why spoil our first evening together? I smiled at him when I saw him returning and put my thoughts away for another day.

We stood in silence for a long time, looking out over the sea. Any harbour at any time has a fascination for me, and of course Singapore is one of the busiest in the world. There was activity everywhere. Ships employing Chinese labour frantically loading and unloading by floodlight before the start of the holiday. Launches, sampans, life-boats, koleks, junks – every conceivable type of craft plied between ships and shore. And the shore itself – more neon lights than ever, and Singapore had always been gay. It was a spectacle.

I had not told Philip until then about the coincidence of the date. And, come to think of it, there had been so many other excitements in our lives when we had first met that I doubt if I'd ever told him in detail what this harbour had been like five years before. It had been to Stan, my Polish boy-friend, that I had unburdened myself – I wonder what happened to him?

Philip listened as I pointed out the oil islands that had been ablaze and tried to describe the extraordinary black pall, mixed with scarlet and crimson, that had hung over the island. And the noise – no, better not to remember.

Suddenly I felt my cheeks wet and his arm tightening about my shoulders.

'I'm sorry,' I said, 'I was only just then thinking that my happiness would be complete if only my father were still alive. He is there, somewhere, buried in a common grave, I suppose. I thought of him this afternoon, but it is only now that the horror of that spell has come back. The Red Cross merely told me that he had died in internment, but I shall have to find out how he died – to lay his ghost.'

Philip said nothing, but I could feel the sympathy in his silence, in his fingers caressing my arm, and the chaste kiss that he planted on top of my head. How lucky I was to have him. My home had gone, my family, but I had him.

62. CHAIRBORNE

James Weatherby

'Helen, Helen.' The voice sounded cheerful and I dared to hope.

I had been watching from the window of the flat as James plodded up the hill – as I did at the same time every evening. In summer I could see him as he rounded the bend at the bottom of the rise, but in winter I had to wait for the light from the lamp-posts to fall on each figure as he or she passed under its beam. If he was in a good mood, I would see him marching up the hill as though on parade, and the first glimpse I would have would be of an outstretched arm swung shoulder-high in the lamplight. But if the mood were bad, the hand would be firmly tucked into a pocket, matching the empty sleeve on the other side. Then the first glimpse would be of a shoulder, or hat brim, pulled well down.

It had been difficult to ascertain his mood this time. His figure had been erect, but slow, idling in the still mild October twilight. And so I had been unprepared for the exuberance in his voice.

'Helen – where are you, woman? Damn you. I've got important news.'

I stepped from the shadow of the curtain and switched on the standard-lamp. I had wanted to watch him for a moment unobserved, to see his expression, but the tone of voice was enough. And so I smiled.

'What are you doing, skulking in the dark?' His right arm had become incredibly strong, I thought, as he circled my shoulders and hugged. 'Honey, guess what? I've got a chance to get out of that blasted chair at last.'

I released myself and took his hat and gloves.

'Get yourself comfy first, while I get us a drink, then you can tell me all about it.'

I closed the kitchen door quietly and stood with my back to it, praying that this was not another false hope. Ever since James had dropped back to his substantive rank and been stuck behind that wretched Air Ministry desk, he had fretted and cursed and made life hell for everyone around him.

He had been in his present job for more than eighteen months and surely it must have become apparent to the powers that be by now that pen-pushing was not his métier? If only he could have got back to a station. Meanwhile he continued to fume about his ill-luck and I stood in the window each day to speculate on what sort of evening lay ahead for me with this unpredictable man. Next door the sound of gurgling bathwater broke in on my thoughts and I realised that I must have been standing there for at least ten minutes.

I went over to the drink cupboard to see what we had. Half a bottle of whisky, three-quarters of gin. Perhaps this time it would really be good news – I reached for the whisky.

I hurried through to the living-room and by the time he emerged, clad in shapeless grey flannel bags and sweater, I had the drinks poured out, the curtains drawn and a pile of chestnuts ready for roasting in the newly-lit fire.

I had never been one to linger in the bath, but to-night I wanted to soak in the hot water and go over the day's events. I'd had my hopes dashed before, but this time I really did think it would come to something. Helen had been marvellously patient with me this past year, but I knew I was being a bastard, both to her and to my staff. Every day I made new resolutions and every day I broke them. God knows, it wasn't Helen's fault that I was cooped up in that dreary office, nor the poor sods under me for that matter, but one frustration after another was driving me round the bend. I had quite given up any hope of advancement in the air force – and with the present government cutting down the armed services on all sides I was not just being a pessimist – but even the civilian channels I had explored had come to nothing. Either the service wouldn't consider release, or there was little chance of being accepted with any physical disability, or I just couldn't see myself in the job offered.

I lay in the bath, listening to the clink of glass as Helen organised our drinks in the kitchen on one side and Angela hummed herself to sleep on the other. Good heavens, I had been so engrossed in my own thoughts that I had neglected to go and say good night to her.

Funny little thing. Button-brown eyes and bright red hair, she didn't look like either of us. 'You're going to be a *femme fatale*,' I told her. It would be fun when she could talk back, instead of gurgling. I pulled the blanket up to her chin and closed the door.

My God, it was good to come home to a wife and child like mine. I looked at Helen, perched on the chair by the fire and pricking chestnuts. She was beginning to look large, must be seven months by now. She was still a beautiful girl, even when she was pregnant. I took in the scene and her alert face and brought out the sheaf of papers which I had held concealed behind my back.

'Take a gander at these,' I said, and held them out to her.

'Colonial Administrative Service? You mean leave the RAF?'

'Would you mind?'

She looked thoughtfully at the forms but shook her head. 'Not in the least – if you are going to be happier in another job. Do you think you'd get in?'

'With these you mean?' I inclined my head on the sightless side and flipped my pinned-up sleeve. A feeling of triumph had been saturating me ever since I left the MO; I'm sure she must have seen it in my face. 'Listen, honey – I heard about this job from another chap who applied. He gave me all the gen a week or so ago – I didn't mention it before because I didn't want you to be disappointed if it didn't come to anything – but to-day I went to see a fellow in the Colonial Office, who gave me these forms to fill in. It wasn't exactly an official interview, but he told me all the pros and cons and gave me a good idea of what the work would consist of. Apparently they're crying out for bodies, so, if they accept me – and he seemed pretty sure that they will – and I pass the medical and get out of the air force, I'm in.' I recalled with some bitterness how he had waved my flying experience and wartime rank aside as being of little consequence. 'It seems that a year or so behind an Air Ministry desk is worth more than all my years of flying.'

She asked quickly, 'Where would we go?'

'Africa, most likely, or possibly the Far East. Would you like that, darling?'

'I loved my trip to India during the war,' she said cautiously.

'I went over to see old Doc Matthews after I got these forms,' I went on, 'he gave me a thorough going-over and sees no reason why I shouldn't pass the medical. Organically I'm sound and, if I can push a pen in AM minus an eye and an arm, what's to prevent me doing the same in some secretariat in Kenya or Swaziland?'

I watched her, this woman whom I knew so well, and knew that she too believed that this time it would be all right. I bent over to kiss her neck and she smiled round at me.

'Let's have another drink,' she said, 'and then I'll go and cook the supper.'

'No. I'll cook the supper and you fill in these forms. I'm bound to make a smudge.'

I stood up, and as I did so a sudden kick reminded me that I was not all that far off from producing our second child.

'I was forgetting John,' I said, patting my middle. 'I'd like to have him here and I doubt if I'd be allowed to travel this size anyway.'

'Don't worry, darling, it wouldn't be as soon as that.'

He went out of the room and a few minutes later I smelled the right smells issuing from the kitchen. I listened for the blasphemy that invariably accompanied most of James's culinary feats and heard him singing instead. His voice was flat as a pancake, but it was better than an operatic aria to me, and I realised with a pang that the last time I had heard him sing like that had been when he first knew that I was to have Angela.

63. LINKED BY A PALE SCARF

Jogindar Singh

Sergeant Gurdial Singh did not recognise me, but I recognised him. That is the crux of this episode, but neither the beginning nor the end.

When my training was completed, I went on leave to Singapore and to take my part in the marriage which had been arranged for me by my uncle, Arjan Singh.

I had not seen my bride before the ceremony, and as we walked round the Holy Book, linked by a pale scarf, I wondered what lay in store for me behind that heavy veil. She was tall and slender, that I could see, and from the skin of her hands and feet, fair.

I had not given marriage much thought until my uncle wrote to remind me that I would soon be twenty-four and that it was high time I did. I left it in his hands and it was not until we reached the temple that I saw even the form of my bride to be. Suvindar Kaur was her name and my uncle had chosen well.

When the ceremony was over and her veil removed, I beheld a demure, docile face of great charm; the eyes large, deep and liquid; her mouth full, and nose long and straight. She was young still, only eighteen, and the daughter of one of my father's friends.

I thanked my uncle and aunt for their solicitude and for the hospitality that they accorded us during my leave. Our bridal chamber, a room in my uncle's house, was decked with silk hangings and paper flowers, and the sweet scents of jasmine and incense intermingled on the air.

I had not had a woman before, but I was aware from the start that our union would be satisfactory. She lay on the couch face down, covered by a silken sheet, but when I pulled this away and placed my hand on her buttocks, I saw that she was as slim and lithe as a boy. She giggled and hid her face, but I could see her watching me from the pointed corner of one eye. I rolled her over then with one hand and removed her own hands with the other.

This was the beginning of my marriage; a marriage I was never to regret.

On return from leave I found myself posted to the Traffic Branch and, regrettably, serving under one Gurdial Singh, Sergeant.

I was but a beardless youth when my father had been led away to lose his head. I was full bearded now and mature in build, reaching the mark of six foot three inches. But those men who had chosen to join the enemy at the outset, who had been spat upon by my father, had already been mature then and had not changed. Gurdial Singh was one of them.

There are no doubt others in the Force by the name of Jogindar Singh, and Pritam, my father's name, is one of the most common of our clan. But Gurdial Singh knew who I was, seeking to ingratiate himself with me from the start; fearful, no doubt, that I might choose to bring to light scenes that were best forgotten.

After only a few months in Traffic, a vacancy occurred and I was promoted corporal – Sergeant Gurdial Singh being careful to point out that it was his doing, his recommendation that had got me my stripes. Perhaps it was.

My conscience was uneasy during these months. I had sworn to avenge my father and yet I knew that to denounce

Gurdial Singh and stir up past mud would do nobody any good. Too many of my compatriots were involved, too many arguing that the government in power at the time was the one to be served, thus covering their defects and making for a smoother life. But every time I looked into his pock-marked, snake-like face, I saw my father's head leave his body and heard the final, eliminating 'thwack'. I had to leave.

After much deliberation, and remembering the interest he had shown in me when I first enlisted, next time I had reason to go out to the Depot, I asked to see the Adjutant.

'I wish for a posting,' I explained. 'For reasons which I cannot divulge, it is not possible to remain where I am.'

After a few minutes of evasive question and answer, I could see the Adjutant was becoming irritated with me. At length he said, rather sharply, 'I don't know what the trouble is, Corporal, but if you wish to be moved for personal reasons you must go through the proper channels which, as you very well know, is through your own Commanding Officer, and no one else. But as you've taken the trouble to come and see me, you presumably have your reasons. The very least you can do is to be honest with me. You may say what you wish in confidence.'

I cast my mind back then to the terrible day when my father, marching at the head of a column of men, had seen the PCs-turned-warders with their white charges. His words still rang clearly in my brain, as clearly as the intoned prayers of the elders and my mother's beseeching, 'Go!'

'You are, I presume, referring to Sergeant Gurdial Singh,' the Adjutant paused and gave me a piercing look. 'Is it your wish to denounce this man? I doubt if it would be wise.'

'Oh no, Sahib. With respect, you have not understood me at all. I do *not* wish to denounce him – as you have said yourself, many of my compatriots did not shine with a clear, pure light – but only to be removed from his presence, which contaminates my soul and my vow to see my father avenged. He was sympathetic, but not prepared to deviate.

'You will still have to go through your CO,' he said, 'but if it will help, I'll give him a ring and explain the circumstances, without mentioning any names.'

'Sahib,' I said, 'I am truly grateful.'

I returned then to barracks and wrote out my application for an interview with the OC Traffic Branch. Now we shall await events. It will soon be the New Year. I wonder if 1948 will be as eventful as 1947 has been for me.

BOOK II

IN WHICH THE STREAMS JOIN THE RIVER

'A State of Emergency has been declared'

64. THE LUCRATIVE CAREER OF MR S. KANDIAH

Ramakrishnan

I am working for more than one year as clerk on Tanah Kuning Estate when my eyes are being opened to potential far beyond realms of clerking.

There are many things I am learning since leaving Mr Ramasamy's silk store. Typing, filing and general routines of office for one thing, and great improvement of English for second.

My wife, Devi, is bringing forth bouncing boy after one year of marriage precisely and I am already making sure that she is pregnant again – which is not difficult seeing that she is still most frolicsome maiden who is greatly enjoying embracings of yours truly.

Mr Ramasamy, father-in-law and father of wife Devi, is paying up monthly without hitch, thereby enabling purchase of radio, sewing-machine and motor bicycle. Verily it was good fortune most that allowed me to become aware of incestuous behaviour of said Mr Ramasamy.

In fact, eyes are being opened in two ways.

Firstly is coming several Chinese to estate and I am being given to understand that they are members of once glorious guerilla band during most clandestine wartime. They are telling all workers that white pigs are exploiting them most foul – in this I am heartily concurring – and that soon great liberation movement will be afoot and all above-mentioned white pigs will be killed or dispatched to own country.

It is time of Chinese New Year and these erstwhile guerillas are handing out ang pows, red paper packets in value one dollar each, to all Chinese workers on estate, at same time requesting support from Indians and Javanese workers likewise.

CC – Chief Clerk – is not believing this and is shaking head, whilst telling workers to remember Japanese times so previously past and stick only to letter of law and order. I am thinking that he is truly old stick-in-the-mud who is too drunken and lazy to remember chains of our people, but I am saying nothing, having learned tact and diplomacy both. But I am being much encouraged by these magnificent hopings and pledge my support without more ados.

In June 1948 great and glorious happenings are taking place. To wit: one European planter killed on first day and all erstwhile glorious guerillas are hiding in jungles again before stupid police are knowing. From hills and valleys they will be harassing enemy as needing.

Truly it is great day when most glorious State of Emergency is being declared.

I am not forgetting humiliations suffered at hands of said guerillas, mind, but am nevertheless approving of all plans and principles.

But not all labour force are understanding actions of said guerillas – now called bandits or Communist terrorists. It is like wartime; there are many stupid fellows who are preferring to continue falling into steps of white pigs rather than join great liberation movement.

I am growing up muchly in six years and am now holding tongue instead of giving vent to feelings true and valorous. Indeed, I am becoming veritable clam and expert in tact and diplomacy both. As soon as I am realising that many workers are not on side of glorious Communist liberating terrorists, I am keeping trap most securely shut.

It is not long before police are coming to estate and explaining to workers about not helping said Communists and soon there are Malay Special Constables living on estate, to guard installations and suchlike. I spit whenever I pass their post.

But second happening, although I am not fully understanding at time, is more important than declaration of glorious Emergency, because it is of great financial benefits.

One day I am checking list of labourers' pay when shadow is falling over shoulder and I am beholding one Mr Menon.

Truly he is most well-dressed gentleman indeed, with many

fine gold teeth, rings, wrist watch, etcetera, etcetera.

'I am Secretary of Rubber and Tin Workers' Union,' he is informing me.

I can see at once that this is most worthy and important gentleman and am therefore giving him my chair and begging him to be seated forthwith. He is most graciously accepting my humble offer and when I have brought forward other chair for self, is explaining his business.

'It is to collect the quarterly subscriptions,' he is telling me, 'and to explain to Union members how their money is being spent.'

Truly he is most pleasant and plausible fellow. All the time I am looking at his clean and well-pressed suitings and brown and white correspondent shoes and thinking that indeed Mr Menon is in post most lucrative. Nylon socks he is wearing, of purple hue, and also purple nylon shirt and yellow tie and purple silk handkerchief is appearing in breast pocket of jacket.

Mr Menon is undoubtedly fine orator and holds all labour bound in spell for long period. I am listening to speech and learning for future reference what is most appealing to labourers' simple minds – for I am hatching plan most devious and bold – but also I am wondering if Mr Menon is indeed *bona fide* trade union official. It would be easy, I am thinking, to hoodwink simple labourers like these – trade unions being in infancy only and many people still unaccustomed to such – and collect subscriptions from all and sundry.

When Mr Menon has finished speaking and is answering questions, his assistant is collecting subscriptions and ticking off names of subscribers in notebook.

Two men lend confidence, I am thinking; where one man is for arousing suspicions, two men are not. Also arrival in limousine most spruce and shining.

I myself am now joining union for first time and paying subscription, for purpose of checking on Mr Menon and also seeing how it is run and what benefits workers are receiving.

I am finding out that Mr Menon is indeed official secretary of Rubber and Tin Workers' Union and no hocus-pocus abounds. But I am wondering nevertheless if correct amounts are always being shown in notebook against subscribers' names and coming to timely conclusion that here indeed is way of making money most beneficial to yours truly, if not to workers.

I am brooding on above-mentioned happenings for several weeks, and then am taking motor bicycle to friend on neighbouring estate, one Mr K. P. Samuel, who is also clerk, to have discussion with him of great import to both.

K.P. is not knowing of my extra monthly earnings and because he is only poor man in unwell paid position is therefore also most cautious. I am not persuading him at first reasoning, I can see, but am suggesting that he is giving idea most serious and formulative thought forthwith.

It is taking K.P. two months over to make up mind and, when he does, I am having to show him that I am in possession of trumping card.

Money received monthly from Mr Ramasamy, father-in-law, is being put away carefully for future use. Now time is come and I am deciding that learning to drive is first essential, so that motor car can be purchased. It is fitting that delegates from powerful union should arrive at estates in motor car, which is in keeping with official dignity. Also stupid Malay police are not so often questioning drivers of motor cars as of motor bicycles. I am therefore, as first step, spending every Saturday afternoon in nearby town, learning to drive said limousine.

Once licence is acquired, I am purchasing discreet but dignified motor car of dark maroon colour. Also suitings of white drill for K. P. Samuel and self ; nylon socks and handkerchiefs of gorgeous hues. Only it is remaining to obtain correspondent shoes, dark glasses and to have gold teeth fitted by Chinese dentist, who are most clever at such work. This last is being done by specialist in far town, as local fellow is most questioning chap.

When all organisations are ready and shipshape, I am asking for two days off to attend wedding of brother, which is being granted by most sleep-laden, toddy-drinking CC without trouble.

Then K.P. and I are driving pell-mell and helter-skelter to distant estate, to approach labour. We are choosing estate where manager is only visiting and name of clerk is available.

K.P. is nervous and all way to estate I am noticing that pink palms are clammy with much perspiration.

'Go faster, Krishnan,' he is urging. 'This is bad bandit area, man. No point in going to all these troubles if we are to be killed getting there.'

'You are not understanding those who you are calling bandits,' I am saying.

Nevertheless, I am putting on spurt, for how are bandits, I mean glorious guerillas, to know that I am sympathetic without asking, and it might be that they will shoot first.

Malay Special Constable is stopping us on roadside before we are reaching estate buildings and I am seeing K.P. bursting out in such perspirations that truly I am becoming nervous myself.

'I am Mr S. Kandiah,' I tell this white man's stooge, with smile to show both gold teeth, 'and this is my friend Mr K. P. John. We are coming to see Chief Clerk, Mr Tetrasamy.'

I too am perspiring now, because I am suddenly remembering that decision to use false name was taken without consideration of National Registration Identity Card. But luckily he is dull fellow and waves us through.

'Thank you, most gracious friend.' I give SC widest smile and hiss at K.P., 'Control yourself, man. All will be going well if we are using bluffings sufficiently.'

I am striding into estate office and holding out hand to Mr Tetrasamy, making sure that gold teeth, rings and wristwatch are all visible.

'Good afternoon, sir. I am Mr S. Kandiah and this is my assistant Mr. K. P. John. We are coming from Estate and Mine Workers' Union to gain members for valuable union support.'

Mr Tetrasamy is looking puzzled and before answering pulls list from drawer of desk.

'I know of no such union,' he is shaking head and looking at us with suspicious frown. 'All labour force here are members of Plantation Workers' Union.'

'You are right, my friend,' I say reassuringly, and sit down on ready chair, exposing nylon socks and correspondent shoes to make correct impression. 'Mr Aru, secretary of that union, is very good friend of mine. But this is new union, offering protection of workers against Communist Terrorist upsets; compensations to relatives when worker is deceased, etcetera.'

'But Plantation Workers' Union is also offering compensations.' Mr Tetrasamy is most cautious and suspicious fellow and is not being convinced, so I can see that it is time for me to be playing trumping card.

'My good friend Mr T. S. Aru is telling me that in future his union will only be looking after estates to north of Kuala

Lumpur; our union will be looking after estates south of this city.'

I mention a few names to impress this most doubting Thomas, then I am looking at gold wristwatch importantly and turning to K.P., who is pulling out list as previously arranged.

'Well, Mister,' I am saying to Mr Tetrasamy, 'I must thank you for your time and courtesy, but wasting no more time. We have already listed members from five estates to-day and still have four to visit. It is not good to be out after dark with such dastardly terrorists in vicinity and accommodation is already arranged on one of estates to be visited this day. We are not wishing to force anyone to join our union, but only asking to be allowed to say a few words to workers and, if anyone is wishing to join, he can do so at entrance fee of one dollar and annual subscription of fifty cents.'

I hold out my hand, and K.P. is putting lists back into most important-looking briefing-case when Mr. Tetrasamy, as I am expecting, is stopping us.

'I have no wish to stop you, friend,' he is saying, 'nor to interfere with honest intentions. You can speak to labour force if you are so wishing. It is only surprise that Plantation Workers' Union is handing over southern areas to other union.'

After that he goes outside and soon small boy is bearing glasses of coffee and we are having chat most friendly and amiable about state of country, etcetera, etcetera.

I am not being student and schoolteacher both for nothing. I am explaining to workers all benefits to be obtained from joining Southern Estate and Mine Workers' Union and K.P. is already pulling out receipt book and official black tin box for money.

'I am not asking any worker to join who does not wish to,' I am telling them at end of most eloquent harangue, 'but for those who wish to join, one dollar entrance fee and fifty cents annual subscription.'

I walk away then and soon K.P. is coping with long queue of workers.

It is already getting dark when we leave and we are driving helter-skelter for state capital.

It is only when we are inside cubicle of Indian lodging-house that we are counting benefits. Four hundred and fifty dollars over. K.P. and I are having most sumptuous meal in town and next day returning to humdrum life of clerking.

'This is only food of chicken,' I am telling him. 'If four hundred and fifty dollars over is being obtained from one small estate, think how much it is we are getting from big estates, man.'

Truly this is most beneficial ruse and soon I am buying wife many gold ornaments, as becomes wife of Very Important Person. For verily, Mr S. Kandiah and Mr K. P. John will be going long ways I am telling you.

65. THE ODDITY

Vincent Lee Chee Min

I had more than two years in Aussie after the VJ-night incident, and it wasn't until June 1948, when the Emergency had been declared in Malaya, that I was able to persuade Dad to let me come home and do as I wished. Dad's a tough nut – he'd survived the war without a scratch – with some pretty definite ideas.

Mum and Rosalie returned to Malaya on the first ship they could get a passage in and I had settled down to swot for my school leaving certificate. But barely a week-end went by without my hot footing it down to the police station, and soon they were making jokes about their latest recruit, and sometimes, when I was hanging around, waiting for my friend Bill to come off duty, Sergeant Williamson would take me into his office and, without him realising it, I'm sure, I was learning a heap.

Sergeant Williamson introduced me to an old retired couple who lived up in the hills, who'd been with the Malayan police pre-war. A real dinkum couple they were, who made me feel at home in their house and encouraged my enthusiasm to join the force.

But it took the Emergency to budge Dad. No good telling him I was an oddity – a Chinese whose *métier* was not maths – it was something he just would not tolerate. So I set to on the accountancy course, hating every minute of it, and then, wham! The headlines announcing that the first planter had been killed were my saving grace. I reckoned it was the time to make Dad change his mind. I pointed out that a son in the police would surely be an asset in these new circumstances. I was now eighteen and, with my education, was bound to get direct entry into the Inspectorate and gazetted rank in time.

To my surprise there was dead silence for a few weeks, then his reply was of a very different tone from usual. He would give his consent after all, he said, provided I was accepted into Special Branch.

This may sound as though Dad were planning his own intelligence network – not that I'd put that past him, if he doesn't already have one – but there is something abhorrent about a uniform to most Chinese. It would not have worried me, but Dad is still China born in his ways, and in China, right through the centuries, there has been no lower standing than that of soldier or policeman. No doubt things have changed with Communism, but, as far as he was concerned, uniforms were out. He said he would be getting in touch with a friend of his, a senior Chinese officer in Special Branch Headquarters, and meanwhile I had better knuckle down and qualify; who knew when I might need a second string to my bow? It never occurred to him, I am sure, that I would get beyond the first interview for the police.

66. THE SHERIFF

Sharif Ahmat

After Hassan's death I had applied for a posting to Negri Sembilan, so that I could be nearer my mother. To my surprise it was refused because, I was told, I had been selected for a course at a Police Training College in England.

Selfish as it may sound, I was glad to go. Hassan had told me so much about Europe and I was eager to see for myself. Besides, it had been a harrowing year, for me as well as my mother, and I looked forward to having something other than family affairs to concentrate on.

I enjoyed the course. I should have been there eight months and I had arranged to take my accumulated leave at the end of it when, with two of my friends, I intended exploring the Continent. But that was not to be.

Imagine my amazement when I heard over the BBC news that a State of Emergency had been declared in Malaya. It seemed dreadful that, only three years after hostilities had ended, my country should once again be plunged into unrest.

As soon as they mentioned Communists, I knew that it was all our old friends of the MPAJA, who had taken to the hills and forests again, as they had said they would if they did not get their own way. This was no secret and I wondered what Special Branch were doing, to let them get away. But how can one understand these things eight thousand miles away?

I had never really gone into Communist doctrine – although Kassim had tried often enough to explain the whys and wherefores to me – and did not know what it was that they wanted. During the war we had been fighting a common enemy. After the war I found their aims difficult to follow, so mixed up in flowery language and jargon. To be honest, I had forgotten all about them, but the news brought them vividly to mind.

It was obvious that with the declaration of the Emergency, every police officer would be needed at home, so I was not surprised when I found myself recalled before the end of the course.

Imagine my surprise, on return to Police Headquarters, to find myself seconded to the army for a year, not to do police work at all.

The life did not seem strange. Of course I had to put up with a lot of banter, such as the soldiers asking me what I had done with my four wives and where did I keep my prayer mat! I didn't mind. They were a good natured lot and, once I got used to their lack of dignity, I enjoyed their company.

The three officers were always meticulous in their address, calling me by my full rank and name. But Inspector Sharif Ahmat was too much for the men and within a couple of days the combination of my name and silver star cap badge caused some wit to dub me 'the Sheriff'. And the Sheriff I remained for a happy year.

The unit I was attached to dealt mainly with air photographs. It was interesting and exciting work and I really felt that I was doing something worthwhile. I have never forgotten Hassan's comment on my early wartime 'see nothing, hear nothing, do nothing' policy. 'Well, you were hardly a ball of fire, were you?' I could hear him in my mind as plainly as though he were there. I had smarted then and I still felt a mite ashamed every time I recalled it.

Perhaps you don't believe in ghosts, but most of us Malays do, and I had a strong feeling that Hassan was close by, watching over me.

I remembered being shown an air photograph of our clearing and Hassan explaining why they had moved a hut after receiving the prints. I told the CO about it one day and he immediately wrote down the details of the area and sent a clerk to see if there were any photographs covering that map reference. He chatted to me in a very friendly manner while we were waiting for the prints, and I soon found myself telling him about our life during the occupation and Hassan's exploits and sad end. (I did not tell him about my sister's wedding, because running amok and suicide are things which anyone would prefer to forget.)

Imagine my joy when the photographs arrived! Not the ones I'd seen before, of course, but taken on a fairly recent sortie. Captain Jones took his stereoscope and started searching the prints for a camp and, as soon as he turned up the print with the huge Sakai clearing on it, I knew it was our clearing straight away. Allah, how my mind leaped back!

I showed Captain Jones exactly where the huts had been – and probably still were – and he searched again. After a while he remarked that our camouflage must have been pretty good, as he could see no sign of it, nor of any path leading to the camp. I thrilled with pride; although, of course, it had had nothing to do with me.

It was terrible to think that Dick Richardson and Hassan were both dead and the Chinese whom I had known were now our enemies.

Only the officers actually interpreted the photographs. I worked with the other ranks who plotted them and made maps and traces and sometimes mosaics of the required areas. But after that session with Captain Jones he often called me in to look at certain photographs and ask me questions concerning them.

I suppose one takes one's own country for granted and, although I had often been half asleep on beat duty, I found that my local knowledge was greater than I had realised.

It was during this time that I met Azizah.

There is quite a famous amusement park in KL, the Bintang Kilat, which means Shining Star. Part of it was out of bounds to the British troops, so, of course, that made it all the more attractive, and for some time the boys had been urging me to take them there.

It was nothing special really. I had been there a few times, but it wasn't one of my haunts. A good old jumble of noisy entertainment. Besides the shooting-galleries and the carnival side, there were a couple of cabarets – these were the main attraction for the BORs – where pretty little Chinese taxi dancers sat two to a table round the floor. You bought a book of tickets and each ticket was worth a dance with the girl of your choice. By rights a girl couldn't refuse, but occasionally they did – and who could blame them when you saw some of the sweaty, beer-sodden drunks looming over them? Then, of course, there would be a brawl and that was one of the reasons why several of these cabarets were out of bounds. The other was because many of the girls were also prostitutes, and there was insufficient control over disease.

There was also Cantonese opera, which is colourful enough if you can bear the noise; various juggling and conjuring acts; the Siamese *ramvong* and the Malay *ronggeng* stages.

It was to one of these last that I led my companions one Saturday night.

The Malay *ronggeng* is our national dance, although I believe it has its origins with the Portuguese. Only professional female dancers take part, and in this case four of them were sitting at one end of a raised platform beside a three-piece Malay orchestra, consisting of a drummer and two violinists.

I remember that evening very well, because it was the first time I saw Azizah.

She sat at the end nearest to where we were standing and she was the tallest, slimmest and fairest of the four. She was dressed in a sarong and kebaya all of one material; both the long-sleeved, tight-fitting bodice and even tighter skirt, of apple green, shot with a silvery thread. She wore high-heeled, red, Western-style shoes, and a silver anklet peeped out of the slit in her skirt. Her hair was thick and glossy and naturally wavy, and it fell in a heavy fold on her shoulders, glistening and swaying with every movement.

She was the most beautiful creature I had ever seen and I couldn't take my eyes off her. I have seen her in many different outfits and with many different backgrounds since, but it is always as I saw her on that first occasion that I remember her best.

We do not touch our partners in the ronggeng, and most

often it is now just a shuffle backwards and forwards, with an occasional turn or sideways movement, but little more. A lot of it is called joget modern these days, and that is just what it is – a sort of aimless jog to samba rhythm, which anyone can do. But there are intricate steps and movements to the real ronggeng, and my father, being quite an expert himself, had taught us all as boys.

I realised with a sudden shock that I was getting on for twenty-seven and still unmarried and that women had played a very small part in my life. My mother was always pleading with me to be allowed to arrange a marriage and I had accepted the fact that I could not remain a bachelor much longer, but I had not given it serious thought.

But now, looking at this glorious girl, I knew quite definitely that I was going to choose my own wife and not to be matched off with some boring frump from the right family.

'Go on, Sheriff – take your eyes off that girl and dance with her!'

All of a sudden I wanted to show off. I bought a beer all round for the band and asked the leader if he would play the intricate handkerchief dance.

At the first drum beat I was on the floor and whirling into the extravagant solo request that is the prerogative of the first dancer on the floor, but more often than not missed out nowadays, especially in public places.

Recognising the introductory strains, the girls began pulling out brightly-coloured chiffon handkerchiefs and a sigh of approval went up from the Malays in the crowd.

I continued my gyrations, every so often approaching the partner of my choice with bent knees and outstretched hands, until such time as three other men had joined me on the platform. My partner remained seated, looking bored and blank, as custom demands, until the band went into the rhythm proper, when all four girls rose.

Luckily I had a rather super white handkerchief with my initials embroidered in one corner, which I had bought in England, and I was able to pull this languidly from my sleeve and face my partner with the required air of nonchalance which I was far from feeling.

The footwork in this dance is precise and there are several moments when one goes down close to the ground with bent knees and ankles, dancing round each other in movements not unlike those of a Cossack dance. This is not easy to perform, especially when rising with slow grace and without losing the rhythm. Each time we went down there were cries of 'Good old Sheriff' from my friends, and applause from the crowd. Every time the band reached the final passage, the crowd roared for them not to stop and they struck up again.

My partner remained as cool and graceful as a swan, but I could feel the sweat trickling down my back and chest and was thankful when the last chord was finally played. The beautiful girl actually smiled at me and I gave her a curt bow.

I knew that this was the moment to leave her, so, jumping from the platform and mopping my brow, I cried out, 'Come on, I'll buy you all a beer. Allah knows, I need one!'

We went on to the cabaret after that but I didn't dance. I never have been able to get used to the Western style of dancing. I had been to many dances in England, but it still seemed slightly shameful to me to clutch a strange woman – or, even worse, one you knew – close like that.

I sat and dreamed dreams of my ronggeng girl.

It became a regular Saturday night routine for a whole gang of us, some of them soldiers from my own unit and two or three of the Malay NCOs, to visit the amusement park and end up with a meal.

After a while I began slipping off on my own on the odd night during the week, and soon I noticed that Azizah's face would light up when I arrived.

She had delicate features; a thinnish, bridged nose, which betrayed a portion of Arab or Turkish blood, and a wide mouth with the most perfect teeth I had ever seen. I never grew tired of looking at her, and when she smiled I felt desire leap in my loins like a shoal of fish.

There was an extra girl, who relieved the others in turn for a couple of dances throughout the night, and it was during one of these breaks that I asked Azizah to have a cup of coffee with me at a nearby stall.

It was the first time I had heard her speak. She had a clear voice, a trifle high, but melodious, with a terrible Pahang accent, but I felt sure I could eradicate that in time.

She seemed impressed when I told her I was a police inspector and, to her credit, made no bones about her own social standing. Her mother, she told me, had also been a ronggeng girl, who died during the occupation. She had no idea who her father was. At first I was shocked by this candid statement, but later I came to respect her for her complete honesty.

After a couple of months I ventured to ask Azizah if she would come to the cinema with me one Sunday, and imagine my delight when she assented.

It was a ghastly film, highly emotional and badly overacted. Something about a pontianak – you know, a woman dies in childbirth and comes back to haunt the place. They are always portrayed as skinny hags with staring eyes, long fangs and claws, and hair like a bale of straw which has come unravelled. Ridiculous, of course, but Azizah was terrified and on several occasions clutched my arm with fright and buried her face in my shoulder. It was wonderful! I made a mental note always to take her to horror films!

Afterwards we went and had a meal of satay and chicken curry; it was one of the best evenings I can remember.

I had told Azizah a little about my family and during the meal she asked if my mother would not be shocked to think of my taking out a girl on her own, unchaperoned.

In truth my mother would have been more than shocked, had she known. But I had taken out girls in England and could see nothing wrong in what seemed to me a pleasant Western custom.

Soon we were spending every Sunday together. I had acquired a second-hand scooter, one of those Italian jobs, and I would pick her up at midday from the room she rented with a couple of other girls in the Malay reserve part of town, and off we'd go.

Mostly we would stroll round the Lake Gardens and have an open-air meal, but we usually ended up in the cinema.

Azizah wanted to go to Port Dickson and swim, but I could not contemplate seeing her in a bathing suit before we were married.

From this you will gather that I had thoughts of marriage on my mind, although I had said nothing as yet to her – nor to my mother. When finally I did mention it, she just laughed and said that as my mother would never permit our union, why even think about it.

I believe Azizah would have given herself to me had I asked – in fact, she almost hinted as much – and this worried me. I wanted her enough, my blood is as hot as the next man's, but loose conduct is something which I have been brought up to abhor and, when I married, I wanted my wife to be a virgin.

I tried to explain all this to her, but I couldn't. Europeans seem to find it so easy to discuss these things – I used to listen aghast sometimes to my English colleagues at the Police Training College when they talked about their love life with such frankness – but, modern as I am, it goes against all my upbringing.

I am sure that Azizah is a pure girl and I have told her that I would not soil that purity – she gave me a funny look, but I think she understands.

67. OF THOSE WHO SURVIVED

Jogindar Singh

I got my posting – traffic branch at Perangor Contingent Headquarters – and no more questions asked. I wanted to write a letter to thank the Depot Adjutant, but I am not very good at writing, so my wife made a fan of gold and silver paper on a bamboo frame and covered it with a mesh of lace and embroidery, which I presented to him for his little daughter. Suvindar is clever with her hands and it was a pretty thing.

It was during the first quarter of 1949 that we boarded the north-bound train from Kuala Lumpur, my wife already with child and suffering from dizzy spells, and our barang, that is, all our belongings, taking up half the railway carriage. It was a relief to arrive at our destination.

Wales is the Chief Police Officer of my new contingent. I didn't recognise him, but I never forget a name and his was on one of my sheaf of letters. I made it my business, therefore, to put myself where he might see me.

My chance came about a week after our arrival. The CPO was already in his car, with the driver walking round to the front seat, when he saw me and leaned out of the window, a puzzled look on his face.

'Just a minute,' he said to the driver, and to me, 'Corporal.'

'Sahib.'

I marched over to the open window and saluted.

He peered short-sightedly at me for a moment. then, 'It *is* Jogindar, isn't it?'

I smiled. 'Sahib.'

He smiled too and held out his hand through the window.

'I can't stop now, I'm on my way to a meeting. Come and see me in my office this afternoon.'

'Sahib.' I crashed my heels again and the staff car drove away.

'Come in, Jogindar, and sit down.'

I hesitated, but the CPO motioned me to bring up a chair.

We talked of the war years, of those who survived and those who had not, of the Japs and of the food, of the tragedies and some of the funny episodes, all the time being interrupted by the telephone and the entry and exit of clerks.

'It's a bit like being on a railway platform,' he laughed, 'I don't get much time these days.' Before I left, he asked me how I liked my job and then advised, 'Traffic's all right, but like most specialist jobs, it's a bit of a dead end. If you want to get on you have to be GD – if I can see an opening for you in a General Duties post I'll let you know.'

That first interview had taken place in June, soon after the Emergency had broken out, and since then the CPO had been busier than ever. He was not young and the years in prison camp had not made him any younger. He looked small and grey as he darted in and out, and there were many lines on his face. It was September when he sent for me again.

'I hear you've become a father *and* done well in your exams since I last saw you. I'm pleased to hear it. And now I have some good news for you. I'm putting you in charge of the police station at Batu Lima. It's a sergeant's post with a corporal and ten men. Only a small station, but it's in a bad area and it's a chance to prove your worth. If you do well, there will be larger stations to follow. No one wants an Emergency, but it opens up endless opportunities for young men like yourself.'

It seemed a long time since Uncle Arjan had mapped out a course for me.

I was thinking about this as I took off my boots outside my barrack-room and tiptoed inside. Suspended from a hook in the ceiling was a spring, which held a sarong and inside the sarong reposed by infant son, not yet two months old.

'Ranjit,' I whispered, gently pulling on the spring. 'Ranjit Singh, son of Jogindar Singh, grandson of Pritam Singh.'

I was still rocking the child and crooning an ancient Punjabi lullaby when my wife came down the verandah from the communal kitchen, bearing our midday meal.

I watched her as she laid out plates and saucers, took the hot chapatties from a cloth and spread them liberally with *ghee*. Soon my meal was ready and she took the child from his swinging crib, to sit and suckle him while I ate.

'You are a good wife, Suvindar,' I said, 'a good wife, a good mother and a good cook. I am a lucky man.'

She lowered her eyes, with the shy smile which she had never lost, and hugged the child to her.

'I also,' she murmured. 'You are a good husband to me.'

I ate in silence for a while, enjoying my meal and the picture of my wife and son.

'The curry is good,' I said, as I folded a chapattie and dipped it in the sauce. 'How would you like to have your own kitchen, instead of having to wait your turn with everybody else?'

'Of course I would like it.'

'You will have one soon – perhaps next week.'

At that her enormous eyes flew wide open and stared into mine, questioning, hopeful.

'A sergeant's quarters has its own kitchen,' I said.

Her brow furrowed and she put the child away from her. 'A sergeant's quarters?'

'Within a short time from now you will be the wife of the OCPS, Batu Lima.'

She smiled then and her eyes shone. She put Ranjit back inside the sarong and moved to replenish my plate.

There was no need to explain to her the meaning of OCPS; she was a police daughter. But for those of you who are unfamiliar with the police formation, I will explain.

At the top is the Commissioner, at Federal Headquarters, then each State has its own HQ – Contingents, the State formations are called – under a Chief Police Officer. Our Contingent was divided into four Circles, each one under an Officer Superintending Police Circle; and the Circles divided again into Districts, each one under an Officer-in-Charge Police District. The circle that I was posted to comprised three Districts, Kuala Jelang, Merbau and Kemuning. Batu Lima was one of the stations in Kemuning District and I was to be Officer-in-Charge Police Station. Of course we never use all these long-winded titles, but refer to the officers concerned as the CPO, OSPC, OCPD and OCPS respectively. There are several jobs that we refer to by initials, and I will tell you about these, then, if anyone in the police is telling you his story, you will understand what he is talking about.

First, let me say that using initials as we do is not laziness, but for ease and clarity; whether we are speaking Urdu, Malay, Chinese, English, or any of the other languages used in Malaya, we always use the same initials. All the uniformed members of the force are General Duties, or GD; the plain-clothes ones are members either of Special Branch, SB, or the Criminal Investigation Department, CID. The lowest rank in either is Police Constable, or PC, and, if he is one of the latter branches, he puts a D in front of it for Detective. Every police station has a Charge Room Officer always on duty and he is referred to as the CRO. Of course there are many others and, now that the Emergency is on, you are always hearing references to CTs, or Communist Terrorists – often called bandits as well – the MCP, or Malayan Communist Party, SEPs, or Surrendered Enemy Personnel – those are the informers – nearly all the estates and mines have Special Constables guarding them, and they are always known as SCs.

I hope I have not muddled you, but you can see from the formation I have explained that I would, in the future, be far removed from the CPO, under whose eyes I had worked for the past few months, but he will still have the last word on my promotion or demotion, depending on how I make out in my first sergeant's post.

I could see at a glance that there would be much to do in my new station. The men, all Malays, were undisciplined, lazy and frightened.

My predecessor was a lily-livered Malay of the worst type. Scared of his own shadow, he had let the very thought of the terrorists get the whole station down. Who cared about a handful of Chinese bandits? I'd seen worse than that during the war. I told the men just that, and it was not too long before I had instilled some discipline and pride into them again and generally tidied the place up.

The OCPD had his hands full and only visited infrequently, but when he did he was quite complimentary and said he was glad to have me. He was very young and rather remote. I would never know him as well as I knew the CPO.

I enjoyed my new responsibility. The CPO had been right; traffic was a dead end. I was grateful for his help but, as I did so frequently, I had to think back and be grateful for the first help, the first guidance, that I had received from my uncle, Arjan Singh.

68. A MATTER OF LANGUAGE

Vincent Lee Chee Min

Dad had given his consent to my joining the police soon after the beginning of the Emergency, in the middle of 1948, and by the end of the year I was in Singapore, with him.

It had certainly looked as though he intended to kill the fatted calf when he wired me that a room was booked for me in the Cathay Hotel and I was to wait for him there.

Instead, he was at the airport to meet me and, if it hadn't been for the letter that I'd received from Mum in the meantime, I would have thought he was afraid I might give him the slip. Mum had said that Rosalie was married and that the union had suited everyone. Two of my elder brothers were already back in Malaya, but the doctor, Anthony, had stayed on in Melbourne to do a post-graduate course. Apparently a friend of his, recently qualified from the same university, had called on Mum and Dad on his return to Malaya and fallen hook, line and sinker for little Rosalie. It was mutual and, as he was the son of one of Dad's important business associates, everything in the garden was lovely. Then, just a month ago, Anthony had written to say he was married too – and would soon be bringing home his Australian bride.

I gather from Mum the old man nearly threw a fit. That was *not* why he had sent us all to Aussie and he immediately panicked in case I should do the same thing. Hence the sudden summons home. Marriage, as far as Dad is concerned, is for one reason only, to unite businesses and to produce heirs to inherit them. The thought of marrying someone merely because you wanted to live with them was, in my father's eyes, sheer lunacy. Marriage was a business contract; you could always find secondary wives for pleasure.

I was thinking about all this while I waited for my bags to be cleared through Customs and responded to Dad's effusive gestures through the iron grille.

'Hi, Dad,' I was able to say at last, 'you look great. I thought you'd be white-haired by now!' I hadn't seen him for more than seven years.

'You look great yourself, son.'

He beamed and patted me on the back, but once we were inside his chauffeur-driven car he said, 'Let's not use a foreign tongue between ourselves,' and addressed me in our own dialect.

I was at a loss. I could vaguely comprehend what he was saying, but I could not for the life of me reply.

My father looked hard at me and grew stern. 'Don't you choose to speak your own language any more – or can't you? I shook my head, mute. 'Your brothers did not forget. And how about your mother – didn't you speak with her at week-ends?'

It was true that Mum had spoken a little Cantonese with us when she had first arrived, but she had soon got into the habit of speaking only English herself. She was better educated than Dad and I guess this was a sore point. But Dad is Fukien and we had always spoken his dialect at home.

'I was only eleven when you sent me to Aussie, Dad,' I reminded him. I didn't want to let Mum down.

'Hm.' He sat in silence for the rest of the drive into town. He had made an effort to learn English himself during the past few years, but it didn't come naturally and it was not a language he enjoyed.

That evening he took me to a businessmen's dinner and excused me, saying that I had almost forgotten my own dialect, let alone Hokkien, but I could see he was ashamed of me. I picked up my chopsticks and my fingers felt stiff too; I would have given a lot for a fork – oh Mum!

It was good to see Mum again, but I only stayed a few days at home.

I had always thought of our house as being fairly vast, but it was even larger than I remembered and I had got out of the habit of being waited on hand and foot. It seemed to me that the luxury was a little oppressive and, for the first time, I really understood why Mum had loved her little apartment, where she could do what she liked when she liked and in privacy.

Rosalie's husband was already practising in Kuala Lumpur and I was glad to stay with them while I looked up Dad's influential friend in the police.

My, it was good to be back to informality. I was already beginning to pick up my Chinese again, but those two spoke English at home from choice and had only one maidservant to attend to their needs.

We spent a happy evening talking about old times and then I was up early to see to my career.

Dad's friend at Police Headquarters was an austere, scholarly type, who greeted me without much enthusiasm. I don't know what rank he was, because he wore plain clothes, but by the deference he was treated with, I'd say pretty high.

'We should not have any trouble getting you into the Inspectorate,' he said, after he'd written down my particulars. 'We badly need more Chinese inspectors in Special Branch You have a good background and education, and languages are all-important now.'

We had used English throughout the interview.

'We like at least three Chinese dialects if possible,' he went on, 'but two will suffice, and of course Malay and English. What's your Malay like?'

'Hopeless,' I told him, 'I haven't used it for eight years.'

He waved that away. 'Not important! you'll pick it up. You've got English. I'd better just make a note of your Chinese dialects though.'

He held his pencil poised and waited. Then he looked expectantly at me.

'None,' I said at last.

'Don't try to be too clever because you've become so Europeanised,' he sounded cross. 'You must have two dialects – and most educated Chinese of your age have Mandarin as well these days.'

'I'm sorry,' I said, 'I shall no doubt relearn them, but at present I have none.'

'Then it seems that you are wasting my time.'

It was obvious that he thought Dad had made a fool of him and his eyes and mouth were hard slits when I stood up to say good-bye.

He barely touched my hand and was already immersed in some report by the time I reached the door.

'Well, good on you,' I said sarcastically to my reflection in the office door; 'so much for Commissioner Lee!'

But I could still join the force; I didn't *have* to go through the back door – although for Dad and his ilk that was the only way to go.

I marched straight down the hill, along the road and the main street, until I came to the first police station. I went in.

'I wish to enlist as a police constable,' I said.

Bugger the old man!

69. AN ILL-CONSTRUCTED TRIANGLE

The first stream joins the river

Donald Thom

'How did it go?'

'All right, I think. When, and if, I graduate.'

Cautious Thom, they call me. Well, I didn't want to sound too cocky, but I was pretty sure it was going to be all right.

A chorus of groans greeted my last remark. Affectation really, because almost all those guys were just one hundred per cent certain they were going to graduate. Only I was afraid of not getting through – because I wanted to so much.

We'd all been through the war, none of us all that young, but they just didn't seem to care whether they passed or failed. There's always next time, they said. Judas Priest, was I ever that carefree?

The interview was for selection into the Colonial Forestry Service and just about every doggone one of us had applied. Sure hope there are plenty of vacancies.

Well, I graduated okay and that sure was a relief plus. The day those results came through we had some shindig and then it was a case of getting down to work.

The Board was as good as its word and I didn't have long to wait before a short, dry letter arrived from the Colonial Office, offering me a post in the Forestry Department of the Federation of Malaya, subject to my being medically fit.

I had no worries on the latter score. It was a long time since I'd broken my legs and I'd been playing rugger and ice hockey since then, so the medical was a mere formality.

Three of us were on the same posting and I guess our faces must have looked like shining Edam cheeses when we left the Colonial Office, armed with lists of what to take and what not to. Then off to get our tropical kit and we were all set for the boat.

I guess I was labelled a wet blanket from the outset. I enjoyed the voyage okay, but hell, once bitten twice shy, damned if I was going chasing the girls, and honestly, the conversation every morning in the bar about who had been caught with whom and in whose cabin became just plain boring after a while. Judas Priest, you'd think those guys had nothing better to think about.

Well, I spent my time sun-bathing and doing PT, doing as much swimming as one can do in those pint-sized ponds they call pools on ships, playing deck tennis, and the rest. I disgusted my companions, but who cares? Probably never see each other again once we've reached Singapore.

I sure feel the heat, though. Gee whiz, this humidity! I thought my home state at harvest time was pretty near furnace heat, but that was easier to take than this. Seems like I change my shirt every half-hour and I'm still wet through. But I reckon if I can keep up this exercise now, actual work shouldn't be too bad when we start.

Well, we're here. That Singapore is quite a place. Noisier than anywheres else I've ever been, and who says the Chinese are a quiet, dignified bunch? Mystic East, my eye – vulgar and ostentatious we'd call them back home, but I guess the old folks are different. Mind you, we only spent the weekend there, then the Monday shopping, and the night mail train to Kuala Lumpur.

We'd heard some about the Malayan Emergency on the boat, but I don't quite know what I'd expected. Certainly not the train with its armour-plated pilot engine, and so many troops and police swarming all over the place. Still, I gather there've been too many derailments for them to take chances. Mind you, the troops guarding the train that night – Jocks they were – were so darned high that they had to be taken off before we were half-way through the State of Johore, the most southern state, and replaced by Malay police. I sure wasn't so proud of my Scottish ancestry that night, but it seems like the Jocks were on the last lap of their tour and they were celebrating the thought of going home.

Jesus, you should see the railway station in Kuala Lumpur! Like something out of the *Arabian Nights*! I guess they built it to look like a Sultan's palace or something, and they sure did succeed. Marble columns and domes and all those little minarets and things. Certainly is quite different from anywhere else I've been. I reckon I'm going to enjoy it here.

And now I'm posted to Kuala Jelang and my head's sure in a whirl. The blurb tells me that it is a district comprising hilly rain forest – isn't all Malaya? – rubber plantations, one oil palm plantation, one tin mine, a rice-growing area, and the rest coastal swamp.

What it didn't tell me was that I was going to receive my baptism of fire on my very first day there. And in the darndest way.

Would you believe it? During the month we'd spent becoming familiarised we'd spent some time on forestry stations in pretty dangerous areas and some on the rifle range at the Police Depot – after all, the forests are where most of the terrorists live. I'd got myself a carbine and been enrolled as an honorary inspector in the Special Constabulary, so what more natural than when seeing a coupla SCs standing by the roadside I should stop to say how do – try out my two words of Malay?

It's a red road from the state capital to Kuala Jelang and I'd been tense as a cricket the whole way down, expecting an ambush at every turn. Then, just a coupla miles out of KJ itself, I see these two guys, so I stop.

One of the bastards loosed off at me before I was even half-ways out of the car, and before I could aim myself they were away.

And so was I. That car sure became a hot rod and I kept my foot right down for the rest of the journey, and to hell with the tyres.

Did I feel a bloody fool, arriving in my first station with a bloodied shirt and my arm feeling a thousand hornets were having a go at it – yeah, the blighters had nicked me, just above the elbow, but I was so doggone mad I hadn't noticed it at the time.

Scant sympathy from the police. Laughed their silly heads off at my being so green – they sent out a patrol nevertheless. Seems a couple of SCs were killed in that area last week and those guys must've had their uniforms – I learned the bandits usually stripped them.

Well, Thom. Lesson number one: this is another war; you're not playing at Boy Scouts.

Kuala Jelang was not at all what I had expected and neither was, or is, the job. I'm not complaining. But I'll sure feel a fish out of water until I get a hold of this language, though, and in a minute you'll see why.

I was pretty glad when I'd been told that once I'd taken over it would be an all-bachelor station, but now I'm not so sure. My predecessor, a middle-aged guy named Leslie, with a young and pretty wife, threw a luncheon party for me when I first arrived, for me and the rest of the European community. That is to say, the District Officer and the OC Police – or DO and OCPD as I've learned to call them – the other two bachelors. Leslie spent most of the time telling me how he sure hoped for a town posting when he returned from leave, because his wife was going nuts here; and the other two kept telling me how they were going to miss having a woman around to stop them talking shop the whole time.

I don't reckon the three of us are going to have much in common. The DO's one of those maidenly old bachelors – you know the type, petit point pictures on the walls and a Malay youth in the servants' quarters. The OCPD, on the other hand, is a womaniser, a great one for the ladies. So where do I fall? I ask you, what an ill-constructed triangle – a stallion, a queer and a celibate monk!

I'd put both Monica and Marijke firmly out of my mind the minute I set foot on that boat, and that's where they were going to stay – I wasn't going to be haunted by any more ghosts. I'd come here to throw myself into my work and, Judas Priest, that's what I'm going to do.

It had been easy while I lived in the Rest House, but once the Leslies had gone and I moved into my own quarters, it was difficult to imagine how I'd cope on my own. And I nearly didn't have to. I said I needed to get a hold of the language, and if I had done so by then I would not have become the laughing-stock that I did – not that I knew what they were laughing at at the time.

Derek King – that's the OCPD – had helped me move. I'd assembled a fair amount of clobber already and my quarters are down by the Forest Station, some distance from the Rest House and the other two bungalows.

We were just standing in the main room and King was voicing out loud what I'd been trying not to think about, that the place sure needed a woman, when in glided Salmah.

Now Salmah was something for which I quite definitely had not bargained. Hell, no. She was Malay, pretty, graceful and of indeterminate age. King laughed when she arrived, seems he'd been expecting her. As I've said, he's a great womaniser that boy. He quite casually slaps her on the bottom and announces to me that she's always good for a roll. How do you like that?

'I won't touch her, old man,' he says, 'She's all yours!

I guess I must have looked pretty nonplussed, especially as it looked to me as though he'd already touched her quite a lot. It was all I could think of and I asked, 'But you?'

He laughed again – irritating laugh that guy has – and then said cheekily, 'No thanks, old man, I like them white!'

I was just about to tell this gal that I could dispense with her services thank you very much, when King caught my arm and shook his head.

'Don't be a bloody fool, old man. She can cook – and that's something that doesn't grow on trees in Kuala Jelang – the other thing does.'

Honestly, I hadn't even thought about eating and having my clothes washed, and all the other necessities which had just happened in the hotels and Rest Houses where I'd been living. So I engaged her, albeit reluctantly, and asked Derek King, my friend, I hoped, to make it quite clear that I required her to cook and nothing else. I didn't quite trust that guy, and with reason.

Well, they went into a long confab and came out of it in peals of merriment. God damn this language! How the hell did I know what he said to her?

'Will you please tell her,' I said, in my most sedate voice, 'that I shall spend my evenings learning Malay and shall require no other entertainment.'

The translation of that brought forth another gust of laughter.

Well, I never did discover exactly what that rotter had said that day, but when I returned from work – and I was pretty shagged after that first day on my own, I can tell you – Salmah quickly filled the tin bath with hot water, laid out my clean clothes, and by the time I was out of it had a drink poured out for me. Never did a Scotch go down so well.

Well, this sure enough is service, I thought, perhaps King was my friend after all. I knew he looked after his own creature comforts pretty well – he was a bit of a sybarite for all his outer veneer of toughness. I leaned back to enjoy my drink, and when Salmah was at my elbow I didn't refuse a refill.

With the aid of sign language and the dictionary, I managed to tell her what time I wanted to eat. Not bad, it was, either. Fish, I remember, with a coconut dessert and local fruit to follow; and properly made coffee. Better than any Rest House fare without doubt. I complimented her – and myself for not being as pig-headed as I nearly was – and settled down to my work while she cleared the table, asked me if there was anything else I wanted, and quietly disappeared.

I worked for about an hour, I guess, and when the print started to blur and I was yawning as often as breathing, I reckoned it was time for bed.

I told you that that King was a double-crossing rotter. She was there all right. I heard a small sound from the bed as soon as I opened the door. No need to turn up the light, but I did, and there I beheld my cook, a flowery sarong rolled up under her arms and long golden legs and arms bare – I hadn't become so celibate that I didn't look. She was all right, all right.

'Please go,' I said; I could manage that much in Malay. 'I thought I made it quite clear.'

'You learn Malay, no?' Her voice was high-pitched and staccato. 'I teach.' She held up her arms and smiled.

'Yeah,' I groaned. 'I've heard all about those dictionaries that always open at the same page. Now off you go.'

It was pretty obvious that Salmah wouldn't, or couldn't, believe it. I reckoned she had every reason to be surprised that her advances were being refused; I bet that son of a bitch had told her I'd take her on.

'You shy,' she said. 'Look, I make like cinema.' She pouted her lips into a grotesque reproduction of what she'd no doubt seen on many a silver screen and held up those gorgeous arms again. If I hadn't been so cross, I might have weakened

'Now come on, git.' I lifted the mosquito net, but she just pouted prettily.

What does a guy do? Okay, okay, don't tell me. Well, I didn't. I picked up my pyjamas and went back to the verandah. I didn't want her to lose too much face for what I had a shrewd suspicion was not her fault, and I had already realised that I would lose a good cook.

I spent as uncomfortable a night as I've spent since the war – and if you've ever tried sleeping on one of those government issue settees, you'll understand – until the dawn came and I heard her creep out through the bathroom door. What a relief. I sank on to my still warm bed and caught an hour's sleep.

At breakfast Salmah was all demure eyes and she never troubled me again. *What* a relief! I still had my cook too.

It was not many days before the OCPD heard on the grapevine that the new Forestry Officer was impotent!

70. THE WILL OF GOD

Omar

Is it possible that I have done some terrible act during my life without knowing it? In what way have I offended Tuan Allah, that I should be visited by tragedy yet again?

We had had two uneventful years in Singapore, years of blessed tranquillity after the horrors and privations of the occupation, and I had been promoted to the rank of sergeant-major, with a pleasant little house.

These thoughts go through my head as I stand in that little house and look at my wife's neatly folded clothes and the children's toys which I still cannot bear to part with.

It had been good to be back in uniform. I had been promoted to sergeant almost at once and we had spent a happy year in Malacca. Politics had never concerned the likes of me, or so I had thought, but when the Straits Settlements and the Federated Malay States ceased to be and became first the Malayan Union, then Singapore and the Federation of Malaya, it threw many of us into turmoil. Malacca became part of the Federation and I had the choice of remaining there or joining the Singapore force, where so many of the old Straits Settlements police were going. I went too.

It took us some time to become accustomed to the life of a big city after the rural areas to which we were used, but once inside the police compound there was little difference. My wife had brought the cats and chickens with her; coconuts and a lime tree to plant – wah! what didn't she bring? It was all I could do to stop her putting a sack of dried fish on the top of the taxi that had taken us to the railway station! There were nine of us on the move. I shall never forget it. Bedding rolls, pots and pans, suitcases, plastic buckets, children's toys – my wife was sure that none of these things would be obtainable in Singapore. Adohi! She was a simple woman, my wife.

We were so happy. Even the plight of Zaitun could not mar our contentment.

The medical authorities did everything they could, but it was no use. Then one day a smart young Chinese lady called on us in our quarter.

'It is about Zaitun,' she said at once. 'I am from the Social

Welfare Department and we have decided, after what the doctors have said, that it would be best if you let her come to one of our homes, where she can be properly cared for.'

Allahumma! You should have seen my wife burst with indignation! Of course the young lady meant well, but my wife would not calm down until she had been chased from our door. Adohi, I was hot with shame.

So the matter of Zaitun was closed and we went on living as we had since the end of the war, a peaceful family, accepting the will of God and praying that no more bad times would come our way.

But the will of God is difficult to understand.

We had returned to Tanjong Mas for my first long leave, and the three months were nearly up when I was recalled to Singapore to be a witness in a court case. There was less than a week of my leave left anyway, so, when the case was over, I did not return to collect my family, but left them to join me on their own.

They were coming by bus, as we had arranged, and I was already at the bus terminal to meet the express when the awful news was imparted to those of us who were waiting. The bus would not arrive; there had been an accident.

The office could only tell me that it had taken place on one of the ferries, crossing a wide river in Johore, and could not say what casualties there were, or if all were safe.

Without waiting, or seeking permission from my superiors, I hailed the first taxi I saw and asked him to drive me to the scene. The driver was a family man like myself and, may Allah bless him, took me post-haste, refusing to accept my fare.

We arrived at the river after about two hours' driving and it was not difficult to see where the accident had taken place.

I went first to the small office, where normally one pays to board the ferry, to make inquiries. Only one survivor, I was told. Of the forty passengers and the driver, only one survivor.

Next I pushed my way through the crowd which surrounded the place on the river-bank where the vehicle should have mounted the ramp to the shore.

Even now I am not clear exactly what happened. Whether the driver misjudged the narrow ramp, or the ferry had swayed out of line from the wash of a passing boat, is still uncertain to me. What matter? All I or anyone could see was the bonnet and front wheels of the bus. The rest of the vehicle was well under water at an angle of about forty-five degrees.

I stood, silent as the rest of the crowd, thinking of my poor wife and children, trapped in their seats, unable to fight the pressure of the water, until it was too late, and now they would be laid out on some mortuary slab. And I knew too, without being told, who would be the one survivor.

Sometimes I wonder if Tuan Allah plays tricks on us human beings.

On the river-bank, swinging her legs and humming a tuneless dirge, sat Zaitun, as unconcerned as though she were waiting for some small, routine event.

How she came to be the chosen one, I shall never know.

She turned to me without recognition and allowed me to help her down from the parapet on which she sat. I left her in the care of the kind taxi-driver while I went to identify the bodies of my wife and other children.

I had hoped that perhaps there had been a miscount of passengers, that perhaps some member of my family might be missing from the pathetic, white-sheeted line. But they were all there. Poor drowned things. I have seen many corpses as a policeman, but when I saw those of my own, I could only wish that Tuan Allah had seen fit to take me as well.

I took Zaitun back to Singapore and cared for her as best I could. It was not long before the Social Welfare worker arrived, the same Chinese lady who had visited us before, but once again I persuaded her to let Zaitun remain with me. I had friends, kind friends, who would care for her while I was on duty and, when I was off, in a way it was a help to have the girl there, albeit silent and remote.

It was some three months before the welfare worker came again, and that time I let her take Zaitun. I was so empty already, what was one more emptiness?

She trotted down the path behind the Chinese lady without giving me a single glance. Smiling, and twirling the inevitable bloom in her hands, she walked out of my life as unconscious of me as when I had first picked her up, a parcel thrown from a passing car, seventeen years before.

And I? I turned to face a life so bleak that I daily committed the sin of asking Tuan Allah in my prayers not to leave me long in this world of suffering and torment, but to take me too, so that I might join my wife and little ones. Purgatory cannot be worse.

71. THE BATTALION GOES HOME

Philip Morrison

In January 1949 the battalion went home, but it went without me.

So much had happened in the two years since we had first arrived in Singapore and yet it had flown. Not everything had gone right; far from it, but when the opportunity arose we both opted to stay in Malaya for another year.

To begin with there was the baby. Sally had been in Singapore about ten months when she became pregnant and, although it had been a mistake in the first place, once she became used to the idea it became an absolute obsession. The air force created merry hell when they discovered she had been married the whole time, but there was nothing much they could do about it, so she had resigned her commission and started making baby clothes. It was a good thing, as it happened, because not long afterwards we were posted up country and she would not have been able to follow me under her own steam.

The colonel had proved to be not such a bad old bastard after all. He liked Sally, which was the main thing, and he'd been pretty decent about giving me HQ jobs when the birth was imminent. We had moved straight into married quarters and I had got my majority, so things would have been rosy if it hadn't been for the baby. It was stillborn, and if you've ever seen the look on the face of a wounded bird, that's how Sally looked and she scarcely said a word the whole time she was in hospital. To make matters worse, the gynaecologist told me that I would be a very selfish man if I ever let her have another – I didn't understand all the technical details, but he made it quite plain that it had been a matter of my wife or the child and that the same thing could happen again.

If only she had taken it better. Sally's always been so full of guts, but it floored her completely; I've never seen her so down. I put all the things she had made for the infant in a top cupboard before she came home and she never once mentioned them.

The only blessing was that just at that time a vacancy for an IO's job arose; it was the type of work which Sally had been doing quite recently in the RAF, so it didn't need much persuasion to have her taken on. I had been worried about what she would do with herself, because, after all, I was a Company Commander and had to get back on the ground. I left with an easier mind, knowing that she had something to occupy hers.

Philip was right, the job was a blessing. Not particularly arduous, but it gave me something to do. I had tried so hard not to let him see how much I cared about losing the baby, but I don't think I was very successful. Of course he isn't fooling anyone – at least, not me. All this hooey about not wanting to risk my having a child in case he's killed. I know that doddering old quack told him there was something wrong with me, but there jolly well isn't and I'll prove it, one day.

I missed him terribly when he went back on ops, but I couldn't expect him to be away any longer. After all, he is a soldier, not a midwife.

1948 was a boring time for wives. Once we moved up country, all the wives, officers' and ORs' alike, were bundled in HQ quarters, while our men lived under canvas and visited us when they could. Sometimes they were only away for a few days, but at other times for more than a month – it was nerve-racking too, not being in the know and hearing odd snippets of information that such and such a company had been in action. Philip never said very much when he came home; he would want to go out to dinner and dance, or a flick perhaps.

A platoon sergeant was killed within forty-eight hours of my return, and two Jocks bought it the day before – a hand-grenade hurled into a coffee-shop – and only one bandit to our credit. As a mere soldier, it's difficult to understand how the civil authorities let all those bastards – known Communists – just scarper off as they did. Extraordinary. One of the police chaps, whose area my company were operating in, told us that they knew all along about it too but were powerless to act. Proves the old theory that the law is an ass.

In fact, we did have a few successes later on, but by that time the battalion was almost due to leave. A pity really; we'd all like to have chalked up a decent score.

A few jobs on the staff came up at that time and Bill Matheson, whom I had been with at the beginning, and I applied and landed two of them. I had never been a headquarters type, but it meant another year here and I knew Sally would be pleased. I was right.

And so there we were. Philip got his job, I was able to keep mine, and we stayed on in the same quarters. What could be cushier? I was all for having a husband on the staff.

I was sorry to see so many of our friends go, but a few Inverness-shires remained and, as Philip so often said, he had started in the wrong battalion, so being ERE for a spell was unlikely to do him much harm. There didn't seem much future in the army anyway.

As soon as he decently could, Philip put in for some leave and insisted on taking me down to see my old home. Why, I don't know, but I had always put off going there – it would have been easy enough from Singapore – but this time he made the decision and booked us a room in a nearby holiday bungalow.

As soon as we were over the border I was glad that he had taken the initiative. What a goose I'd been not to go before. As the first familiar landmarks came in sight my excitement rose and I kept stopping him to point things out. He was looking smug as anything, and if he hadn't been driving I'd have given him a big hug.

The old house still looked wonderful; timbusu trees bordering the drive and the lawns even greener than I remembered. We had rung up the present occupant, who had invited us to stay. I declined, but it was marvellous having someone so nice to take us round.

We didn't stay long, though, and next morning drove to the kampong where our servants used to live. They still did. Daddy had built a house for them before the war and, except for the trees that had grown up round about, I had no difficulty in recognising it.

Ja'afar and Siti, looking very much the same as when I had last seen them, were leaning over the railing of their small verandah, talking to someone below. They looked up as the car stopped, surprised to see Europeans, no doubt, but without a flicker of recognition on their faces.

They, of course, had already been middle-aged when we had left during the shambles of 1942, but I had only been sixteen.

Both came down the steps, their expressions of surprise changing first to puzzlement, then wonder and incredulity.

'Missy Sally? It *is* Missy Sally.'

Then they were all wide grins and Siti wrapped her arms around me and shook hands demurely with Philip, and a small boy was dispatched for cakes and bottles of orange crush.

'But why didn't you let us know you were back? We would have come to work for you.'

We were sitting on the verandah by that time, Philip feeling a bit of a lemon, I could see, because I'd made him take his shoes off! I made some feeble excuse about moving around, but they were not to be put off.

'We shall come now!' Ja'afar was quite firm. 'Next month. That will give you time to give notice to whoever you are employing at present.'

I was amused by their arrogant self-assurance and translated for Philip.

'Why not?' he asked. 'It would be nice for you. But you must tell them it will only be for a year.'

I did.

Ja'afar was unimpressed. 'Time he found another job then,' he snorted. 'Fancy not speaking Malay and leaving the country after such a short time. Whatever would the Old Tuan have said?'

Irrespective of what Sally's father might have said, there was no doubt who was going to be boss in the house in future, and it wasn't going to be me – it wasn't going to be Sally either!

I was amused to see her meekly doing what she was told by the two elderly Malays – I say elderly because they were both wrinkled and inclined towards toothlessness, but Sally said they could not be much over forty-five.

To cut a long story short, Ja'afar returned to Kuala Lumpur with us at the end of my leave and within ten days we were being thoroughly organised and I found myself having to start understanding Malay. Not a bad thing, as events proved, but I didn't know that then.

72. TO BE A HERO

Abdul Karim

The time came for me to leave school and one morning the headmaster asked me what I wanted to do.

'I want to be a mechanic,' I told him.

'A mechanic?' Inche Yacob, our headmaster, raised his eyebrows. 'Lucky all the boats have sails, because you would put paid to their outboards in no time!' He was always saying things like that.

'A mechanic?' my father asked. 'And where could you be a mechanic here?' It was true. There were no real roads, only a few tracks that jeeps and Land-Rovers could use in dry weather. No garages, no workshops. 'And what do you expect to learn on, your mother's sewing-machine? You'd better put such notions out of your head and become a fisherman like me.'

But I didn't want to be a fisherman.

I did go to sea, however, and, quite the opposite from Inche Yacob's prediction, I kept most of the outboards in good running order; the inboards too.

'It seems that the boy has a bent for engines,' I heard Inche Yacob remark to my father one day, as they sipped coffee on our verandah. I was supposed to be mending nets, but of course I stopped and strained my ears to hear what else he might have to say. 'Have you thought of putting him into the police? There's a big recruiting drive going on – here, let me see, I think I have the dates of the team's visit to this district in my pocket.'

The police? I had time to think while Inche Yacob went through one pocket after another and then said he must have left it on his desk. What would I want to join the police for? No one from Pasir Perak had ever joined the police that I knew of. I wanted to be a mechanic, not a policeman.

Pak made no mention of the conversation and I had almost forgotten it until the next time the OPCD visited our kampong. It just so happened that his Land-Rover drew up outside the police post as I was passing. I looked at the driver with new interest. Of course he was a policeman, although he was a driver – I'd not thought of that.

When the officer had gone inside the post, I approached him, suddenly feeling that he was rather grand.

'Excuse me,' I asked politely, 'but are you a mechanic as well as a driver?'

'Why do you ask? Want some old outboard mended?' He was rather a cheerful fellow, with a mouthful of gold teeth and a Kedah accent that I could hardly understand.

'Could you mend an outboard?' I asked.

'Of course.' He grinned, but at that moment the officer

called to him from the doorway and we were unable to converse further.

It made me think, though.

By the time the recruiting team arrived in our area I was seventeen and a half years old and had been out of school and messing around with the fishing fleet for more than a year.

'Could I be a mechanic?' I asked the Recruiting Officer.

'If you show aptitude and a vacancy exists,' he replied. I wasn't quite sure what he meant, but at least he hadn't said no.

The team were to be there all day. I would think about it, I said, and went home to talk it over with my father.

'Karim, wait for me,' I turned as I heard Rokiah's voice behind me. 'Oh, Karim, is it true? Are you really going to join the police?'

'I want to be a mechanic,' I told her, 'as you well know.'

'But the police, Karim – you might get killed. I know the Emergency hasn't touched us here yet, but hundreds of police are being killed on the other side.'

Musah had left the kampong, and it was generally thought that he was making his fortune in Singapore. I had been jealous of Rokiah's admiration for him.

Quite suddenly I wanted to be a hero in Rokiah's eyes.

'Men are needed,' I said shortly. 'It is better that I should serve my country rather than mess around here as I'm doing now – besides, I'm bored.'

'Oh, Karim, I do hope you won't get killed.'

She took my hand and we walked together down the road to my house, as we had walked nearly every day since she was nine and I was ten years old.

73. A COMMISSIONER'S COMMENDATION

The second stream joins the river

Jogindar Singh

It was in May 1949 that we moved again.

I had had seven months as OCPS Batu Lima when, one day in April, the OCPD visited the station. He had inspected everything, the books, the barracks, the arms and ammunition, before he told me that I was posted.

'You've done a good job here, Dato,' he said, 'and if I were not moving myself I would probably jib at your posting – except that it's on promotion, so I couldn't.'

I should explain here that sergeants and sergeant-majors are called 'Dato' in the force; it means 'Grandfather'. In the same way, inspectors are called 'Inche' and officers 'Tuan', which mean 'Mister' and 'Sir' – although many of us have kept the terms of respect from our own language and still call European officers 'Sahib'. It is just one of our customs.

'Sahib?' I now inquired, and to be polite, although I was burning with curiosity regarding my own future. 'The district will be sorry that you are leaving.'

He laughed then, and looking at him closely I saw that he was not, after all, so young.

'Jungle training school for me. It'll be a rest cure after a district. But aren't you interested in your own posting?'

'Sahib.'

'Well, you're only moving next door – OCPS Kuala Jelang. It's district headquarters, so it'll be promotion to sergeant-major for you. Both the OSPC and I have been very pleased with your work here and there'll be a Commissioner's Commendation for that amok case last month. Congratulations.'

The episode he referred to was an unpleasant one, when a Javanese in one of the nearby kampongs had run amok. Two of the man's immediate relatives were already dead and a third one near-fatally slashed when we were called. I had seen him coming at me like a crazed bull, parang raised, and put up my rifle to take the blow, in the same way as we use our staves as weapons of defence. It had not been difficult then to disarm him with one hand and drive my free fist into his jaw. He had gone down as though dead – and indeed I was afraid that I might have hit him too hard – but he regained consciousness soon after we had him locked in the police station cell. It had been an incident in the normal line of duty and did not to my mind merit a commendation, but I was pleased to have it.

So once again we were on the move. Only a matter of some 40 miles to the coast and the OPCD let me use a troop-carrier to transport my family and belongings. Once more my wife was near her time and I was glad that she was able to ride in front of the van with little Ranjit, now eleven months old. The back was piled high with our bedding rolls, pots and pans, and furniture that we had acquired, and I followed in a hired lorry, carrying the fruit trees in pots that were nearly ready for planting out, and our three cows. These last I had purchased when first coming to Batu Lima, in order to obtain fresh milk for my wife and child. The Health Sister, who comes round with the Mobile Clinic, insists that it is unhygienic and has done her best to dissuade Suvindar from drinking it, but some of these young women are very ill-informed. I had travelled to Kuala Jelang on the first day off after being informed of my transfer and made sure that there would indeed be sufficient grazing ground in the vicinity of the police station for the cattle.

It had been a business, pulling the unwilling beasts up the ramp and on to the lorry, but at last we were under way, with instructions to the driver to keep an even, steady pace and not go too fast – he might worry about ambushes, but I did not want to risk any broken legs.

Kuala Jelang was not unlike the coastal station where my father had ended his days as OCPS, only on the opposite side of the peninsula.

I was pleased to see that the police compound was well out of the town and away from the other government quarters. This made for both privacy and security and I believe that the police should always remain aloof from the civilian departments.

First I saw to the off-loading of the cows, then I saw my wife and child installed, changed into uniform, and reported to the OCPD.

On my recent visit I had come to an arrangement with a Chinese *towkay*, who owned a strip of grassland not far from the barracks, to let me graze my cattle there and provide him with milk in return. I knew I would never have to give him the milk – which he would not have touched anyway – but the offer had been made and he in his turn was pleased to be in favour with the police.

Poor things, they were badly scared and would undoubtedly not yield much milk for the next few days. I patted their rumps and noses and spoke gently to them until they were soothed and their great eyes were questing the juiciest grass, instead of staring in panic at the confining walls of the lorry.

Although still OCPS, I would no longer be my own master in the way that I had been at Batu Lima. Being a District Headquarters, the OCPD had his office in the station and there were a couple of Malay inspectors. Nevertheless, I was sergeant-major now, probably one of the youngest in the force ; I could not complain.

The OCPS's quarter was a small wooden house, raised on concrete pillars and standing alone to one side of the parade ground. My predecessor had planted many flowers in kerosene tins and Suvindar was already adding ours. I was glad that we would be installed before the second child was born. I hoped it would be another son.

74. KUALA JELANG – A BACKGROUND

Until the outbreak of the Emergency in June 1948, Kuala Jelang had been a veritable sleepy hollow.

The remains of the Portuguese fort slept on the top of the hill, the grave of Rajah Adnan, the last inhabitant of royal blood, reposed under its soft mantle of grey-green moss and the tide slid gently in and out of the mangrove swamps.

Sometimes at high tide the steamers of a local steamship company could be seen alongside the riverside wharf, loading bales of rubber and sacks of copra and pumping the liquid latex and palm oil into their tanks. Machinery would be offloaded and stores for the local shops and estates, and occasionally a few deck passengers would disembark. Irrespective of what the ship was doing or having done to her, there would always be a crowd, because the weekly visits were an event.

On Sundays, the planters and miners would come into town to play cricket on the padang, and to foregather afterwards at the atap and timber shack that was the local club. There were no other amusements and the club was the focal point of entertainment for all around, government servants, those living on the nearby estates and mines, the shopkeepers and anyone else who felt inclined to pay the modest entrance fee. Once a fortnight a film show was held and then all those inhabitants of Kuala Jelang who were not members of the club would crowd around the open windows, standing on orange boxes and home-made stilts, and sometimes taking it in turns to stand on each other's shoulders! The films were in Malay, Chinese, English, Hindi or Tamil – it made no difference, as the soundtrack could seldom be heard above the din.

Into this peaceful and somnolent way of life the Emergency had swept overnight, like some evil tidal wave.

Incidents erupted on the surface of the district like boils, while below, the pus of fear seeped steadily and mercilessly from estate to mine, to market garden and *padi* field, controlled by the pulsing head inside the jungle itself.

First a planter was shot at point-blank as he walked from his office to the factory; none of the labourers saw or heard a thing, despite the fact that it was a busy time of day. Then the bodies of two Tamil tappers were found, their hands nailed to the trees on which they had been working; they had been hacked to death. Fastened to one of the latex cups was a note warning their friends to expect similar treatment if they continued to tap the white man's rubber. Once again, there were no witnesses.

While King was out investigating these murders, a Javanese padi planter brought news of strangers in the rice fields; Chinese, some of whom were armed. They were demanding monthly subscriptions, clothing and food, and had issued a warning enjoining silence on the part of the subscribers. The Javanese, brave enough to inform the police in the first place, bravely returned to his land and was never seen again.

From the other side of the district came information of an illegal still and the inspector who went out, to investigate what he considered to be a routine crime, was shot in the stomach as he approached.

It was no use King, or any other OCPD, urgently demanding reinforcements from their circle or contingent HQs; there were not the men, and almost every district was in a similar plight. It was soon clear that what had appeared to be isolated incidents were, in fact, part of a well-organised pattern of violence, intended to disrupt the government and industry of the country as a whole.

After four incidents in as many days, a planter and his clerk were ambushed as they returned from the bank. On this occasion, through skilful driving, a good deal of luck, and the swift action on the part of the Tamil clerk, who threw the payroll out of the window, they escaped unscathed, but shaken.

'What are you going to do about it?' the planter demanded, crashing his fist down on the OCPD's desk. 'Sit there and take my statement?'

King was almost too tired to hear the sarcasm. He was, in fact, at his desk for the first time since the initial shooting had taken place, and then only to use the telephone.

'What the hell do you expect me to do?' He had not been to bed for three nights; had not even had time to atend his inspector's funeral. He was at his wits' end, and his superiors could not help.

'Come and see my car.'

Wearily King had followed the planter outside, noted the shattered windscreen and the bullet-scarred bodywork. 'Lucky they didn't get the tyres,' he observed, and returned to his office to flop, head in hands, until his call came through.

The planter drove off in a fury.

Next day King himself was ambushed on the main road as he drove towards Circle HQ, but this time he and his escort debussed and fought back from the ditch. There had been a yell and a body fell from an overhanging tree, and moments later a wounded man emerged, hands on head. He was their first SEP (Surrendered Enemy Personnel), prepared to turn King's evidence in return for his life.

The man had been well treated, clothed and fed, and as soon as he was fit, led King and a police party to his camp. Only the sentry and one man had been killed, the remainder getting away, but it was a beginning. These were the first corpses to be put on show to the public outside the police station and they marked the turning point in the utter helplessness that had previously prevailed.

During these weeks, terrorist incidents had continued; a young Chinese squatter had been nailed to his own wall, the nail passing through his head; two PCs were burned alive in their jeep; and a woman and child were killed when a hand-grenade was hurled into a coffee-shop. Feelings ran high, and the police bore the brunt of it.

And then there had been a sudden lull. The ambushed planter had apologised to King, who in turn had gone to his estate to supervise the erection of defences. Wire mesh, with a barbed wire vee on top, went up round the police compound and various installations; round estate managers' bungalows, factories and labour lines. Planters beseeched their principals for funds for wire, guns and generators.

Although caught out so badly in the first instance, it had not taken long for the wheels to turn and soon there was action everywhere. Special Constables were recruited to guard estates, a call for recruits into the regular police went out, and European officers and sergeants came from Palestine to help. More army battalions were posted out to boost the civil power, but it was still the police who bore the brunt and in the early days stood it almost alone.

There was action and there were men, but the danger did not lessen. Every day came news of ambushes, intimidation, thefts of arms and identity cards, and killings among the labour. The Chinese who did not co-operate suffered worst, but any European was automatically a target and an armed man a definite aim.

It was into this atmosphere of tension and intense activity that Donald Thom and, a few months later, Jogindar Singh, were propelled.

At first Thom was peeved to find that his movements were curtailed and he was hampered from visiting most of his area. The police on their side had no men for escorting a new government officer round his domain. It worked itself out in time, but for the first few months he had to be content to concentrate on the Forest Research Station and stay near home, only going into the jungle when the police were going anyway and were prepared to take him with them.

Meanwhile, a District War Executive Committee had been set up with the DO as chairman, and Thom found himself, along with the OCPD and others, a member. He had intended appealing to this committee until he realised, long before the first session was over, just what the police were faced with and the task in hand and then, being by nature of a reasonable disposition, he gave them his wholehearted co-operation instead.

It had not taken the police station long to feel the hand of Sergeant-major Jogindar Singh. His predecessor had succumbed to the general flap, but the unrufflable Jogindar had seen the OCPD and two inspectors going to and fro and decided, once again, that his job was to clean things up. It suited him that his seniors were sufficiently occupied with the Emergency to leave him with a free hand and he set to with a will.

Barrack-rooms were scrubbed – mud coming in on jungle boots of tired men was no excuse; equipment cleaned – wearing jungle green without any brass was no excuse either; everything polishable was polished. And woe betide the man who was seen playing the fool in a public place, whether in uniform or not.

The men groaned, but some of the older hands were pleased to have this rock standing so firmly in their midst.

He anchored them to the peaceful world of discipline, drill and parades – and seeing the sergeant-major, never anything but smart himself, watching with scornful eye the sloppy figures of jungle-green-clad PCs padding softly in their high jungle boots, they felt that it would take more than the bandits to dispatch *him*.

Suvindar Kaur had given birth to another boy within a month of their arrival and, when her husband marched across the compound with stern countenance and ramrod back, she would see his eyes soften as he beheld his sons. The OCPS was a different man from the husband and father that she and the children knew. They were content.

Donald Thom too had settled down. He had had no cause to worry about his privacy being disturbed. Perkins, the DO, was already looking at the calendar and sighing. His leave was only four months away and there was more than the district from which he had to tear himself. He had little interest in the self-imposed solitude of the young Canadian. And as for King, although the Emergency had now been going on for a year and he had his district under control, he was still too busy, despite his nonsensical talk of living on one long blind, to worry overmuch about the personal feelings of a man whom he considered quite old enough to take care of himself.

75. AN AMBITION ACHIEVED

Stanislaus Olshewski

Take deep breaths! It seemed that I never entered a ward without hearing a nurse telling a patient, for one reason or another, to take deep breaths. And that is just what I was doing myself.

For the first time in my life I stood at the railing of an ocean liner and listened to the seagulls fighting and screaming, as we eased our way down the Thames estuary from Tilbury.

It was a wonderful feeling to have come to a decision at last and to be looking forward to the future with no regrets. The DP camp – where I had intended working – was behind me and soon the whole of Europe would be. It was a sick continent, I thought, and needing more than doctors to cure it.

I spread my hands on the railing, thinking back, and as I looked at them a clear, high, Glaswegian voice interrupted my reverie.

'A penny for them, Doctor?'

It was Kathy MacKinnon, the little round-eyed, curly-haired Scottish nurse, who was one of my table companions in the dining-saloon. A pleasant companion in a coquettish way, no doubt, but I had no wish to become involved, especially as we were bound for the same destination.

I had been thinking about that destination, and of the person who had first mentioned it, when Miss MacKinnon joined me. But the occasion demanded flippancy.

'I was thinking of a wee Scots lassie, no less!'

'Och, Doctor, you've got it just right! But I'll bet the lassie was no' Kathy MacKinnon?'

She positively bridled with coyness, but I was in too good a mood to retort.

'The same tribe, I imagine. Sarah Catriona MacCallum Gunn, to be exact.'

Not bad, remembering that mouthful after all these years. I doubt if I'd given much thought to my future when Sally Gunn had remarked that I had hands like a Malay. But here I was, on my way to Malaya and, thinking back, trying to remember all she had told me of her home.

'We all know what you medical students used to get up to ; I'll bet ye've known many a lassie, Doctor!'

'Och aye! But never one more difficult than her – nor one as pretty as you!' I might as well give it up and resign myself to nonsensical small talk. 'What would you like to drink? I'll bring them out here.'

'A wee cherry brandy would do fine.'

She was part of the scene. The brightly-lit deck – hardly necessary that clear June evening – the old hands already reclining in deckchairs, the bridge fours in the smoking-room – partners from many voyages, no doubt – the crowded, noisy lounge behind.

By the time I returned with the drinks, the Thames had begun to spew itself into the open sea and the rolling and pitching that I had heard so much about began.

It was difficult to talk with the increasing wind, and I enjoyed the silence as the day died and the long dusk blew softly into night. The motion changed and, with my eye on a distant light, I felt us turn, leaving the North Sea to enter the Channel. How intimately I knew that sleeve of water.

After four years of hard work, indecision and a good deal of soul-searching, it was easy to relax in the holiday atmosphere of the big ship and the easy companionship of Kathy MacKinnon.

We ate and drank, played deck games, danced and made love – after a lot of coy refusing, naturally. Of course I realised that I was getting myself into deeper and deeper waters, but I was lazy, and by the time we left the Red Sea and entered the Indian Ocean, Kathy and I were unofficially engaged.

I took her ashore at Aden and went out to the RAF Station, where I had landed so often during the war. I took her ashore at Bombay and we went out to the beach where I had swum so often during the war. But it had all changed. I hadn't thought of Helen for years and, when we passed the block of flats where we had spent that leave, it was difficult to believe that that other world and its inhabitants had ever existed. Kathy was a great chatterer and I was able to sit back and dream most of the time and let her prattle on.

Don't get the idea that I was wallowing in a morass of nostalgia. Far from it. As far as I was concerned, the war was a world I had escaped from and nothing would induce me to return to it. I'd achieved my ambition career-wise; it was unlikely that I would ever pilot an aircraft again – wouldn't even go up in one if I had my way; what was wrong with the sea? I had concentrated too hard on qualifying to worry much about the future beyond that goal, but I wasn't going back.

I had never tried to visit Poland – had no desire to do so – but I had spent two of my long vacs working in camps for displaced persons in Germany and that was enough to put anyone but a sadist off war, I can tell you.

After a short spell in a London hospital, I explored several possibilities and, just as I had almost finalised acceptance as junior partner in a general practice, I saw an advert of vacancies in the Colonial Medical Service. Well, I made sure that it would cause no hold up in my naturalisation and applied. It would appear that they were short of doctors at the time!

'Och, it would be fine if we were to work in the same hospital.' Kathy had expressed these sentiments at frequent intervals throughout the voyage.

But it was not to be. Our posting orders awaited us in

Colombo; she was to disembark at Penang for a northern post and I was to continue to Singapore, for a hospital in the south of the Federation.

I had been as disappointed as she at the time but, once settled into my new job, there was much to do, to see, to learn. Hard work and a new language to tackle soon drove Kathy from my mind.

The wards of the hospital to which I was posted in Johore were a perpetual fascination. Heaven alone knows I'd seen enough shapes, sizes and colours in London, but I'd never visualised being called upon the perform the tasks which were soon to become everyday routine. And in London everything had been too efficient, too clinical, to enjoy the human side.

'I'm sorry, Doctor, it happens all the time.'

The sister, who was escorting me round male medical, drew my attention to a small Chinese nurse who was trying in vain to chase a brood of chickens from under a patient's bed before I arrived.

I laughed outright.

The ward was broad and long with open doors on both sides, opening on to a covered concrete surround, which in turn opened on to grass. Cobwebs festooned in an inaccessible, gaping hole in the ceiling and many of the supports were wafer thin from the onslaught of white ants.

I had been thinking back a few months to the London ward; the starched sister; starched, make-upless nurses, the spotless patients, general cleanliness and strict visiting hours. The comparison had already been making it difficult enough to keep a straight face, but the chickens were the last straw.

'It's wonderful,' I said, 'I only wish I could sketch.'

'It has its frustrations. But I laugh too when I think back to my training days.'

The sister was a pretty girl, with starched veil pushed well back on her ginger hair, and showed a good deal of suntanned arm and leg. I could not visualise her in a London hospital either.

But we had arrived at the first bed.

I listened while my escort translated the old man's complaints, pleased that I could already understand the gist of what she said, then prescribed a stringent diet.

As soon as I turned away I saw an old Indian woman, presumably the patient's wife, who squatted on the concrete flange, fanning the charcoal under a batch of chappaties.

'Oh really,' I said, and it was impossible to keep the exasperation from my voice, 'that's going a bit too far. What's the use of putting the old fool on a diet if he's going to stuff himself with those the minute my back is turned?'

The old man must have understood my tone and let forth a veritable torrent of thick, fast Malay.

'He says his wife is only cooking for herself and the children who will come at lunchtime from school. They are not for him.'

'And do you believe that?'

The sister shrugged. 'If you frighten him enough, perhaps. We have an occasional blitz on relatives, but everything's so open here it's almost impossible to prevent them, and honestly, when you see how some of these people pine, I think in the long run the relatives do more good than harm. As I told you just now, it has its frustrations.'

We continued down the ward then, my companion telling me the race and religion as well as the case-history of each man.

I shook my head in amazement. 'I had no idea this country was so diverse.'

'Wait until you're in a district,' she laughed, 'you'll probably have cows and goats in the ward as well!'

I raised my eyebrows. 'I should have become a vet!'

But there was no chance for further levity. At that moment a young Chinese dresser came hurrying towards us.

'You are wanted urgently in Outpatients', Doctor,' he said, and we followed him out.

A Gurkha soldier was being carried in as I arrived. He was swathed in various cloths, but the blood still seeped through. He clutched his abdomen as though afraid to let go, but there was no fear in his face, only mild surprise.

A Naik who was escorting him crashed to attention.

'At least one bullet has entered stomach, Sahib.'

A senior hospital assistant came out, hypodermic poised, and gave the man a cursory glance.

'The theatre is being prepared, sir,' he said to me as he bent to swab the man's arm.

'Where is Mr Lawrence?' I asked, a tingle of apprehension already shooting through my brain.

'He is attending the surgical conference in Singapore, sir. He will be back at 3 p.m.'

'You'll have to operate, Doctor.' It was the soft voice of

the sister, who had followed from the ward. She smiled. 'It'll be all right.'

76. TO HELL WITH FRIENDS AND NEIGHBOURS

The third stream reaches the river

James Weatherby

God, was I glad to get on that bloody boat – and off it.

The voyage out was gruesome. Of all the unkind things the Crown Agents could have done, they had to go and book us on a troopship. I shared a cabin with an elderly major in the Education Corps who never uttered, and a couple of infantile pilot officers who never stopped. Two good reasons for leaving the service if nothing else – what types are they commissioning these days? I could have forgiven them a lot if they hadn't whistled at Helen, but at that I blew my top.

Then eight equally gruesome months in a boarding-house in Kuala Lumpur – woman who ran it ought to be strung up if there's any justice. Not that it worried me much, I was seldom there, but I felt for Helen with the two kids. No need for her to have panicked about having the baby in England; John was eleven months old by the time their airships finally released me and spent his first birthday being sick in the Indian Ocean.

As a matter of fact, I became quite nicely dug in in the Secretariat and would not have asked for a district if it hadn't been for the fact that Helen was so damned miserable in those digs. I wasn't too happy about going out-station either – wouldn't have minded if I'd been a bachelor, but hell, people are being shot up every day and I didn't much like the thought of my family living under those conditions. Not that Helen could have cared less; all she wants is a house, but when I used to see all those grim-faced planters coming into town, armed and looking as though they belonged to a different world, it made me uneasy.

Anyway, in October '49 my posting came through and we set off for our new station.

Kuala Jelang was not everybody's cup of tea, I had been told, and I could see their point without having to delve too deeply.

My predecessor was a neat, finicky type, ten years my senior at the very least, I should say, and odd, to put it mildly. Wouldn't hand a thing over in the office and talked in a whisper, looking over his shoulder half the time. They might have warned me about him. 'Secretive type, old Perkins,' was all I had been told, 'but you'll find everything in apple-pie order.' Well, I suppose that was true.

Oh James, James, please be happy here. I closed my eyes and said a silent prayer before opening them again to look at our house. *Our* house. We'd been married for three and a half years and now, at last, for the first time, a real house.

The man James was taking over from was a precise old woman with a great air of 'hush, keep it dark' about him who had insisted on handing over his confidential files in the seclusion of the house instead of the office. So I had been banished and I can't say that I minded.

Everything was still. We had spent the night in a neighbouring district, having been advised not to travel after dark and, I don't mind admitting it, I've never been so scared in my life as I was on that journey; it didn't need much imagination to see a terrorist behind every tree. We arrived in Kuala Jelang while the morning was still cool, now it was afternoon and John was blessedly asleep. I took Angela by the hand we wandered away from the men's murmurous voices and surveyed our future domain.

The two government quarters, ours and the one belonging to the OCPD, James's counterpart in the police, shared the summit of a highish hill between the river and the sea with a formidable lighthouse, the design of which had specifically been drawn for the Outer Hebrides! In contrast with this monstrous structure, the two wooden bungalows looked flimsy in the extreme.

At the back of the hill there was a Rest House, also of ancient origin, and a road leading a couple of miles to the Forest Research Station, where the Forestry Officer had his house.

On the river side of the hill nestled the town – one main street of Chinese and Indian shops, bordered with magnificent flame trees, and two smaller streets leading off at right angles to the main road. At the seaward end, immediately below the hill and unseen from the town, the police station squatted, surrounded by its barracks, parade-ground, canteen and games field. At the other end of the town a small hill was crowned by the District Office, and between the two, bordered by the town on one side and the river on the other, lay the padang, that open space found in every Malayan town, no doubt laid out by the first Britons, homesick for their village greens. It serves as football field, cricket pitch, meeting place, market place, the home of the annual county fair – in fact, not only does it resemble, but also serves the purpose of a village green.

Perkins was a bachelor and, being ready for leave, had packed up and moved into the Rest House before we arrived. I sighed with pleasure as we reached the top of the hill again and sat on a garden seat to look at the dilapidated old bungalow that was to be our home.

The dank smell from the mangrove swamp, the enormous scorpion I had found in the kitchen sink, and the myriad cockroaches; nothing was going to put me off. Even the oil-lamps would be fun; the mangrove shapes were quaint and the fact that the house looked liable to collapse at a puff of wind merely seemed to make life more exciting! James might be worried about the Emergency and the danger that surrounded us, but I was not at all.

'What does the European population consist of?' I asked.

'Actually resident, only the OCPD and the Forestry Officer besides yourselves. PWD and Agriculture visit once a week from the next district, Kemuning, and a doctor comes when he can. Socially, of course, there are a fair number of planters and miners around, but few people move around after dark unless they have to, even when the curfew isn't on. It'll be a bit lonely for your wife, I'm afraid.'

'That's what I was thinking.'

At that moment I saw Helen's face, eyes shining and lips pursed with suppressed laughter, peering at me round one of the verandah screens. Her expression had been enough to tell me that having a house was going to be more important than company and I turned back to Perkins with an easy mind. I could concentrate on taking over; domestic problems, thank God, did not exist.

I lay in bed, listening to James prowling round the garden and wishing he would come to bed. This job was not going to be easy for him, I knew. He had never been a 'hail fellow, well met' type; never a good mixer at the best of times, he'd become increasingly intolerant of his associates during the past few years and I could see he would have very little in common with our two bachelors.

But now I wanted to forget everything else, everything beyond ourselves. I wanted him to come and take possession of me as I had taken possession of the house; to love me and want me and be as happy as I intended that he should be, instead of growling about outside like an angry bear.

My thoughts were interrupted by an overwhelming smell of burning oil and I could see the silhouette of smoke against the open door.

'James,' I called, 'please turn down the light. I don't want to get out of bed in the dark with bare feet.'

I had left the light on the verandah; there were too many creepy-crawlies, and besides, I had nothing on.

Helen's voice forced me inside. I hadn't noticed the lamp going up, although I'd been watching its glow from the garden in a vague sort of way. Christ, if we set fire to the house it really would be the last straw.

The filthy thing was black and stinking, and by the time I reached it there was already an oily, discoloured mark on the ceiling. I looked at it with distaste; the last oil-lamp I had had to cope with had been in Libya.

'Better turn it right out,' Helen called, 'there's enough moonlight for you to see to undress by.'

I sighed and stood with closed eyes for a few moments, letting myself become accustomed to the gloom.

It had been an utterly bloody evening, spent in the company of people whom I could quite frankly do without. If leching at my wife was going to be a favourite pastime, I would have to ask for a posting; I just wasn't going to put up with it.

I suppose the Forestry chap is all right – looks pretty solid and doesn't say much – and I needn't worry about the few days we shall have with Perkins – that's another thing I don't go for overmuch. Helen seemed to think her discovery of a harem of flowery young men wildly funny, but I was disgusted. Yes, disgusted. God knows I'm no prude, but Christ, at least I'm normal. What must the locals think? How are they going to react to me, expect me to behave?

And as for that Brylcreem boy. I never could abide his type – typical Fighter, all dash and no sense of responsibility. He'd be better placed selling something on the Edgware Road than the job he's doing here. Whoever put a creature like that in charge of a district this size and with that number of men needs his head examined. And the infuriating thing is that Helen seems to find him amusing. Well I don't, and that's flat.

'Do stop rumbling, James, and come to bed.'

'I'm not rumbling.' But I was.

Then quite suddenly the moon crept round the edge of the bedroom window and a shaft of light fell on the mosquito net, suspended in the middle of the room from invisible wires and moving slightly in the faint breeze that was breathing through the wide open windows. It brought me into the intimacy of our home and away from outside thoughts.

I dropped my clothes on the bare floor and watched the moonbeam picking out the hideous, heavy black furniture and sombre walls. It was all bare and impersonal, but it would not always be so. Helen was right. We had ourselves, the children and, at long last, a house. To hell with friends and neighbours – we didn't *have* to see them once the offices were closed.

I felt as though I were parting the wings of some great hovering white moth as I drew aside the mosquito net. And there, naked, lying on borrowed white sheets, was my wife, as white as the moonlight and as beautiful. My madonna lily. She held out her arms and I went into them gratefully.

77. JEALOUSY UNFOUNDED

It did not take James Weatherby long, after all, to get the hang of the job, despite his wife's fears. The crops and buildings, strange at first to one from the West, were now familiar, and he had broken the back of his first struggles with Malay.

As far as Helen was concerned, after the dreary months in a boarding-house, Kuala Jelang was sheer bliss. At most times it was hot and humid, and at low tide the mud-flats steamed and the sand flies rose in their swarms, but when the tide was high and the wind blew in from the sea, it more than compensated for the bad spells.

The only real fly in the ointment, it appeared, was the young OCPD. As James said, they had to work hand-in-glove and he just could not take to the chap.

After only a few weeks James marched in to lunch one day, his face alight with the arrogance which Helen remembered so well. It had made his juniors dislike him in the days when he had first been promoted Air Commodore and had nearly driven the hospital staff mad. It bode no good and she was wary.

He sat down with a thud and glared at his still empty plate.

'I shall report him to his superiors,' he fumed.

'Who?'

'Young King. I won't *have* that chap around.'

'What has he done?' Helen was aghast, terrified that her husband was going to make a fool of himself because, despite what else he might have to say, she knew in her heart what was the real cause of this outburst.

"It's his manner,' James muttered. 'He's out to sabotage me in every way.'

'James, you have no right. He may be younger than you and in the despised part of the RAF as far as you were concerned, but that was years ago. He's been in Malaya ever since the end of the war, speaks fluent Malay and is considerably senior to you, even if he isn't in the same job.'

He looked stunned. He had expected sympathy, not an attack.

But his wife had not finished. 'His superiors would laugh at you,' she sneered.

She had to hurt. She knew very well what was at the bottom of all this and the sudden explosion merely served to confirm a suspicion which had been growing lately in her mind.

It all went back to their first night in the district when she, never dreaming that there were still places without electricity, had come to Kuala Jelang unprepared. They were to inherit the Chinese servants with the house, but they had gone on a fortnight's leave. Having no lights and unable to cope with the wood range, she had called on Derek King for help. He had lent them a lamp and insisted that they eat with him.

He was a bit smooth, it was true, but Helen was amused by his over-obvious charm and played him at his own game – until she had noticed her husband's sullen face.

Derek had seen it too and, to make matters worse, had deliberately picked up her hand and said, 'Ma'am you don't know what a difference it's going to make to Kuala Jelang, having a woman around – even if we do have to have her husband as well!'

She had laughed and drawn her hand away, but James had glowered and remained silent until they started for home.

'No need to come,' he had said icily to their host, 'I am quite capable of lighting my wife home.'

He had taken the light and stalked off without a single word of thanks.

The next morning she had written a short note to Derek King, thanking him and apologising for her husband's mood, saying that he had not been feeling well. But King, insensitive and typical of his breed, cared not a jot for what James thought or felt and, besides paying obvious and exaggerated court to his wife whenever the chance arose, took every opportunity to aggravate him in other ways. He was, by most people's standards, an infuriating young man. Happy-go-lucky, couldn't care less, he always managed to be at the right place at the right time and always fell on his feet.

Why, James asked himself, seething with irritation, should King always manage to reach his goal without any apparent effort, when he had to slog? Popular among the locals; respected by his men; and somewhat grudgingly reported well on by his superior officers. If it came to open conflict between the two of them, there was very little doubt as to who would win.

In his own mind James knew all this – which made it so much worse – and was aware too of his own jealous nature and how unfounded all his suspicions were.

Sometimes when walking along the tow-path at Richmond, he had imagined that they were being followed, or that some man on the farther bank was eyeing Helen as he had no right to do. He would hurry her home and spend the rest of the day sulking, knowing within himself that there was no foundation for his rage.

He felt like that now. He knew Helen was right 'His superiors would laugh at you,' she had said. What the hell did she see in the man? She must see something, or she would not have made a remark like that. He knew that she really didn't see anything at all, but he could not bring himself to admit it.

'Can't you stop those bloody kids from making such a row?' he snarled. 'I don't want any lunch.'

And with that he walked out of the front door and got into the car.

Helen sighed. She had been patient enough, God knew, but this time she rebelled – but only mentally. Her hands were tingling with rage and it was only with the greatest self-control that she prevented herself from picking up the nearest object and hurling it at the retreating car.

Back in his office, James sulked. Putting his head in his hand, he sank forward on to the desk. His head began to ache, as it always did on these occasions. It was a long time before he heard the sounds of exhausts and bicycle bells, heralding the return to work of the clerks. He sat up then and hit his head with his clenched fist, telling himself, as he invariably did, not to be such a bloody fool.

If he had had his way there would have been no more social contact with young King, but Helen, as soon as their china was unpacked, had insisted on inviting him back. Thom, the FO, had come too – thank God he could feel no jealousy there. A dour chap, he thought. He hadn't been in the district all that long and did not speak very much Malay either – *how* that young King liked to show off his knowledge of the language; cracking jokes at every opportunity, knowing full well that he could understand neither the speed nor the idiom. He ground his knuckles into his eyes; Helen apart, he could not like the man.

'What is it?' he called wearily, as he heard a respectful knock on the half open door.

It was Balasingham, his Jaffna Tamil Chief Clerk, carrying a pagoda-like pile of files. James watched him carefully off-load them on to the desk. Nothing for it but to forget King and lose himself in work, he thought with resignation.

78. A MAJOR RETIRES

Philip Morrison

'It could be that I have an early Christmas present for you,' I told Sally one lunch hour, 'it all depends.'

I held out the copy of Part II orders that had been floating round the unit for weeks, and waited until she'd read them through.

'As you see, the army is allowing transfers to the Colonial Service. Anyone who is accepted may retire.'

She said nothing for a minute, but turned them over and looked at the date.

'But these aren't new.'

'No. I wanted to find out all the pros and cons first.'

That was the understatement of the year. There were so

many of us becoming fed up with the army that the whole subject had been gone into and thrashed out in almost every office – I was surprised that she hadn't heard it. Perhaps they were all contented Labourites or National Service in her section. It wasn't only the lack of prospects, it was the whole attitude. Even the RSM had admitted he could no longer keep proper control. As far as I was concerned, my mind had been made up the week before. It was a very small incident; I had kept the unit working late on an extremely urgent job and I vaguely remembered one of the sapper draughtsmen moaning that he had a cold – most of us had, there was one going the rounds. I thought nothing of it at the time but, before I knew what had hit me, I was on the mat, answering questions by post from the man's MP. Well. When the army reached that stage, I'd had enough, and I wasn't the only one.

'What job would you do?' Sally asked.

'Admin and police are the only ones I'm qualified for. From what I can gather, admin would mean Africa; but they want police here – so, police it is – if you agree.'

I could see that I had taken her completely by surprise.

After a while, she asked, 'But you're always so rude about the civil government; would you really want to join them?'

'We've had quite a lot to do with the police,' I told her, 'it's a para-military set up and I'm hardly complimentary about the army either these days.'

'What's the pay like?'

'Considerably lower than ours, I'm afraid.' The pension would be better, but I wanted to paint only the black side at this stage.

'Oh God!'

'And I'd go in as a cadet – two pips.'

'Oh God, again. What a come down.'

'I don't think you can really compare ranks; their responsibilities are quite different. In the district where we were operating last year, the OCPD only had two pips up, but he had more than a thousand men under his command, all told.'

'It's up to you, Philip. I've never thought of you having any career other than the army.'

'Career? With this ruddy Labour government cutting down the whole time? Times have changed since Father commanded a battalion. Think about it, Sally. The applications have to be in by the end of the year – you've got a month.'

I had been surprised to hear the bitterness in Philip's voice.

It was difficult to work that afternoon. For the first time I realised that other people were talking about the merits and disadvantages of transferring – I suppose they had been talking about it for some time; I just hadn't listened before.

The largest item in favour was, of course, the fact that we would be able to live together without the continual threat of separation. The battalion was on temporary duty in Berlin at that time, without wives, and I knew it was something I would have to face sooner or later. I knew nothing about the police – except that few days went by without some reference in the newspapers to an ambush or patrol where someone had been killed, and they were usually Europeans.

I hardly spoke for a week, so busy was I with my thoughts.

'You could keep Ja'afar and the animals,' Philip said one day.

Of course that was the second major point in favour. We had adopted three stray cats, whom I loved dearly and dreaded having to leave behind, and the past months, with Ja'afar and Siti in charge, had been very pleasant. Undomesticated creature that I am, it suited me down to the ground to go off to work knowing that the house would be well run; and Ja'afar was a superb cook. And, when and if I ever did have a child, they would be there to help me care for it, just the same as they had cared for me. I had a feeling that Philip was trying to prod me into giving an affirmative answer.

But I didn't want to leave army life. I had grown up in uniform myself and I was very happy being spoon-fed. I didn't want to be thrown out into the great, wide, open world.

I had just reached a stage when I was going to say 'no' to the idea when Philip rushed into my office one morning, looking very bright.

'Bill Matheson's applied and been accepted,' he said, 'he's retiring next month.'

I couldn't care less about Bill Matheson, or what he did. He was a contemporary of Philip's, in fact, they had been commissioned together and bosom pals until Philip had been taken prisoner, then they had met up again after the war, both moaning about the colonel and the first battalion. He was a bachelor still and lived in the main mess; he came in for the odd meal and occasionally invited us out, but we didn't see all that much of him.

But what I did see was that Philip really did want to transfer and was using every subtle argument to persuade me. I sighed.

'All right,' I said, 'we'll go too.'

79. LIKE THE EDGE OF THE OUTBACK

The fourth stream enters the river

Vincent Lee Chee Min

A full year passed before I saw Dad again.

He had been furious when I joined up, but I think that secretly he was glad I had chosen to stand on my own feet and not gone crawling back to him.

In fact, I haven't done too badly for myself.

The recruits' course at the Depot was shortened because of the Emergency and I was already earmarked for Special Branch before it was over. My Chinese is still pretty stilted, but it's coming back and, when I went on leave after the course, I made a point of not speaking a word of English to the old man.

Actually I enjoyed my leave. There's a lot of good in Dad. He made quite sure that I understood what I was missing by choosing not to join one of his business concerns, the whole time with an amused glint in his jet-black eyes. But I wasn't taking the bait.

He's in far more than just tin now. Rubber, cars, hotels, import/export, and messing around on the stock exchange. You name it. He still lives in the same house, but he has offices in Ipoh and KL now; plush, air-conditioned jobs. Like his air-conditioned cars.

We only had one clash of wills and that was on the last day. The evening before he'd become positively benign over his XO – no three-star brandy for Dad – and announced that he was making me an allowance of two hundred bucks a month. My first impulse was to refuse it, but Mum had shaken her head and told me afterwards that he was giving the same to all his sons – even the one with the Aussie wife – and that I'd only make him lose face by refusing. The clash came the next morning when I was going to Ipoh to board the train. Dad had insisted that I be driven to the railway station in state, but not in my PC's uniform! So I said I'd walk, or go by bus.

Perhaps, although he was loath to admit it, he was glad

that I too could be a chip off the same block and he partly relented, ordering the driver to drop me outside the station precincts – he wasn't going to have anyone seeing an ordinary PC alighting from *his* car! In fact, the driver took me the whole way – he's a Malay, there's nothing wrong with wearing a uniform for him.

I filled a sergeant's post, with acting rank, at one of the main police stations in KL for a few months, but it was soon apparent to me that if I were really going to get my teeth into Malay and Chinese I would have to be in a smaller station, where I would be using them the whole time, instead of spending half my day sitting behind a desk. Of course, I did go out a good deal, but too much of my time was spent on observation. I needed more interrogation and mixing with the local people.

After some thought, I asked the Deputy Superintendent if I could be sent to an out-station and explained why.

Kuala Jelang came my way just at the right time. It was a new post. To date, the SB officer from Circle HQ at Kemuning had visited the district a couple of times a week, but it had been decided to post a sergeant there permanently, who could get in touch with the officer when needed.

'Just the thing for you,' the DSP told me. 'It will give you a chance to prove your admin ability as well as being right on the ground. Stroke of luck for you that it became available just now; normally they would have sent someone more experienced.'

So Kuala Jelang it was, or is. My, it's a little hack town all right! About the size of some of the ones you find way out in Aussie; like the edge of the Outback. Real sleepy colonial, I should say, until the Emergency woke it up.

The OCPD seems quite a good bloke, but a bit leave-happy. Can't say I blame him, reckon the bright lights will call me too after three years in this joint. I can see the job will be all right though, once I get my teeth into it.

I settled down straight away to write and tell Dad the news. I don't think I've done too badly for myself one way and another. Fourteen months only since I arrived in Singapore and now I'm a sergeant with my own office and a fair whack of responsibility – and I've got here without anyone else's help.

I must write to Sergeant Williamson too, back in Aussie – his remarks on my becoming an acting sergeant in next to no time were pretty caustic, wonder what he'll say to this lark?

80. THE TROUBLE SPOTS

Chee Min was nervous. Infiltrate yourself into the squatter areas, King had instructed him, and glean what information you can. And now he was on his way, in a borrowed private car, an elderly Chinese detective sitting beside him. But soon he would be on his own.

The OCPD had given him a couple of days to settle in, lending him his own annotated map of the area to study. Chee Min had studied it and it had not taken him long to put his finger on the obvious trouble spots.

Kuala Jelang was a large, pear-shaped district, with the river, the Sungei Jelang, running east to west along the approximate core, cutting it in two. Roads ran parallel with the river on both sides, with turnings off both north and south, and meeting on the one bridge some ten miles upstream. A ferry served to connect the two coastal halves of the district, which contained most of the cultivated land and population. There were several rubber estates in both halves, and one tin mine towards the eastern boundary. The remainder of the district was jungle.

The township of Kuala Jelang itself nestled on the south side of the mouth of the river and, owing to the rock formation and an inlet which curved round the hill, was almost on a peninsula.

But it was neither the rubber estates nor the town that worried Chee Min. There were two squatter settlements, one on the same side of the river as the town and covering a roughly triangular area of low-lying ground, a moderately compact formation if he deciphered the OCPD's hieroglyphics correctly, and another on the far side of the river which was far from compact. Chinagraph dots speckled the talc and straggled on both sides of the road for more than a mile, terminating at the forest edge. He was not surprised when King stubbed his finger on that portion of the map and announced, '*That's* the area I don't like. There are three main sources of supply to the Communists: squatter areas, timber *kongsis*, and estates. I want you to take them in that order of priority.'

Until the squatters could be controlled and their help and food denied to the terrorists, government was waging a battle already lost. From his father and his few months in Special Branch, Chee Min knew that these people, China-born for the most part, and owing allegiance to no one beyond their immediate kin, had no intention of co-operating. How many actually had Communist leanings and how many gave their support under duress, it was impossible to say. Riddled with secret societies and protection groups, they had lived since time immemorial in fear of losing what little they had. Small chance then that they would be prepared to betray the greatest secret society of them all, Communism, and risk the consequences.

Thankful that he had dropped Mandarin as his third dialect and studied Hakka instead, Chee Min questioned the detective at his side. He had taken the precaution of providing himself with a civilian identity card to enable him to travel by bus – too often they were burned and the passenger's belongings and identity cards scrutinised and stolen – but first DPC Chin was showing him the ground.

Chin, jealous possibly of the rank of the young man behind the steering wheel, took pains to point out the dangers of moving unescorted among the squatters. A quick cord round the throat, a knife; no one would see, no one would hear. And if he were taken alive? Who more hated by the CTs than a Chinese member of Special Branch?

'If we stop here, you can walk back to the bus stop we've just passed,' he told Sergeant Lee. 'Ask for Ulu Pandanus; the fare will be twenty-five cents. I'll take the car back.'

Chee Min stopped, got out and walked straight back. He could feel the cold sweat trickling between his shoulder-blades and his hands were clammy. Never before had he been so conscious of quiet. They were in open scrub country, flat, with stunted bushes. In the distance a kite was flying.

The road remained deserted although he waited nearly half an hour. Not a vehicle passed. He saw the bus approaching at such speed that he was afraid it would not stop. He stepped into the road and held up his hand, and with a screech of brakes the vehicle halted just long enough to allow him to cling on to the first step, then took off again, throwing him into a vacant seat. None of the few passengers seemed surprised.

For more than a week Chee Min walked through the vegetable gardens and orchards, asking questions about the crops and the soil and attempting in every way to get himself accepted.

Not that the squatters welcomed him with open arms. Far from it. They knew what he was about and told him nothing. He only had to be seen entering or leaving the police station once, he knew, for everyone to know exactly what he was and what his job. He knew too that he remained unmolested because the CTs might be hatching plans to use *him*.

He made no attempt to overcome the squatters' suspicions, but while he was amongst them he was able to listen and observe. The sideways glance, the lifted eyebrow or quietly closing door; all signs of furtiveness or guilt were noted mentally, to be committed to paper at the end of the day.

King studied his report, queried one or two observations, and knew that it confirmed his own conclusions. He had not told Chee Min that a police lieutenant and four jungle squad PCs had been killed there during the past month; that they were sure the area was being used as a rest camp and supply depot; he had wanted him to find out for himself. Resettlement of the squatters was the only solution, he was sure. He had said so at the last meeting of DWEC, the District War Executive Committee, but met with little response. The trouble was the head-on clash of personalities between himself and the DO and, although the police were responsible for security, the DO was chairman of the committee and as such held an excellent weapon for impeding progress. The planters' representative had been heard to remark that the only time the committee reached agreement was when either Weatherby or King was absent.

King tapped Chee Min's report with irritation. He despised Weatherby and did not bother to disguise his feelings; that they were mutual was equally apparent. Who cares? he thought. He was due for leave; it would be his successor's problem. To Chee Min he said, 'I'll take it up with the Special Branch Officer next time I go to Circle HQ. Now for the timber-cutters.'

The timber-cutters were a different kettle of fish. Known providers, and whether voluntarily or not mattered little to the police.

King asked the Forestry Officer to come round to his office that afternoon and introduced Chee Min. Donald Thom was in an affable mood and delighted to have the chance to spend some time in the timber camps. Of course he would accompany the new detective-sergeant. Only too glad.

'Say, you sound kinda Australian,' he remarked, after a few minutes of conversation. 'Howcome you've picked up an accent like that?' Chee Min explained and Thom held out his hand. 'Shake, pardner, we're colonials together in this Imperialist set-up!'

They had all laughed and Jogindar Singh, looking in as he made some excuse to walk past the OCPD's open door, made a mental note that he would have to tell Sergeant Lee to have a little more respect for his superiors. He strongly disapproved of the way the young Chinese was leaning on the desk and talking in such familiar tones. Upstart!

They set off the next day, and the reception from the first timber kongsi they reached was cool, to put it mildly. All questions were dealt with in a masterfully evasive manner, and Chee Min noticed considerable surreptitious coming and going.

It was the same all along the line, and as they penetrated deeper and deeper into the forest Chee Min was glad of their strong, armed escort.

In fact they were safe, he was pretty sure, because the death or disappearance of a policeman and a government officer would almost certainly spell closure to the timber *kongsis* and cut off a valuable Communist supply line. He said as much to his companion.

Thom looked wistfully at the great trees surrounding them. He knew the police were keen to close the deep camps and in his heart he knew they should. It was only the revenue they provided for a government already overtaxed by the financial commitment of the Emergency that had allowed them to operate for so long. It was just his luck that he should have arrived in Malaya when he did. He would have so loved to spend long periods in the forests, free to go where he wished, unescorted and without fear.

He sighed. 'I suppose you'll recommend they be closed down?' They had visited seven camps and were on their journey back.

Chee Min shrugged. 'That'll be up to the OCPD, but it's certainly what I'd do.'

Chee Min's third assignment, the estates, had been the easiest of the lot but, as he sat drinking a beer with Snowy White –

no relation of his friend Bill White, but from the same place – he was still smarting.

He had been warned not to expect much co-operation from the police lieutenants, but he had not been prepared for the rebuff he received on the first estate. He had jumped out of the police jeep and advanced with outstretched hand towards the uniformed European standing with the Scs.

'I'm from the police station,' he announced, smiling broadly. 'I'm the new SB sergeant, Vincent Lee Chee Min.'

Police Lieutenant Moriarty had looked him up and down, ignoring the hand. 'Bugger off,' he said, and turned away.

Chee Min's hide had not been toughened sufficiently by his Australian schooling. He had returned to the jeep, quivering with rage and humiliation, and gone straight to the managers' office after that. But, coming out of the office on the fourth estate, he found a police lieutenant standing by the jeep. He stiffened and walked warily towards him.

'Hey, cobber, could you give me a lift into town?'

This one had held out *his* hand, and after finishing his business with the OCPD had invited Chee Min to join him in a beer.

'You don't want to take too much notice of Paddy,' he remarked when he had heard about the clash with Moriarty. 'He can be as mean as hell, but you know he's got the George Medal for gallantry? He's a bastard, all right, but a good man to have on your side in a fight. The best.'

'I hope I never need his help.'

'Aw, trouble with you Asians is you're too touchy. Never heard the old saying, "sticks and stones can break my bones, but words can never hurt me"? You see,' he explained, "we're such a mixed bunch. Most of the lieutenants are the ex-sergeants from Palestine, then when they needed more they advertised. A lot of applicants were attracted by the rank and were disappointed when they got here and found it was non-commissioned – bloody silly, misleading rank anyway, if you ask me – then there are the ones like me. I took the job for the money – make no bones about it – besides, it suits me better than the desk job I had in Sydney. So there we are, the professional thugs, the disappointed hopefuls, and the ordinary mercenaries, like me!'

'I'm glad there are some like you,' Chee Min murmured, and meant it.

'Wal,' Snowy looked at his watch, 'you'll get along all right. I've got to get back to the estate. See yer, Vin.'

Snowy White had, in fact, summed up his colleagues very well.

In Kuala Jelang district there were eight police lieutenants, all but one lodged on various estates, in charge of the Special Constables on their own estates and those within a certain radius. The odd man out, O'Brien, looked after the jungle squads. Some of them were first-class, responsible and reliable men; others were just plain bolshie. But almost all of them were fiercely loyal to their own men and although the bolshies were a permanent thorn in the flesh of the OCPD and the regular police, even they would stick up for them if it came to a fight with outsiders. King frequently remarked that there were several of them whom he could have done without, but, in fact, without replacements, he could not have done without a single one of them.

81. A UNION REPRESENTATIVE MEETS HIS MATCH

Ramakrishnan

For the whole of 1949, K. P. Samuel and I are representing Estate and Mine Workers' Union at estates far and wide and collecting subscriptions most satisfactory.

I now have rented garage in nearby town, where car is kept most secretively, and forged identity cards in names of S. Kandiah and K. P. John. It is not being difficult to leave estates for toddy-soaked CC is spending all days, except when manager is visiting, drinking with equally sodden cronies. I am therefore in charging of office duties and giving self time off whenever conveniently required.

Truly my brethren are individuals most cretinous and sheep-like, which is lucky for us. On each estate I am visiting it is only necessary to be obtaining one follower and all rest of stupid fellows pay up, although most are already paying to real union. Truly I am despising them for being doltish fools – I was telling my father this always, but he was not believing me.

I am telling you, K.P. and I have milked all estates in area conveniently far from Tanah Kuning and far enough apart not to be having new union discussed. Fellows on our own estate are not asking questions as we are always returning by nightfall and wife Devi is most lazy and lustful still, and only accepting gold ornaments and marital caresses without using brains at all.

All is going well until we are collecting subscriptions for 1950. Now we are going to fields farther and looking after area to the north.

We are no longer bothering about managers, for I am soon finding out that if chief clerk can be won over and is telling manager that genuine union official is visiting estate, manager becomes like putty.

Only I am not being given correct information regarding one estate and I am standing on forty-four-gallon oil drum, delivering honest and usual harangue to workers when manager arrives.

This is first time that manager has attended such speaking to workers and I am waxing eloquent when he is interrupting most rudely.

'Get off that drum and off my estate,' he shouts.

Now is the time to show workers that I am not being intimidated.

'I am telling you, Mister,' I am shouting back, 'you do not have right to throw me off estate. Law is forever on my side also. I shall take civil suit and criminal suit against you for causing grevious bodily harm if you are for throwing me anywhere.'

At that, said manager is coming towards me with look most unpleasant upon face.

'Speak your own language so that all can understand,' he is saying in Tamil, 'or I shall have to teach you to speak proper English.'

At these insulting words many of the workers are laughing and I am quickly seeing that my audience is attending to this white pig more than they are to me.

'Take no notice of this white slave driver,' I yell at them, 'he is oppressor of the workers, like all his kind.'

From the corner of my eye I am seeing K.P. sneaking towards car. Lucky he cannot drive, I am thinking, or he would be leaving me in veritable lurch.

'Get off this estate without further nonsense, or I *shall* throw you off.'

'Yes,' I am jeering, 'you will be calling toadies to do dirty work, I bet.'

I see then that there are no SCs with manager and he is advancing towards me on own, but with manner menacing most.

'Shoot,' I call out, 'you will be using pistols on poor defenceless representative of workers, I bet. You are big man, I see, ready to fire at inferior being.'

'Get off that drum,' he is saying, and quietly now. 'I have never yet hit a man smaller than myself.'

I am getting down then, to avoid humiliating indignities which appear to be impending. I see at once that manager is only small man of height like mine much of muchness. He looks at me with expression most scornful which I do not like and is undoing belt which holds pistol in holster and is removing stainless steel watch and spectacles.

'I am tell you once more, and for the last time, get off this estate.'

Manager is wearing khaki shorts and shirt and jungle boots. He is already dirty and will not be minding dirt more, but I am looking at my clean white suitings and correspondent shoes and recalling time most humilitous after affair with Muriani and state of clothes thereafter.

'You will be sorry, Mister, for such high-handed actions,' I shout, but already half-way to where car is parked and relieved that no one is following.

'Thank your lucky stars that you are being allowed to go scot-free,' he calls out and laughs, 'but justice will no doubt catch up with you in due course; it always does.'

I am making no further reply when sudden pain on side of head is making me aware that several labourers have picked up stones and I am target. Truly I am ashamed of my fellow-countrymen.

Next stone is cutting cheek. K.P. is lying in long grass beside car with face pressed to ground and hands over ears. I can see at once that his suiting is already stained and I give him feelingful kick in ribs.

'Get up,' I say, 'fair weathering friend.'

Then I am starting car and proceeding at leisurely and dignified pace along estate road until out of sight of jeering workers.

'What is happening to you?' Devi is asking when she sees my cheek already swollen and with blood higgledy-piggledy on side of face.

For answer I am saying nothing, but at once seizing her bangles from her and earrings and pendant which is suspended round neck.

'Quick, Devi,' I say, 'give me your nose ring and your

anklets and all other jewels. There is bad rumouring that Communist terrorists are in vicinity and all such trinkets gold and silver will be taken. I am hiding these in place secure and you are not to be telling anyone that I have taken same.'

Devi hands over remaining jewellery and I add my rings, wrist-watch, cigarette case and lighter, and am wishing I could remove gold teeth also. All these things I am stowing in powdered milk tins and burying behind quarter. Then I am burning identity card of Mr S. Kandiah and coming to unfortunate conclusion that it is necessary to return to life of clerk most ordinary and that S. Kandiah and K. P. John can no longer be existing.

82. THE BETROTHAL

Abdul Karim

Once I had done my six months' basic training at the Depot, I was allowed to go on leave. Of course I had not yet realised my dream of becoming a driver/mechanic, because so far we had only square-bashed, but there would still be a lot to tell them back home.

There was Kuala Lumpur for a start. Wah! I wondered if they would believe me when I told them about the tall buildings and wide streets and the traffic. I wish they could see us in our walking-out dress going on Mosque Parade on Fridays; wah, that was something! All the traffic held up while we passed, the inspectors marching in front in their black and silver and us behind in our blue and white.

It was a long journey home and it made me realise why we had been left alone so much, during the occupation and since. Wah! When we had had discussions about our kampongs, I had felt like an orang-utan compared with some of the sophisticated recruits from the western and central states. I might have boasted that my picture had appeared on the front page of the leading newspaper if I hadn't looked so like an orang-utan in it, but I kept quiet about that one!

I felt quite sophisticated myself, though, when I walked into the Police District Headquarters and asked if there would be any transport to Pasir Perak in the near future. I was in luck, because the OCPD was visiting the next door kampong that very same afternoon and would drop me off.

When I went outside and looked around I wondered why I had ever felt ashamed of coming from the ulu, the back of beyond. The sight of my home, the boats drawn up on to the wide beach and the nets laid out to dry, the tall coconut palms and the feel of sand between my toes were better by far than anything to be had in the city. It was wonderful to see my parents' familiar faces and to touch the familiar objects in the home. For the first time I appreciated how my mother must have felt when we first came back from Kelantan at the beginning of the war.

After I had told them all my news, I went to see Inche Yacob and then to find Rokiah.

Rokiah was like a stranger. She who was as familiar to me as my own parents. My companion in so many scrapes and adventures, who had romped with me in the surf, climbed trees and pelted me with jambus, stood by the hibiscus bush at the foot of her steps, smiling shyly.

I always pictured Rokiah in her patched and faded old blue and white school uniform, but of course she had left school now and it was a young lady who stood waiting quietly for me to approach. The old Rokiah would have rushed forward, heedless of dignity or decorum, but this one, clad in a flowered sarong and kebaya, remained modestly at the foot of the steps.

Perhaps I looked different too. Six months of uniform and drill had given me a new deportment and the Depot barber had seen to my unruly hair.

I went forward and held out my hand. She put hers into mine, but her eyes looked demurely at her feet.

'Rokiah, you *are* pretty.'

I said it on impulse and knew at once that it was true. I had never really noticed girls before going to Kuala Lumpur and I had never thought much about Rokiah being a girl!

She giggled and put her hand shyly before her face. I caught her eyes for a second but she dropped them at once and would not look at me.

Was it Musah? I wondered. Rokiah had always been my special friend, but I had been the stay-at-home while he had ventured into city life.

I clenched my fists at the thought of his large pale face – surely Rokiah couldn't find it attractive? – and quick brain. He'd been back to the kampong recently, Inche Yacob had told me, talking very big. My old headmaster had spoken to me as a man for the first time. A smart Alick, he had called Musah, and not to be trusted. He had been sly and spread ideas among the kampong folk that Inche Yacob did not like. Surely Rokiah could not care for a chap like that?

My thoughts were interrupted by a tactful cough and Che Fatimah joined us. We sat and chatted till the sun went down.

I went home then; my thoughts with Rokiah, my tomboy friend who had so suddenly blossomed into a woman.

Her face was powdered now and her pigtails coiled up into two heavy buns, one behind each ear. She would be considered old-fashioned in KL, where nearly all the girls wore their hair short, but I like it that way. I'll never let her cut it, I thought, then wondered at my own impertinence. What right had I to let her do or not do anything? I was no longer the elder brother of our schooldays, but a man. Welcome as a casual friend, no doubt, until such time as she was betrothed.

At that thought my stomach did a flip. Rokiah must be almost seventeen. It had not been mentioned, but without doubt she would be married soon. She had admired Musah; did she admire him still?

For the first time since joining the police, I sighed for my schooldays; days that I had not realised until now had been so happy and carefree.

There was a good meal at home that night, but not the feast with all our friends and relations present that I would have expected on my first day home. But I was soon to understand the reason.

My parents looked at each other, then my father nodded and my mother spoke.

'There is no kenduri for you to-night, Karim, because one is already prepared for three days' time,' she said. Then she looked at Pak again, as though expecting him to take over, but he signalled to her to continue. 'We wanted to speak to you before you went to see Rokiah, to save you both embarrassment, but we saw you crossing over from the school and it was too late.'

My heart was thumping. What had happened that this should be necessary? What had happened to account for Rokiah's downcast eyes? My earlier thoughts returned and I felt sick with apprehension.

My thoughts must have shown too, because my mother frowned and put a hand on mine.

'Karim, please don't be so upset. It is only right that we should arrange a marriage for you, and the kenduri will be a feast to celebrate both your betrothal and your homecoming.'

Then my heart really sank. The betrothal would not be a hundred per cent binding – people had opted out before – but in a conservative community like ours it simply wasn't done. I was still only eighteen and the wedding probably would not take place for a few years yet, but I knew that I must be content with whatever arrangements my parents had made.

It seemed that among the urban Malays they could pick and choose for themselves these days. It was a subject often discussed and I knew that if my parents had chosen someone whom I knew but could not stand, I could refuse – but they would not do that anyway. I cast around in my mind for the possible girls from amongst whom my betrothed would have been chosen.

The meal continued in silence until my mother said, in a disappointed voice, 'You don't seem very interested in the celebrations, Karim.' I smiled politely but said nothing. 'I know you are young still, but Rokiah will soon be seventeen and as Che Fatimah was willing, your father and I – '

'Rokiah?' I jumped up, rudely interrupting my mother, who looked up at me, a puzzled frown clouding her face.

'Of course. Who else? It has always been understood that you and Rokiah. . . .'

I sat down again then, cut my mother short with a big hug, and burst out laughing with relief.

Both my parents looked so upset that I told them what had been on my mind. We all laughed then and as soon as we had finished eating, Pak slapped me on the back and said, 'Come on. son. We men will celebrate now – we'll go to the coffee-shop.'

Wah! *What* a relief!

I had only been back at the Depot for a month or so, this time training to be a driver/mechanic, as I had so ardently desired, when I had the surprise of my life.

We were walking down the main street of Kuala Lumpur one Saturday afternoon when I saw a newsvendor holding out a copy of the *Malayan Times* and there, on the front page, were enormous headlines: STUDENT RIOTS IN SINGA-

PORE. That wasn't so surprising in itself; it was not the first riot of students – I think they were avoiding call-up, but I'm not sure – and I wouldn't have taken much notice if it hadn't been for the photograph below.

It was a terrible picture. A man and a woman lay dead beside the wreckage of a car, and standing over them, a large stone in his hand, was Musah.

I loked again to make quite sure. There were several young men, some who looked like boys only, and the print was a bit blurred, but there was no mistaking that face – hadn't I sat next to it for long enough to know?

That someone from my kampong should be involved – although he had been neither my friend nor even Malay – made me feel quite sick.

'Are you feeling all right, Karim?' It was my friend, Hashim, who spoke a little English, so I bought a copy of the newspaper and asked him to translate it for me. We took it to a bench on the padang and while he read the article to us, very slowly, it went through my mind that I had always hated Musah and that I had not been such a bad judge of character after all.

We looked at the other pictures. Not all the rioters appeared to be Chinese. I hope I never have to fire on a mob, I thought, even if it did mean the end of men like Musah.

'Which vehicles do you think we'll be working on on Monday?' I asked.

83. THE LITTLE CHILDREN

Omar

'Fire!'

The word echoed dully through my brain and then the same imperative voice, a note of irritability and slight undertone of panic in it this time.

'Sergeant-major, order your squad to fire.'

But all I could see were the little children. I was told in court that there had been no children; small men maybe, men crawling through legs to reach the front of the crowd, but no children.

I had been upset all day – it always upset me, the anniversary of Zaitun's ordeal. Eight years ago, and so many others gone, but I can never forget.

I do not understand what started the riots. They say it was students. But why should students riot? They should be in school, studying. But then I am a simple man; I do not understand half of what goes on amongst the young these days.

I was told there had been no children. But they had been young people – all children to me.

'Sergeant-major, give the order, damn you. Fire!'

Three waves of riot police had charged, wielding batons and rotan shields, but still the mob came on. I saw the grey-blue shoulders of one of my colleagues go down, his steel helmet rolling in the dust and baton flung wide as he sprawled before the oncoming surge. But still I could not act.

It was the children. We were in the normally crowded shopping district. The alert had been given as soon as the mob had been sighted, marching from the junction of the two main streets, and we had hastened there in our trucks, sirens blaring and tyres squealing, in order to prevent catastrophe.

But it was no use. The crowd was armed. My own cheek had been opened by a sliver of flying glass and blood mingled freely with the sweat on shoulders, legs and arms of my companions and on those of bystanders who had not been quick enough in entering shop doors.

And then, in the forefront of the men, as they marched down the empty street, small figures, running, crawling, and when we, the police, had taken up our positions, they were there, in the front. The children – or those whom I thought were children.

There should have been tear gas. Something had gone wrong. The rioters did not give before the charging men. Baton fell on head and shoulder and the mob did not falter.

The cries for holy war flew hysterically above us. Slogans that made the blood run hot – or cold. I heard them, but the court said there had been no cries for holy war.

And then, heedless of warning, a small car turned in at the opposite end of the street. Two Europeans sat in the front seats, a man and a woman. I could see their horror-struck, unbelieving faces as they swung into the kerb, even from where I stood, more than a chain away.

Motioning the woman to remain where she was, the man opened his door and got out. As he did so a flying rock hit him on the side of the head and he fell, like a stunned bullock, into the road. This seemed to be the signal for all sanity to disappear and the mob surged forward, over the man's prostrate form, to attack. I saw the woman's eyes widen with fear as the crowd began to rock the car.

'Fire!'

The car seemed to roll over in slow motion and the mob were upon the woman, hauling her out, tearing at her clothes and hair.

I saw her go down, blood scarlet against her white skin, and heard the mob's triumphant roar.

My command had been superseded; my men had fired, obeying the orders of that imperative voice. Whether they had fired into the crowd or over their heads, I cannot say.

The sight of the children, the woman's torn body and the mangled mass of metal that had once been a car, sickened me. The strap of my steel helmet bit into my chin and my mouth was dry. I had had enough.

Laying down my rifle, I turned away and walked through the ranks of my men.

'Where the bloody hell do you think you're going?'

I looked at the red, angry face and the massive shoulders towering above me and they were part of a dream; hovering, unreal.

A brown hand, a Malay hand, fell on my shoulder and spun me round and Red Face ordered, 'Put that thing down.'

I looked down at the broken bottle in my hand. How I came by it I do not know – the court didn't believe that, and how could I expect them to? – I must have picked it up when I put my rifle down, but I don't remember doing so. Bewildered and puzzled, I raised my hand to see what I held and at that moment a fist crashed into my jaw.

84. OUT OF THE FRYING PAN

The fifth stream flows into the river

Philip Morrison

We drove out of Kuala Lumpur in the chilly grey dawn, Philip and I in our own car with Siti and the animals, and Ja'afar following in a hired lorry with all our goods and chattels.

Neither of us spoke much, we had a long drive ahead and too many thoughts behind.

Once I had resigned myself to the idea of Philip leaving the army, I had done my best to see all the benefits, and luckily, being a born optimist, it was not long before I began to share his enthusiasm.

'As a matter of fact,' I said, 'I might be able to help. Daddy had quite a lot of government friends; he was a member of Legco for years and was director of hordes of things – he was quite a bigwig, you know.'

'If I hadn't realised that before, I would have done when I saw the house,' he replied.

'Oh, that wasn't ours; it just went with the job.'

'That's what I mean. But I don't need any help, Sally; if other people have been accepted, I don't see why I shouldn't be.'

He did however accept my help in teaching him Malay, and Ja'afar and I pounded it into him at every available moment. Two and a half months did not get him very far though and, by the time we left the army, it was still hopelessly inadequate.

Out of the army one day and into the police the next. We had twenty-eight days' leave, but Philip wanted to take the plunge and start his new job at once, and I suppose he was right. We weren't given much chance to linger anyway; the new occupants of our quarters started moving in even before we were out and, remembering our days in boarding-houses, I couldn't really blame them, but I would have enjoyed a more graceful exit. And so we were off.

It had been difficult to gauge Sally's thoughts. I had done this really because of her, knowing how she hated living in England, hated the cold, hated the separations – and there would have been plenty of those ahead of us.

'Ever heard of Kuala Jelang?' I had asked her a few days before. She had shaken her head. 'Well, you have now; I'm it's new OCPD!'

What I was letting myself in for I dreaded to think. Happily motoring out into the blue, with my immediate family beside me and everything else in the ancient lorry trundling along behind. Bill Matheson had been posted to a staff job at a Contingent HQ and was learning the easy way; it had never occurred to me that I might find myself put in charge of a district straight away, but I suppose that with the Emergency getting steadily worse they were becoming a bit short of bods.

I was growing tired and wished I could put on a spurt, but I didn't want to lose the lorry. Sally had offered to take over, but I couldn't bear being driven and she knew it, so I plodded on. She was going to be tired before the end of the tour. We had already done our three years in Malaya and Singapore that the army allowed, and now we were starting on another three. Six years without leave would be a long time. Sally's only comment was that her father had once done an eight-year-tour. She's a good kid. I hope I've done the right thing.

There was very little difference between Kuala Jelang and a score of other little Malayan towns. A long drive in through the usual government quarters, an avenue of flame trees here and another of jacarandas there; sleepy old government offices on the one hill and ancient government bungalows on the other – I'd seen it all a hundred times before. One row of shophouses and lagastroemas surrounding the padang.

The one thing that made it different was the deep river mouth, where quite large steamers were able to load and unload. I brightened up at that, it was more like home – I have always loved ships and I was born by the sea.

The police set-up looked terrifying. PCs – or mata-matas as I had always known them – crashing to attention all over the place, and literally millions of wives peering at me from the barracks' verandahs; we had already gathered that it had been a bachelor station for some years. I sat in the car while Philip went in meet the man he was to take over from. Derek King, his name was, and I hoped he was nice, because we should have been there the evening before. We'd not reckoned with a curfew.

It was a relief to see them come out, Philip and a bright-faced cocky little man who, even at a distance, reminded me of a cheeky sparrow. He was smiling and made a wry face at the police wives.

'All the monkeys aren't in the zoo,' he said, when Philip had introduced him, 'As you've no doubt already discovered. May I hop in and I'll take you up to the house.'

We made room for him in front and began to climb the hill.

'You've certainly picked an opportune moment to arrive,' King commented. We were in his office, having dropped Sally and the servants at the house. 'Take a look at this.'

He pushed a signal across the desk, the gist of which was a warning to expect a spread of the Singapore student riots to the Federation.

'They're terrified of being called-up,' he explained. 'Personally, I'm all for letting them go – put them on the first boat to China, which is what they want, and good riddance. Provided we don't let the little buggers in again.'

'How does it affect us?'

'We've only one Chinese school in the town, but it's a hotbed of Communism – those bastards sure know how to corrupt the young. A fortnight ago two boys disappeared for a couple of days and the last bandit leaflet to be found was printed on the school press. Some of the pupils come in from the squatter areas and there's altogether too much coming and going. That's one of the reasons for the curfew; that and the fact that a contractor's lorry was ambushed the day before yesterday, just outside the town limit. Driver and escort killed, everything stolen – a month's supply of rice for one of the estates and a hell of a lot of tinned stuff – and the vehicle set on fire. It was still smouldering when we got there and – of all the damned cheek – nailed on a tree nearby was a bloody great star; made, incidentally, from materials from the school art-room.'

I chewed this over while King answered a phone call.

It was a long call and appeared to be mainly one-sided. During the course of it he dug a file from a drawer and passed it over to me. It contained his handing-over notes. Pinned to the cover was a square of paper marked 'most urgent' and listing: squatters, timber-cutters, estate defences, army – lack of. I began to read.

'Old windbag!' King put down the receiver at last. 'Wotherspoon, of Bukit Merah Estate. Never stops complaining about the SCs on his estate – I scarcely listen any more; he'll be on to the DO now. Hang on to those notes and we'll go through them as soon as we can. And now you'd better see the set-up and meet the staff.'

As we walked across the parade-ground he remarked, 'You must have been driving pretty slowly – there was such a long gap between two police posts reporting your passage that I almost took out a patrol to look for you!'

I blinked. I doubt if either Sally or I had given the Emergency a moment's thought; there had been so many other things on our minds. A year on the staff had lulled me into a false sense of security.

By the time we returned to his office, my head was in a complete whirl.

There were two Malay inspectors, the elder, Zainal Abidin,

due for retirement, and the younger, Zukifli, just recently posted there – there should be three apparently, we were under strength – a Sikh sergeant-major, Jogindar Singh, and a Chinese Special Branch sergeant, Vincent Lee Chee Min – this last I felt I would find myself leaning on ; language was going to be a terrible problem. There were also two clerks, both Indians, the chief clerk called Maniam ; I didn't get the name of the second one – must ask.

Derek had arranged a lunch party for us at the Rest House, to meet the other Europeans, and that evening, having apologised because he was committed to a stag party, we were having dinner with the DO and his wife. Frankly, I wish we had not been so organised.

In my giddier and more ignorant moments I had said how much I was going to enjoy living in an old colonial-style bungalow.

The huge, rambling, barn-like house was painted throughout in a heavy, margariney shade of cream, picked out wherever it could be in chocolate. It really was rather nauseating. Things were a bit bleak.

Ja'afar too was regarding the house with disgust when a really rather beautiful woman arrived.

'I'm Helen Weatherby,' she introduced herself, and laughed – she told me afterwards that the expression on my face was a real picture. 'We took over from a bachelor too, but after a boarding-house in KL it was sheer bliss – I just couldn't find anything wrong with it. I'm sure you'll be able to do something with the house.'

I liked her immediately.

'I won't waste your time now,' she said, 'I can see your husband leaving the police station ; I expect he'll want to change. We'll be meeting at lunch anyway quite soon, but I just wanted to pop in to say hallo and to ask you to have a meal with us to-night.'

She was gone almost before I had time to thank her, and I turned my attention to my heavy-faced husband, slowly ascending the long flight of winding steps up to our house.

I cursed myself all the way up those bloody steps. We had had Ja'afar for over a year and if only I'd started learning Malay when he'd first come to work for us, instead of leaving it until I had to, I wouldn't be in such a predicament.

Of course I had only seen the operational side of the

police in the army; perhaps if I'd had an overall picture I might have had second thoughts about transferring. I shuddered when I thought of the responsibility – imagine a brand new two-pipper in the army being put in charge of an area this size, and with all these men – it was ridiculous. I wasn't worried about the operational side; anyway, there are eight police lieutenants, Europeans, in charge of the Special Constables. But everything's so strange. I know nothing about law and it's all very well King showing me through this ledger and that register – how can I possibly have a clue what he's talking about?

I did my best to muster a grin when I saw Sally's worried face, but it was no use, I'm afraid. She's such an optimist – thinks I can get the hang of things in two minutes flat. I know she'll help me with the language, but I can hardly keep her chained to my side as my unpaid interpreter.

I enjoyed our lunch. The DO and his wife are a charming couple, a little older than us. I'm sure we'll get on famously. Derek and the Forestry Officer, a rather gauche, blundery sort of person whom I'm sure I've met before somewhere, excused themselves to go to a meeting, and we had our coffee and fruit on our own with the Weatherbys.

It was really too funny watching those men. Sniffing around each other like a couple of suspicious dogs! Then they discovered that they were both thwarted regulars, who had joined the Colonial Service for similar reasons, and it was Helen and I who had to break up the party and remind them of the time.

Helen raised her eyebrows as she left. 'Thank God you've come,' she said. I don't know why, but no doubt I shall find out. It was fairly obvious, I thought, that there was not much love lost between her husband and Philip's predecessor, so I suppose that's what she meant.

Philip was in much better spirits after lunch and drove off to the office in quite a light-hearted manner.

How I blessed Ja'afar and Siti. By the time Philip brought Derek King up for a beer that evening we were actually able to produce beer mugs! Of course the whole place would be shambolic for days, but they had already unpicked three crates and our pictures were stacked along one wall, waiting for me to hang.

'How goes it?' I asked. Philip, I thought, looked all in.

'So-so. A bit 'ard, I reckon, asking anyone new to take over in three days. Ah, well, here's to my boat. *I'm* all right!' Derek lifted his mug.

Philip grinned wanly. All my maternal instinct was aroused and I longed to cradle his head and stroke his hair. I wasn't sorry when Derek got up to go.

'Well, hope you enjoy yourself with the nobs as much as I intend enjoying my Chinese chow.'

He was obviously as smart as a cartload of monkeys, but I thought a little of him would go a long way. As soon as he had gone, Philip slumped forward with his head in his hands and I thought for a dreadful moment that he was going to cry.

'How *am* I going to cope?' he asked at length. 'King admits the senior inspector's an old dead-beat, and the young one's too new to help much. There's no one to whom I can turn.'

'You'll manage,' I said, and I was stroking his hair by then. I certainly hoped I was right.

85. FIRST BLOOD

While the Morrisons and the outgoing OCPD were discussing the district, the Weatherbys, on the other side of the hill, were discussing the newcomers.

Helen had been bubbling ever since lunchtime and James could not remember seeing her so frivolously excited before. She remarked, for the umpteenth time, that it would be nice to have another woman around, what a pity they didn't have any children and what fun it would be helping Sally to unpack and move in.

James sat on the edge of his bed, listening to her with one ear while she splashed around in the bath and chattered on. The other ear, as usual, was on his job.

'Brush my hair for me, James.'

She seated herself on the stool before the dressing-table in bra and pants and handed him the brush. With no one locally to cut her hair it had grown quite long. James picked it up and looked at it before wielding the brush; still as blonde as ever and her skin as white, despite the sun. He took up a firm stance and began to brush with long, sweeping, rhythmic strokes, smiling at her in the mirror as he did so.

It was ages since he had brushed her hair. He seldom suffered pangs of conscience, but it suddenly occurred to him that she must have been bored to death these past six months, and lonely too. What company there was had largely been barred – by him. He knew that he had nothing to be jealous about, and yet he could not bear another man looking at his wife and unfortunately, when you looked like Helen, people did look at you, especially men. He was proud of her and yet he hated it, sometimes wishing that she were ordinary and plain. And then there was his work; he was so bound up in it that even the odd evening in the local estate club seemed a waste of precious time and he made sure that they gave the weekly club night in town a miss if they possibly could. It could not have been much fun for her though. As far as he was concerned the Morrisons could only be an improvement, and first impressions had been good. Thank God he was married, if she and Sally got on it would make all the difference for Helen.

'I'm glad I asked them for supper on their own,' for an awful moment James wondered if she had only just spoken, or if he had been miles away while she had been talking. 'I suppose I should have asked Donald as well, but he's such heavy going and I thought it would be fun just the four of us.'

He made some non-committal sound.

'I'm sure we're going to have lots in common – isn't it strange that you and Sally should have been in the air force and Philip and I in the army?'

'Not really. Most people of our age were in one uniform or another. You're going to be late.'

'Oh James, you can be a wet blanket. You know you liked them – even if you never will admit to liking anybody.'

He slapped her on the bottom with the hairbrush and muttered something about tying his tie – something he had never managed to cope with one-handed.

In fact, they did find plenty in common and were still talking when the clock struck midnight. By that time they all had a synopsis of each others' careers, moaned about the lousy pay of government servants, the disgusting colours that the PWD chose to paint their houses, and argued hotly about service matters. What a pleasant change it will be, James thought, to have someone here who knows even less about the district than I do.

The next morning Derek King was up at the house before Philip had even finished shaving.

'Anyone awake yet?' he yelled. And when Philip emerged, 'I didn't want to use the phone, but I've got an informer in the office. Came in from one of the timber camps. I'm taking a patrol out in half an hour; are you fit?'

'Never fitter.' It was a relief to tackle a job with which he was already *au fait*. 'I hope Ja'afar's unearthed my jungle-green. Have a cup of coffee?'

'Thanks.' While they drank, he outlined the plan.

An hour later they were walking in single file down a narrow-gauge light railway, running into the jungle from a roadside timber camp. The informer led, a sack with eye slits over his head and shoulders, police issue jungle-green below. Immediately to his side and behind came two jungle squad PCs, stens at the ready, then Morrison and King and some fifteen men.

They had walked for nearly three miles before the high-pitched whine of an electric saw reverberated through the forest. The informer stopped dead and held up his hand.

'He says we are now less than half a mile from the cutting area,' one of the PCs whispered to King. 'The men will be with the first trolley coming down.'

'As good a place to ambush as any,' King said to Philip. 'With any luck we'll get them as they come round that bend.' He waved his carbine in front of the sack and said to the Chinese-speaking PC, 'Tell him no nonsense or he'll be the first to die.'

It was eerie waiting in the intense gloom, Philip thought, the only sounds besides the insects the heavy breathing of his unseen companions and the occasional distant whine of the saw.

From where he lay the rails were above him and immediately in front. Quite suddenly they began to hum, and a moment later to shake. A trolley had started on its way.

A twig fell on the line; signal from a PC high in a tree that the trolley was within fifty yards. Philip licked his lips and counted.

The firing was practically instantaneous. Three men fell dead, and with a high-pitched shriek of rage the fourth person, a woman by the voice, attempting to use the trolley as a shield, flung her weapon on to it and pulled a hand-grenade from her shirt. With one movement two PCs grabbed her and she fell with them, kicking wildly and tearing at them with her hands. The trolley hurtled down a slight incline and the grenade rolled harmlessly along the line.

A third PC caught the woman's hands and tied them, but she was not beaten; she twisted round and spat, full in his face. The man hit her across the mouth and she started up a screeching that must have lasted five minutes, all the time thrusting her chin in the direction of her hooded compatriot, before King shouted, 'For Christ's sake, gag the bitch.'

When she was firmly bound and loaded on to the trolley with the three corpses and their weapons, the party started back.

Later that afternoon the woman's screeched invective could be heard all over the police compound. Chee Min came out of his office, mopping sweat from his brow and grinned at Philip. 'She could teach an Aussie truck driver a few words!'

'What did you get out of her?'

'That men may turn informer, but a woman never. We can gaol her, torture her, offer her cash, and string her up, but she'll never split. I believe her. Incidentally, she's accusing the two PCs who grabbed her of rape!'

When the men were told, their remarks would have shamed an Aussie truck driver too!

Sally had turned away, sickened, when she saw the three corpses being laid out on the grass verge outside the police station, but as soon as Philip came home she sensed that he had found his confidence. The first blood had done the trick.

The next day King handed over; they attended a stupendous farewell party for him and the day after that Philip was on his own.

Within days of taking over, and bearing the priorities in mind, Philip Morrison visited the Ulu Pandanus settlement with Detective-Sergeant Lee Chee Min. He looked with interest as they moved slowly along the raised, flat road, with squatter huts and market gardens on either side.

'They seem well established,' he observed, pointing at the sizeable coffee bushes and fruit trees.

'I believe they've been here ever since the end of the war.'

At that moment a middle-aged man wearing a large topi and pushing a bicycle with a heavy-looking sack on the carrier emerged from one of the orchards and attempted to push his overloaded cycle up a makeshift ramp and on to the road.

He looked at them with an expressionless face and called out to a boy, whom Philip judged to be about twelve years of age, to help him push.

The police vehicle continued to crawl through the settlement, until they were past the last house and already within the confines of the jungle.

Philip told the driver to turn round and stop. They all sat in the stationary jeep for a couple of minutes while he asked a number of questions, then said they would return the way they had come.

'Drive slowly,' he ordered, 'I want to have another good look at the area.'

Back they went until they reached the man and the boy, still heaving and pushing the heavy bicycle with much high-pitched abuse at each other, but little success.

Philip laughed. 'Go and give them a hand,' he said to the two PCs sitting at the back, who immediately jumped off the vehicle and ran towards the quarrelling couple.

As soon as they saw the police coming both man and boy abandoned the bike and fled down the path, past a couple of houses, through the market gardens and into the jungle fringe.

The PCs needed no orders to give chase and, picking up their rifles, dashed after the fleeing pair, closely followed by Philip and Chee Min.

At the jungle edge the man turned, pulling a revolver from his waist band as he did so, and fired, hitting one of the constables in the shoulder.

Philip and the other PC fired at the same time and the man fell.

'Get the boy,' he called to Chee Min, and went to the body lying on the path.

The man was dead, with two bullet wounds in the chest, and Philip stood up from examining the corpse to find the boy, with Chee Min holding his arm, looking down at it with a look utterly devoid of any emotion other than curiosity.

'Ask him who the man is.'

Chee Min interpreted.

'My uncle.' The boy shrugged. 'Can I have a cigarette?'

'No,' Philip stifled the impulse to hit the youngster, 'you're too young.'

Then he turned his attention to the wounded constable, who was sitting by the side of the track holding the blood-stained sleeve of his shirt.

'Nothing much, Tuan, only a small wound.' The man

grinned but he was obviously in pain.

'Where's the nearest doctor?' Philip asked Chee Min.

'Kemuning. But I expect the dresser will cope – he's removed bullets before.' He turned to the wounded man and spoke in Malay, 'Can you walk, Ismail?'

The man rose, unaided. Incredibly nimbly Philip thought, and marvelled at his stoicism. 'I'll take your rifle,' he said, and turning to the other PC, 'yours too; you carry the body.'

They walked in single file back to the jeep. Chee Min leading with the boy, then the wounded PC, the PC carrying the corpse, and Philip bringing up the rear.

Not a soul was to be seen. Every house appeared to be empty, every garden deserted. But they could feel the eyes watching as they made their silent way back.

The body was thrown into the rear of the jeep with scant ceremony and the boy seated beside it under the guard of the able-bodied PC, while Philip and Chee Min examined the contents of the sack.

Rice and dried fish, tins of bully beef, pilchards, sardines, jars of chicken essence by the score and several well-packed bottles emerged. Philip carefully unwrapped one.

'Good God, look at this,' he held up a bottle of Benedictine. 'Whoever would have thought they had such sophisticated tastes?'

'It is a powerful body-builder and most strengthening to the constitution,' Chee Min remarked and, just in time, Philip realised with amazement that he was serious.

Back at the police station, Chee Min and a Chinese detective interrogated the boy.

There was no question of his trying to run away; escape was far from his mind. He looked around him, picked things up and showed no emotion whatsoever. After half an hour, Chee Min went into Philip's office to report.

'The boy's father is with the bandits proper in the jungle. The deceased, his uncle, was only Min Yuen, who kept that particular supply line going.' He paused for a moment, not knowing how *au fait* the new OCPD was with the local Communist organisation. 'You understand, sir? The Min Yuen who don't wear uniform, but keep the fighting terrorists supplied. They are the ones who collect food and money and act as contacts; the men in the jungle couldn't survive without them.'

'Sort of combined RASC and Ordnance Corps,' Philip murmured.

It was Chee Min's turn not to understand. He gave Philip a slightly puzzled look but went on, 'I cannot make out where they were actually heading when we happened to pass. But the boy will tell.'

'You can't beat him up,' Philip said hastily.

Chee Min gave a mirthless laugh, 'Not necessary, sir. He will lead us to his father's camp – depending on the amount of the reward money involved.'

'I don't believe it. No child would lead the police in – why, his father might be killed.'

'This one will. He's a hard little bugger, make no mistake.'

'We'll have to be on the alert for a trap.'

Inspector Zainal Abidin, the elderly senior inspector, who had been with Philip when Chee Min came in, murmured, 'Europeans find this mentality difficult to understand.'

'By God I do. It's horrifying.'

Both inspector and sergeant shrugged their shoulders and Philip told Chee Min to get what details he could to enable them to plan a raid.

By the following evening all plans were completed and a little before midnight two troop-carriers and a jeep, carrying the OCPD, Chee Min, the boy, Police Lieutenant O'Brien, and fifteen members of his jungle squad, set off from the police station in the direction of Ulu Pandanus.

Still incredulous that any child could be sufficiently callous to engineer the possible death of his own father for a cash reward, Philip had come well prepared to be led into a trap.

The vehicles separated before reaching the squatter huts, passing through the inhabited area at intervals, to rendezvous on the jungle-enclosed road beyond.

After a quarter of an hour's travelling, the boy called a halt and announced that a track began from behind a tall Ipoh tree a couple of chains farther on.

Philip held a sheet of paper on his knees in the front of the jeep and, beckoning the police lieutenant and Chee Min to his side, he flashed his torch on to it. The boy had drawn the plan in the police station that afternoon and Philip still marvelled that one so young could be so sure.

'We're here,' the child stabbed the map with a grubby forefinger, 'and this is the beginning of the track, here.'

There was one main track, the one they would be starting

on, used by the Min Yuen and terrorists making direct for the camp, the boy had told them, but there were many hidden tracks, branching off and surrounding the camp, which the bandits used as escape routes. The only sentry was posted on the main track.

O'Brien, ex-Commando and Palestine policeman, had volunteered to take one of his men and deal with the sentry but, if the boy could be trusted, Philip's plans were otherwise.

If as many hidden tracks existed as marked, he intended that they should branch off the main one long before reaching the sentry and half encircle the camp from the opposite side. The moon was in the last quarter, giving them a glimmer of light by which to travel. A two-hour walk to the camp, the boy had said, and Philip allowed three, to enable them to be in position and ready to attack at dawn.

They had been moving in silence and in single file for about an hour when the boy suddenly stopped. He pointed to a large, moss-covered boulder and whispered to Chee Min.

'He says that one hidden track begins the other side of this rock; it goes to the left. A few yards farther on there is a rotting log, on the right side of the path, and another hidden track starts there. Which one do you want to take?'

Philip fought down his exasperation and said. 'Tell him the easiest one to get *behind* the camp.' He was still not altogether happy about their guide.

Without any hesitation the boy scrambled under a bush by the side of the rock, stood upright on the other side, asked for a torch – which was reluctantly passed – flickered it around the ground at his feet, gave an exclamation of satisfaction when he found a largish stone with a fern growing out of it, and parted the bushes immediately above it. On the other side was a well-used path.

'Oh for some aerial photographs,' Philip remarked, almost inaudibly. 'We'd never have found this in a month of Sundays.'

Trap or no trap, it was clear that the boy knew his way. After half an hour's fairly swift moving, he stopped again and pointed. In the remains of the moonlight is was possible to see the jungle thinning into secondary growth, and a few minutes later they were able to see the clearing itself.

Philip and O'Brien edged forward until they could make out the boundaries of the clearing and the outline of a long atap hut, nestling on the edge and sheltered by overhanging trees.

'Whole area must have been a Sakai clearing,' O'Brien whispered. 'Look, you can still see the remains of their tapioca over there.'

After a few more moments of examination of the area, they returned to the main body of the party.

'You stay here with the boy,' Philip instructed Chee Min and ordered that the rest of the men, led by the police lieutenant, should take up positions a short distance apart in a half moon round the back of the hut. He drew his whistle on its lanyard from his top left-hand pocket and held it up, the pale moonlight glinting on the shiny metal. 'This will be the signal to attack. When you hear me whistle, open up. If what the boy says is true and we are on one of their escape routes, at least some of the terrorists should run from the hut in our direction – that is the time to pick them off.'

The men began to spread out and Philip concealed himself in the fork of a low tree some twenty-five yards from the hut. There would be about half an hour to wait.

Dawn came very suddenly, and as soon as it was light enough to aim, Philip blew his whistle and the men of the jungle squad opened fire.

Bandits came popping from the huts like peas from a ripe pod. A few ran through the door and down the steps, but mostly bodies came hurtling through the flimsy atap walls, dropped through trap doors in the floor and on to the ground, and Philip dropped one man who thrust a ladder through the roof and tried to swing into a tree.

The firing lasted for about a minute, by which time it was daylight and, calling to a man near him to give him cover, Philip walked warily into the camp.

Nothing stirred. Complete silence reigned. The camp was deserted except for the dead.

Soon a great pile of weapons, uniforms, food and documents was being divided into portable loads and six corpses were laid out on the ground.

Three separate blood trails had been followed up and soon two PCs walked into the clearing carrying a wounded man, whose groaning rose above the excited chatter of the other men. They laid him on the ground, telling the OCPD that they had first come across his rifle, then, a few yards farther on, the man himself. The boy walked over and looked at him.

No sign of guilt, recognition or accusation was expressed on either face.

'Is he your father?'

He shook his head and pointed to one of the six corpses. 'No. My father is over there.' He showed complete disinterest. Then, brightening up, 'Do I get the reward money now?'

Sally dashed to the verandah railing when she heard the vehicles grinding along the road. Watching townsfolk had seen the gruesome cargo of the last troop carrier and were already flocking to the police station in droves.

'Oh my God, how horrible.'

She turned away as she saw the six bodies being off-loaded and laid out in a row on the side of the road. Ja'afar was at her elbow, grinning.

'It is good luck for the Tuan,' he said. 'Nine bodies in as many days.' He started towards the front steps.

'I will not have any ghouls in this house,' Sally commanded, 'just you go and organise the Tuan's breakfast and leave the spectacle to the town.' Nevertheless, she knew he would go down as soon as her back was turned.

Ja'afar grimaced, said nothing, and continued to watch. So did Sally herself, but keeping her gaze averted from the gory sight. The morning air was crystal clear. She could even see the white smile in the beard of Jogindar Singh as he greeted Philip, and his clicking heels and call of attention to the Charge Room cracked up like pistol shots.

Then at last Philip himself was leaving the police station and ascending the steps to the house.

He dropped his muddy jungle-boots at the front door and padded across the room in blood-soaked socks.

'Philip, you're wounded,' Sally hurried towards him, and only then did he look down at his gory feet.

'Leeches,' he said. 'Bloody place was full of them.'

'Ugh!' They were one of the few things that she never learned to take in her stride.

Standing by the front door with Philip's bloody boots in her hand, Sally glanced over the heads of the milling crowd below and at the river, then raised her eyes to the blue hills; the hills where Philip would spend so much of his time.

Because she was so close to her husband, she was able to visualise the long night vigils and slow, weary, plodding through undergrowth and hampering vines that had to be cut, inch by inch, before success could be achieved. She understood the furtive rustle or sudden bird-screech that sent the adrenalin coursing through the blood. She knew the tense moments of apprehension that caused the throat to go dry and the palms to sweat; the terrible heartbeats that thumped in rhythm to the stranger's step; the moment of fire and the fleeting question, Will it be them or us?

She looked down at the boots in her hand and there, wriggling obscenely on the blood-soaked canvas, lay a satiated leech; pinkish, grey-white, bloated on blood. It was so like a segment of the entrails that had once been spewed over her lap that her memory betrayed her and she had to dash for the drain.

A minute later Ja'afar was relieving her of the boots and pushing back her hair. 'She must be pregnant,' he told his wife, and they both smiled with pleasure.

Sally washed and rinsed out her mouth in the spare bedroom, pulled herself together and turned her attention to the breakfast-table.

The plates and coffee-pot were squeezed to one end and she sighed as she looked at the great pyramid of files cluttering the major part. Philip was slowly wading through them whenever he had a break and she was doing her best to précis the long reports for him, but how could anyone be expected to spend hours and days in the jungle yet still cope with the weighty routine work? And yet scores of OCPDs must be doing just that.

Philip was singing under the shower. Will he still be singing in a year? she wondered.

'Aren't you going to get some sleep?' she asked when he emerged from the bedroom, looking a new man in clean shorts and shirt.

'Can't. The mail's in already and there's a pile in my tray I haven't looked at yet. I'll go to bed early though; we're going out again before dawn to-morrow.'

'Another camp?'

'No. We brought in a wounded man; he's told us where the escapees were heading. Also where there's a lot of equipment to be found. Chee Min was keen to go straight away, but if we give them time there should be a better haul.'

He ate a couple of slices of toast, swallowed only half his coffee and was gone.

Sally took another piece of toast – she's hungry, a good sign, Ja'afar thought, as he cleared the used crockery away

– and thought how important it was to keep one's mind on mundane things. She spoke to Ja'afar on a number of household matters, but her thoughts kept wandering.

She had never appreciated how far removed from reality she had been as an army wife – and she had thought it nerve-racking at the time; nor how much worse it would be, being married to a policeman instead of a soldier. How much more down to earth. It wasn't only that as a police wife she herself was living in the danger zone, but that she knew too much. When Philip had gone out on ops with his company she had not known what was going on, or the area, and when he returned to their quarters he was always clean and shaved and neatly dressed. Reality was much closer when you saw your husband lacing his jungle-boots and picking up his carbine. Then the roaring of trucks away down the road and, once the sound had died away, the awful waiting. Not going to bed until the small hours, in case he should come home, and the ever-listening ear for voices or vehicles on the road below. And when they did return, sometimes wounded men were lifted from the trucks and sometimes corpses.

She took her coffee to the verandah rail. The crowd had dispersed; only the corpses remained, mangled, torn and bloody. She could almost hear the buzzing of the flies.

The information led them, needless to say, to the Ulu Pandanus squatter area.

Philip's whole body tingled with apprehension. They crept through dense, white, pre-dawn mist and arrived at the first houses as the first cockerel crowed. There was something sinister in the sound.

Faint and fleeting above the mist rose a kite.

'White,' Chee Min whispered. 'I haven't worked out their signals yet, but I think it means they have info to pass.'

The stillness was uncanny. The houses looked blind in the pale grey light, the mist sweeping them in ribbons, passing, circling, swishing on. Eyes seemed to be watching, narrowed, in every swathe of vapour. Suddenly a nightjar rose, squawking, in a flurry of feathers, at their feet, its crimson eyes glaring through the gloom. Philip caught his breath, Chee Min gave a faint, nervous giggle, and the man beside him swore.

And then, as though the curtain had been lifted on a stage, it was light. The cockerels crowed in unison and the search began.

Uniforms, material, sewing-machines, flags, arms and ammunition: all came from under floorboards, in tins tied to beams and to branches of trees. Babies were found lying on bundles of money; curtains weighted down with ammunition and pieces of dismantled weapons in every conceivable nook and cranny of the apparently poverty-stricken huts.

But of the escaped CTs there was no trace. Not a young man was to be seen. Chee Min looked reproachfully at his superior.

Philip, too, was furious with himself. The boy had said that about twenty men normally occupied the camp. They had accounted for seven. What had happened to the other thirteen?

On first entering the squatter settlement he had noticed something unnatural about one of the gardens, but could not pinpoint what it was. The house had been searched along with all the others and yielded nothing, but he was still not satisfied. While one of the other houses was being gone through he had walked back to take another look, and while he was doing so Chee Min joined him.

'What's different about this garden?' Philip asked.

Chee Min looked, then he walked to another garden and came back, shaking his head.

'I thought perhaps that it was that they are growing flowers instead of vegetables,' he said, 'but in fact most of the huts have a few flowers as well.'

It was the zinnia bed that stood out so startlingly, Philip realised, and then, quite suddenly, he saw what was wrong.

It was still early morning and the zinnias were growing in the shade of the hut. Standing like guardsmen, straight and bright, they bloomed, row upon row.

'No green,' he pointed out, 'no leaves.'

He strode forward and plucked one of the heads from the bed. It came straight out at the first tug, its stem cut clean about a foot down.

'Have it dug up,' he ordered.

The elderly occupants of the hut came out while the police dug and stood there watching, quiet, expressionless, flat-eyed.

The body was not more than eighteen inches down. Still in uniform and with a gash across the neck, he must have been one of the wounded terrorists who had come so far only to die on arrival.

'Do you know this man?' Chee Min asked the old couple.

'He was our son.' The disinterment continued and Philip

was wondering at the humility of the old people when the man spoke again, a wistful note in his voice, 'His politics were not our politics, but he was our son.'

86. THE PRIORITIES

Donald Thom looked thoughtfully into his Scotch and listened to Philip laying down the law. This was no ordinary dinner-party; the Morrisons had asked him for a reason.

'I don't see how we can achieve anything until we get the supply lines under control.' Philip, the only person standing, emphasised his point with a cutting gesture. 'Cut them off. Get the squatters resettled and the timber camps closed down.'

'Steady on,' Donald interrupted. 'Regrouping was the intention, not closing down.' He drained his drink and Sally rose to refill his glass. He smiled at her. 'Taking the forward camps out of the deep forest and regrouping the various kongsis, sawmills and all, in an area where they can be guarded – '

'Guarded by whom?'

'You.'

Philip sat down with a loud humph and asked, 'And where, do you suppose, the men are coming from?'

'Gee, I dunno; guess that's a police problem. Thanks, Sal,' as she handed him his replenished glass, 'I can see your predicament, Phil, but it was all gone into before you arrived; the same throughout the state. The idea is to have these regrouped camps and then the cutters go into the jungle each day, having been searched – by the police – for supplies, then escorted – by the police, of course!'

Philip grinned then. 'Okay, Don. I'm not really being obstructive, but I want to have my facts and figures clear before the CPO comes down. We're hopelessly under strength anyway. I wanted to talk this over, amicably, with you and James, somewhere where we wouldn't have the phone ringing the whole time – '

The phone rang.

'Sorry,' Philip said, a minute later. 'Scare on Belimbing Estate. I'll have to go. God, how I wish we had some troops here. James, can we discuss the squatter problem tomorrow? CPO'll be down in a few days.'

Sally spread her hands in a gesture of resignation as they heard Philip's jeep drive away. 'And to think I *wanted* to stay in Malaya.'

Philip tackled the DO on the resettlement problem the next day.

'It has been brought up with DWEC,' James admitted, 'but the trouble is finding land.'

He knew in his own heart that he had disliked Philip's predecessor so much that he had done very little to co-operate with him. King had been going on about resettling the squatters for some time and, not without malice, James had always found some other matter to take priority. On the other hand, land was a genuine problem. There was no Crown land available in a suitable area; it would mean buying land – funds would be forthcoming, but who was prepared to sell?

'To date it only appears to be those isolated squatters across the river at Ulu Pandanus that we can pin anything on,' Philip continued, 'but I suppose the Pasir Hitam crowd are helping too – although we have no evidence as yet.'

Pasir Hitam was the settlement to the south of the river.

'Obviously it must become number one priority,' James agreed. 'We'll have to have another go at finding a site.'

'And then, my next task will be to lay down the law a bit over defences.'

'Making yourself popular with the planting fraternity?' James raised an eyebrow.

'Well, perhaps it's my army mind, but it strikes me that if you're going to have SCs on the estates, paid by Government, then there must be reasonable defences to help them do the defending. Don't you agree?'

'On the whole I do.'

'Oh well, better get back to the grindstone. I have a new inspector arriving, I hope, on the bus and I'm going out on an overnight patrol. At least it can't be said that we lead idle lives.'

James sat for a while after Philip had left. It was a relief to be able to work with someone he liked for a change. Sally was company for Helen too. If only his eye wasn't giving him such hell he would really enjoy this job. His arm too.

He rolled up his empty sleeve and examined the stump. A mass of small ulcers covered it, that would not heal whatever he tried. This bloody climate, he thought. It had been all right in Kuala Lumpur, where he had had an air-conditioned office, but here there was not even a fan. He glanced up at the ceiling, where two hooks showed where a punkah had once hung. He had been amused to see on one of the old account books that had survived the war what the wages of a pre-war punkah wallah had been – everything was so penny-pinched he doubted if they would pay *that* now.

He called his clerk and asked for a file, then looked at his watch. He would have to go across the river to settle a dispute between two headmen after lunch; what a bore. He would have preferred to be going with Philip; he didn't feel like talking all afternoon.

Philip did not return to his own office at once, but went to the Forestry Station instead.

'I'm going to take out patrols and penetrate every cutting area and the surrounding jungle,' he told Donald, ' – having read the riot act to the towkays first – and hope we have the odd encounter at the same time. Do you want to come?'

'You bet!'

As Philip left the office he rubbed his hands. Action at last. Then he realised that he was aiding and abetting his own redundancy.

87. NO DENIAL

Sharif Ahmat

My year with the army came to an end and although I was sorry in many ways to leave them, I was still ambitious, and sensible to the fact that being out of sight was out of mind.

I was posted to Special Branch and it seemed that Hassan had been right about the inspectorate being a mere stepping-stone for me. Of course I was no keener than the next man to see my country plunged into virtual war again, but, as any regular soldier will tell you, there is nothing like a war for personal advancement – always providing that one survives.

These sentiments were echoed by the senior SB officer who interviewed me on arrival at my new post. I must say he was extremely friendly and told me that, with the sudden expansion of the force, I stood a better than ever chance of early promotion to gazetted rank. He also told me that my war-time background, knowledge of the Communist guerillas and my recent experience with the army, would hold me in good stead.

I can tell you, I walked out of that interview already mentally buckling on my Sam Browne and considering myself Tuan Allah's gift to the force!

My ego did not remain inflated for long though. I was to share an office for a week or two with a Chinese inspector, to learn the routine of filing, classification, etcetera, before going on an SB course. This man was my senior in both years and service and it was clear from the start that, as far as I was concerned, he was not impressed.

I suppose I was a mite cocky. I repeated the gist of the interview while he sat, picking his nose and jogging a knee – in that infuriating manner of many Chinese. Then he asked me just one damping question.

'Just exactly how long *were* you with the guerillas?'

The army had helped me to believe that I was one hell of a fellow, but when I stopped to think about it, I had to admit that I had spent far more time as an ordinary PC, maintaining a negative 'no see, no hear' policy than I had either as a go-between or in the jungle.

I felt my ears growing hot and I suppose I stammered some sort of reply. I can't remember now. I never did learn to like that particular colleague of mine, but I had one thing to thank him for – he taught me to stand on my own feet and not rely on Hassan's reputation.

I cannot tell you much about my work with Special Branch, partly because I had signed the Official Secrets Act and partly because it would be difficult to explain – I was, after all, a pretty small cog in a large wheel and my job was only a part of the whole, dovetailing in with other people's.

I went on seeing Azizah as much as I could, but I no longer worked regular office hours and was unable to maintain the weekly dates each Sunday.

We talked about marriage quite often and I finally won her over, but there was still the stumbling-block of my mother.

I think Azizah was quite looking forward to the status of being an inspector's wife – for I had made up my mind to marry her, whether my mother gave her consent or not.

And then the blow fell.

I must have been working in SB for about a year when I was summoned to the presence of my immediate boss.

I could see it was going to be a painful session as soon as I opened the door, and I was right.

He was a bluff, burly man, rather a jovial character normally, but now he was frowning and tapping a pencil agitatedly on his blotter.

'Sit down, Ahmat. I'll come straight to the point.'

He handed me a cigarette and lit his own.

'There has been an anonymous letter written about you. I abhor these things at any time, and even more so when it concerns one of my own men. But we can't be too careful with this confounded Emergency on and the Head wants your comments before it goes any further.'

Of course my mind leaped to Azizah, but I could not have been wider from the mark.

'The letter accuses you of being a Communist.'

'But – '

'No, wait. Let me finish first.'

'But, sir, I'm not a Communist.'

'It accuses you of having deliberately set fire to a police station in 1945 in order to facilitate the escape of a wanted Communist. Now what have you to say to that?'

What was there to say?

'Well?'

'I have nothing to say.'

'You don't deny having set fire to the police station?' The incredulity made his voice rise.

'No.'

'I never, for one moment, expected to hear that reply from you. In the circumstances, you can hardly expect to remain in Special Branch.'

'I am not a Communist, sir. Nor have I ever been one.'

'And yet you helped them.' It was a statement, flat.

There was a long silence before he spoke again.

'To say that I'm upset and disappointed in you would be putting it very mildly. Both the Head and I had taken your denial for granted – the letter seemed utterly ridiculous. Now I have no alternative but to suspend you from duty until such time as the Head decides what action to take. Inspector Nordin will take over from you temporarily. That's all.'

I returned to my own office and buried my head in my hands and nearly wept with the bitterness and injustice of it all. Hasbullah was behind it without a doubt – but how could I prove that he wrote the letter, or caused it to be written? And anyway, what it said was true. The escape of Ah Keow seemed a hundred years ago and even Hasbullah had not been in my thoughts since the inspectors' course.

I must have been sitting like that when my office mate, Shau Lee, came in, and it was a relief to pour out my troubles to him.

'But my goodness, man, that was during the occupation. Plenty of people went into the jungle with the guerillas who weren't Communists. Didn't you tell him that?'

'How could I prove it? Hassan is dead, Richardson is dead, and I've no idea what happened to the army officers who were with us. There is only Kassim, and I don't know where he is. Everyone else *was* a Communist.'

'I don't believe that. There must have been others who weren't Communists.' I shrugged. 'But who could have written such a monstrous letter?'

'Oh, I know who wrote it all right. But even if I could prove it, it would be his word against mine.'

'But why didn't you explain? Old Hopper would have listened to you.'

I shrugged again. 'What could I say?'

'Oh, you Malays. When you get proud and stubborn like this it just makes me lose my patience.'

He slammed out of the office and I was left alone once more with my very uncomfortable thoughts. If it came to interdiction, I supposed I would have to fight, but if it were merely a posting it could be worse. The thought of leaving SB did not upset me much – in fact, I would prefer a more active job – but I saw all hopes of reaching gazetted rank receding from my grasp, and the unfairness of it all hit me all over again.

Soon afterwards Nordin arrived to take over. I went straight to the Bintang Kilat that evening, but I didn't dance. I did my best to smile at Azizah, but she was no fool and I could see her ill-concealed look of puzzled concern. At the first break she came over to where I sat.

'Whatever's wrong, Mat? You look awful.'

'I feel awful. Azizah, please come with me for a walk or something after you've finished – I've got to talk to you.'

'We're not busy to-night; Munah will take over for me. I'll come now.'

I didn't even buy her a cup of coffee. We went straight to the Lake Gardens and there, sitting on a bench in the kind, velvety darkness, I told her what had happened.

'You know, Mat, I'll marry you even if you are disgraced.

After all, being the wife of an inspector isn't everything.'

'But even if I'm not disgraced, I'm bound to be posted out-station.'

'Oh yes,' she replied shrewdly, 'that's inevitable.'

I cannot tell you what a surge of joy and relief swept over me. I suppose at the back of my mind there had lurked a nagging, insidious little thought, that Azizah's interest was in my rank and position rather than in me myself. And of course I knew she liked the bright lights.

What a wonderful girl she was. I jumped up and hugged her and when I felt the softness of her cheek against mine and the scent of her hair so close to my nostrils, it was all I could do not to make love to her there and then.

After that we walked, hand-in-hand, over to the open-air restaurant.

'Are you a Communist, Mat?'

I stopped, open-mouthed in astonishment. I could not see her expression in the dark, but she had sounded casual, as though it were not at all important.

'Of course not.'

I had never told her about my war days, but when we had reached the restaurant and were settled at an isolated table with glasses of iced coffee before us, I told her the whole story from beginning to end.

She listened carefully and at length made a pertinent remark. 'If you can't find Kassim, don't you think the Ceylonese dresser might still be alive?'

Old Ratna. Of course. Why hadn't I thought of him? I had been so busy all afternoon hating Hasbullah that I had let my feelings cloud my judgment. There were several Jaffna Tamil clerks of his age in HQ; someone there might know him. I would make inquiries the very next day.

When the restaurant closed, we strolled again out into the black night and lay on the soft warm turf under a laburnum tree. You could see the carpet of bright yellow petals showing grey against the darker ground. Azizah sat with her back propped against the tree, gathering the petals into her lap and soon we were talking of other things.

I suppose I must have fallen asleep, for the next thing I knew was Azizah shaking me and seeing the first pale streaks of dawn reflected in the lake.

'Oh Mat, we're soaked with dew and my shoulder's bruised from cushioning your heavy great head all night!'

I could just see a glint of light on her eyes and teeth. She smelt good. I leaned down and touched her lips with mine, Western style, as we had seen on the movies. Then I pulled her up and brushed her down. She was right, we were wet.

'Come on, hurry. I'd better get you home before daylight.'

The noise of the scooter sounded vibrant and alive in the cool morning air. There was no traffic to speak of and I brpt-brpt up the middle of the road to reach her lodgings in record time.

Then I went and showered and changed into a clean uniform – the first time I'd worn uniform for more than a year – happy to face whatever the day might bring. Man, I felt good.

In fact, it brought nothing and I had to wait for nearly a week before a clerk told me that I was posted to Kuala Jelang as senior inspector.

During this time I had had several interviews with officers of varying seniority. I just kept quiet most of the time; I could not see any point in trying to explain myself. And anyway, I didn't care. I had Azizah behind me and in my heart I knew I had done nothing wrong. Tuan Allah knew that my conscience was clear, so why should I worry?

If my punishment was merely to be returned to general duties, and with what appeared to be promotion to boot, it was no great tragedy. But when the clerk also told me that the Chief Police Officer of Perangor, the state to which I was posted, wanted to see me first, my heart sank. Normally I would have gone straight to the station and reported to the OCPD. It was most unusual

The next morning I set off to report to my new contingent, and find out the worst.

Berembang, my destination, was only a morning's journey from Kuala Lumpur, and as I hung around the railway station, waiting for the day mail to start, my head was full of memories.

Allah knows, I've been on KL railway station often enough during the past few years, but I never go without remembering the sight of Mahmood walking down the platform the day after my father ran amok.

Mahmood. Allahumma! If only he had remained a little more stable, a little more conventional, life would be easier for me. He had never had much interest in the police, and when the RAF Regiment (Malaya) was formed, he left the force and went straight off to Singapore to join it. He had

had a few months in Singapore, then a session up-country, where he'd been involved in a few skirmishes with the bandits – which was more than I had – and then his squadron had been posted to Hong Kong. Nothing much wrong with that; the pill was that in next to no time he had written to say he had married a Chinese taxi dancer and hoped to make his home in Hong Kong when his time was up. I gather he had not even insisted on her becoming a Muslim.

Needless to say, I had not imparted all Mahmood's news to my mother. Marrying taxi dancers was altogether too close to home and in my numerous requests for permission to marry I had not dared mention Azizah's profession. I bet Mak knows though – there's nothing she doesn't find out, whether she's told or not.

It was no good hoping that when she met Azizah she would change her opinion. She wouldn't consider one of the Sultan's daughters once she'd made up her mind that I was going to marry a girl of her choosing. I believe women of all races can be obstinate and stubborn, but there's nothing to touch a Malay woman once she digs her heels in. And my mother is the arch stub! We have a very good word in Malay – *degil;* the e is almost an English i and you pronounce it with a very hard g. You can really get your jaw muscles round that one – I know, I use it in connection with my mother frequently!

While these thoughts were running through my head, the train was making ready to depart. It was almost like the beginning of the war again to see all those soldiers boarding it. First the armoured pilot engine got itself into position, filled with Gurkha soldiers and Malay police, and then the ordinary engine shunted behind it and a platoon of Scottish soldiers, our escort, took up their places in various parts of the train. I thought I'd try and find a seat near one of them – by the time I'd finished my year's army attachment I'd learned their jargon pretty well and it always amused me to see the astonished expression on a BOR's face when I addressed him in his own language.

The CPO was a dapper little man with grey hair and piercing blue eyes.

'Sharif Ahmat? Welcome to my contingent. I knew your brother well. Glad to have you. Sit down, won't you?'

The CPO did not smoke but gave me permission to do so if I wished. In fact, I was dying for a drag but thought it politic to decline. I read his approval and knew I had done the right thing.

'Now, Ahmat. I've asked for you especially, because the senior inspector in Kuala Jelang is due for retirement shortly and you're just the man to take his place.' This was a lie, of course. Perhaps he didn't know I'd been thrown out of SB, or maybe he thought I didn't know. 'The OCPD Kuala Jelang is just out of the army and he's having a tough time, learning both police work and Malay from scratch. Your English will be an immense help to him and, by taking a lot of the routine work off his hands, it will leave him freer to concentrate on the operational side.'

He looked as though he was expecting me to say something. I was a bit rusty on routine police work myself, but he must know that, so there seemed no point in commenting.

'Inspector Zainal Abidin isn't due to leave for another month and there's no point in both of you hanging around the station all that time. I see you have a lot of leave due to you, so I suggest you go down to Kuala Jelang to-morrow – make your number with the OCPD; then off you go on fourteen days' leave – unless he has other ideas – and report straight back there at the end of it. How's that?'

I made no attempt to conceal my grin of pleasure. I couldn't have done so anyway.

'That's fine, sir. Thank you very much.'

'Good. I'll write a note to the OCPD; you can take it with you.' He stood up and we shook hands, the interview was over. 'I hope you enjoy your new post. Send the clerk in when you go out, will you?'

Just as I was opening the door he spoke again.

'By the by. You should get on well with your new OCPD, you have something in common – he was with the partisans as well – not here though, Italy. Believe his wife was too.'

So he did know. I saluted and shut the door.

As the door shut the CPO lifted the telephone and put through a call to Kuala Jelang. The conversation was brief.

'I'm sending you a replacement for Zainal Abidin – Inspector Sharif Ahmat. I suggest he reports to you, then takes fourteen days' leave. He'll be on the bus to-morrow morning – if it's not burnt. Sorry I can't let you have any transport – we're too short.'

Turning to the clerk, he said, 'Prepare an envelope for the OCPD Kuala Jelang; Personal and Confidential. The new inspector will take it with him.'

Then, with a sigh, he set to to write a difficult and careful letter.

My dear Morrison,

Re our telephone conversation this afternoon.

This inspector has been removed from Special Branch because of suspected Communist leanings. I should tell you to watch them, but I have no intention of doing so, because I do not believe they exist.

I have agreed to have him in my contingent, partly because there seems to me to be a smell of injustice somewhere, and partly because I had the greatest respect for his brother – a GO who died a few years ago of TB. He comes from one of the oldest police families in the Force, his father being Chief Inspector at the Depot pre-war. He himself is, or was, earmarked for gazetted rank and, if he puts up a good show in your district, I see no reason why his promotion should be retarded.

I met Sharif Ahmat myself for the first time this afternoon and liked what I saw. He has a bright, open face and is obviously intelligent. I am sending him to you for two good reasons. Firstly, because, as a newcomer to the force, you will be better able to judge him with impartiality and, secondly, because his English is excellent. He is well educated and young, and I feel sure will be of great help to you. His police work may not be up-to-date, as he has spent the past two and a half years with the army and SB, but I am sure that a fortnight with his predecessor will enable him to catch up.

I shall look forward to hearing your opinion when I next visit your district.

Yours sincerely,
P. R. Wales.

I boarded the Berembang-Kemuning bus early the next day and, after a short wait, the one for Kuala Jelang.

Perangor was a new state for me, but little different from the ones I already knew. We passed first through tin tailings, rubber, then a stretch of jungle, climbing, with some nasty hairpin bends – I didn't much care for that and nor did the driver. He went as fast as he could, but I doubt if he got out of second gear for at least a couple of miles. Just my luck to be ambushed to-day, I thought, then we were travelling through rubber again and I heaved a sigh of relief.

Too soon. Almost before I realised what was happening, we were entering a cloud of black smoke and the stench of burning diesel oil was overpowering. We all started coughing as the suffocating waves rolled in through the open windows. But mercifully the driver had the presence of mind to keep going, murk or no, and we were soon through the pall.

I drew my pistol and prayed that the bandits had gone. I'd be a sitting target anyway and in uniform – it didn't bear thinking about. I slipped the safety catch as the driver stopped.

A pathetic group, all Chinese, stood by the roadside, looking lost and bewildered, and three women wailed over the bodies of an older woman and a boy lying in the ditch. Empty suitcases and cardboard cartons littered the verge and one old man was rooting through them.

It was apparent, thank God, that the CTs had left and I got down to question the occupants of the burned-out bus; the earlier one from Kemuning.

It did not take long to ascertain that all identity cards and clothing had been stolen and I was just taking a statement from the most responsible-seeming passenger when a police troopcarrier arrived on the scene.

A police lieutenant and half a dozen men jumped from the vehicle. I introduced myself.

'Looks as though the bastards have got away again.' The police lieutenant was clearly disappointed, but on this occasion I was grateful.

There had been too long a delay to make a follow-up worthwhile, so we crammed the unfortunates into the second bus and I climbed into the troop-carrier with the police.

Bus-burnings were so common at that time that I soon put the episode out of my mind.

I am not a creature of change. I never move voluntarily and, when I do, usually like to take some part of my previous station with me.

But in Kuala Jelang it was different. I don't know why. It was no different from a number of semi-coastal towns situated between Muar and the Dindings. I say semi-coastal because there was no beach, but only mangrove and bakau swamps along the coast itself and, although it is shown on the map as a port, in fact the life of the small town centred around the river. From the police station, although we were almost on it, we couldn't see the sea.

The town itself was similar to most small Malayan towns, with a few rows of Chinese and Indian shophouses, a padang, a few jetties, and a wide avenue of flame of the forest trees leading to most of the government offices, and a tiny hospital.

The police station was at the far end of the town, away from the other government buildings, and was flanked on one side by a highish hill, which boasted the remains of a Portuguese fort, a lighthouse and two senior government quarters. The OCPD had one of these houses and the DO the other. All this I learned from Zainal Abidin, the elderly inspector whose job I would inherit in a month's time.

Perhaps it was sun after rain, giving the grass that vivid green look, or the flame trees being in flower, or the lively river traffic. I just don't know. But there was something light and airy about Kuala Jelang, and before I had even alighted from the troop-carrier I was beginning to look forward to being stationed there. I was glad to have shaken the unhealthy atmosphere of Special Branch from my shoulders; I felt I was coming home.

I arrived just as the sentry slung his rifle and stepped forward to hammer out the hour on a curve of old railway sleeper – a custom I had forgotten in HQ. The sergeant stood up behind the counter and called the Charge Room to attention, and at that moment a smooth-looking Chinese in white shirt, black trousers and dark glasses came out of an office and passed through. No mistaking *his* job. He gave me a quick look up and down but made no attempt to come to attention, so I presumed he, too, was an inspector. On inquiry I found that he was Detective-Sergeant Lee. Detective-sergeant indeed. I made a mental note of at least one change which would take place in due course.

The station was standard pattern; a squarish, white building with the main part of the police station, Charge Room, cells, etcetera, in the front, and the remainder, consisting of offices for the OCPD, Station Inspector, OCPS, CID, SB and a general office for the clerical staff. The compound was surrounded by a hibiscus hedge and high mesh fence and had raised barracks on three sides. One side was bordered by the road and the others by open ground, mangrove and the river. In the middle there was a large parade-ground, which doubled as a games field and football pitch. At one end of this stood one small house on its own, facing the river and surrounded by its own hedge of many-hued hibiscus and several creepers.

This was the Station Inspector's quarter and I realised with a quickening heart that it was to be mine.

The house was, in fact, pretty shabby. Zainal Abidin had been waiting to retire for some time and had lost interest. I would be prepared to paint it myself and, if PWD would only change some of the battered furniture – I could already see it with gay curtains fluttering in the windows and gay cushion covers on the chairs, a home that Azizah would cherish.

As I waited in the Charge Room for the OCPD to be free, I heard a few sentences of stumbling Malay coming from his office and knew that the CPO had not lied in one respect – he certainly needed help language-wise! It appeared I would have my uses.

I had quite a short interview. The OCPD seemed pleasant enough, but a little harassed. He kept looking at his watch and told me not to think him rude, but he was shortly leaving on a patrol. He seemed interested in hearing about my year with the army; he knew my Captain Jones and told me that he himself had asked for aerial cover on a couple of occasions.

He asked me where I came from and if I were married.

'No, sir,' I replied, 'not yet. But the main reason for my being keen to go on leave now is to try and obtain my mother's permission.'

'Your mother's? I thought the men ruled in Asia.'

'Not in my state, sir.' And I told him a little about our matriarchal laws.

'Good heavens,' he laughed; 'better not tell my wife that. She was born in Negri Sembilan – might give her ideas.'

'In which case, sir,' I pointed out, 'she most probably knows.'

He gave me a shrewd look and we said nothing for a moment or two. We were summing each other up. I felt that I was going to get on with this man and I believe he was thinking the same. I hope so.

At that moment there was a knock on the door and Zainal Abidin came in to tell him that all was ready.

'Right, Bidin. By the way – ' he turned back to me, ' – what do I call you? I'm not yet *au fait* with Malay names – it took me a full week to discover that Inspector Bidin and Zainal Abidin were the same person!'

'Ahmat, sir, or just Mat. I used to be called the Sheriff in the army.'

'Were you? Yes, obvious, I suppose – especially with those

star cap badges you used to wear. Well, Mat, see you in two weeks' time.'

I spent the rest of the afternoon wandering round the compound and the town, and in the evening had a meal in the canteen with the bachelor inspector, Zukifli.

The next morning I returned direct to Kuala Lumpur, and when the Bintang Kilat opened I was there.

Azizah was not quite as enthusiastic about life in Kuala Jelang as I was, but then she hadn't seen it.

'And anyway,' I told her, 'it won't be for ever. Just getting back to an ordinary police district was like a breath of fresh air for me. I realise now that I was never cut out for dark glasses and tight black pants – the operational police is my background and, thank God, I'm returning to it. You know, Azizah, the future looks better than ever. I'm sure I'll be gazetted soon and then you'll be an officer's wife. That means you can be a member of all the clubs and go into the Officers' Mess on Ladies' Night – how will you like that?'

She just smiled.

The next day I caught the southbound train on leave.

88. A TALE OF TWO FATHERS

It was on one of the evenings when he was trying to catch up with the mail and cursing the flickering oil lamp that Philip opened the letter which the inspector he had interviewed briefly the previous day had handed to him.

'Good God, Sally,' he passed the letter to her, 'look at this. Do you know, I must be going ga-ga or something – the CPO rang me up and told me he was sending a replacement for Bidin and then this chap arrived yesterday and I didn't really take it in. What do you make of the old man's letter?'

'Fair. Could be a blessing, or could be a problem child. What did you think of him?'

'Seemed pleasant enough. Tall, good-looking chap – spoke beautiful English certainly, what little I heard of it. He was in my office for less than ten minutes and I must admit I had my mind on a number of other things.'

'Oh darling, I do so hope he's going to be a success.'

'You're not the only one. Lucky I opened this this evening though – look at the last paragraph: "I shall look forward to hearing your opinion when I next visit your district." He said he might be down in a couple of days.'

He worked on in silence for a while, until Sally interrupted him to say, 'There seems to be a light in your office, Phil. Don't you usually lock it when you leave?'

'I do, but the key's kept in the Charge Room – I suppose it's the CRO.'

'Whoever it is, he appears to be having a good snoop around. The shadow's moving all over the place.'

'I think I'll go down. I wanted another file anyway.'

To avoid having the Charge Room called to attention, Philip waited until the sentry was busy sounding the hour and could not slap his rifle-butt, then slipped into the station by a side door.

The door of his office was slightly ajar and he could see the shadow of a turbanned head on the far wall.

'What are you doing, Sergeant-major?'

Jogindar Singh whipped round and Philip heard the slap of something falling on to the desk.

'Just checking, sahib.'

Both top drawers of the desk were open and then Philip saw that the slap had been made by a passport. He looked inquiringly at Jogindar, who smiled sheepishly in his beard, nodding his head slightly from side to side and showing his empty hands.

'Just curiosity, sahib.'

Jogindar was telling the truth. It would never have entered his head to take anything, but, in the same way that he liked to know everything about the men who served under him, so he also liked to know about those in command. All sorts of interesting snippets could be gained from the odd letter left around, even if it was only the occasional word that he could understand. He had found something of interest too.

Philip suppressed the desire to tell him to get the hell out of his office. He was finding the job hard enough without alienating one of his senior NCOs.

'I appreciate your diligence, Sergeant-major, but I would not wish to put you in a position where you might be held responsible for any missing document.'

'Sahib.' Despite the fact that he was in civilian clothes, Jogindar came rigidly to attention. The OCPD had got his mark; he looked at him with a new respect. He was young and not long in the police, but he knew how to handle men.

So did he.

'I'll lock up; I just want to collect a file. Good night, Sergeant-major.'

Philip picked up the passport and proceeded to close the drawers. Jogindar did not move.

'Sahib?'

'Yes. What is it?'

Jogindar pointed to the still open drawer, where the passports now lay.

'The Memsahib's passport, sahib – I see that the Mem was born in Malaya and that her own name was Gunn.'

'Well?'

'I knew her father. He was a fine man, sahib.' Philip was surprised to see the sergeant-major's face working with emotion. 'I was with him the day they led him away. It was a terrible day. Ten men they beheaded that morning. Please, sahib, will you wait here for a moment? There is something I want to show you.'

He left the office, but was back straight away, clutching a bulging wallet. He leafed through it excitedly and chose a scrap of paper which he held out to Philip, who took it and read:

'To whom it may concern. This is to certify that Warder Jogindar Singh has done everything in his power to help the internees for the past two years. If I am unable to testify to his courage and loyalty in person, I shall be grateful to any of my fellow-countrymen who will help him in turn.'

The hand was spidery and weak and it was signed 'George Gunn, Member of the Legislative Council.' It was Sally's father without a doubt. There was no date on the note, but it must have been written while they were with the partisans.

'There are many more, sahib.'

Philip glanced through the sheaf of papers on the desk before him. Torn scraps of brown paper, tissue paper, newspaper, the odd leaf from an exercise book, a couple of opened cigarette packets. All bore the same testimonial: loyal, trustworthy, prepared to risk his life, helpful, kind.

Thank God I didn't tear a strip off him, he thought He held on to the note written by George Gunn and passed the others back.

'May I show this to my wife?' he asked. 'She will be very interested. It was quite a long time before she knew how her father died.'

'Sahib.'

'I have been a prisoner myself. I know very well how much help a friendly warder can give.'

'Thank you, sahib.'

'Good night, Jogindar Singh.'

'Good night, sahib. Please tell the Memsahib her father went bravely to his death. He was a fine man. I had the greatest respect for him.'

'He appears to have had the greatest respect for you too.'

'Thank you, sahib. My own father was beheaded by the Japanese – he was a sergeant-major also.'

'I'm sorry. Terrible things happen during wars. I'll tell the Mem.'

'Don't forget the CPO's coming down to-morrow, Sally. I've invited him to lunch.'

'Oh hell. I wish he could bring something with him. Unless there's some fish in the market, we'll have to have curried beef again.'

'I don't expect he'll mind.'

'Well, *I* mind. It's ridiculous not being allowed to keep anything in the house when, here we are, a stone's throw from the police station.'

'We're still outside the specified area.'

'Specified area my bloody foot! If the Big White Chiefs worried a little more about the squatters and less about a handful of Europeans, just because our hill isn't surrounded by barbed wire – '

'Squatters. That reminds me. Sorry for interrupting, but Chee Min has something on his mind that he wants to tell me this morning and I have to be at a meeting by nine. Better hurry.'

'Sir, the squatter settlement at Pasir Hitam. . . .' Lee Chee Min paused to let his words sink in..

What about it?'

'I'm sure they're supplying the CTs.'

That was that conglomeration of huts and vegetables on the Sungei Belimbing road, where the people turned away as cars went past and went furtively about their work in silence.

'I've had men watching for the past three nights. The Min Yuen have visited them twice.'

'You're sure?'

'Quite sure, sir.'

'We'll go and take a look at it this afternoon.'

As soon as they were seated in Philip's car, Chee Min began to tell him how his suspicions had been aroused in the first place and how the visitors had been recognised as known Min Yuen.

'And if we guarded the settlement?' Philip suggested.

Chee Min shrugged. 'Useless, sir. They would just take the stuff out during the working day – most of them work as casual labour on the nearby estates.'

'We've *got* to resettle them,' Philip muttered, half to himself, 'not only this bunch, but all those stragglers across the river and all the isolated houses. The DO's looking for land, but it doesn't appear easy to find.'

The squatters were settled on a low-lying stretch of land between two roads which eventually met. The area was roughly triangular. After they had driven to the fork in the road, down the other side and back, Philip stopped the car and thought for a minute.

'We could wire it in as a temporary measure,' he said, 'at least until we get a proper resettlement area organised. What do you think?'

'It would give them protection, sir, if we guarded the wire. I do not believe many of these people really *want* to help the bandits – they are just afraid.'

'We would have to have a small police post and search the people as they go to work each day. I'll discuss it with the DO.'

That evening Philip drove James over the same ground as they had covered in the morning and told him what he had found out.

'I'll have to get the CPO to agree first though,' he said, 'because, unguarded, the whole idea would be pointless and the station's under strength as it is – I just haven't the men for even the tiniest police post.'

'If we can get government to cough up the necessary funds,' James mused, 'it would seem the best solution for the time being. If he agrees, perhaps you could get the CPO to put some pressure on at his level.'

'I'll try.'

The guard having been inspected and the customary courtesies with the senior NCOs exchanged, the CPO settled himself behind a large glass of sweet, milky coffee and, remarking that, after thirty years in Asia he still could not get used to having the spoon in the glass and most of the coffee in the saucer, they got down to business.

'Now, Philip, tell me, what did you think of that inspector I sent you, Sharif Ahmat?'

'I only saw him for about ten minutes, sir. He seemed all right. A trifle arrogant, I thought.'

Philip could see he was het up and wondered why.

'There was so much I wanted to tell you about him before you met him, but I couldn't put it in a letter. By the by, have you had SB's report on him?'

Philip coloured. 'To be honest, sir, I have, but I haven't read it yet.' He extracted a sealed envelope from a drawer and put it on the desk in front of him. 'It's not that I make a habit of leaving mail unread, but I've been so busy the past few days and, as the chap is still on leave anyway, I thought it would keep.' It sounded a lame excuse.

'May I read it?'

'Of course.' Philip passed it over.

With meticulous care, the older man polished his reading-glasses and went through the letter with ever-tightening lips.

'Do me a favour, my boy. Don't read this until you have had Ahmat under you for a week or two.'

'Certainly, sir, if you so wish.' He returned the letter to the drawer.

'Special Branch would have you believe he's an arsonist, a murderer – and after all, weren't our commandos? – and, worst of all, a Communist. You see, the whole trouble is that he won't deny anything. You know what those cloak and dagger merchants are like – tape everything they hear. Well, they taped all his interviews and, I must admit, were good enough to let me hear them. They reminded me of some of the Moscow spy trials. He could have cleared himself so easily, but would he? Would he hell – didn't say a damned thing. Just the occasional "Tuan" or "Sir," but most of the time he remained silent. Well, if you're assuming that a non-denial is an admission, then he's guilty. If it hadn t been for the intervention of one senior SB officer who, thank God, thinks like I do, he'd have been interdicted. Then I was called in and, between the two of us, we managed to persuade the Commissioner to give him a trial.'

'What do you want me to do, sir?'

'Just that – give him a fair trial. You know, my boy, many people in the force consider me to be an old dead-beat, and perhaps I am; I don't pretend to know much about cloak and daggery, but I do pride myself on knowing the Malays. You know, they're proud people, stubborn people, and if they think they've been done an injustice, they just close up like clams and remain silent. Not like your vociferous Chinese and Indians – and a lot of Europeans for that matter – who clamour for sympathy and call in lawyers at the drop of a hat. No, the Malay just bottles it up and then, one day, if he's an unstable type and things become too much for him, he runs amok. By the by, one thing you had better know, that won't appear on Ahmat's record, and that is that his father ran amok – with the greatest provocation, I believe.'

'I'm beginning to wonder what you're letting me in for, sir.' The CPO, however, was not amused..

'I'm letting you in for a damned good man – and I'll stake my reputation on it. I do so hate injustice. Nearly all those chaps who interviewed him may have been experts at their jobs in Palestine or Scotland Yard, or wherever they've come from, but only one understood the mentality he was dealing with here and to him young Sharif Ahmat has a lot to be thankful for.'

'He seemed pretty cheerful, I thought.'

'He was all right with me too, but then it was an absolutely straightforward interview. I'm hoping that sooner or later you may win his confidence – you were with the partisans, try and get him to talk about the war. Chap obviously needs a safety valve. Pity he's a bachelor ; I'd have gone stark raving mad years ago if I hadn't had my wife to pour out my troubles to.'

'Me too.'

'Ah yes. I'm looking forward to meeting your wife – if you hadn't asked me to lunch first, I was going to ask you both to come to the Rest House with me. I don't mind telling you, Philip, that I'm probably talking to you like this because I had the greatest affection and respect for your wife's' father.'

'You knew Sally's father, sir? She never told me.'

'She doesn't know – yet. We were cell mates. And by the by, that brings me to someone else I wanted to mention. That sergeant-major of yours, Jogindar Singh ; he was one of our warders. I've only had him under my direct command for a few months as a policeman, but during the war he was a first-class *man*. Pity he's so poorly educated ; might make inspector if he learns a bit more English, but he won't go any higher.'

'He always seems a bit smarmy to me, but I've seen a sheaf

of glowing testimonials from ex-POWs. I gather his own father was killed by the Japs.'

'So he was. But Jogindar's all right; your predecessor had a lot of time for him. I shall never forget his description of Jogindar's arrival here. The driver was a nervous wreck! he only transferred from Kemuning, but, as you know, that road has always been bad. However, that didn't worry our sergeant-major one jot; along he came, troop-carrier with wife and barang in front and he himself following in a lorry with those blessed cows on the back and doing about five miles per hour all the way! King said he looked like a scruffy old bullock-cart driver, turban askew and torn shorts, but within minutes of his arrival and getting his cattle organised – before wife and child, mark you – he was reporting in uniform, bandbox fresh. As King said at the time, from that moment on he felt he was leaving the station in the hands of a most able administrator!'

Philip laughed with the older man and thought once again how glad he was that he had not handled Jogindar Singh differently.

'Well, so much for personalities. Now, let's have your problems – you mentioned something about a squatter settlement – and perhaps there will be time for a drink before lunch.'

'What did you think of Grandpa Wales?' asked Sally later that evening.

'Bit of an old fuddy-duddy, but rather nice.'

'He's certainly worked himself into a state over this new inspector. Only hope he's as good as he thinks he will be.'

89. A MARRIAGE HAS BEEN ARRANGED

The sixth stream flows into the river

Sharif Ahmat

Whatever feelings I had had about this leave and confronting my mother, I was glad to see her again.

I fingered the carving on the verandah railing which my father had started on his leaves and Hassan had finished; played with the cats and sniffed the roses.

I sniffed at the good smells issuing from the kitchen too – my favourite chicken curry, with plenty of coconut, belachan and pineapple sambal. My mouth watered and Mak smiled

– she still thought of me as a schoolboy, as all mothers do.

Normally the men eat alone, but my mother ate with me and we were served by one of the women. Azizah and I would eat together like this, Western style, and I would buy her plastic flowers for the table. I smiled across at my mother, picking delicately at shreds of meat.

I did not mention Azizah for a couple of days. I spent the first day in the house and the second visiting my friends and relations and hearing all the gossip.

'Did you visit your Uncle Jalil?' Mak asked.

'Yes, I did. We went to the coffee-shop together.'

'And did you see his daughter, Maimounah?'

'I think I did.' There had been a couple of girls feeding the chickens and giggling a lot.

'Maimounah is nearly eighteen now. She has grown into a lovely girl. An obedient girl, too.'

'Has she?' I was not particularly interested in my plump, girly, second cousin. But, of course, I should have guessed where the conversation was leading.

'Maimounah will make you an excellent wife. I have already approached her parents and a marriage contract is being drawn up.'

'But, Mak, I do not wish to marry Maimounah.'

'Nonsense. Of course you will be very happy with her. Young men seldom know what they want.'

I was no longer all that young. 'I am not going to marry her,' I said.

My mother sighed. 'You are tired, Ahmat. We shall talk about it later.'

I went to bed fuming and the next morning I told her that I wished her permission once and for all to marry Azizah.

'She does not sound a very suitable person,' Puan Sharifa, my mother, remarked, very much on her dignity, 'I do not think I wish to meet her.'

Before leaving Kuala Lumpur I had insisted that Azizah have her photograph taken and the photographer had done her proud. It was an excellent likeness and the portrait showed her delicate features, gleaming hair and beautiful teeth to perfection. I passed it to my mother, who put on her glasses and gazed at it for some time with pursed lips and dead straight back.

'You must admit that she is beautiful,' I ventured..

'Skinny. I doubt if she would give you many children.'

'I don't want many children.'

'Nonsense. Every man wants plenty of children.'

She folded her glasses away carefully and announced that it was time for her rest.

What can you do with a woman like that? Etiquette did not allow me to talk things over with my Uncle Jalil and I spent a miserable few days. Every time I broached the subject of Azizah, my mother would either find some excuse for cutting short the conversation or retaliate by extolling the virtues of my cousin Maimounah.

It was impossible.

I had made up my mind that I was going to marry Azizah, permission or no, and towards the end of my leave I pinned my mother down and asked her to terminate any and all arrangements for my betrothal to Maimounah.

She was rather pathetic in a way and looked up at me imploringly with her great eyes, rheumy now, although she can't have been all that old.

'Give me a grandson, Mat,' she pleaded, 'I am an old woman and I have lost all my men but you. I do not wish you to be unhappy and I can see from her photograph that Azizah is very comely, but I want a grandson.'

'She will give you grandsons, Mother. Azizah is strong and healthy and will make me a good wife.'

'That type of woman seldom has children – but many miscarriages.'

'She is a ronggeng dancer, Mak, not a prostitute.'

'Yes. Well.' She didn't say it was the same thing, but the implication was there.

She remained quiet for a long time and I began to think she had fallen asleep, then she raised her eyes, a smile of sweet content lighting her face, and announced, 'I have decided. We must make cakes and prepare a kenduri. We shall celebrate your betrothal the day after to-morrow – I must send a message at once to your Uncle Jalil. As I have said, Sharifa Maimounah will make you an excellent wife.'

It was then that I lost my temper.

'I am twenty-eight years of age,' I banged the table with my fist and shouted at her, 'and you cannot stop me from marrying whom I want.'

Puan Sharifa rose to her feet with great dignity and looked down upon me, an expression of scorn in every wrinkle.

'It is true,' she said, 'you are twenty-eight years old and I cannot stop you.'

And with that she beckoned to one of her women and left the room.

It is unpardonable for any son to speak to his mother as I had, but in my case it was worse than unpardonable; it was a sin for which I would have to beg forgiveness.

I avoided her the next day, the penultimate of my leave, but when the time for my departure came I had to swallow my pride. I knelt before her and touched her folded hands with my forehead.

All the time she sat there, still as a statue and seeming more than ever like an angry old tortoise.

There were always a great many women hanging around my mother, near and distant relations, and some just hangers-on. She spoke not a word to me, but said to one of them, 'Tell my son that I wish him a safe journey.'

I was dismissed.

But the old lady was not going to be shamed by having me marry outside the kampong. She might have met her match in stubbornness – and, after all, I am her son – but she was going to have the last word. Azizah was an orphan, so there could be no case of my being carried to the bride's house. A week or so later, just as I was taking over in Kuala Jelang, I received a letter from my Uncle Jalil which read:

'Your mother instructs me to tell you that, should you still persist on going ahead with this highly undesirable union, she will make the necessary arrangements for the marriage.'

Allahumma! What an ordeal that is going to be!

90. A SUCCESSFUL DAY

'How's the new inspector, darling? And how's the famous English?'

Sally had worried about Philip, seeing him grow thinner and thinner and more harrassed, and was afraid, too late, that after four years without a proper break, and a new job and a new language were too much in one go. If Sharif Ahmat lived up to the CPO's expectations, it could make all the difference.

'Well, he can't be anything but an improvement, that's for sure. He's a bit piano at the moment – mother trouble, I gather. The old bag apparently won't give her consent to his marriage, so he says he'll marry the girl anyway.'

'Good for him.'

'Agreed – depending on the girl. As to the English – well! Of course I only heard a little of it before and it's certainly very fluent, but I'm not sure that it's benefited from a year of British Army influence!'

'Fruity?'

'Well, yes, but that's not quite the adjective I'd use. There was a hell of a rumpus going on outside my office this morning – whole gang of Tamils, all yelling at once in the Charge Room – and Ahmat went to sort them out. He's a very stately person, you know, and when he returned he said, with the most serene dignity, "I instructed the complainant to make his statement quietly and told the other buggers to shit off"!'

In fact, Ahmat was not only 'piano' because of his mother, but also because of the rustiness of his police work.

He still had more than a fortnight's leave due to him and had hoped that he could apply for it as soon as his marriage was arranged. But Azizah and police work did not go together and he put her firmly out of his mind for the time being and concentrated on learning all he could from Bidin, while he was still there.

The Sikh sergeant-major seemed a tower of strength, he thought, thanks be to Allah that *he* was OCPS – the station was clearly in capable hands. He didn't think much of that Special Branch sergeant; a smooth type and too familiar by half. Still, he was junior enough to be kept in his place and he need not have too many dealings with him. He liked the OPCD.

Philip, in his ignorance, had thought that Ahmat and Chee Min were bound to hit it off. They had so much in common, he had remarked to Sally, a good education, they'd both been overseas and both were ambitious men. For his part it was a tremendous relief to be able to hold a three-sided conversation in his own language and know that everything that was said would be understood. He looked forward to smoother waters, once Mat had settled down, and said so to Chee Min. But for the moment they were concentrating on squatters.

In fact, Chee Min thought Ahmat a proud, stuck-up Malay and longed to trip him up, but he was sensible enough to keep his feelings to himself.

DWEC had agreed that fencing in the squatters was a sound plan, and in due course much hammering was to be heard around the huts of Pasir Hitam, as the wire went up.

The squatters looked at each other and said nothing. The wire might protect them or it might present new problems. Each family was quietly paying subscriptions to the terrorists and keeping mum. The police were continually snooping round for information, but the squatters saw no one, said nothing, and minded their own business. Informing to the police was a profitable game if you could get away with it, but it was safer in the long run to keep quiet and produce when the Min Yuen demanded.

The squatters worked, ate, slept and paid, and the fence went up around them. Now the Min Yuen were asking questions. Who was putting up the fence? Why? Who had squealed to the police? Woe betide the family who had.

Each family looked at its neighbours and wondered if they had received informer's money. Signs of wealth were dangerous, and if anyone had suddenly become rich they were unlikely to broadcast the fact.

The day came when the fence was complete and a small police post was erected by the only gate. Several Chinese-speaking government officials explained to the squatters that the fence was there for their protection and that now they need no longer hand over clothing, food and funds to the bandits. Their days of extortion were over.

The squatters heard all this but their faces remained blank. There were many ways of getting money out of a man, in case the government officials did not know.

The first morning after the completion of the fence, Philip went with Chee Min to supervise the searching of the workers.

Each man or woman stopped at the gate, hands above their heads, while the searchers ran their hands over their bodies and examined their bicycles, tools and bags. The supply denial operation was in full swing.

'Tell them we're sorry, but they will not be able to eat or drink anything but water until they return from work,' Philip said.

Chee Min walked over to where a man was arguing volubly with a Malay special constable, who had just removed his billycan of rice. Behind him stood a young girl with an impish smile and Chee Min was immediately attracted by her face.

She was covered from head to toe against the sun and carried only a tapper's knife. Her head was swathed in a nun-like coif and she laughed openly as Chee Min peered round the edge.

He smiled at her and went on to pacify the man. She was soon out of sight, cycling down the road, her narrow back trim and erect on the old-fashioned bicycle.

Philip followed the sergeant's glance and was amused, but said nothing.

When everyone who was going to work that day had gone, the gate was closed and they drove back to the station to start their routine work.

'I think I had better check again,' Chee Min said the next morning, 'once they get into the routine there will be no need, but until they get used to the idea . . .'

'Of course.' Philip smiled and thought to himself, I bet you'll go every day yourself, you fox.

That morning Chee Min asked for names, pretending to tick them off on a list. It was not long before the girl came along.

Rose Cheng, aged seventeen, occupation rubber-tapper.

'Find out which house that girl comes from,' Chee Min ordered one of the SCs. He had already made a rough plan of the squatter area and numbered all the houses, in preparation for this opportunity.

A few days later a kite was reported flying over Pasir Hitam. Chee Min was delighted; it gave him an excuse. He said to the OCPD, 'I think we should carry out a search of Pasir Hitam, sir, to make sure there are no arms or documents in those squatter huts.'

'Right. Go ahead – you know the correct procedure.'

The Chengs' house was small but neat, with curtains at the windows and flowers by the door. It was surrounded by raised vegetable beds and a few yards away an old man was hoeing.

Chee Min wanted to search the house. He produced his warrant card, but the man waved it away. 'I can't read foreign characters,' he said. 'My wife's inside – don't scare her.'

Chee Min and the constable took off their shoes and entered the house. At the back there were sounds of clothes being slapped on stone. A round table, covered with a pea-green velvet cloth with bobbled fringes, took up most of the space in what was obviously their living-room. There were schoolbooks on the table, English and Maths ; on one wall a vivid print of the Bleeding Heart and on the other a crucifix.

'Old Aunt,' he called, and the washing noises ceased abruptly, 'may we look round your house?'

A middle-aged woman in blue samfoo, the pyjama-type clothes worn by many Chinese women, appeared in the doorway. Her eyes were round with fright and her mouth opened and shut, but emitted no sound. She had soapsuds to the elbow and was rubbing her wet hands up and down the sides of her trousers with nervousness.

'Don't be scared. We are police,' Chee Min told her. 'We are helping you ; you must try and understand.'

The woman nodded but still made no sound.

'Whose are the books?' he asked, and a voice from the outer door answered him.

'They are our daughter's books.' It was the old man who spoke. 'You must forgive my wife. Our son was killed by the terrorists less than a year ago – they came here, just as you come now, and when he refused to join them they drove a six-inch nail through his head.'

The woman gave a wailing moan and rushed from the room.

'Please explain we mean no harm and not to be frightened if she sees us again,' he called, and left the house.

So it had been their son. Well, they were hardly likely to be Communist sympathisers, but no doubt paid up to the Min Yuen, just like everybody else.

The next morning Chee Min stopped Rose Cheng as she came out of the gate and asked how her mother was.

He asked her about the books. Yes, they were hers. She had been to the convent in Kuala Lumpur but had had to leave when her father's shop was burned down. They were not insured and had lost everything.

'This is very fertile land,' she told him, 'so now my father grows vegetables to sell and I earn good wages as a tapper. Perhaps one day we shall move back, but meanwhile I'm trying to continue my studies in the evenings.'

'The convent?' Chee Min was surprised. 'You must speak English then?'

'A little,' she said in clipped, staccato syllables, 'but I get no practice now.'

'I'm Vincent Lee,' he introduced himself, also in English, 'I could help you sometimes, if you liked.'

The girl smiled shyly and said that if she did not hurry she would be late for work. He moved aside to let her pass, happy in the knowledge that contact had been established.

Back in the police station the OCPD was happy too. But for a different reason. The army had arrived.

Chee Min had only just left for Pasir Hitam, and Philip was blessing the sudden lull and hoping to catch up on some routine work, when the sound of a jeep drawing up outside had made him groan. But it had contained a most welcome visitor.

'Mike Harrington,' and a thin, wiry little major of the Gurkhas had thrust out his hand. 'We're moving a company down from Berembang; hope to be here next week. I wondered if we might discuss a site for a camp.'

Philip blinked. 'Well, it's nice to know what's going on in one's district,' he remarked dryly, 'but I shan't take um – too pleased to see you.' He spread out a map of the area. 'When I asked, some months ago, if there was any chance of having troops stationed here, I had this piece of land at Sungei Belimbing in mind as a possible site for a camp. It's central and not too far from the bridge, you see, which would give you easy access to both sides of the river.'

'Could we go and see it?'

'Of course. I'll just give my wife a ring – you'll stay to lunch?'

Later that day Philip and Sally stood on their verandah, the dying sun in their eyes, waving as Mike drove away.

'Nice chap,' Philip remarked. 'I'm glad he accepted the offer of our spare room. I shall be happier knowing that at least sometimes, when I have to be out for several days, you won't be alone. Not that I imagine he'll use it much.'

Mike had approved the camp site, where he would have his Company HQ, and there would be a platoon under a Gurkha subaltern under canvas in the police compound in Kuala Jelang itself. It had been a successful day.

Willing hands helped or hindered as the Gurkhas put up their tents – the Gurks were popular with everyone – and the police compound was a hive of activity.

Sally had asked the other Europeans to lunch.

'I suppose you'll be starting patrols soon,' James said.

'To-morrow, with luck,' Mike replied.

'Good God!'

To Philip it put the Gurkhas in a nutshell. 'If I hadn't been an Inverness-shire, I'd like to have been a Gurkha,' he had often said.

As he had predicted, although Mike had gratefully accepted the offer of their spare room as a *pied à terre* and a place to dump some kit, he was seldom there. But always the round, brown, smiling Mongolian faces were around.

91. TO TIMBUKTU

The seventh stream meets the river

Omar

In due course a Court of Inquiry was held, but it was not until some months after the riots that my fate was decided.

Dismissed.

A sergeant-major with twenty years' unblemished service. Unblemished until that terrible day, when I could not fire.

Dismissed.

Dismissed for believing that little children were in the forefront of the rioters. There had been few Malays amongst the rioters, I was told, and the leaders were known agitators, Chinese, Indonesian and Indian Communists. Perhaps if I had known that at the time I would have ordered the squad to open fire. But would I? To me it had had the appearance of an ordinary crowd of young people, angry perhaps, but ordinary. Youths, women – children. There had been no women or children, I was told. Only men, a mob of uncontrolled, fanatically-led men, who had murdered without motive a helpless woman and her husband.

I had entered the court a sergeant-major still, ashamed, contrite and regretful, but prepared to plead my case. I left a civilian, disgraced, unwanted; a pariah.

I hung up my uniform for the last time, fingering the crown that had been my ambition and achievement, while my head buzzed with the dreadful words that had preceded my dismissal. Words of scorn and derision. Cowardice, treachery, unfitness to hold such rank, ignominious conduct. I had listened to the defending officer pleading instability; I had heard again the sad history of Zaitun and the untimely demise of my family, but it had meant nothing to me. What had those events to do with cowardice and treachery? Better to have kept my wounds to myself; I was still dismissed.

But they were in my thoughts, those little ones. As I lay down to sleep for the last time in the quarters which I had entered so jubilantly with my wife and children by my side, I wondered why our lives are planned as they are and why a man like me, who loved his fellow-beings, should be left so alone.

I was given a railway warrant back to my kampong, but when the train stopped at Tampin station I didn't get down.

I couldn't go back to Tanjong Mas.

It was not only the disgrace, but the thought of the empty house that was too much to bear. If my wife and children had still been there, perhaps it would have been different. But at least they were not there to witness my disgrace.

Dismissed with ignominy.

The tears rolled down my cheeks as I gazed at the dear, familiar sights. A young Chinese girl walked up and down beside the stationary train, hawking peanuts, langsats and bananas, and I thought tenderly of my dear, departed ones. How often I had given in to those clamouring hands. How many peanuts I had bought at so many station platforms.

The train gave a jolt and I sighed. A couple of Indians flung open the door and climbed into the carriage just as we began to move. They jabbered excitedly and took no notice of me, the only other occupant. I hastily wiped my eyes and stared out of the window as the scenery changed from buildings to countryside and the fresh green of the foot-high padi came into view.

Where I was going, or what I was going to do, I had no idea.

I shut my eyes and prayed that the all-merciful Tuan Allah would show me the way, and then I must have fallen asleep.

'Kuala Lumpur, Kuala Lumpur.'

I must have slept right through Seremban and all the intermediate stops. I could not remember whether this train went on to Ipoh and Prai, or if this was the end of its journey.

Without thinking, I scrambled up and dragged my two suitcases from under the seat. To my surprise, besides the two

Indians, there were several Malays and Chinese getting down, all of whom must have joined the train while I had been asleep. I waited for everyone else to leave the carriage, then I walked slowly to one of the platform benches, to sit and think out what I must do.

I had a friend, a sergeant from the same kampong, who was stationed in Kuala Lumpur. His wife was my second cousin. Perhaps I could stay with them for a night or two and discuss my problems with them.

Leaving my suitcases at the station, I walked the short distance to the main police station and inquired if Sergeant Othman was still stationed there.

Never before had I entered a Charge Room feeling like a fugitive. Of course I wore civilian clothes and, as has always been my habit, was neatly dressed, but I felt that every person there must have known that I was an NCO dismissed from Singapore. I looked at the 'wanted' posters on the walls, almost expecting to see my face amongst them.

The young constable on duty was very polite. He called me 'Father' and came to the door to point out my friend's quarters to me.

He would be off duty now, so thanking the young man, I walked across the compound and called softly at the foot of the steps.

Malay hospitality would not allow Othman to turn me away, but he could have been chilly. But he was quite unperturbed and invited me in as though he had been expecting me.

I was still stiff from my long sleep in the train and took some time untying my shoe-laces. While I was bending down, Othman's wife, my cousin Saloma, came chattering out of the doorway, helped me with my shoes, shook hands, and pushed me into a chair almost in one movement.

I had forgotten what a great chatterbox and gossip she was. She went to fetch cold drinks and cakes, keeping up an incessant flow of small talk the whole time.

'Poor Omar,' she piped, 'we were so sorry to hear of your trouble. Fancy dismissing you after all those years. They ought to be ashamed of themselves. Ai-ee, there's very little justice, I sometimes think.'

She took a deep breath and held out the plate of cakes.

I shook my head. I was too filled with emotion at this sudden burst of friendliness to either eat or remember my manners.

I had seen Othman frown at his wife and had wondered how they already knew about me. Then I understood.

'Abubakar told us everything.' Of course. Abubakar was a taxi-driver from Tanjong who plied between Kuala Lumpur, Malacca and Singapore. He was a well-known gossip and carrier of messages. I should have known.

I found myself having to wipe my eyes again.

Othman gave my shoulder a gentle shake. 'Come on, man, eat something. You know Saloma's cakes – better than those you can buy in a coffee-shop.'

I smiled at them both and took the proffered cake this time. Adohi, it's good to have friends.

'When you've rested we'll go to the station and pick up your things, then this evening we'll discuss plans.'

'You know you are welcome to stay here as long as you like,' Saloma chipped in. 'It's an honour to put up a man like you.' She gave an indignant snort, just like my wife. In fact, she was very like my wife; perhaps she was her cousin and not mine – I always get mixed up with relationships.

Othman was still in uniform and begged to be excused while he bathed and changed. 'We'll go to a coffee-shop before we fetch your cases,' he suggested. 'The children will be home from school soon and we shan't be able to talk in peace here. Besides, if I know my wife, she will want time to prepare a really good meal for you to-night.'

We spent several evenings discussing my future and, as I could already drive, had come to the conclusion that if I could get myself accepted into one of the kongsis, or partnerships, perhaps I could become a taxi-driver.

This was almost decided upon and we were awaiting a visit from Abubakar for his advice, when Othman came home one lunch hour full of a new idea.

'Wouldn't you rather have remained in the police than become a taxi-driver?' he asked me.

'Of course, but – ?'

'Forgive my interrupting. A tremendous recruiting drive is about to start – with the Emergency getting worse we need all the men we can get and men who are already trained will be doubly useful. Weren't you a marksman in your younger days?'

I puffed with pride, my disgrace quite forgotten. 'I still am.'

'So much the better. I've spoken about you to my inspector and he thinks you stand a good chance of being taken on by the Federation Police – no rank though, it would be as a PC.'

I thought about this for some time. It was twelve years since I had been a PC; it would be difficult, especially when it came to taking orders from men in every way my junior. Still – it was a way to acquit myself and, on the practical side, free board and lodging. Allah knew where I would live as a taxi-driver; I could not sponge on Othman for ever.

I felt very old compared with most of the young men waiting to enlist, and when a PC from my kampong saw me and asked in surprise, 'Hallo, Dato, what are you doing here?' I felt hot with shame. 'Dato' means 'Grandfather,' but it is a courtesy title we use for senior NCOs in the police. He could not have known and addressed me in ignorance, but I saw the officer's head lift with interest and I tried to pretend I wasn't there.

Of course, when it came to my turn it appeared so odd that a man of my age should be joining up for the first time that I had to explain.

'Sergeant-major, eh?' The Admin Officer had a very pink skin and ginger hair; he looked at me shrewdly and I stared through the ginger hair to a thin spot on his scalp. 'Are you prepared to serve as a PC, realising that your previous rank can have no influence on promotion in this force?'

'Tuan.'

'Very well. If you're prepared to serve, we're prepared to have you.'

It was as simple as that.

After a short spell at the Depot I was posted to Alor Hijau. I had not wanted to work in my home state, but there was nothing I could do. Thank goodness it was some way from my kampong.

It was good to be in uniform again and fall into the orderly life of station routine. This was a quiet area and all went well until one day when there was a bandit scare.

The inspector was rushing round, getting all off-duty men into jungle green, and soon had us all lined up for roll-call by the main gate. Just as my name was called the OCPD emerged, slinging his carbine and pulling on his floppy, jungle-green hat.

'I won't have that man,' he called to the inspector. 'No one comes on a patrol with me who doesn't shoot when he's ordered to.'

There was a terrible silence. My colleagues stood as though turned to stone and the inspector looked most unhappy. I felt hot with humiliation; I felt I must faint with mortification. No one moved.

'Get that man off parade, Inche. We haven't got all day.'

I hated the OCPD. The whole station had heard him make me lose face.

I was still sitting on my bed, brooding over the incident, when the patrol returned, several hours later. It had been abortive and the men were hot, tired and ill-tempered. I could hear the OCPD shouting as soon as he got down from his jeep.

'Don't take any notice of him,' the first man to enter the room remarked. 'He's the most uncouth European I've come across – but he's brave.'

'Trouble is, he's a Chink-lover,' put in another. 'Makes it quite plain that he thinks little or nothing of Malays. Unfortunately for him the few Chinese in the force are nearly all detectives or in Special Branch – the only ones who go jungle-bashing are on the wrong side!'

Everyone laughed. Everyone except me. I was still too humiliated to find it funny.

I couldn't sleep that night and at the first opportunity next morning I got hold of the inspector and asked for an interview with the OCPD.

'Do you think it wise?' he cautioned. 'He'll only say something to upset you more. He can be a cruel bastard, you know.'

But I was determined, and by the time I heard a bellow of 'Send in our brave sergeant-major then,' I was quite unafraid.

The OCPD spoke very fluent Malay, but he didn't bother with any formalities.

'So you wanted to see me, did you? Why?'

'I wish to explain, Tuan, that when I disobeyed an order, it was not because of fear or cowardice, but because I could not – '

'I am not interested.'

'But Tuan, if I may – '

'You may not.'

He pointed to a livid scar which ran down one side of his face, ending in a cavity a little below the ear.

'You see that?' I remained silent. 'And that?' He opened his shirt to reveal another scar. 'I have two more which I do not propose to show you. Do you know how I got these?'

'A bullet?' I ventured.

'*A* bullet my foot. A whole bloody magazine. And do you know why?"

I shook my head. My mouth was dry.

'Because my patrol, consisting of a bunch of bloody useless, cowardly Malays, ran. That's why. Just one man, a Sikh, stayed with me and he was killed. So I was left to fight it out on my own.'

I wanted to say that I would not have run, but who knows, perhaps I would. I stood there, silent.

'Now do you wonder that I won't have a man behind me who's been *proved* untrustworthy?'

'But Tuan – '

'Get out of my sight and keep out of it. If I'd been the recruiting officer I wouldn't have taken you on. You've been sent here, so I have to keep you, but the less I see of you the better it'll be for both of us.'

'Perhaps it would be better if the Tuan transferred me to one of the other stations in his district.'

'You can go to Timbuktu for all I care.'

The interview was over. I saluted, but he was already writing a letter.

I spent a most unhappy couple of months. Just when I was bitterly regretting having joined the Malayan Police and was passing the open door of the OCPD's office one morning, I was amazed to hear a cheery hail.

'Good news for you, Sergeant-major. It seems that the powers that be have decided that I have too many men for such a quiet place – I'm to lose six and you will be one of them.'

'And to which of the Tuan's stations is he sending me?'

'None of them. Right out of my district; right out of this contingent, in fact. Can't remember which state you're posted to – Perangor, I think – the inspector will tell you. One of the trouble spots – that should suit you.'

'Tuan.'

I was so pleased to be leaving Alor Hijau that I did not care where I was sent, and for once I had been able to ignore the sarcasm in the OCPD's voice.

All six of us were posted to stations farther north and were told to pack our kit and be ready to catch the northbound mail train that evening. I could not get away quick enough.

My posting was to Kuala Jelang – I don't think I had ever heard of it.

92. AN ORCHID FOR SALLY

Jogindar Singh lifted his third son in his arms and smiled.

The small boys, Ranjit and Ojagar, looked on and at their mother, swathed in many scarves and shawls, lying on the wooden sleeping-platform.

Suvindar Kaur had put on a lot of weight since her marriage three and a half years ago, but her face was still the face of a girl and her eyes shone with pride.

'Those are your brothers and that is your mother,' Jogindar told the infant, and gently laid him down beside his wife. He stooped then to push the sweat-sodden hair back from her forehead and gently wiped her brow with a towel.

'So many sons,' he murmured, 'so many sons.' Then, turning to his first-born, 'Ranjit, go and fetch Puron Kaur and ask her to mind the baby while your mother sleeps; I have to go to work now.'

He was late on duty for the first time in his life. Through the open door of the OCPD's office he could hear Philip Morrison talking to the clerk, and the Special Branch sergeant was on the telephone. The elderly PC on duty in the Charge Room rose to attention and smiled at Jogindar"s radiant face.

'Good morning, Dato,' he said, 'I hear your wife has safely given birth.'

'A son.' He looked keenly at the old man who, rumour had it, had once been a sergeant-major himself. It would have been indelicate to ask. The man had only been in the station a week, but it was apparent that he knew his way around the books and registers in a way not expected from a PC with only two months' station experience behind him.

'Dato,' the call came from the OCPD's office, and both men rose.

So it was true. Omar quickly sat down again and Jogindar called, 'Coming, sahib.'

'Dato, will you find Inche Mat and tell him I want to take a few men out this afternoon.'

'Sahib.'

From the Charge Room, Omar heard. He rose to intercept the OCPS on his return.

'Dato, if the Tuan is taking a patrol, I would like to go.'

Jogindar shrugged. 'If you wish. I will give the inspector your name.'

It was after they had returned from the patrol, late the following afternoon, that Omar appeared at the OCPD's house, bearing an orchid for Sally.

'Oh, what a beautiful thing,' she gasped with genuine pleasure. 'Wherever did you find it?'

Omar's grin spread wide. He was still muddy from the jungle and he pointed at his eyes. 'The Tuan sent me up a tree to scout. My eyes did not see any terrorists, but they did see this. It was in another tree, so I climbed up and got it down.'

He handed the little plant with its lush green leaves and long white bloom to Sally. Poor old man, she thought, he looks much too old to be a PC, and so tired and hot.

'Sit down,' she said indicating the front step, near where she was working, 'I must go and hang this in the shade, then I'll get you a cold drink.'

Omar was shy; he had not had much contact with European women, although he noted with relief that her Malay was good. He ran his tongue over dry lips – a drink would be welcome – but he did not sit down.

Sally returned with two long glasses of orange squash. 'I'm thirsty too,' she said, and sat down on the grass.

After hesitating for a moment longer, Omar too sat, and asked her how she came to speak Malay already when the Tuan was still learning.

Sally told him about her childhood and how she had left Malaya in 1942. In fact, he already knew from the servants, but it made a good excuse to talk.

To her surprise, the old man suddenly shot to attention, nearly spilling his drink as he put it down in haste. Shoulders squared, feet at an angle of 45 degrees, thumbs to the front and down the trouser seams. Good heavens, she thought, he's exactly like the flight-sergeant drill instructor at OCTU! His face stared woodenly into space and in a moment she saw the reason for all this show, as Philip's shoulders appeared at the top of the steps. She had not heard him on his rubber-soled boots, but Omar, who was sitting on a higher level, had been watching him ascend.

He looked surprised and Sally explained, 'I've just been given an orchid – do you see it hanging over there? Isn't it a beauty?'

Ah, Philip thought, this was the old boy who has obviously been trying to get me on my own ever since he arrived. The orchid and holding Sally in conversation were a good excuse. The station had recently been brought up to strength and this was one of the new arrivals, but damned if he could place them all yet – which one was this?

He sighed to himself. His hair under his beret was wet with sweat and he longed to have a shower. Best to get it over with.

'That was very kind,' he said, and smiled at the old man, motioning him to relax. 'I'll just get myself a drink and then I'll join you.'

Sally rose to get it for him, but he frowned at her and slightly shook his head. As he brushed past he whispered, 'Try and find out his name.'

Omar stood first on one foot and then the other until Sally asked him outright if he wanted to speak to her husband.

He nodded eagerly. 'Yes, but please, Mem, stay. The Tuan must think I am very stupid, still to be a PC at my age – I used to be a sergeant-major – I want the chance to explain. Please, Mem, I don't speak any English, would you help?'

Sally's eyes popped wide. 'Oh,' was all she said, and they remained silent until Philip returned. 'Omar has been in the police for many years – he wants to tell you about it.'

Oh God, now? Philip thought, I shall be having my bath at midnight. He sat down.

'The Singapore Police,' Omar began, 'but I want you to understand, Tuan, that I am not a Singapore Malay. I come from Malacca, which is only a small state, with not enough land for everyone to cultivate – it produces many soldiers and sailors and police. Before the war, as the Mem knows, Malacca was part of the Straits Settlements, with Singapore and Penang – I was in the Straits Settlements Police then. Then, after the war, when the Federation was formed, I found myself in Singapore.'

He looked up to see if the OCPD had taken it in. The latter nodded and he went on to tell his story, hoping that this time it would not fall on deaf ears. Philip groaned silently.

Omar was terribly long-winded and, although both his listeners were sympathetic and Philip assured him several times that he quite understood his reluctance to shoot, he still repeated himself *ad nauseam*, until they both began to wonder if he was ever going to go home.

'It seems a pity that you are here in barracks on your own,' Sally remarked, getting up from her chair and hoping that he would follow suit. 'Have you no family to join you?'

'Only one daughter left, Mem, but she is in a mental home.'

'Oh, how sad. Was she born mental?'

Omar gave a great gulp and his eyes filled with tears. And then out it all come, the whole tragic story of Zaitun and how he lost the rest of his family.

Sally sat down abruptly and Philip lit a cigarette, which he placed in the old man's trembling hands.

There was no question of their attention wandering this time. Omar was more eloquent than he knew and the rape of Zaitun became as vivid in its horror as the night it was committed.

When he had finished, he hastily wiped his eyes and looked at his watch, embarrassed by his own emotion.

'I am deeply grateful, Tuan and Mem, for listening to me. Now I must go.'

'Don't you think that perhaps a drink of something stronger than orange squash might do you good?'

'No, thank you, Tuan. It is forbidden.'

'Yes, I know, but – '

'I have never touched alcohol, Tuan, and if I had before, I never would again after I saw what it did to the Japanese.'

They were silent for a long time after Omar had left; his presence still very much with them, like a sad ghost.

'Well, there's one Malay who doesn't bottle things up,' Philip remarked at last, 'and luckily, I should say.'

'How *can* life be so unkind to one man? And to think how I've fretted and pined over losing one baby whom I never even knew.'

93. TRULY THERE IS NO JUSTICE

The eighth stream reaches the river

Ramakrishnan

I am sorry most that it has not been possible to continue in lucrative role of Mr S. Kandiah, but with large nest-egg now put aside and monthly remuneration still being received from Mr Ramasamy, father-in-law, I am not poor man and have much dignity in being.

I am now father of three children and wife Devi is rounding nicely with fourth.

One evening, after long and tiresome afternoon spent in company of visiting manager, I am returning home to find strange man with Devi, and my wife is beating breast and wailing and tears are running through ashes which she has smeared on cheeks and forehead.

At first I am suspecting bad doings of this stranger, before seeing said ashes, but Devi beckons me and says, 'Oh, Krishnan, my father has died, seemingly of a stroke or heart attack.'

For me this is good news, for my bargain with Mr Ramasamy, no relation at that time, was to be left all in last will and testament.

'I must go to Rembang at once,' I say.

Rembang is much changed since days when I am lowly employee in silk store and I am wondering now why I ever thought it grand town indeed.

Mr Ramasamy's wife, all other ripe daughters and many friends and relations both, are weeping and wailing and all making din most terrible to hear. Body of Mr Ramasamy, deceased, is already being cremated and male relatives are just now returning to abode.

'What is content of late deceased's last willing and testament?' I am asking, and am surprised to see widow's puzzled face.

Then Mr Ramasamy's brother, Nathan, whom I am not knowing existed, but turns out to be most notable attorney, speaks.

'There is no will and testament.'

'But what of me, Ramakrishnan, also son of Ramasamy, although no blood relation, but son-in-law?' I am asking. 'Deceased is promising me great beneficiaries when time is coming for him to pass away.'

'I am sorry, man,' lawyer brother is saying. 'This lady here is sole beneficiary under the law. And if it is not too impolite to ask, why should he leave anything to you?'

'For services rendered,' I reply, 'for great number of services rendered.'

Lawyer brother Nathan is again shaking head. I can see

that he is not believing me.

My God, man, after all such work and careful planning, truly there is no justice in this world. I am telling you, I could easily kill both widow lady, ripe daughters and all brothers and sisters both.

Instead I return to estate and beat my wife.

'Your incestuous and evil-living father was not man of good word,' I am shouting, 'but you will pay for sins of father instead. Every dollar which your mother is receiving you will take and hand to me, or I shall tell all most foul happenings that are taking place before marriage.'

But Devi is truly stubborn. 'I shall give you nothing,' she is yelling, 'nothing, you hear? I know you have been bleeding my father all these years, but no longer. I am glad he is dead now and can pay you no more.'

Truly then I am losing my temper most incredibly and hit Devi across face, breasts and abdomen.

'You will do as I say,' I hiss, 'or I shall tell secrets most vile.'

'Tell them,' she screams, 'I do not care,' and runs from quarters to outside.

Already many labourers and their wives have gathered to investigate sounds of quarrel most shrill. Devi runs into middle of them, hands clutching belly and hair falling over eyes.

'Tell them,' she is screaming again, 'no, I will tell them. You are not going to blackmail me.' Pushing hair from face, she stands upright in light from many windows and doors and shouts, 'Because my father was first man to enter me, Krishnan here has been receiving money all these years. I am not ashamed; I don't care, I am not first daughter to be entered by father before husband. When sacred bull mates with cow who is daughter, is there so much fuss, man?'

I am hitting Devi then, again and again, and soon I feel hands pulling me away and face of chief clerk is peering into mine.

'So it was you,' he is hissing at me like most malevolent snake, 'it is you who has been bleeding my friend Ramasamy. I should have known. All those golden ornaments you are buying, while my friend is selling cattle and dispensing with services of assistants in silk store.'

This is truth, for I have been putting veritable screw on Ramasamy, ex-father-in-law, until one hundred dollars is becoming one hundred and fifty, two hundred, etcetera, until now three hundred and fifty dollars each month I have been receiving. I am rich man, with many catchings of money put away in secretive hiding-places on estate, but I am afraid to leave job in case foul white pig of planter who is threatening me has reported said incident to police.

All this time CC is shaking me like dog with rat. 'If it were not for Devi, I would be making sure you are being given sack,' CC is saying, 'but because she is daughter of old friend and I am not wishing to see her without roof over head of her and children, you shall retain employment of clerk without report of such incident being made to manager. But, on condition, man, that you apologise to your wife, understand, and be causing no more trouble on this estate.'

He is shaking me until teeth are rattling in head and I am knowing that I have to go with him when he is marching me off to apologise to wife, otherwise I am most undone. Verily there is no justice. Why am I apologising to girl who has enjoyed overtures of father most vile?

But Devi is not to be found and quarter is only full of wailing children and remains of rough housing and uneaten dinner both.

'I am calling midwife.' It is neighbour's wife who is speaking. 'You kicked your wife in belly, and now she is in travail. Your fault, Mister, if mother or baby dies.'

At that moment I am being glad if everybody dies, but CC is again shaking me in manner most threatening and unfriendly and hissing again in ear.

'You will take care of your wife now, Krishnan. If she dies in childbed, it will be murder, man, and it will be a pleasure taking you to police station.'

But Devi does not die. She is being delivered of seven months' child most frail and premature, but who lives also.

She is cooking my food and washing my clothes, but truly she is now most sullen and unattaching wife. Submitting to marital rights without pleasure or lust, she is for driving me away from job, I know. But I cannot leave.

When I have been putting up with said situation for three or four months and Devi is once more pregnant, suddenly there is coming to estate one Tamil police inspector with two Malay constables in uniform and one Tamil constable in plain clothes – I know he is constable because he is showing warrant card and saying he is detective from Criminal Investigation Department.

First inspector is asking to see lists of labour, payrolls, etcetera, etcetera, then is asking if anyone is knowing Mr S. Kandiah.

I am telling you, man, truly I am quaking in shoes and glad now that CC and wife are being under impression that all monetary rewards have been coming only from Mr Ramasamy, ex-father-in-law.

Everyone is showing ignorance of Mr S. Kandiah and then inspector is saying, 'On information received, car has been discovered belonging to S. Kandiah, garaged in rented shed in nearby town. That is why we are making inquiries from all estates in vicinity.'

'And what has this Kandiah done that inquiries are necessary?' I am asking.

'Impersonating official of non-existent union and thereby receiving money under false pretences from labourers.'

'How is it a crime to impersonate man who does not exist then?' I am asking, but realising too late that it is indeed stupid fellow to be smart with police. Inspector is turning cross eye on me and next words are making perspiration break out all over body.

'Kandiah's assistant, known as K. P. John, has turned King's evidence and confessed all,' he says.

I am trying hard to stand still and not to run, and then inspector is asking if anyone has seen this man and reads out official description. I am listening carefully then, but description could fit at least one-third of labour on Tanah Kuning, let alone other estates, and I am most thankful of having taken precaution of having gold teeth covering removed after last act as S. Kandiah and doubly thankful that K. P. Samuel is in ignorance of said precaution.

Next, inspector is reading out description of car. 'Registration number is BA – ' But I am not waiting to hear more, but sliding away from crowd and hot-footing it for K.P.'s estate on motor bicycle.

I stop only to pick up identity card and driving licence, but it is long enough to see Devi, who has been listening at window without emerging from room, give cunning smile.

As I am leaving quarters, she is calling out in voice most provocative, 'I can tell them who is Mr S. Kandiah,' and, as I move towards her, 'No, don't hit me, Krishnan – I don't *have* to tell them, but I can. It will go the worse for you if you turn on me again.'

'Verily thou art stupid daughter of a she-goat,' I say, and lose no more time in prattle.

But when I am arriving at K.P.'s estate, he is not there.

No one is knowing where he is gone, but only that he is left estate one week ago. Wife, children, bag and baggage also.

Indeed, then it is panicking that I am. How do I know if K.P. has in fact divulged true identity of S. Kandiah? Maybe it is that inspector is playing cat and mouse game, already being in possession of relevant facts and evidences. But if he is knowing already, then surely he would have been arresting me outright, not giving chance to escape?

With such thoughts giving me much needed hope, I am riding as hard as motor bicycle will speed me back to own estate.

Devi must be forgiving and protecting both when she understands that I have money and many golden articles and that she will have nothing if I am being denounced. Thus reasoning, I am relieved to reach estate and find no further sign of police party.

But Devi has gone. Neighbour's wife, the same who helped deliver Devi of last child, is standing by doorway, smiling. Verily I could have kicked said smile from face.

'She has gone, Mister; children and all belongings,' she says.

I cannot afford to be arousing suspicions, so I ask civilly, 'Where? And when?'

'She telephoned for taxi to come to estate,' I am being informed, 'and left about one hour ago. She said she had important information to give to police, too important to wait until morning.'

'They are coming back, then?' I am asking, and trying to sound most casual.

'Inspector said to-morrow morning they would be returning for sure.'

There is no time to lose. I am throwing clothes, towel, etcetera, into case, all the time under direct gaze of neighbour's wife.

All the time I am thinking that if Devi left one hour ago and is being believed straight away by police, then they could be back here in less than one hour more, or even less. I am thinking too of the many cachings on estate where I am secretively hoarding funds and knowing there is no time to reach them. I am having one cache in fireplace, but how can I dig up bricks with woman watching? Truly it is most frustrating time I am going through.

'I must follow Devi,' I am saying, by way of excuse for unnatural rush, 'she will have gone to her mother's house in Rembang for sure.'

Still woman does not move, watching me like mongoose watching snake, and I am unable to retrieve money or any golden articles. Only one milk tin which is conveniently near case under sleeping-platform am I able to take, this containing about two hundred and fifty dollars over.

Soon time limit is up and I must travel at top speed, only hoping that Devi is calling bluff and giving such sayings to neighbour's wife to cause my unease. I have been dropping many hints to get rid of woman, including leaving her to relieve nature outside, but on return she is still there. Now I cannot delay if I am to be avoiding police and so all money and golden articles both must be left behind.

Soon I am out of estate wire and speeding northwards on motor bicycle, with heart in mouth and only two hundred and fifty dollars over in pocket. Verily there is no justice.

I am lying low in railway lines in Kuala Lumpur for one month over before hearing of vacancy as clerk in District Office, Kuala Jelang.

Many police stations are displaying among 'wanted' posters one showing face of S. Kandiah. Picture is taken from group photograph, showing self and K.P. in places of honour. I am being fat at that time and now thin, also picture shows me smiling to show gold teeth – verily I am grateful that precaution was taken to remove said teeth.

No one in railway is recognising me, so I am hoping all is safe. Kuala Jelang is in Perangor state, well away from former residence of yours truly, so I am applying for said vacancy. First, for one hundred dollars, I am obtaining certificate of leaving from Railway School and changing date of birth thereon, to give impression of younger man, luckily being of stature small.

It is now just new year of 1951 and I am resolving to turn over new leaves and trying to forget many cachings of money and golden articles rotting on Tanah Kuning Estate. I am now becoming plain Ramakrishnan, son of Ramasamy, respectable government clerk. I am travelling by train and omnibus to said district and making straight for office of Mr

Balasingham, chief clerk of District Office, whose name I am careful to learn, presenting credentials and making first good impression most necessary for future employment.

94. A CLERK FOR THE DISTRICT OFFICE

'Sir, there is coming a young man who is after wanting a job.'

The DO stopped writing and asked his clerk to repeat what he had said. Pausing just inside the door, Bala did so.

There was a vacancy for a junior clerk, it was true.

'What's he like?' James asked.

'He is a youngish man, sir, only just leaving school, he says. He has a bright face, sir.'

James tried to sound more interested than he was. 'If you think he's all right, I'll take your word for it,' he said, 'but now the Emergency's on, he'll have to be vetted by the police before we can take him on. What's his name?'

'Ramakrishnan, sir. I am already asking the police to vet him, sir.'

'Good. Well, I'd better see him, I suppose.'

Ramakrishnan, who had been listening behind the half-open door, came in. He was bowing and smiling and washing his hands with invisible soap, but his thoughts were flying like pigeons suddenly released from a loft. Police vetting was something he had not bargained for. To date nobody had connected S. Kandiah with Ramakrishnan, and if either Devi, K. P. Samuel or the chief clerk of Tanah Kuning had informed the police, he would have been arrested by now. It would appear that they had not informed. His only worry was if they had taken fingerprints from the car – it was something he had not thought of when he'd been driving along so happily with K.P. beside him and another haul of subscriptions in the brief-case on the back seat. The whole populace had been fingerprinted at the outset of the Emergency, when identity cards were first issued. In time, no doubt, if the police were diligent enough, they could find out that the prints of S. Kandiah also belonged to him, Ramakrishnan. But surely fingerprinting was only connected with murder and theft? He was worrying too much. Bluff had always been the best way; it was unlikely that they had bothered about fingerprints. He swallowed and gave the DO his most toothsome smile.

He was a small man, quite unlike Balasingham; a Tamil from south India, James supposed.

'Have you been a clerk before?' he asked, as a matter of routine.

'I have only just left school, sir, as I heard my good friend Mr Balasingham here telling you, sir.'

Bala winced. James was not much taken; he seemed an oily little man, but Bala had assured him that they were desperate for a clerk.

'All right,' he said, 'if the police clear you, we'll take you on.'

Krishnan's head rolled and his hands spread, 'I am forever your most humble servant, sir.'

Bala too spread his hands; a gesture in his case of resignation. James laughed. Bala was a good egg.

But the mixed-up mind of Ramakrishnan could not settle to the disciplined routine of a junior government clerk. Thoughts of all that beautiful money going to waste on Tanah Kuning Estate were too much for his peace of mind. Within a few weeks he was casting round for a diversion.

As usual, bitterness and hatred played their part and he decided that here, in a district with three European government officers, a perfect opportunity to get even with the hated white pigs must present itself.

It did not take him long to find a victim. Although not particularly intelligent, Krishnan was gifted with more than his share of low cunning and he discarded at once the DO, his immediate boss. Nor would he be so foolish as to risk entanglement with the police. The OCPD therefore was also out, and the Forestry Officer was too infrequently in Kuala Jelang itself. There remained only the wives.

He soon found out that, whereas the DO's wife had come from England with her husband and was in Malaya for the first time, the OCPD's was not only Malayan born and bred, but the daughter of a planter to boot – the most hated of all breeds in Krishnan's mind.

So Sally Morrison forthwith became his target.

Satisfied with his knowledge, Krishnan waited for a suitable occasion to pounce – and he did not have to wait long.

From the office window he had a clear view of the main road out of the town, and within twenty-four hours of selecting his victim he saw the largest of the police vehicles, a three-tonner, wending its way slowly along the road with the OCPD seated next to the driver. Standing at the back were several men. Undoubtedly they were going on an operation.

Making some excuse to leave the office, he went at once to the post office and ensconced himself inside the public telephone booth.

The OCPD's wife answered his call.

Speaking through his handkerchief, Krishnan said, 'Your husband is on way to certain death. He is recently leaving here with many men on way to dangerous area, where Communist terrorists are already setting ambush. He will be killed, man, and nothing you can do.'

He was sweating when he returned the receiver to its hook and wiped his face and hands before hurrying back to his desk.

Sally put down the receiver with feelings composed of a mixture of incredulity, unease, puzzlement and a sense of having touched something dirty.

The voice had been Indian without a doubt, despite the attempt to disguise it. Obviously someone who wished her or Philip ill. A PC with a grievance perhaps, but who? She thought quickly; the Pakistani driver was on leave – Philip had mentioned it, because he always drove his jeep – and also the junior Tamil clerk. That left only three possibles in the police station: Jogindar and another Sikh – who had only just arrived – and the civilian clerk, Maniam. The new man was too new; it was hardly likely to be Jogindar, which left Maniam. Unlikely, but Philip might have upset him in some way.

Taking the bull by the horns, she went straight down to the police station, hoping to tell by the expression on the clerk's face whether or not he was responsible.

To Sally's relief, Maniam showed neither surprise nor guilt on her arrival in the office and, rising to greet her, said in his usual voice, 'There are some letters for you on the OCPD's desk, Mem.'

'Thank you,' she lied, 'that's what I came down for.'

She continued on into Philip's office, picked up the mail and was just leaving the room when the telephone rang. Maniam came through to answer it and, as she went back through the main office, she saw the open door into the SB section. Sergeant Lee was writing with bent head; the opportunity seemed too good to miss. Quickly she slipped inside and closed the door.

'Hi, Ma'am,' Chee Min rose, and Sally thought, not for the first time, what an attractive smile he had, 'anything I can do for you?'

'Well, yes and no. Only please, what I want to ask you must remain absolutely confidential.' Chee Min nodded and pulled out a chair for her. 'I have just had a rather horrid phone call and I was doing my own bit of detective work.'

She told him what had been said and of her suspicions, but he firmly shook his head.

'Not Maniam, Ma'am. My door's been open all morning; I haven't moved and nor has he.'

'I'm glad.'

'And don't you worry, Ma'am, the OCPD's only gone to the Forest Office. He should be back any minute now. Do you want me to look into it?'

'No, thanks. But what did he mean by going out with "many men"?'

'Just hang on a minute; I'll ask the OCPS.'

Sally heard the brief voices of Chee Min and Jogindar Singh, then he was back.

'The "many men" were those who went on board that Indonesian ship that was in – they're now on their way to the hospital for cholera jabs in consequence; I expcct he was dropping them off *en route*. He usually takes his own car, but it's being serviced.'

'I'm so relieved,' she said, 'and please don't tell my husband, I don't want him to make a fuss.'

'Okay. Just as you wish.'

Sally went out then, smiled at Maniam and returned home. She was only half-way up the steps when the police truck returned. She saw Philip jump out, say something to the driver, and walk towards his office. Thank God, she thought, and resolved to put the incident out of her mind.

Three days later an anonymous letter arrived. Written on lined paper torn from an exercise book and in thick pencil, the capital letters read: 'YOUR HUSBAND WILL BE KILLED TODAY. IT IS YOUR FAULT. YOUR PAST AND THE PAST OF THOSE LIKE YOU IS YOUR UNDOING.'

Philip had, in fact, gone to a particularly dangerous part of the district that day and told her that he was unlikely to be back before evening. If Ramakrishnan could have seen her, he would no doubt have danced with glee. Poor Sally, it was pointless telling anyone; there was nothing she or anyone else could do, only wait.

When Krishnan had overheard the DO and OCPD discussing a visit to this area, he had written the note with much care and posted it on the crucial day. But Sally stayed at home; he did not have the pleasure of gloating over her strained face.

On the rare occasions when Krishnan did see Sally, he gnashed his teeth at her calm manner – as though he had expected her to turn grey overnight – and decided to try new tactics. Obviously she did not care whether her husband lived or died. Something more drastic was needed.

The first opportunity came at the annual Agricultural Show.

As Sally and the wife of one of the Malay schoolmasters entered a marquee to judge the handcraft exhibits, a sudden commotion at the entrance caused them to pause.

'It is your father and his kind who are being responsible for dilemma of yours truly. Chained we are and chained forever shall be. But you, lady, will shortly be paying just price.'

Sally swung round at the extraordinary words. Behind her were a bunch of giggling schoolchildren, a couple of Boy Scouts and a neat, well-dressed little Tamil, whom she took to be a shop assistant or a clerk. Surely none of them had spoken?

'Did you hear anyone speak just now?' she asked her companion, but the woman shook her head. He had, in fact, been several feet away and the voice was only a whisper.

Unaccountably, Sally did not connect the mysterious voice with either the phone call or the letter. This time she did tell Philip.

'Imagination,' he shrugged, 'why should anyone want to say anything like that to you?'

And there the matter rested. Both had plenty of other things to occupy their minds and gave it no more thought.

It was nearly a month before Sally received another telephone call. Krishnan, in his warped way, was determined to make her sweat. So far she appeared to have kept her troubles to herself, but this time he would send her running to her husband, whose work would go to pot in consequence – the possibilities were endless – and he would exult in the mental torture of those hated Europeans.

With memories of Muriani, Devi, his ex-father-in-law and many estate stories in mind, he rehearsed his speech once more and asked the exchange for the OCPD's house.

Sally listened, almost hypnotised, and when she put the receiver down she was not only white and trembling but very near to tears.

It was in this state that Helen found her. Amazed that her normally cheerful friend should so give way, she hunted in the Morrisons' medicine chest for some aspirin and refused to hear a thing until Sally had swallowed them and a glass of water. Then she asked Ja'afar to make some coffee and sat down.

'Now tell all,' she commanded.

Sally shook her head. 'I can't. It was too horrible. Oh, Helen, I've never heard any man say things like that before. He must be sexually deranged, a pervert. It was revolting, obscene.'

'We'd better ring Philip.'

'He's out. He'll be away for two or three days. It always happens when he's away.'

'Always?'

Sally told her then of the previous call, the note, and the voice outside the marquee which, to her own surprise, she now connected for the first time.

'Well, if anything else happens and you don't want to involve Philip, at least tell me. It's always better to get it off your chest to someone, even if they can't do anything.'

Sally promised that she would and, Ja'afar having arrived with the coffee, they talked of this and that until Helen brought out the purpose of her visit, a dress that required the hem putting up.

Although she did her best to concentrate, first with helping Helen do her dress and then gardening and a pile of letters she had to write, the obscene words kept floating back into her mind, disgusting her again and again. She slept little, jumping at every sound, and finally woke late, feeling tired and heavy.

The office orderly brought up the mail. There was only one letter; an ordinary buff-coloured business envelope with a local postmark, probably a bill.

But it was not a bill. Sally turned the letter over, put it down and picked it up again. Before she finally opened it, her heart began to thump and her guess was not wrong.

'I AM COMING TO GET YOU,' was written in the same pencilled capitals as before, 'YOU KNOW WHAT FOR.'

In a moment of sheer, panic-stricken terror, she rushed for the telephone and called Sergeant Lee.

Chee Min sensed her agitation before the first sentence was completely out and interrupted her, 'Now hold on, Ma'am. I'll come up.'

He gave her a few minutes on purpose and, as he had expected, she had herself under control by the time he arrived at the house. She thrust the offending letter at him without preamble.

At Chee Min's look of inquiry, she told him all that had happened since she had first sought his aid, only asking to be allowed to gloss over the actual wording of the phone call. He did not press her.

'Would you be happier if a PC slept in the house while your husband is away?' he asked.

'No, I don't want to make a fuss. I'm sorry I troubled you – you must have so much work to do – I'm afraid I panicked.' She was feeling embarrassed by then and genuinely wishing that she had kept her head.

'A lot of OCPDs have a guard posted on their houses when they're away. It wouldn't be anything unusual, you know.' Sally still shook her head. 'And I'm sorry, Ma'am, but this time we shall *have* to tell the boss.'

'Oh no, please not. I don't want to worry him. He has such a lot on his plate just now; all this resettlement and the Malay language exams next week. No, please don't tell him.'

Chee Min smiled. 'Me and the OPCD have something in common – struggling over languages. I have a couple of Chinese ones ahead of me.'

'Chinese? You're joking!'

'I'm not.' And he went on to tell her of the ludicrous position he had found himself in.

'What a lot of nonsense, especially after such a good education.'

'Too right!'

'Gosh,' Sally laughed, 'that takes me back. I was at school in Australia too, you know – not for long though, less than a year in fact, thanks to the Japs.'

They had parted with Sally in a more normal frame of mind, but Chee Min still told Inspector Zukifli, who in turn told the sergeant-major, and Jogindar himself made sure that the house and grounds were patrolled each night until Philip's return.

Sally was grateful but embarrassed, and Ramakrishnan, who watched the steps to the house from a coffee-shop near the end of the town, hugged himself with delight at the thought that he was responsible for upsetting the police station routine.

But then he had a sobering thought. He had already sailed close to the wind with the police on more than one occasion. Here he was, watching the house; but what if someone were watching him?

He looked round the coffee-shop hastily. He recognised no one. Any one of them could be a PC in plain clothes. Or perhaps two, or three, waiting to pounce as he left the shop.

And what if they had checked the fingerprints on the car and had married them up with his? Or they might still be checking; he had no police record – as yet – and there would be a lot of prints to wade through if they relied on identity cards. There might still be time.

At that moment a young Chinese whom he *knew* was a detective-sergeant came in and Krishnan nearly sent the table, with his half-finished cup of coffee flying, as he jumped up to leave in such a hurry.

Several customers looked at him curiously and he sat down again, trying to muster some self-control.

'Your mosquitoes are bad, towkay,' he tried to laugh the incident away as the coffee-shop proprietor brought him the cake which he had ordered. 'One bit me so hard, I nearly upset my coffee just now.'

The man made no reply and Krishnan settled back to drink his coffee and try to appear nonchalant.

Chee Min had wanted to help Sally, but he was quite unaware that he had done so by the simple act of walking into a coffee-shop that evening.

He noted the incident of the nervous little Tamil, but was quite oblivious of the fact that he was the cause and that one spilled cup of coffee and a barked shin had spelt 'finis' to the anonymous phone calls and letters.

95. A FRUSTRATING INTERVIEW

Chee Min had waited a week or two after his 'search' of the Cheng house and then dropped by casually one day and asked if he might come in.

This time he received a very different reception. The family were all smiles and invited him to drink some tea with them.

Rose shyly produced an exercise book and asked him to correct her English, which he did without much difficulty, but was better pleased with himself for being able to chat to her parents in their own dialect.

Mr Cheng was delighted on both counts.

'A teacher *and* a sergeant,' he exclaimed, and mother and daughter beamed.

Chee Min beamed too, but soon he got up to leave – no point in outstaying his welcome. He left, satisfied that they were genuinely sorry to see him depart, thus ensuring a welcome in future.

In fact, this was the first of many pleasant social interludes, and it was not long before he began spending most of his off-duty time in the Cheng household.

It was not long either before the friendship blossomed into something more – as everyone except Chee Min himself, or Vincent, as he was called by the Chengs – could have foreseen.

She would make me a good wife, he thought, and once the idea had taken hold in his mind, he was convinced that he could not marry anyone else.

He was still only twenty and sparks would fly at home, he had no doubt, but that was something he was confident he could overcome.

Meanwhile he confided in Sally and asked if she would meet Rose.

'Of course,' she said, 'bring her along any time you like. I'd love to meet her.'

But not so Rose. She was quite overcome with shyness at the thought. Chee Min did not press her; after all, it might not work. Sally was kind, but she was blunt. He was used to bluntness, heaven knew, but Rose was not.

Sally shrugged when he told her; she was not upset. 'Only one bit of advice I would proffer,' she said, 'which, of course, you can ignore, and that is, if you haven't already proposed to her, don't until after Chinese New Year.'

She could well imagine the set-up at Chee Min's home and had no doubt that his father would already have a prospective daughter-in-law in mind. If Chee Min burned his boats before talking to 'Dad,' she could see him being hurt on both sides.

He pondered her advice, chewed on it, and found it sound.

Chee Min had learned sufficient tact not to approach his father during the holiday and for that reason he had asked for an extra day. But he did tell Mum.

She merely raised her eyes to heaven and said, 'God help you when the explosion comes! I've been waiting for this. And you'll have your way, no doubt – you're as pig-headed as your father!'

The festivities over and everyone in genial mood, he bearded his father in his office the following day, but realised within five minutes that it was a mistake.

Lee Chee Onn sat with his hand on one telephone while he spoke into another, at the same time motioning with his head to his son to sit down.

Chee Min shivered slightly in the cold air-conditioning and hoped he would not have to stay in there too long. He wondered how much money his father had to pay the Communists to be allowed to remain in an office like this.

'Nice to see you here, son,' Mr Lee put down one receiver and picked up the other. 'Be with you in a minute.'

This time it was only a short conversation, then, with a surreptitious glance at his watch, he leaned back and smiled at his youngest son.

'Now, what can I do for you, Chee Min? How much leave have you got?'

'I have only to-day, Dad, and I had to see you urgently. I want to get married.'

'Married? Nonsense. You're far too young –' A telephone rang.

'Dad, I'll be twenty-one in five months' time.' He got it in quickly, as soon as the phone was down and before his father could start another conversation.

'Maybe, but I have plans for you. Anyway, who is it you want to marry?'

'A girl I've met in Kuala Jelang. Her name's Rose Cheng.

'Cheng? Do I know her?'

'I think it most unlikely.' The phone rang again before he could go on – he was beginning to feel very frustrated. He stood up and, as soon as his father was free, asked, 'Please, Dad, could we discuss this at home this evening?'

'Sorry, boy; got a business dinner to-night. You'd better tell me now.'

Chee Min sat down and prayed that the phone would not ring again, but his prayer went unanswered.

'Now,' his father seemed settled for a spell, 'this Rose Cheng. Where does she come from? What does her father do?'

Chee Min took a deep breath; he had reached the tricky part.

'Her father came originally from Kuala Lumpur, where her father owned a shop. She now lives in a squatter settlement, where her father market gardens.'

No point in beating about the bush. He sat still and waited for the fireworks display to commence.

But not as still as his father. He sat so quiet and so still and for so long that his son began to wonder if he had had a stroke. Then he came to life and began roaring like a wounded tiger.

'*Squatter* settlement, did you say?' Before Chee Min could get a word in edgeways, his father made a gesture of finality with both hands and shook his head so violently that his chops wobbled. '*No!* I don't want to hear another word – not one. D'you hear me?'

Chee Min heard but, as his mother had so recently remarked, he could be as pig-headed as his father.

'I intend to marry her whether I have your permission or not – I shall soon be twenty-one.'

Something in his tone made his father give up his blustering for a short while.

'Now, Chee Min,' he pleaded, 'think. I have let you have your own way over joining the police – the last career *I* would have chosen for you – and you will go far. To-day you are only a sergeant, but to-morrow an inspector; you'll be gazetted in no time. Think what a handicap it will be then to have an illiterate wife, however pretty she may be. Besides,' he added as a last resort – which was sheer hypocrisy for him – 'we are Christians.'

His son grinned; this was one of the things he had been keeping up his sleeve.

'She is a Christian too,' he said, scarcely able to conceal

the triumph in his voice, 'she is convent-educated and speaks English – they have only been driven into their present environment through hard times – and no doubt lack of business acumen. At least her father could read and write before Rose was born!'

He should have resisted the temptation to make that last quip, he knew, but he couldn't. His father still only signed his name to dictated letters, never putting pen to paper if it could be avoided, and certainly not when anyone else was around. Chee Min had probed a sensitive spot. As a younger man, Chee Onn would tell people proudly that his father had come from China as a coolie and that he himself could neither read nor write for many years. But times had changed – and he with them. To be a well-educated, rich tycoon, with secretaries, mistresses and an air-conditioned car was one thing, but to be an illiterate tycoon was to be the laughing-stock of the younger generation and that was something which Lee Chee Onn could not have stood. His face went a deep plum red and he stood up and shouted at his son.

'Make her your mistress if you like – if she's pregnant, I'll pay – but if you marry her I'll cut you off. No more allowance, no car for your twenty-first. If you marry her you can expect no further help from me. Do you understand?'

Perhaps it was Chee Min's police training that came to his aid, or maybe his natural control, but whatever it was, he handled himself with admirable restraint and dignity. He had no intention of shouting back.

'Very well, Dad,' he said in an even voice, 'I am sorry that I have earned your displeasure and not gained your consent. However, your threats will in no way alter my intentions – as soon as I am twenty-one I shall marry Rose.'

He gave his father a slight, old-fashioned bow and left the room.

He had intended spending the evening with his mother, but now he was no longer in the mood to stay at home. If he left at once, he could still make Kuala Jelang that night.

As he eased himself behind the wheel of the borrowed car, he had a momentary pang that now he would not soon have his own, but it did nothing to lessen his determination. He would propose to Rose as soon as he returned; his mind was made up.

96. TO LIVE IN PEACE

James had just about given up hope of finding a suitable site for a resettlement area, without requisitioning or forcing someone to sell, when he received an unexpected visit from one of the planters.

It was Wotherspoon, manager of Bukit Merah Estate. An elderly bachelor, he was always making complaints about government, and the police in particular. James was wary.

Extraordinary, he thought, as they shook hands and the older man seated himself, how many people seem to find pleasure in playing one government servant off against another. With King it had rankled, and he had been too new at the time to know it was just a local pastime. With Philip it was different; they were able to compare notes and laugh about it.

'What can I do for you?' he asked.

'I understand you are looking for some land.' Wotherspoon had a high-pitched, rather querulous voice.

'Indeed I am.'

'My company has about twenty-five acres that they want to get rid of, possibly more. Any use to you?'

It seemed too good to be true. In wartime, James had climbed partly through efficiency and partly through luck, but a good deal through ruthlessness. He had often been criticised for being too high-handed; it was strange that he should now be the very opposite. The police seemed to requisition things left, right and centre, and DWEC, or its state equivalent, SWEC, had powers that could so easily be misused. All along he had been determined to avoid requisitioning, shunning the power that could put it into effect. He looked steadily at Wotherspoon, still warily, but with hope.

'Can you show me where it is exactly?' He walked over to the map of the district which hung on the opposite wall, below the photograph of the King.

The area was part jungle and part disused rubber. It adjoined Bukit Merah Estate.

'No use to me,' the old man said, 'estate's already too large for me to cope with single-handed – be glad for government to take it off my hands.'

'I'll have to have the police opinion first, then we'll raise it in DWEC.'

'The police,' Wotherspoon sneered. 'All that Morrison's interested in is making me spend more money. Do you know, the blighter had the cheek to threaten to withdraw my SCs if I didn't improve the defences?'

'That's up to him,' James said quickly; he had no intention of becoming involved. In fact, he did think Philip was antagonising the planters rather unnecessarily, but they were his men.

As soon as Wotherspoon had gone he rang Philip up. 'Let's go and have a look at it this afternoon,' he suggested.

'Well? What do you think of it?'

Philip leaned against the jeep and stroked his chin. Ahead and behind them men of the jungle squad stood, weapons at the ready, alert against the ever-present menace. It was not the most salubrious of areas. He did not, in fact, think very much of it at all, but James was so het up about this wretched land that he was not prepared to make matters worse by saying so.

'I could wish it were in a better area as far as security is concerned,' he said at last.

James sighed. 'Well, we've got to find something and this seems the best bet so far.'

Reluctantly Philip agreed.

It was true. They had no hope of clearing the CTs from even part of the district as long as they continued to prey on the squatters, forcing food, funds and information out of them. To resettle all the squatters in the area, where they could be guarded, was the only possible solution. Communal kitchens would be set up and the workers searched every morning when they left the area, to ensure they were not carrying food for the bandits. Information was another problem, but at least cutting off their material needs would be half the battle. It had worked in other districts, it must work here.

He turned to the back of the jeep where his detective-sergeant and an SC were already installed.

'What do you think, Chee Min – you spend enough time with the squatters?'

Chee Min lowered his eyes and gave Philip a slight smile. He would not be happy with Rose in this area, so he must let that be his guide.

'I think it is a dangerous area, sir.'

James slapped at the side of the vehicle impatiently. 'Special Branch,' he spat out, making it sound like a curse.

Chee Min was not going to be rude, but his opinion had been asked. He coloured slightly, but his voice was steady.

'Until we can be sure there are no bandits living on Bukit Merah Estate,' he said, 'I do not think it will be safe.'

It was exactly Philip's own opinion, but it was one of the few matters on which he and James did not see eye to eye.

'Who says there are bandits on Bukit Merah?' James snapped. He was looking very hot and cross and kept dashing the sweat from his forehead with his one good hand. 'Christ, it's hot,' he added in a less belligerent tone of voice.

They all agreed.

'Wotherspoon – ' Philip began, but was cut off in mid-sentence by a frown and an impatient gesture from the DO.

'Can't discuss it here,' he interrupted, meaning not before Other Ranks. 'I've got a bloody meeting at five o'clock. Come and have some grub to-night, Phil – pot luck; I'll ring Helen as soon as we get back – we can discuss it in the cool of the evening while the women talk about their knitting – or whatever they do talk about.'

Over coffee and as soon as the servants had left the room, James turned to Philip without preamble.

'I know the police have had it in for old Wotherspoon ever since he refused to spend any more money on his defences,' he said, 'but have you any proof that there are bandits living on his estate?'

'When we moved in after that last ambush and caught the CTs on the hop, amongst other things that they left behind was a typewriter. The fact that all the recent propaganda leaflets had originated from that machine was not difficult to prove.'

Philip looked James straight in the eye, who in turn stared back at him.

'Go on.'

'Wotherspoon denied ever having seen that typewriter before and even made a statement to the effect that nothing had been stolen from his estate. On the bottom of the machine there was a label – stuck on by the agents in KL, who certified that it had been repaired and serviced on such and such a date. Of course we checked to see who had taken it in – Wotherspoon.' James opened his mouth, obviously to protest, but Philip shook his head. 'Let me finish first. I went into the office myself when I was last in KL. There is a very efficient Eurasian girl running that side – she remembered Wotherspoon coming in and described him very well. There is absolutely no doubt that that typewriter belonged to him, or to the estate, but he slipped up – if he had admitted that a typewriter had been stolen, we should probably not have given it a second thought.'

'Is that conclusive proof?'

'No, it's not. But don't most managers deal with one shop for the bulk of their estate supplies?'

'I should imagine so.'

'Wotherspoon runs three accounts at three shops – one in his own name, one in the name of the agents, and one in the name of the estate. The combined amount of rice he draws each month would feed more than twice the strength of his labour force.'

James was now sitting up very straight and staring not at Philip but out into the night.

'I wish you'd told me this before,' he said.

'I should have done so soon, but we're still investigating – I'll let you have the whole story as soon as I can.'

'Do you consider your Special Branch to be infallible?'

'Far from it, but in this particular instance I agree with them. In fact, I'd go so far as to say they are merely confirming my own suspicions.'

The two women had been listening intently.

'You don't think he's actually "in" with the bandits, do you, Philip?' Sally now asked.

'A Communist?' ventured Helen.

James stood up. His head was aching. 'Convince the girls, Philip,' he said, 'I'm going to get us a drink.' He hated the whole business and women could be such ghouls.

'He's old,' Philip told them, 'old, a bachelor and alone and like most old men, he's selfish. Anything to be left in peace – you leave me alone and I shan't see you. Do you agree, James?'

James was behind a screen, where they had a small bar. Four splashes of soda were heard before he replied, and then he sounded tired.

'I suppose so. It's the only charitable view we can take. What do you propose to do?'

'Let him know that we know. Suggest politely that he mends his ways – at least that is how I would like to handle it, but the CPO is coming down in a few days; I shall ask his advice.'

'Hm. Old Wotherspoon wouldn't take it kindly from you – say you were too young to know what you were talking about, too new in the country, too new in the police. I think he could be difficult.'

Philip's face went hard. 'We've had too many police killed,' he said, '*and* planters, to put up with any nonsense. I feel sorry for the old boy, all on his own up there, and I'll handle it in the kindest way I can, but I'm not prepared to risk men's lives so that Wotherspoon can live in peace.'

'Hear, hear.'

Philip gave a mock bow to the wives. 'And having said my piece,' he grinned, 'let's let the CPO sort it out.'

'And the land?' pressed James.

'I suppose it will be all right, if we can clear sufficient space around it.'

'By the way,' asked Helen, 'on a lighter theme, is it true that we're getting a quack?'

'Well, how the devil did *you* know?' James looked at her in surprise. 'I haven't mentioned it to a soul yet, because if we can't find anywhere for him to live, he won't be posted here after all.'

'The servants know,' Helen looked smug, 'they always do. Do you think he will come? It would make such a difference, not having to worry when the children are ill.'

'If they can find a bachelor, I'm hoping to persuade Donald to let him share his bungalow. I've just written to the Medical Department to find out.'

'I hope he does come,' Sally put in, 'then we can have six for dinner instead of always the four of us, and Donald the odd man out.'

'Our social Sal,' James smiled at her. 'I'll be glad to have a doctor in the district, period.'

'I'm not an easy man to live with,' Donald was saying.

He was horrified at being asked to share his bungalow and yet, at the back of his mind, a little sneaking thought insinuated itself: perhaps company would be, could be, pleasant. Someone to talk to in the evenings, someone to drink with, perhaps someone with whom he could play chess. But supposing he got a TT or a God-botherer? He might even be a queer. He looked across the desk at the DO.

'I'm not too keen,' he said.

James was becoming exasperated. 'I can't force you, Don,'

he said, 'but you'd be doing the whole district a favour and it would only be temporary – until we can find somewhere else for him.'

Then there was Salmah. She had been mistress to at least one of his predecessors and he remembered well how she had expected him to take her on – what a rat that King had been! He had only kept her on because she could cook, but it had taken a long time to convince her that that was all he wanted of her. Well, she probably thought *he* was queer – or impotent, more likely – he'd heard the rumours. Supposing this new chap should accept her advances and take her on? It could be damned embarrassing.

'I understand that he's not an Englishman,' James's dry voice cut through Don's thoughts.

Oh boy, these bloody, superior British! That did it.

'I'll share,' he said abruptly, and stood up to go.

James smiled at his retreating back. Helen said he was hard, but in his air force days he'd always been able to handle his crew. He picked up the telephone and asked for his house.

'Helen, can you water down the soup? Don's coming to lunch!'

Donald swung round just as he reached the door. The two men grinned broadly at each other.

'Well, you old bastard!' was all Don said.

97. THE GRASS GROWS GREENER

The ninth stream enters the river

Stanislaus Olshewski

A lot of water had flowed under the bridge since the day when I removed my first bullet from my first Gurkha rifleman.

I had removed a lot of bits and pieces since then. I'm not quite sure what I had expected my job to be; leisurely encounters with Malay, Chinese and Indian civilians during office hours? And learning Malay in the evening? I suppose so. Well, it certainly didn't take me long to find out that that was just part of it. The Emergency had already been on for more than a year when I arrived in Johore, and we were hardly in the healthiest of areas. We were, in fact, a good deal nearer most of the fighting troops than any military hospital, and I soon found myself, at all hours of the day and night, treating wounded British, Gurkhas and Malays, soldiers and police.

After I'd been working flat out for more than a year, I took some local leave and visited Penang. Kathy and I were still engaged and she had written to me every week since leaving the ship, but I noticed she wasn't wearing the ring I'd bought her in Colombo. Her eyes followed mine as I looked at her empty hand.

'I didn't think you wanted to be tied, Stan. I thought you'd consider it just a shipboard romance and I'm not one to force myself on any man.'

I really felt a heel then – I think I had written to her twice. The Emergency had doubled the work at the hospital, but not the staff. And I really had devoted every spare moment to learning the language. Not that languages ever presented a problem to me, but I was determined to know it thoroughly and not get by with the bazaar Malay that half the Europeans considered sufficient. But there was no need to make excuses to Kathy; she waved my explanations away with an impatient shake of her head.

'It's enough that you're here, Stan. You wouldn't have come if you hadn't wanted to.'

It was true; I had looked forward to seeing her – when I'd thought about her at all. I enjoyed Penang and I enjoyed her company, but after a week I was fretting to get home.

'You want to get back, don't you, Stan?' Kathy knew me; I hadn't said a word. 'I love Penang, but I wish I could come with you.'

Well, why couldn't she? I only had to say the word. I would have liked to have had her with me, and yet I was jealous of my solitude, my privacy. That, I suppose, is what happens when you're still a bachelor at thirty-five. I pressed her hand, but said nothing.

Back in my bachelor bungalow, which boasted no luxuries, no adornment whatsoever, I missed her intolerably. It would be pleasant to come home to a civilised house, have someone to discuss my problems with. We were so short-staffed, she could help out in the hospital too; she'd not be bored.

But it was equally pleasant to sit in dirty shirt, unchanged, unbathed, and unnagged at. To sit in the velvet thrum of the Malayan night, for company cicadas and the toc-toc bird.

What happened, of course, was that I just let things slide.

And then my mind was made up for me. I was posted. And posted to Berembang, up in Perangor, to a bachelor mess, so that a married couple could have my bungalow in Johore. Accommodation was such a problem at that time that it influenced postings a good deal.

I accepted my transfer with a fatalistic shrug, but once there I was miserable. Work and responsibility had been the very savour of life and suddenly they were removed. I was one of a number of junior MOs and every case of interest I had to pass on.

The Emergency seemed a hundred miles away – although, in fact, it was just around the corner – and the mess was foul. No privacy, lousy food, and no kindred spirits.

And then Kathy was posted to Kuala Lumpur. It was only a few hours' drive and I thought things would perk up. We saw each other perhaps a couple of times a week and still I made no move. Then, one Sunday morning, when we were sitting by the Lake Club pool, she pushed a letter over.

It was a love letter and I didn't want to read it, but she read it out to me anyway. It was from a doctor in Penang.

'I didn't think you were interested in him.' I couldn't even feel jealous. She had said she was thirty and as things were going would end up on the shelf if I didn't make up my mind. 'Are you in love with him?'

'Are you in love with me, Stan?' I'd asked for that.

'I don't know, Kathy. I just don't know.'

'So what do I tell him?'

I was silent a long time then, not knowing what to say. On impulse I nearly said to hell with him, marry me, but a terrible lethargy was descending on me.

'It's all my fault – I just seem to have lost interest in everything. Most of all myself.' I must have sounded like one of those ads for vitamin pills; night starvation or something. By God, I wasn't even interested in that any more.

'Which means I tell him "yes".'

I said nothing. She rose from the grass and I saw the tears filling her eyes. There have been many times in my life when I've hated myself; that was one of the worst.

'Kathy, I'm sorry.'

She shook her head violently. 'Please don't say any more, Stan. Just try not to see me again, that's all.' And she walked away, a small dignified figure, straight-backed and proud.

The next morning I approached the CMO for an out-station posting. I had done so before, but there had been no go.

'There is a district that's badly in need of an MO,' he told me. 'But the trouble, as usual, is lack of accommodation. There's already a small hospital there, run by a senior dresser, but now that the Emergency has made it so dangerous to send patients by ambulance for any distance, a doctor is badly needed on the spot. The post has been approved and the Director is keen to fill it as soon as possible, but . . .' he spread his hands in a helpless gesture; hell, I could happily have lived in a tent.

'Isn't there a Rest House?' I asked.

'There is, but you couldn't live there for ever – only two rooms and they're nearly always in use. The DO is trying to organise something and, as it will have to be a bachelor posting, I'll keep you in mind.'

Whether is was the prospect of leaving Berembang or having made the final break with Kathy – severing a connection which I never should have made – I don't know, but quite suddenly the lights shone brighter, the grass grew greener and my patients, if it were possible, less drab.

I celebrated the arrival of the New Year with a surge of hope and a thick head. One thing was for sure, no year could be as dreary as 1950.

Kathy had been a Christmas bride; my conscience was clear. And if the photo of her wedding in the local rag was anything to go by, she looked a lot better off without me.

Time went fast after that, and it seemed no time at all before I was back in front of the CMO. My posting had come through at last.

'It'll mean sharing a house, I'm afraid,' he said, 'but it may not be for long.'

I was as excited as a schoolboy and couldn't have cared less where I was going to live, just as long as there was a decent job of work to go with it. The thought of being my own boss again was exhilarating. I said as much to the CMO and was just about to thank him and go when it occurred to me that I didn't know where I was being sent!

We both laughed at the absurdity of the omission and the CMO duly enlightened me.

'Kuala Jelang,' he said. 'Not a bad little place.'

It would not have worried me had I been posted to the moon,

so pleased was I to get away from urban life. Piling my belongings into the old second-hand Ford I'd bought in Johore, I set off, singing at the top of my voice and generally behaving in a manner unbecoming. I had been advised not to travel alone and to get myself a gun, but I had the feeling my time was not yet up and I'm afraid I politely ignored the well-meant counsel. I cocked a snook at every high bank and concealing tree and thought, to hell, you can shoot at me another day.

Kuala Jelang was on the coast and for the last few miles of the journey I was travelling along a raised road, the ridge down the centre of a narrow peninsula, hemmed in on both sides by mangrove swamp. It was my first encounter with mangrove and there seemed something infinitely evil about its devious, intertwining roots and the black oozing mud in which they lived. It was a relief when the swamp opened out and the first buildings came into view.

There's one thing about British colonial town-planning – you can never lose yourself! Once inside the Town Board limit notice, everything began to fall into place. A wooden building on my left bore the sign Forest Checking Station, and stretching out behind was what appeared to be a forest nursery. Behind that again, built on a low hill and with a long, winding drive, stood an old-fashioned bungalow almost entirely grown over by bougainvillaea of varying shades. A typical old government house; the Forestry Officer's quarters presumably, and if so, my temporary home.

Within a couple of minutes a ramshackle conglomeration of low, whitewashed buildings appeared and I slowed down, knowing that they could only be the hospital.

Resisting the temptation to go in – it would be unfair, when I was not expected before the next morning – I stopped the car on the opposite side of the road and looked at it with satisfaction. I saw at a glance that most of the buildings could do with a coat of paint, the grass needed cutting and a few well-kept flower-beds would not come amiss. A couple of young nurses, who looked smart and cheerful enough, flitted between the buildings like trim, starched butterflies, and an elderly Chinese in a white gown, whom I took to be the Senior Hospital Assistant, emerged from an office and went into a ward. At that moment I noticed that some of the mobile patients were clustered on a verandah and watching me watching them, so I decided it was time to make a move. Brief though the glimpse had been of my future domain, it had been enough to fill me with plans of pleasurable anticipation and I started the engine with spirits soaring.

Through a suburban area of junior government quarters. like so many flower-surrounded boxes in dotted rows on either side of the road, until I came to a fork with a two-armed signpost pointing to 'The Town' in one direction and 'Government Offices' in the other. Taking the latter turn, I came across just exactly what I had expected – an avenue of flowering trees ascending a small hill, crowned by what could only be what they were, the government offices.

It was so similar to so many of the districts I had visited in Johore and passed through on my way down that it was like coming home. I smiled to myself as I read the boards: District Office, Treasury, Public Works Department, Survey Office, Agriculture and, slightly on its own, Post Office.

At that moment I heard a familiar sound as well, the clanging of metal against metal as the police sentry struck the hour. Judging by the sound, the police station must be some distance away; the other side of the town apparently.

There was a great commotion as doors and windows were shut and clerks began hurrying from all directions, Chinese and Indians mostly, with a couple of Malays and one tall, thin Eurasian. Only then did I realise that it was five o'clock. I had been driving all day and forgotten about the time. Smiling at the curious stares that I received from the home-going clerks, I ran up the steps and knocked at the wooden swing doors marked 'District Officer'.

The DO was on the phone and motioned me to a chair. I was glad of the chance to size him up and also to relax for a moment, for I had suddenly become very tired.

He was a short, squat man, with one arm, a glaringly obvious glass eye and a lot of brown crinkly hair, which I suspected he tried unsuccessfully to subdue, as I did my own. He grunted monosyllabically at intervals into the receiver, which he held between shoulder and neck while doodling on the blotter with his one good hand. There was a hint of ill-humour in the face and more than a hint of pain. He must have a bloody temper, I was thinking, when he suddenly put the receiver down and smiled.

I looked at him with fascination as he walked round the desk with outstretched hand, amazed at the transformation of his face. There are smiles and smiles. This one lit the whole face and I wondered how many women it had enslaved.

'I'm Weatherby,' he said, 'and you, I take it, are the new quack. As you will no doubt find out when you see the amount of work awaiting you, you are a very welcome addition to the district.'

'Thank you. I hope I shall fulfil your expectations. My name is Stanislaus Olshewski.'

'So you really are Polish? My God, your English is bloody good.'

'Thank you again.'

'I suppose you know you're sharing a bungalow with the FO, Thom – only a temporary arrangement, I hope. I'll take you round.' He looked back at his desk and sighed then and said, rather wistfully, 'On second thoughts, I don't suppose you could find your own way there? I've got such a pile here – ' he indicated the laden desk ' – and once I leave it, I find it so hard to start concentrating again. This is the only time one has any peace. You've already passed the house – '

'On the hill behind the Forest Checking Station?' I interrupted, 'I'll find my way.'

'Good man. Glad you've arrived before the week-end; the police band is coming down to beat the retreat on Saturday. The whole district will be coming to town. You'll be able to meet everyone in one go; most convenient.'

Right at that moment all I wanted was a shower and my bed. It had been a tiring drive and the grit and sweat were causing my shirt to stick to my back and chest, a feeling I detested. But I said it was indeed most opportune and turned to go.

A small Austin was parked beneath and through the porch, leaving room for my car. A considerate character, I thought, thank God.

And then I saw him.

Large, gingery and familiar. His name meant nothing, but as soon as I heard his New World voice, the tantalising buzz in my brain increased. He was unlikely to be an American, so the accent must be Canadian, but where? He looked at me without a flicker of recognition at first, then a puzzled cloud descended over his face as well.

'Wait a minute,' he said, large paw still pumping mine, 'we've met before.'

'I know we have.'

'Judas Priest, my doggone memory's gone. Were you in the army?'

'No,' I replied, 'air force.'

'Pole? I never met no Poles. Holland?'

'No. UK, Middle East, East Africa, India,' he shook his head at each one, 'and finally Germany. Were you a POW?'

'No. You a partisan?'

'No.'

We both stopped and thought. Then, "Were you at Edinburgh?' he asked.

'St. Andrews.'

'I've got it! That Hogmanay party at the Wallaces'. I got blind drunk and when I woke up we were in a huddle on the floor – if I remember rightly, I was holding your head!'

'I was poleaxed by one of those kilted fiends!'

'We have one here, the OCPD – dances round like a dervish on tribal festivals! You were bragging about vodka if I recall aright!'

'I carried you home – and cooked the breakfast!'

'Well, Judas Priest! Talk about a small world. Glad to have you share my home for a second time, Doc! Say, how's about a shower and a drink and then I'll drive you round the rest of the metropolis before it gets dark. We get quite a spectacular sunset this time of year from the top of Nobs' Hill.'

As expected, Kuala Jelang continued to follow the usual pattern.

Hedged in by mangrove, I had been unaware when driving down that such a broad river ran so close to the road. I had been told it was a peninsula, but I hadn't appreciated that the water on one side was not sea.

Thom drove on, beyond the government offices and along the river bank. Two quite sizeable steamers were loading rubber and beyond them I could see several boats of the fishing fleet chug-chugging out of the river mouth to the sea.

'Good fish here,' he remarked, 'you want to see the rest?'

I nodded. It was wonderful to be away from the big town and the shower and a beer had momentarily banished fatigue.

Conforming, the town was centred round the padang. Good old traditional English village green. It was all so right.

'Do they play cricket on Sundays?' I asked, a trifle maliciously, not expecting to evoke a rush of enthusiasm.

'Sure thing. Some of the Indians are first-class. One of your sports, Stan?'

'Not too keen,' I murmured. 'I imagine I'll have a fair amount of work to do.'

'The wall, we can't all have the same interests. I suppose.'

He was clearly disappointed and I was sorry I had brought the subject up. He wasn't the first overgrown schoolboy I'd met.

The usual Chinese shophouses bordered two sides of the padang and at the end of the main street stood a war memorial and to the left of it a mosque. After that the road curved round the base of a sudden hill and we began to climb.

Immediately the jungle noises of the night rose around us with the gathering dusk, bullfrogs and cicadas taking up the chorus where, for me, they had left off a year before.

'OCPD's house on the right, DO's on the left, Rest House straight ahead.'

We were at the top of the hill now and lights were beginning to come on in windows seen vaguely at the end of the tree-shrouded drives. The road was terrible and I felt for the little car as we lurched in and out of potholes and ruts. It was a relief when we were past the Rest House and he stopped.

'We'll walk from here. You should see this road when it's rained – sometimes you can't take a car up here for weeks, then they all have to walk. Does 'em good, I say, they none of them get enough exercise.'

God preserve me from professional keep-fitters! I knew one subject to avoid!

As though to prove his point, Thom set off with great strides to cover the short distance to the lighthouse, a solid grey stone tower that looked as though it would be more at home in northern seas than the tropics. Perched on the very edge of the escarpment, it afforded an excellent view of the seaward side of the town. He beckoned me to follow him on to the parapet and pointed down.

Immediately below us a fringe of mangrove ended abruptly at a bund, beyond which nestled the police compound. Station and barracks and a few individual houses bordered a central parade-ground and, to the left, a line of khaki tents.

'Army contingent,' Thom explained, 'we have a few Gurks stationed here.'

'Good.' Things were getting better all the time.

Figures moved like ants down below and the hum and throb of a myriad radios mingled with the engines of the fishing boats leaving port and the insect life above.

'The silent and inscrutable East,' I laughed. 'I never thought that so many people could own radios and find so many different stations to tune them in to!'

'Yeah, they're a noisy bunch. But look at those clouds.'

I raised my eyes to one of the most beautiful sunsets I had ever imagined, let alone seen.

A shoal of fishlike, silvery clouds, reflecting lilac, turquoise and soft green, sailed into a salmon and crimson patch, arched round by cerulean blue with purple depths. The sun itself, crimson, orange, gold, majestic, hung like a god amidst the splendorous shafts of pagan light. Then to sink, slowly at first, then faster, faster, faster into the brazen sea. And suddenly, with that heart-pulling stab of sadness which so often follows beauty, I looked out at the now black, empty sea and shivered.

Neither of us spoke as we walked quickly back to the car and drove in silence to a silent meal.

'Sorry I'm such poor company,' I excused myself. 'Fact is, I'm dead beat.'

He nodded and I went to bed.

The DO was as good as his word and arrived at the bungalow while we were still having breakfast.

He frowned, and with a glance of manifest displeasure at Thom's unshaven face, remarked curtly that he was a busy man and if I didn't mind – I got the message and, picking up my bag, joined him in the car.

I myself had noticed the empty bottle and overflowing ashtray where I'd left Thom sitting the night before. The few words he had spoken at breakfast had been truculent and aggressive, and confirmed my suspicions that he was a soak.

Weatherby introduced the Senior Hospital Assistant, handed over a few files and left.

My day was spent between alternating periods of satisfaction and dismay. The staff seemed fair and eager to please, but the equipment, or lack of, presented an impossible situation.

'Perhaps, now that Doctor is here, he could request these.' The dresser laid a list before me of indents which had, he told me, been consistently ignored.

I groaned as I went down the list; items of the most elementary necessity, I would have thought. The hospital, which had appeared so promising from the outside, was merely a shell. I did my rounds grimly, making copious notes, then I went over to the District Office to try and borrow a clerk and a typewriter.

I gave lunch a miss and, by the time I returned to the bungalow, my voice was hoarse from shouting down the telephone over impossible long-distance connections and my arm stiff from writer's cramp.

At least I returned to find my stable companion in a different frame of mind. It appeared that once his hangover was past, he was all right until the next morning.

'How did it go?' he asked, and I was glad that there was someone there to whom I could moan. 'Pretty frustrating, eh?'

'That would be the understatement of the year.'

'Wal, you can't blame them not putting too much in the hands of these guys. Having seen what our driver can do to an engine, can you imagine some of your blokes playing with a microscope or an X-ray machine?'

'I suppose so.'

'Aw, come on, Doc, don't be so low. It'll all change now that you're here; it'll sort itself out, but you can't expect the whole caboodle to fall into place and spring up over night, now can you? Bring your letters over to me until you get a proper clerk and my girl will do them.'

'Well, thanks, Thom, Don, that would be a help. I was wondering how to cope.'

Our conversation was cut short by the entrance of a stunning Malay girl. Plump and pretty, her sarong was so tight and her slippers so high-heeled that she could hardly walk, but minced in with tiny steps and swaying hips. I reckoned her kebaya was even tighter than the sarong – if that were possible – and as she insinuated herself into the room and past my chair, my eyes practically left their sockets.

'Wow!' I exclaimed, 'falsies, I bet!'

I was aware of the fact that Donald had been eyeing us in turn, tight-lipped and dour, and when he spoke he sounded positively prim.

'I really couldn't tell you,' he said.

'You mean you have no claims?'

"No claims at all.' I didn't know then that he was falling back on someone else's remark, 'I like them white!'

'We-ll. Purely for research, of course!'

'Of course.'

The girl swayed so far that she almost overbalanced and I laughed. However, she recovered herself and tottered out with a fair semblance of dignity. To my relief, Don laughed too, and I had the impression that, after all, he couldn't care less whether I slept with her or not.

'Let's have a drink,' he said. 'No vodka. I'm afraid.'

98. THE PAST CATCHES UP

'You haven't forgotten the band's coming down this afternoon, have you, Sally?' Philip called, as he left the house after breakfast. 'Hat and gloves and all that?'

'No, darling, I hadn't forgotten.'

Half-way down the hill he turned, thought for a moment and went back.

'I forgot to tell you, Donald's bringing the new doctor along this afternoon – do you think we should ask them to dinner? We shall have Mike and the bandmaster anyway.'

'Oh yes, that'll be fun. I'll ask Helen and James as well. Better pray that the bus doesn't get burnt to-day though, or heaven alone knows what we'll give them to eat.'

Ja'afar stood by the linen cupboard, waiting to make up the bandmaster's bed, amused by the antics of his charge – as he still thought of her – as she alternately sang and muttered to herself.

'I like to be a Clerk SD and make controllers cups of tea,
And then I'll get my LAC,
It's crafty, but it's done.'

Sally sang, high and slightly flat, as she pulled clean sheets from the cupboard and hunted unsuccessfully for a towel without a darn.

Parades were fun – and the band in full dress too. What ages since I was on a parade, she mused.

'I like to be a Clerk SD and sit on the controller's knee,
And then I'll get tapes, one, two, three
It's crafty, but it's done. Oh damn, where *did* I put those new pillow-cases?'

'You sound happy, Mem,' Ja'afar murmured, as he took the sheets.

'It's just a silly wartime song – I don't think I can translate it. I love parades – didn't even mind going on them myself – looking forward to this afternoon. Do you know, Ja'afar, the last parade I took, I open-order marched the rear rank over the edge of a bank and they all went for six!'

'Yes, Mem.' He hadn't the foggiest notion what she was talking about, but she was the Old Tuan's only child and he was pleased to see her happy. A pity that her father was not alive to see her married and settled down – even more of a pity that she had no children of her own.

He stood aside to let the DO's wife come through the open door and smiled to see Miss Sally strike an operatic pose and sing even louder.

'Squadron Leaders and Wing COs are easy ways to wealth,
I'll work on them from morn till night, although I'll wreck my health.
In my off times to bed I go,
I've found out all I need to know,
I'm bound to get my ASO,
It's crafty, but it's done!'

Helen sat down on the edge of the bed and shook her head, laughing.

'How you take me back, Sally. They were good times, weren't they?'

'Luckily it's usually the good times that we remember.' She paused to close the cupboard doors, then turned to face her friend. 'But do you know, Helen, it's an extraordinary thing, but the air force keeps coming to mind to-day and for some unknown reason I'm really excited – the parade this afternoon, I expect – but although I was only in the ranks for less than a year, it's that time that I keep thinking of. I can see the Ops room and the plotting-table as clearly as though they were just next door – keep thinking I ought to be getting ready to go on watch!'

'I try not to think back too often – James was so different then.' She changed the subject abruptly, but Sally had caught the momentary wistfulness and wondered. 'But that's not what I came over about and I must hurry back – I just wondered if you wanted any help this afternoon; teas or anything.'

'Not to worry, thanks all the same. The men are having theirs in the canteen; I doubt if I'll even have the bandmaster to cope with. But I'm glad you came because I wanted to ask if you'll have dinner with us. Don's bringing the new doctor over, so there'll be eight of us. One odd glass and two plates, and I'll have to borrow a couple of knives if I may, but I don't suppose anyone will mind.'

Helen's face clouded. She was too loyal to James to dream of discussing him. She had nearly made a slip only a few moments ago, and anyway, would Sally ever believe it if she told her that, when they got home, James would undoubtedly accuse her of flirting with Philip, or say that he hadn't liked the way Don looked at her, or suspect her of having an affair with the bandmaster? There was no rhyme nor reason for his dark moods; nothing that anyone as uncomplicated as Sally could be expected to understand. He lost more than his eye and his arm in that crash, she thought bitterly.

She raised her head to meet Sally's compassionate eyes.

'I'd rather not,' she said bleakly, 'I'd love to accept, but. . . .'

'James?'

'He's not well. It's difficult to explain, but things upset him - little things. He was never like this before that last crash - it did something to him.'

'Maybe, but I think it goes deeper than that.' Helen looked at her friend in surprise and listened intently as she went on, 'You know, I used to have nightmares early on in the war - awful dreams about leaving Singapore.' She paused for a time, looking out of the window, and Helen began to wonder what was relevant to her and James in Sally's thoughts. 'When I have nightmares now, they are different; now it is because I once attracted a man's attention so that another man could strangle him. I was proud of myself at the time, but I'm not now, so many years later. He was a German soldier.'

'But that doesn't seem so terrible - after all, it was war and thousands of people were being killed the whole time.'

'No, it's not very terrible in itself, just a tiny pinprick in a great hole of destruction. But it's terrible to *me*. I can't even bear to kill a centipede these days. I remember once a boy friend of mine suddenly getting cold feet - he wept on my shoulder, literally, because he had strafed a railway platform with women on it. I thought he was rather wet at the time - now I'd be more sympathetic. It's a pity that we only learn tolerance so gradually. But he was a fighter pilot don't you think a bomber pilot must wonder sometimes how much of the destruction, how many lives lost, were due to him? Why have so many turned to religion or good works of one sort or another?'

Helen stirred uneasily. Sally was becoming too intense and she wasn't sure what she was getting at. James had been no worse than anyone else during the war.

'Don't you see,' Sally persisted, 'we all have our quirks? I don't believe that any of our generation have been left completely unscathed by the war; only some of us were affected more than others. You've told me often enough that James was on some of the largest raids and you've implied – though never said – that he was pretty hard and ruthless in his job. I've no doubt he had to be and I'm sure it's telling now. All this bitterness – it must stem from something. Oh dear,' she grinned suddenly, 'I'm becoming involved and I'm not going to spoil my day worrying about a war that's already past history. Come on, Helen, stay and have a cup of coffee while I polish Philip's medals; I'm sure you have time.'

Helen rooted around in the cardboard box from which Sally had taken the medals, while waiting for her coffee to cool.

'We're a magpie race, aren't we?' She smiled as she picked up a square of tartan and fitted a badge to it. 'What did that go on?'

'Philip's balmoral. Can't think why we keep all this junk.'

'This looks familiar.' Helen was holding up a brass button, its heraldic eagle looking strangely medieval beside the simple thistles and albatrosses. 'American?'

'Polish. I swopped it with a boy friend's, years ago. Oh, damn these corners – whoever designed campaign stars never thought of the person who'd have to clean them. I'd leave them to Ja'afar, but he will polish the oak leaf and clasps as well.'

Helen looked wistfully at the medals. 'That's another thing,' she said, 'medals. James can't bear them. I put his out to wear on our first Armistice Day here and he was furious – flung them into the WPB and said he never wanted to see them again.'

'It all adds up, doesn't it?'

Helen finished her coffee and walked slowly home. She was seeing Sally in a new light and realising that, after all, there was someone on whom she could lean, someone who did not condemn James, but who sympathised. She sighed with something near satisfaction; it had been a good day for them when the Morrisons arrived.

It's as good as Ascot, Sally was thinking. The padang was looking as green as it could and the late afternoon sun slanted out of a cloudless sky. A warm breeze stirred the bunting with which the area had been squared off, and a gay crowd milled in all directions.

Two or three rows of folding chairs faced the band and she noticed that a sprinkling of European women, Helen and some of the planters' and miners' wives who had come in for the occasion, were already seated.

If you closed your eyes to the fact that the road was lined with armoured vehicles, jeeps, and large American Ford V8s with armoured protection, if you considered the number of SCs in town to be normal, and if you did not know of the piles of serviceable clothing littering the two rooms of the Rest House, you really could believe it was a normal, peaceful, social gathering.

The women, who seldom met or left their estates these days, were dressed to the nines, all with hats and gloves and some with the odd parasol as well. Helen sat in the front row, alone except for the two children, looking strangely cut off, and the men were gathered in groups behind the chairs. With the exception of Mike Harrington, all were dressed in Palm Beach suits and might have been discussing the prospects of the forthcoming race; but in fact they were discussing their defences, the merits of various types of wire, and the latest gun to be imported from Australia.

A planter's daughter herself, Sally had found it easier to fit into this setting than Philip had done, although he was sure of himself now.

'Ah, you are all most bountiful lady. But how about the oppressed slaves, I am asking you? Is it that you are seeking to chain us for ever then?'

Sally whipped round at the whispered, venomous, hissing words. A small Tamil confronted her, face and hands ebony against his white, long-sleeved shirt and trousers. Huge eyes rolling and accusing finger pointing, he darted in her direction again, only to fall over a large police boot.

Jogindar Singh, standing on the fringe of the crowd, had seen the incident and stepped forward to trip the man.

The Tamil was shorter than Sally and Jogindar was a very large Sikh. He picked the little man up by the collar of his shirt and held him, struggling, as a mother cat holds a recalcitrant kitten.

'Oh please, Dato, put him down!' The last thing she

wanted was a scene on a day like this.

'He was annoying you, Memsahib. What did he do? What did he say?'

'Well – nothing really. Nothing that means anything. I think he's a bit tiga suku – not all there.'

'I should take him to the police station.'

'Please, no.'

'If it is the Memsahib's wish, I will let him go then.'

Clearly thwarted, Jogindar strode off with great dignity, head and shoulders above most of the crowd, while Ramakrishnan retreated, muttering threats against all comers and Sikhs in particular.

Sally glanced round to see if the incident had been noticed, but it seemed that only the immediate onlookers had paid any attention and the seated spectators were oblivious of what had occurred. Relieved, she greeted the assembled women, gave a casual wave to the men and sat down beside the DO's wife.

'Thank God you've arrived,' Helen whispered, 'I seem to have been here for hours. Government servants' privileges are all very well, but sometimes I feel such a dreadful snob.'

James and Philip, from the far side of the padang, had, in fact, seen Ramakrishnan dart up to Sally – appearing like a diminutive fighting cock from that distance – and the latter had been about to intervene when he saw that the sergeant-major had the matter in hand.

'I'll swear that's the clerk I've just sacked,' James remarked, 'but I thought he'd left the district.'

'Why did you sack him?'

'Bala said he was a trouble-maker and was keen to get rid of him and I'd always accept his word. He was only em-employed on a monthly basis anyway.'

Sally settled into her chair and looked around.

'We were just saying, Sally, dear that your Philip is really a very handsome man.' It was one of the elderly planter's wives who spoke, leaning forward to tap Sally's shoulder as she did so.

She turned, childishly pleased. 'Oh, do you think so?' Then she looked towards the band, who were seated in a crescent, playing light music. Philip and James stood chatting to the bandmaster a little distance away from them. She was so used to him in uniform that she took it for granted, but I suppose he does look good, she thought; still, I wish he were in full dress. Because of the Emergency, the local police were in everyday khaki; only the band was on parade. In their blue and silver sarongs, white shirts and trousers, white webbing and black velvet songkoks, they were a pleasure to the eye. She turned again, 'I don't think he's too bad myself!'

As the two men walked across the padang towards the knot of Europeans, the newly-arrived doctor looked around him as though in a dream. Was it possible that this could be the 1950s and in the midst of an Emergency?

It was the first time he had been stationed in a small district and the atmosphere was so exactly as he had imagined a pre-war district *en fête* to be that it hardly seemed true. The women all decked out in garden-party hats and gloves, those of the correct seniority sitting in the prescribed seats, the men standing behind, more uniformly clad than the one man in uniform.

It amused him to note the two solitary occupants of the front row; government wives, no doubt, who would be joined by their husbands in due course. Two children, offspring of one of them, he supposed, climbed on and over the chairs until their mother scolded and they sat down primly beside her. Stan smiled. Then he saw the other woman and, as she turned, he caught his breath and stopped.

Was it possible? They were within fifty yards of the seats now and there was no mistaking the identities of the two European women who sat together and apart.

'Something wrong?' Don turned, puzzled, to his companion.

'No. I just wanted to digest the scenery, all this colour, before I became involved in polite conversation.'

God, what were the next ten minutes going to be like? Bumping into a casual acquaintance, as he had with Don, had been a welcome surprise, but meeting up with two of the women with whom he had been on such intimate terms as these was a bit shattering. Of course, there had always been the possibility of meeting Sally, ever since he came to Malaya – although he had no idea that she had returned – but to be confronted with a double slice of one's past so unexpectedly was enough to take the wind out of anyone's sails! Helen would probably be all right, but Sally – oh Christ! She might well refuse his hand or make some crushing remark, such as colonial ladies were always supposed to make.

'Say, you sure you're all right? You look quite queer.'

The twangy voice was a welcome intrusion into his thoughts and Stan shook himself, both mentally and physically, before he laughed.

'That's one thing I am not!'

'Yeah. No fear of that. Thought you were going to burst a blood vessel when Salmah came in last night! There was a real beauty when I first came here though. Judas Priest, what a guy!'

'I suppose that is the OCPD, the one in khaki talking to Weatherby?'

'Yeah. Philip Morrison.'

'What's he like?'

'Okay. A bit too good to be true sometimes, but okay. But Jesus, you should have seen the previous bunch – can't complain about these two guys. DO gets a bit "English" on occasions, if you know what I mean.'

'He was very pleasant, but I had the impression he didn't like me much.'

'Foreigners and colonials – bad as each other in his eyes, I guess; that's what I mean.'

'Wonder when he lost his arm.'

'During the war, I guess. He never talks about it.'

'Which one was the bomber pilot?'

Don looked surprised. 'Why, the DO. But how did you know one was?'

'I guessed.'

Stan looked at the two women again and decided that he had procrastinated long enough. Better get it over with. He took a deep breath.

'I suppose we should make a move,' he said.

'Yeah. The men'll start sitting down as soon as the band begins to move.'

Helen drew Sally's attention to the two lounge-suited figures approaching across the grass.

'That must be the new doctor,' she said, 'James said that he'd moved in with Don.'

Sally looked up. The sun was in her eyes; it was difficult to tell whether the newcomer was grey or fair. Then she heard Helen gasp and turned to see the colour drain from her friend's face.

'Oh no,' she whispered. Then, quickly busying herself with Angela's dress, 'The children shouldn't be occupying these seats; I'd better take them back and leave them with Ah Ling.'

Sally was puzzled. True, the men would be sitting down soon, but there were still plenty of empty chairs. Helen had already moved when she heard Donald's voice close by.

'Sally, can I introduce our new MO? Dr Ol – '

'Stan!' Sally, eyes and mouth wide with amazement, stood up abruptly, handbag and gloves falling to the ground. He bent to retrieve them, and by the time he straightened up she had recovered her composure; her face split in an incredulous smile. 'Stan! I don't believe it!'

Stan felt the sweat of relief break out on his forehead, and as he bent over her hand he whispered, 'I hope you have tropical weight PKs for this climate!' Aloud he said, 'Charmed, Mrs Morrison.'

'Oh, Stan, you haven't improved!' Sally felt the hot colour spreading up her neck and put her hands up to her face. So I can still blush, she thought. Good grief, after all these years.

Stan was regarding her with an amused grin and she turned away, embarrassed that she should be the focal point of so many eyes and wished that someone would say something.

Donald came to the rescue. 'Say, do you two know each other?' he asked. 'You know, it's the darndest thing – first I meet this guy and recall getting drunk with him in Edinburgh, and now you too. Who next?'

Who next indeed? Stan looked up to meet the eyes of Helen as she rounded the rows of chairs. James was coming towards them. She gave a little frown and tried to mouth a warning without being seen as she put her hands up to adjust her hat. Bless him, he had understood.

No sign of recognition passed between them as she held out her hand, and Donald continued with the introductions.

'Mrs Weatherby?'

'How do you do?'

James had arrived. No ruddy foreigner was going to kiss *his* wife's hand. He quickly held out his own.

'Ah, Ol – , Ol – , old man. Nice to see you here. I can see that Thom is doing the necessary, but they're about to begin the *Retreat*, you'll have to meet the others after the parade.'

Stan looked at him keenly. Was this *the* famous bomber pilot? The bastard who had given Helen such a bad time? She had never mentioned him losing an eye, nor an arm.

'My first name is Stanislaus,' he said, 'but most people call me Stan, they find it easier.'

'Well, er, Stan, as I remarked before, your English is perfect.'

'Thank you,' Stan inclined his head in a gesture which was not English at all. 'I spent much of the war in England.'

James's eyes narrowed. If he had only been there a minute sooner he would have heard how Helen greeted him.

Stan had turned away and, seating himself beside Sally, asked, 'Is that your husband over there?'

She nodded. 'Yes. Don't you think he's good-looking?'

Stan shrugged. 'What does it matter, Sally, as long as he's kind?'

James stiffened. Sally already. Not backward in coming forward. He looked at Helen, but her eyes were intent on the band, who were stacking their chairs at the edge of the padang, preparatory to beginning the *Retreat*.

The men formed up, the bandmaster took his stand, and Philip walked over towards the chairs.

Sally leaned across Stan to where her husband stood. 'Philip, this is – '

He nodded and motioned her to stand as the band struck up 'The King.'

The band played and the crowd clapped. Marching in intricate patterns, back and forth, in and out, the flash of blue and silver weaving through their own shadows on the grass, they were the only moving things. Soon the last of the sun was glinting across the sea and the bunting waved briskly in the sudden evening breeze.

As Philip marched across the padang and the flag came down, Sally smiled a small, secret smile to herself. How lucky I am, she thought, her mind flowing back to the turbulent affair with Stan and the trials and tribulations before, how lucky I am to have married the man I did. Stan was right; it's more comfortable remaining within one's own race and creed. Not everything had been perfect; they had their rows – tempests, one of Philip's colleagues had called them – and they were both stubborn, but they had a lot else as well. I'm proud of him, she thought, and, taking his arm as soon as he returned, completed the introduction she had attempted at the beginning of the parade.

There was general upheaval as soon as the *Retreat* was over. Most of the planters wanted to return to their estates before it became too dark, the band were putting away their instruments and the crowd drifting away. With a feeling of anticlimax, Sally looked up at the flags hanging sadly down and watched the backviews of the few club-bound Europeans. But Philip was soon tugging at her sleeve.

'Sally, is the room ready for old Jones? I want to settle the band.'

Driving back to the house he asked her about the incident with the Tamil.

She told him. 'It's the same man who spoke to me before. Do you remember? You thought I was imaging it. I suppose he must have been one of Daddy's clerks or something. But he looked too young, and anyway, Daddy was always so good with the labour.'

'James thought it was a clerk he had just sacked.'

'Maybe. Oh well, the world's full of cranks. Let's forget about him. I'll have to hurry if dinner is going to be anything like organised.'

'I think I'll look into it, just the same.'

Helen and James drove home in silence and it was not until they were on the last half-mile that James, who had been staring moodily ahead, asked in a grumpy voice, 'Why didn't you marry him?'

Helen did not take her eyes off the road.

'Marry whom?' she asked.

'That Pole, of course. He is the one, isn't he?'

Could he know? How long had he studied that photograph for, before tearing it into shreds? Not long enough to recall the face, surely? It must just be intuition. She thanked Providence that firstly she was driving and, secondly, that a buffalo should choose that moment to wallow out of the ditch and on to the road. She had to swerve and it gave her a moment's respite.

'Of course not,' she lied firmly, once they were beyond the lumbering beast. 'Don't be so ridiculous, darling.'

Clearly James was not convinced. 'He looked at you as though he knew you,' he grumbled.

'I don't think so.'

'What was the name of your Polish boy friend, anyway?'

Helen said the first name that came into her head, 'Paderewski.'

James raised his eyebrows in disbelief and she went on quickly, before he should comment, 'You can imagine what he had to put up with, with a name like that. Everyone reacted in the same way as you've just done, whenever he tried to reserve a table or anything.'

At last he seemed satisfied and said no more until she changed down to take the hill.

'He seemed pretty familiar with Sally, I thought; actually whispered in her ear when they were introduced, and she went as pink as anything. Funny chap, Philip, he must have seen, but he didn't appear to mind at all.'

'Why should he?'

'Well, I can tell you, if it had been you I'd have been bloody furious.'

Helen sighed. 'You would have had no reason to be. Anyway, as he was RAF, Sally possibly knew him during the war – she was a WAAF, don't forget.'

'Who said he was RAF?'

Oh God, she thought, now I've done it. Aloud she bluffed, 'You did, didn't you? I know someone said he'd been in the RAF.'

Thank God, they were home and there were John and Angela rushing down the steps to meet them.

James was soon fussing over the children, who were cross because they had been sent home for supper before the end of the parade. Helen went into the bedroom to remove her hat and have a quick think. When she emerged she stopped to watch as James, his blind side towards her, swung the children in turn between his legs and over his head. Why can't he be like this always, she wished, and put his futile doubts and jealousies away. If I'd ever given him cause. A great wave of fondness swept over her, but it was tinged with fear.

'That's enough; off you go.'

He clapped each child on the behind and straightened up.

'More, Daddy, more, more,' they chanted.

'That's enough, I said. You'll be sick. Off you go.'

He turned to Helen and smiled. 'Whew, I could do with a drink after that.'

She smiled too, but mainly with relief.

'I got a bottle of wine in the last cold storage order,' she said, 'shall we have it with supper?'

'Good idea; I'll go and decant it now.'

Thank God, she thought, that I refused Sally's invitation.

'Do we dress up?' Philip called from the bath.

'Just ties, I think. I shall wear a long skirt. Thank God the food turned up; I want this to be a nice party to-night.'

'Weatherbys coming?'

'No.'

'James, I suppose.' He stood dripping on the bathroom steps. 'He can be a cussed devil all right. I wonder what gets into him?'

Sally finished putting on her lipstick before she said slowly, 'Helen came nearer to-day to discussing him than she ever has before – I rather imagine she has a pretty sticky time. Of course, he's frantically jealous – did you see how he dashed in to prevent Stan from kissing her hand? Still, I think we should be very tolerant of our James – I'm sure that, besides everything else, he has a lot of pain.'

'You're probably right. Nice chap, that Pole. Stroke of luck your knowing him already; he won't be so shy.'

'My dear,' Sally had starting brushing her hair, 'you don't know the half of it – he's one of my old boy-friends.'

'Oh, indeed?'

'Indeed! Poor man. I was beastly to him and he was such good fun – kind too. He tried to rape me once.'

'And did he succeed?'

'You know he didn't.' She turned to him, her eyes soft in the lamplight, 'You were the first – and I'm glad.'

He came over to put his hands on her shoulders and kiss the top of her head as they looked at each other in the mirror.

'It's a long time ago. Watching you brush your hair just now took me straight back to the night Enrico cut it off. From the pine-woods of Piedmont to the mangroves of Jelang – that sounds rather good, I'm sure one could make something out of it.' He looked at his watch. 'Hurry up, old girl, we're going to be late.'

It was some hours later, long after they had finished the wine, that James rolled over and gently stroked his wife's neck. Outside the rain poured down, but inside they were snug and secret behind their white mesh of fragile security. There is nothing more intimate than a mosquito net, he thought, and pulled Helen towards him.

'I'm terribly glad that Pole isn't the one,' he said softly. 'He's probably a very nice fellow and I've no doubt we shall get on. Thank God he isn't Paderewski though – if he had been, I should have had to request for a transfer. Oh Helen, I've been eaten up with jealousy all afternoon – hating him, hating myself – you've no idea what an awful day it's been.'

He buried his face in her neck and Helen stroked his hair

some time before replying.

'You never have any reason to be jealous, darling,' she said at last. 'You know that.'

She kissed him and caressed him and drew him to her, but at the same time she was thinking that she must get hold of Stan before he and James met again, to explain the lie of the land.

What an extraordinary day it had been.

Stan lay in bed, listening to the rain, and going over in his mind the events of the past twenty-four hours.

The parade to start with: the colour and provincialism – just exactly as he had imagined it. The women's clothes and the small talk – although, to give them their due, much of that covered deeper subjects. He was a stranger amongst them, an unknown quantity still, not to be admitted without reservations to their inner circles. He'd know them in time. But the quite incredible, the extraordinary coincidence of meeting up with two of his old flames in one day! It was strange, thinking back, that of all the affairs he had had in his lifetime, some casual and some not so casual, the two women involved in the least casual of all should be those he had re-encountered that afternoon. Sally had been part of the most emotional phase of his life; Helen of a more tranquil period, a time when his collapse was over and he had been finding himself. He and Helen had never been in love; completely in accord, but never in love. His feelings for Sally had bordered on hysteria. He felt the thin, slightly-ridged scar on the back of his hand and frowned in the dark as he remembered with shame the degrading culmination of that love. He would never show her the scar. He was grateful to her for her reception – he was sure he had detected genuine pleasure in her greeting and the evening had gone smoothly enough. The only reference that had been made to the past had been when the Malay boy was handing him a dish. As he was helping himself, Sally had remarked, 'Do you remember I once said you had Malay hands, Stan? Now you know what I meant.' It was true. He had looked at his hands, then at those of the man serving him, and his hostess had made a remark to Ja'afar. He had been irritated by the arrogant way in which she had taken it for granted that he would not understand and had retaliated by making a quip himself. Donald had grumbled that he seemed to be the only person who had never caught on to the language, and Sally's husband had made some comment on his murky past and everyone had laughed. He and Mike Harrington had discussed mutual acquaintances in Johore, while Sally questioned the band-master on various aspects of the police, and Philip and Don had talked shop for a few minutes, but otherwise the con-versation had been general throughout – he would have to catch up on Sally's history another time. She had been seven-teen – and only just seventeen at that – what was she now? Twenty-five, twenty-six? She had grown up – and so had he.

But what of Helen? That was odd. Obviously her husband was a jealous type, but surely, behaving as she had, was carrying it too far? He tried to recall the name on the news-paper announcement that had upset her that morning, so long ago, in Bombay – he had not heard anyone use his Christian name. Was this the famous bomber pilot? She hadn't talked about him very much, but he remembered him as James. Oh well, perhaps one day soon she would explain and, until then, he would play it her way and pretend they had never met.

The rain had stopped and, putting his thoughts aside, he stretched out and listened for the first onslaught of the bull-frogs to begin and the high whine of the mosquitoes after rain. He was content. Content to be away from urban life, back to a district where the jungle was nearer, the problems smaller – but greater by comparison – it was like becoming a name again after an age as just a number. Ah, there was the first frog; there should be a chorus soon and it would be cooler after the downpour.

Whilst listening for the amphibian choir to get up steam, he heard another sound, a light scratching on his bedroom door.

He smiled – and Sally would have remembered the cynical down-turned corners of his mouth. He had no doubt but that it was Salmah. She had been eyeing him ever since his arrival. Not a dish had been handed nor drink poured out with out a coquettish glance and giggling withdrawal; playing hard to get. Well, she could go on playing as far as he was con-cerned, he was not bent on any chasing game. But, of course, if she were to come to him outright, he'd think about it, give it his due consideration.

The scratching continued. He feigned a groan, a 'just woken up' noise.

'Masok,' he called, in his most sleepy voice.

Salmah came in. She carried a small lamp and there was jasmine in her hair. A short sarong was pulled tight across breasts, ending above the knees.

Stan's eyes opened with interest and appreciation. The soft light showed her flawless, pale-brown skin, the lovely limbs; she held it with good effect to highlight the gleam of her long, black hair.

She stood for a moment, motionless, saying nothing; then she lifted the net and, sitting on the edge of the bed, put out a tentative hand to touch him.

Why not? he thought, and aloud he said, 'Tuck in that net, you're letting the mosquitoes in.'

99. A BUSY DAY FOR THE NEW MO

More than a week had passed since the advent of Stanislaus Olshewski on the Kuala Jelang scene and Helen was growing desperate.

She dared not ring him up, because the telephone exchange listened to all personal conversations and gossip had a nasty habit of reaching the wrong ears.

She thought of confiding in Sally and asking her to speak to Stan, but it seemed too disloyal to James.

What extraordinary twist of fate had brought Stan, of all people, to Kuala Jelang, God alone knew, and He was not being particularly helpful just now.

But in fact it was only a few minutes after these thoughts had been running through her head that she was able to quote the proverb of the ill wind silently to herself.

She had been sitting at the desk, trying hard to write letters, when a high-pitched screech announced the arrival of Ah Ling, the Chinese amah whom they had inherited with the house.

'Look, Mem, look –' Ah Ling dragged her bleeding son in front of her and thrust him forward at Helen. 'Your dog bite my boy.'

It was useless, with her limited vocabulary in Malay and Ah Ling's English, to go into the subject of provocation, but she had seen the little brat throwing stones at Mollie, their young Alsatian bitch, and on two occasions the dog had yelped and the child had been seen running away. Helen had warned Ah Ling that it would be the sack for her and her husband if she caught them or the child maltreating any animal, but this time it suited her to be merciful.

'All right,' she said, 'I take you by car to hospital = doctor inject.' She made the appropriate mime – muttering, 'And I hope it hurts,' to herself – and the child yelled twice as loudly.

Ah Ling looked smug. 'Your dog him bite.' No doubt there would be a great exaggeration of the incident told to all and sundry when they arrived at the hospital.

'She doesn't bite my children,' Helen retorted. 'Go and get ready; I'll ask Tuan for the car.'

It was a God-sent opportunity. Even if she did not have the chance of seeing Stan, she could pass a message to him. She sat down to write a note.

Stan,

Please don't ever let on that we knew each other before. I will try to explain when I can. And please, whatever you do, *don't* mention having been in Transport Command.

H.

PS Don't reply.

She rang up James, explained what had happened and waited for the car.

Helen left the boy with his mother in the small dispensary to have his anti-tetanus jab and went in search of Stan.

Seeing the queue of people waiting to see him, she soon gave it up as a bad job, but in answer to her query a dresser told her. 'The doctor is examining a patient now, but I can ask him to see you next.'

'No, don't bother,' she replied, 'but perhaps you would give him this note.'

The dresser took it and she waited until he came out of the office again and, through the open door, saw Stan smile and hold up a hand in acknowledgment.

Her heart felt light with relief. Now that he had been warned it would not matter what James said to him. Really, this jealousy was ridiculous. but she had come to the conclusion that there was little she could do about it other than try to prevent any incidents.

Stan glanced at the note between patients. So he had guessed right, it was a jealous husband. Whatever did she mean about not mentioning Transport Command? Why did women have to be so melodramatic? Still, he had to admit that Helen had been one of the more sensible ones he had known.

His mind was drifting back briefly, but with pleasure, to that happy fourteen days in Bombay, when the nurse announced the next patient. He looked up to see a Malay PC being wheeled in, blood oozing from a sketchily bandaged wound in his chest. Immediately his thoughts returned to the present.

'Emergency, Doctor,' said the nurse, 'he's just been brought in. The OCPD is here; he says it is a gunshot wound.'

'Ask the OCPD to come in.'

Philip strode in, his jungle green shirt filthy with blood and sweat. His hair was matted and there were deep scratches on his face and arms, but he was cheerful. A good man in a fight, Stan thought.

'Hi, Doc,' he said, 'I'm group O if he needs any blood.'

Stan nodded. 'How did it happen?'

'We flushed a camp – cheeky bastards, not more than half a mile from the main road. We killed three –' his teeth grinned white in his dirty face and Stan thought how long it had been since he too had been able to smile about killing, '– and none of ours.'

He gripped the Malay's shoulder. 'Tahan, Omar, you'll be all right. You have some of my blood, that'll put strength into you!' He imitated the growl of a lion and Omar managed the glimmer of a smile.

While they were talking, Stan and the nurse had been carefully uncovering the wound.

'How did you get him out?' Stan asked.

'Carried him piggy-back.'

'You deserve the VC.'

'Nonsense. He'd have done the same for me. As a matter of fact, my sergeant-major carried me out like that after Tobruk. I only had to get him to the road anyway – I sent a couple of bods ahead to organise some transport.'

Philip watched in silence for a few minutes, then whispered behind his hand, 'Is he going to be okay?'

'I hope so,' Stan replied. The man's face had turned a deathly grey and he saw that he was not as young as he had first thought. 'I may well need that blood though, will you stand by?' Philip nodded. 'Perhaps you'd like a wash – there's a bathroom through there.'

'Thanks, I would. And I'll use your phone too if I may. Don't want Sally to get some garbled message.'

Sally's not done so badly for herself, Stan thought, as he heard Philip ask the telephone operator for his house.

'Nurse, call the senior dresser, please. We'll do the rest under anaesthetic.' He turned to Omar, whose great spaniel eyes were moving from one face to another. 'We're going to put you to sleep,' he explained, 'we have to dig the bullet out and then perhaps we'll give you some blood – make you strong, like the OCPD says.'

Omar smiled.

Hot and dirty as he was, Philip went straight to his office from the small hospital. There he took a sheet of paper and sat for some time staring into space and fingering the square of plaster on his arm.

He went back over the events of the morning, trying to fix them clearly and accurately in his mind. He could not, with any honesty, go as far as to say that Omar had actually saved his life, but he had shown, quite definitely, that he was no coward.

He always found it difficult to put facts of this type on paper. That's what comes of generations of regular soldiers, he thought ruefully, no good at waffle.

The element of surprise was the most difficult to convey. It had not been a planned raid; none of them had expected to stumble on a bandit camp so near civilisation and, for a split second, as they had entered the clearing and taken in the small thatched huts and knot of men sitting down, cleaning their weapons, no one had moved. They, of course, had had the advantage, because their weapons were already in their hands and ready for firing and they had put their fire-power to good use. But it was Omar who had pushed forward and received the only wounds inflicted by the terrorist sentry.

He had not had Omar under him long enough to put in a confidential report on him, but he would very much like to put him up for promotion – not only because of that morning's work – but because of his conduct generally. If he had had a good report from his previous OCPD it would not have been so bad, but when Philip opened his personal file he was horrified to read that he had been labelled cowardly, lazy, untrustworthy, and unfit for promotion.

The official report was easy enough, but it was Omar who was on Philip's mind. You cannot write 'his previous CO appears to have been lousy at handling men,' even if that is your opinion.

He concocted a short synopsis of the incident but was soon

stuck. He was still staring at the sheet of paper when Sally came in.

'Don't you think it's time you came home for a wash and something to eat?' she asked gently. 'It's ages since you left the hospital.'

He looked up at her with gratitude. She had been so much part of every aspect of his life, his work, for so long. He rose from his chair and sat her down in it.

'Here, Sally, have a go at this, will you? I'm flaked.'

She read through what he had written, asked a few questions about the incident and about Omar generally. Then she wrote a couple of concise sentences and ended with, 'When a vacancy exists, I recommend that this constable be considered for promotion.'

He had not mentioned promotion to her, although he knew that she too had a soft spot for Omar.

'You read my mind,' he said. He showed her Omar's file then and added, 'Better seek the CPO's advice in the circumstances, but knowing the old man's penchant for justice, he should be sympathetic. I think I'll ring him now.'

When Philip had finished speaking, the CPO remained silent for a moment and then said thoughtfully, 'I'm sorry. I hadn't realised you'd been sent another problem child. I don't know this man's case, but I do know the OCPD Alor Hijau – hard and intolerant in many ways, but he's a first-class officer. Got the CPM for gallantry in Pahang. Probably been shot up once too often – people become biased, you know. Anyway, put your chap up, with the details, and I'll see what I can do.'

If he had sounded only faintly interested and somewhat non-committal to Philip, it was a good act. In fact, old Wales was delighted.

He had taken a chance with Sharif Ahmat and been proved right. That young man's doing well, he thought, it's time I paid him another visit.

Stan thought he had seen his last patient and was preparing to leave his office when the nurse announced that Detective-Sergeant Lee was outside.

He groaned inwardly. 'If it's about that PC, tell him he's all right.'

But the nurse held her ground. I've already told him that, sir, but he says he's come on a personal matter.'

Stan groaned again. In his comparatively short experience,

he had found out that, when someone sought him out after office hours, it was usually, in the case of a woman, an unwanted pregnancy and, in the case of a man, VD.

'Send him in then.'

He got back into his white coat and began to wash his hands. He was not sure if he had met Sergeant Lee, but he seemed to have had half the police on his hands to-day. He was surprised when the good-looking young man, neatly dressed in civilian clothes, was ushered in.

Chee Min sat on the edge of the indicated chair and smiled shyly. He was not sure how to start.

The doctor looked at him inquiringly. 'Well, Sergeant, what's your trouble?'

Chee Min cleared his throat and straightened his tie, which was already as straight as it could be. Strangely enough, he had not felt half as nervous when he had approached his father.

'I am not coming to you because you are a doctor and I a policeman,' he began, 'but because we are both Catholics.' He paused. 'Please, Doctor, I want your advice.'

Oh God, what is he going to ask? Stan wondered. He looked over Chee Min's shoulder at the blank wall, and in his mind's eye saw the tall, foaming glass of Tiger beer which he had been looking forward to for the past half-hour.

On the spur of the moment, he asked, 'Is it something that must be discussed in the consulting-room, or could we talk about it over a glass of beer?'

He had glanced briefly at his watch; Donald was playing tennis this evening, he would not yet be home.

Chee Min's face relaxed. 'I'd be happy to talk over a beer, sir,' he said.

'Good man. I thought you would with that accent!'

Stan hung up his coat again, told the nurse to lock up, and they both got into his car.

'Ahhh!' Stan smacked his lips as he put down the empty glass. 'Nothing like a cold beer when you're really hot and thirsty. Now, when I get myself a refill, you shall tell me all your troubles.'

He held out a hand, but Chee Min shook his head; he still had more than half a glass left and did not want to become cloudy.

After Stan had heard all about Rose, he counselled, 'Don't be too impatient with your father. You are young. On the other hand, if you are quite sure that she is the girl for you, then I'd go ahead and marry her. But I reserve judgment until I've met the young lady myself – when may I have the pleasure?'

Chee Min noted the time. 'She will just be returning from work – in about half an hour would be a good time.'

'This evening?' Stan had not been quite that enthusiastic. 'Well, why not? Make yourself at home while I have a shower.'

Chee Min listened to the doctor singing while he showered. It sounded sad and in a strange language. It must be awful for him, Chee Min thought, not to have anyone to speak his own language with. In fact, Stan had not spoken a word of Polish for more than a year and would have been surprised to learn the sergeant's thoughts – it did not worry him in the least!

At the main entrance of the squatter settlement the guard came to attention and opened the gate for them to pass.

Chee Min led the way to the Chengs' house. It was the first time Stan had been inside a squatter area and he looked around him with interest. The industry of the Chinese never failed to impress him, and wherever his gaze wandered there was someone, man or woman, hoeing or digging, tending chickens or pigs.

'This is the house, Doctor.'

Stan had almost forgotten the reason for their visit until Chee Min's voice cut into his thoughts. They stopped outside the front door and, in answer to Chee Min's call, Rose came out and Stan noticed how her eyes lit up when she saw who it was.

'Hallo, Vincent,' she greeted him, 'I am glad you have come.'

She looked shyly at Stan and held out her hand, lowering her lids as she did so, and gave a little bow when he was introduced as 'my friend the doctor, who happened to be with me.'

She looked freshly scrubbed and wore a flowered samfoo. Stan liked what he saw. Rose was petite and pretty, but it was not a doll-like prettiness. She had a ready smile and her eyes were lively and intelligent, shining black in a clear, pale skin. Her face, he thought, was unusually strong for her age.

Briefly she introduced her parents, who exchanged polite nods and smiles and retreated into an inner room. Rose dismissed them with a youthfully intolerant, 'They speak neither English nor Malay,' and sat down.

'Vincent has been helping me with my English,' she explained.

'I didn't know that you were called Vincent,' Stan remarked, for want of anything better to say. The visit showed all the signs of becoming sticky.

Chee Min shrugged, 'Sometimes I am called Vincent, sometimes by my Chinese name, Chee Min – it makes no difference, I answer to both.'

Stan listened obediently while Rose read out a passage from *Jane Eyre* and asked for correction of her pronunciation afterwards. Chee Min immediately opened his mouth to speak, but Rose held up her hand, 'No, no. The doctor must correct me,' she said.

'He's not English either,' Chee Min remarked a trifle sulkily, 'but of course he speaks it very well.'

'Thank you,' Stan was amused at the condescension in his tone.

After an hour had passed, Stan said that he must go. It was a genuine excuse; he wanted to see how Omar was getting on. Calling good-bye to the unseen parents and promising to come again, he walked out into the warm night.

'I like your Rose,' he told Chee Min. 'If you father doesn't relent after a month or two, I should marry her anyway – but try and persuade him or your mother to meet her first.'

Chee Min asked to be dropped off at the hospital; picked up his borrowed car and drove back to barracks feeling well pleased with himself.

100. SUPPER FOR THREE

'Anyone at home?'

'Damn,' Sally muttered, straightening up from the flowerbed where she was working. She wiped her earthy hands on the grass and calling, 'Coming,' walked round to the front of the house.

'Oh, Stan, it's you.' She was both surprised and relieved; glad that it was not anyone with whom making conversation would be an effort. 'Come in; I'll just wash my hands.'

He's aged, she thought, as she brushed her hair and put on some lipstick; there were streaks of grey in his fair hair and the habitual expression of cynicism had left his face.

'I came to see if you and your husband would come and have a drink with me at the club.'

'Philip's off on a five-day patrol,' she told him, 'otherwise we would have loved to.'

'He should not have gone out so soon after giving blood.'

Sally shrugged. 'He's tough; pig-headed too.' In fact, she had tried to persuade him not to go.

'And foolish it seems. A pity he's not here though, I wanted to tell him that that PC he brought in, Omar, is making good progress.'

'Is he? Good. Philip's put him up for corporal; it would be awful if he died now. He was a sergeant-major once – did you know?'

'No. But I thought him a little old to be a PC still – he doesn't appear dim.'

Stan was interested and Sally told him Omar's story.

Afterwards he looked at the sky; it was beginning to get dark. 'Well, Sally, how about you coming to the club?' he suggested.

'All right, I'd like to. Give me half an hour to wash and change.'

An hour soon passed while they caught up on each other's news. So much had happened in the years between. For Sally, her time in Italy, her wedding, the baby, and the years since. For Stan, his transfer to Transport Command, D-Day, and the prison camp, then St Andrews and Kathy. He made no mention of his breakdown, nor of Helen.

When she said it was time she left, he urged her to return with him to supper.

'Do Don good,' he said, 'he's such a morose bird – he'd enjoy the company, honestly he would.'

Donald stood awkwardly as Sally came up the steps. He was still in shorts and a rather sweaty shirt, a towel round his neck.

'I hope you don't mind, Don,' she said, for she too felt awkward, 'Stan insisted that I come. Philip's away.'

It was the first time that she had been inside the Forestry bungalow. Her glance took in a typical bachelor establishment. Nondescript curtains and cushion covers, chairs set squarely round the table, the lot resting on a much-weathered coir mat. Odd calendars were tacked up at random and the table was littered with an untidy mass of magazines.

A curtained screen partitioned the verandah from the dining-room and, before she had even sat down, this was pulled aside and Sally was aware of being inspected from head to foot by a pretty Malay girl. She began to wish she had not come. It was a relief when Stan returned with the drinks.

'Well, if you'll excuse me....' Donald indicated his attire and made to leave.

'Please don't bother on my account.'

'Nonsense,' he looked suddenly brighter and took a gulp of his drink, 'I was about to change anyway.'

'Do you know,' Sally turned to Stan as soon as Donald had left the room, 'ever since we came to Kuala Jelang, I've been trying to place Don, and it's suddenly come to me where I've seen him before.'

'Another boy-friend?'

'No. It was in Piccadilly on VE-Night. He was very drunk and insisted on having yet another with me. Kept muttering about his wife and someone who had been killed.'

Stan looked thoughtful and unconsciously fingered the note that he had received from Helen, which was still in his trouser pocket.

'I wouldn't mention it unless you're absolutely sure he won't be upset,' he said, 'not everyone leads such straightforward lives as you and Philip, you know.'

Further discussion was cut short by Donald's return. 'Surprise,' he called, and disappeared in the direction of the kitchen.

There were raised voices at the back of the bungalow and a few moments later the Malay girl flounced in and banged down a third plate on the dining-room table – it remained for Donald to add a knife and fork – glared at Sally, pouted at the men and swept out again.

Donald was grinning from ear to ear. 'Don't know if we'll get anything to eat,' he said, 'but we have this to drink.' He held up a bottle of claret and very studiously drew the cork.

'I don't know which one of you she belongs to,' Sally murmured, 'but I do wish you'd tell her that I already have a husband, or she might put arsenic in my soup!'

'Oh, Salmah – don't take any notice of her; she goes with the house. She's always the same when we bring in an unexpected guest. God alone knows why, it only means frying another egg and opening a larger can of baked beans. I must admit she usually glides though, in a sulky sort of way; this is the first time she's banged and crashed so much, but then it's the first time the guest has been a lady. Say, Sal, can you eat baked beans?'

'I went through the war too, you know!'

'So you did.'

Sally smiled at Salmah and thanked her politely as she was served, but received a corn cob in the lap and a bruise on the ear from the water jug for her pains. Both men glowered and Stan jumped up to fetch a sponge for Sally's dress. Salmah snorted and Sally found it hard not to laugh. She was eaten up with curiosity – the girl was so obviously the mistress of one of them, if not both, but she could hardly ask. She was not, however, left in doubt for long. Going through Stan's bedroom to use the bathroom, she almost tripped over a pair of tiny, high-heeled slippers. A gauze scarf was thrown carelessly over the back of a chair and a flowered sarong, neatly folded, reposed on the pillow next to Stan's checked one. Had they been put there deliberately during the meal, she wondered, or had Stan merely made no attempt to remove them?

The two men rose on her return. Sally looked thoughtfully at Stan, who was pouring out the coffee. There was no sign of Salmah.

'Sally has black, I know,' he remarked, and passed her cup with an intimate smile.

But Sally had just seen the slippers and the scarf; she had no intention of being coy. 'I see you use your eyelashes to as good effect as ever,' she remarked dryly.

'*Touché!*'

They both laughed.

'What's going on?' Don shook his head in a fuddled way. 'All this is lost on me.'

'Just getting my own back,' Sally explained. 'Stan caught me on the hop with a most unfair crack when we first met at the parade – I couldn't think up a suitable retort at the time – although I've thought of several since!'

'So you two really did know each other before?' he looked from one to the other. 'I've a good mind to open the other bottle.'

'As a matter of fact, we've met before too,' Sally chirped; it seemed a good thing to mention it after all, 'but it was only just now that I remembered where and when.'

'Go on!'

'Piccadilly on VE-Night. I supported you to a bar, where you proceeded to become even more drunk than you already were – if that were possible! Not that everyone wasn't pretty high.'

'Go on!' Don said again. He peered at her quizzically, then stood up. 'I remember you now – you were in uniform. Only time I was guilty of fratting with the RAF!' A cunning smile touched his face fleetingly and was gone. 'Yeah, I remember you – wasn't as drunk as you thought I was. Stop me if I'm wrong – and Scout's honour I won't blackmail you – but didn't you tell me a rather odd story about getting married in a Swiss mountain village or something?'

'That's right,' Sally grinned, and he looked relieved.

'Well, I'll be darned! I don't remember a word I said to you though.'

'Nor do I,' she lied, 'you were far too incoherent.'

'Was that Philip who was still with the partisans?'

'It was.'

'Judas Priest! I *will* get the second bottle.'

'You see?' Sally laughed happily when Donald was out of earshot, 'it was all right.'

'I've yet to see him in such a good mood,' Stan replied, 'it needs – ' he was about to say Helen, but checked himself in time, 'Philip, and you'd be able to tie up all your men!'

Plop!

'Ah,' murmured Donald with satisfaction, 'that came out beautifully. Now I shall sit back and drink myself into a stupor and you two can tell me how the air force won the war.'

'But what did you do during the war, Don?' Sally asked.

'Me? What did I do? Well, let me see now. I was trained as a commando, then I went on a super-duper course, I was commissioned, I was a mountain warfare expert and a parachutist, but I'm not sure that I actually *did* anything.'

'Oh, don't be so silly,' Sally teased. If she had known him better she would have heard the underlying bitterness in his voice and stopped. As it was, she merely thought he was being modest. Stan heard it, but made no attempt to stop her; he was hoping that Donald might talk. 'You were with the partisans too – you told me so.'

'I was *with* the partisans certainly.' He appeared to have forgotten what she had said before, or at least did not take her up on it. Stan leaned forward with interest.

'And you had both your legs broken – you told me that too.'

Don nodded assent and refilled his glass.

'Where were the breaks?' Stan asked. It looked as though they might be getting somewhere at last. Broken legs were unlikely to be the cause of his mental attitude, but they might be tied up with it. 'Were you injured on impact?'

Don nodded again and, with a guillotine-like motion of his forearm across the thighs, indicated the approximate place. 'I was very well looked after.'

'Bet you had a jolly pretty nurse!'

He looked at Sally and raised his glass. 'Hm. Here's to her.' Then quite suddenly his expression changed. She thought she had never seen such a look of pain in a human face. 'Can we change the subject, please?'

'I'm sorry, Don. I didn't mean to pry.'

' 'S'all right.' He drained his glass, refilled it and drained it again, and was now holding the empty bottle upside down with an expression of disgust. He went to the cupboard, filled his glass with something else, then, sitting down again, began to hum a maudlin dirge.

Sally glanced at Stan who nodded, and they both got up.

'Good night, Don. Thanks for the supper.'

But he did not hear her. He still gazed straight ahead, his eyes glassing hastily, and continued to hum.

'You see how it is?' Stan remarked, as he helped Sally into the car. 'If only he'd talk, get it off his chest. I'm a good listener, I might be able to help him – I helped you once, you know. I cured your nightmares, didn't I?' She nodded in the dark. 'Only through listening, making you talk about them. If only I could do the same for him. Beyond the fact that he's divorced – and I heard that from my dresser – I know nothing about his private life. He said more to-night than he's ever said before. I was hoping you'd go on – either drag it out of him in the way that women do, or make him lose his temper or something.'

'Thanks!'

He smiled ruefully and gave her arm a slight pinch. 'It wouldn't have hurt you and it might have helped Don. He's terribly bitter about the war – perhaps he was passed over for promotion or something, who knows? Perhaps I'll get to the bottom of it if I'm here long enough. Pity he didn't take on Salmah – a woman might make him relax. As it is, he just gets drunk, night after night, and his staff bear the brunt of it next day.'

Sally made no comment and they drove the rest of the way in silence, each busy with their own thoughts.

Stan stopped the car at the police station. 'Hope you don't mind walking up the steps,' he said, 'after that rain I daren't take the top road – might get stuck.'

'Not at all.' She got out and was starting to say good night when he interrupted her.

'I'll come up,' he said, 'see you to the door. I've got a torch somewhere.'

'Will you? Thanks. I'm terrified of snakes.'

They climbed the long, winding path to the house and stood panting a moment by the front door.

'Philip must be fit,' Stan commented as they reached the top step, 'going up and down all these so many times a day.'

'Yes, he is. Good night, Stan. I did enjoy the evening, although I'm sorry old Donald was upset. Despite your psychology, I'd prefer not to be the cause of his breaking down.'

He made no answer to that, but putting his hands lightly on her shoulders asked, 'May I kiss you good night, Sally? Just for old times' sake?'

'We-ell. I suppose so. Oh, all right.' Demurely she held up a cheek.

Stan's hands slid down from her shoulders and his arms encircled her. Then moving her face with his head, his mouth came down on hers, gentle at first, lingering, then searching, forceful and strong. It was no use, she had to respond. He was kissing her as he had first kissed her nearly ten years before and, like then, she clung, her whole body crying out for him.

For a fleeting second, the temptation of the empty house behind them crept into Sally's mind, to be instantly dismissed. She pushed him away.

'You wicked, sinful creature,' she said, as much to herself as to him, 'go away. And never do that again.'

'I shan't,' he said, 'I never meddle with other men's wives – besides, I like your husband. But I had to, once – I had to know. Good night, Sally.'

'Good night.'

She watched his back view, silhouetted against the shifting torch, descend. With breasts taut and her stomach turning somersaults, she saw the light throw back the pale outline of his blond head, cream slacks, and shirt, as he wended his way through the ferns and under the rain trees, but in her mind she saw him again in blue, walking through the beech trees and fields of Devon. I was a fool, she thought, a prude and a fool; I did neither of us any good and now I shall never know what I missed.

Turning, she pushed the ill-fitting door and went into the house.

Strange, she thought, that the servants did not leave a light for me, then seeing the glow under the bedroom door, presumed that they had put one in there instead. She went in, running her hand through the hair that Stan had just run his hands through and stopped in surprise. Philip was lying in bed, reading.

'Darling,' she gasped, 'you gave me a fright. But I'm glad you're home,' and was pleased to realise that she was. 'But how come?'

'One of the boys went sick – malaria, I think – and sending a couple of men back with him would have left the patrol too short. So we all came back. I had covered the area I most wanted to anyway. Where were you?'

She told him. 'But I rang Ja'afar from the club; he never told me that you were home. Have you had anything to eat?'

'The servants had already gone to bed when I came in, so I had some mee with the boys in the canteen.'

'Good.'

He had already put his book down when she came out of the bathroom, but Sally was not deceived. She lowered the light and crawled under the net and into his arms.

'Love me, Philip,' she demanded, 'love me hard.' Was it imagination or did she detect a glint of amusement in his eyes?

'Of course, my darling, always ready to oblige! But why so earnest?'

For answer she lowered her mouth hard on his. You do not tell your husband when another man's kiss has set you on fire – you let him reap the benefit.

She leaned across him and turned the lamp right out.

As soon as he was clear of the town, Stan stopped the car and lit a cigarette.

He had not meant to kiss Sally like that. He had only intended it to be a friendly peck; but then he could not resist it. The spark was still there all right, in both of them, and it would not take much to ignite it. He looked up at the starlit sky, listening to the frogs croaking in the swamp and the chorus of cicadas in the trees that lined the road, mixing the present with the past. She had not changed much. A little older, perhaps, a little wiser – she should be – but physically much the same.

He sat for a long time, recalling the summer of 1942. Sally singing, Sally crawling under the wire, Sally with headset and plotting-rod, Sally in the punt. He smiled.

A passing car brought him back to the present with a jolt. He looked at his watch. Good God, it was after midnight and there would be the usual stream of patients to cope with from crack of dawn onwards. Well, I've achieved my ambition, he thought with satisfaction, it's the life I wanted. He lit another cigarette and started the engine.

His room was dark, but he knew that Salmah was there.

'Off you go,' he said, 'I'm not in the mood.'

He heard her stir, but there was no reply. Possessive women were something he could not stand, and in these circumstances he was not prepared to put up with it.

'I know you're jealous,' he sighed, 'but you are also stupid, and if you ever behave again as you did this evening, you will have to go. Tuan Thom has no interest in you and we can always find another cook.' Silence. 'Mem Morrison is an old friend of mine and you insulted her. It will serve you right if she complains about you to her husband, the OCPD.'

She was silent as a cat, but he heard the floorboards creak once and a slit of lighter grey appeared as she disappeared through the bathroom door.

He undressed and lay down, noting with irritation the hot patch that she had left. What a bore to have a woman always sharing your bed; thank God he had never married, he thought.

101. FROM EAST TO WEST

The tenth and final stream joins the river

Abdul Karim

It was near the end of 1950 before I returned home again, and then I was there for a long stay.

After completing my training as a driver, I was posted to

Batu Tukul, a station in Johore, and had my first real taste of the Emergency.

It was so bad there that the bandits had even captured one of the stations in our area and held it for several hours. Wah! There were a lot of police killed and I was glad I was a driver and not with a jungle company – not that I was all that safe, as you will see.

I had been taught to drive several different types of vehicle at the Depot, but the whole time I was at Batu Tukul I drove only a jeep. It was quite exciting – better than the war, because then I had been too young and now I can only remember feeling hungry. When the OCPD asked me if I was frightened one day and I said no, he laughed and said that was because I was excited, which was a good thing.

Most of the roads round us were 'red' roads – that meant that there must always be at least two vehicles – and the day I caught it, the second one had broken down and we had just been back to fetch the fifteen-hundredweight to tow it in.

It was on the return journey and, going round a bend that we'd already passed twice that day, that we were ambushed.

'Put your foot down, Karim,' the OCPD, who was sitting beside me, ordered, as he opened up with his carbine and the two PCs in the back with their stens.

As I did so there was a ghastly scream and a body came hurtling down the bank.

'That's one bastard less,' remarked the OCPD, 'get the one that's running, Zainal.' Another burst from behind me and a satisfied, 'Good shooting, man,' as the OCPD fired again himself, told me that Zainal had found his mark.

I don't know how many there were but, just as I thought we were out of it and on to the straight and I was changing back into top, the sound of automatic fire spurted from all around us and I skidded furiously into the ditch.

'Christ, they've got the tyres. Out and run, all of you.'

There was no need to repeat that order. We were out in a flash and running towards the shelter of a pile of timber stacked, waiting for collection, on the side of the road. I shouted as I saw a figure leap to the top of the bank with raised arm.

The next moment the grenade hurtled through the air and I felt the most agonising, burning pain along my right side.

'I've been hit,' I yelled. And yelled again as one of the other PCs flung himself on top of me.

'Try and be quiet; I think they've gone.'

We waited in absolute silence for what seemed an eternity, then the OCPD took off his hat and stuck it on the end of his carbine.

'We'll try the age-old trick,' he said, and raised the hat slowly to the top of the wood pile.

Nothing happened and he motioned Zainal to do the same a little farther along.

All was quiet, and after a short while the OCPD got up and came over to me.

'Now, young Karim, we'd better see how much lead you've stopped.' He began to move me and, hard though I tried not to, I yelled again. 'Good God, it's not a bullet at all; you're impaled.'

The blast from the grenade must have flung me against the pile of logs and a protruding splinter had passed through the flesh between hip-bone and rib cage.

I looked down at the jagged wood emerging from my shirt and the OCPD drew a penknife from his pocket and began cutting the cloth away. By this time my companions were all standing over me and discussing what to do. I felt sick.

'My God, you've been bloody lucky. If only we can get you off it. Grit your teeth and we'll try.'

I did grit my teeth, but the pain was awful. Searing, white-hot, I'd never known such pain.

'Stop, Tuan,' I begged, 'I can't stand it.'

They stood back and the OCPD said, 'The only thing to do is to cut the wood from behind and get you to hospital as you are. It'll be hell, but not as bad as trying to extract it.'

There was an axe in the jeep and Zainal set to work, but the wood was several inches thick at the point where he would have to cut and he was unlikely to manage it in one blow. I shut my eyes and clenched my fists and waited for the worst. He did it though. The OCPD and Ramil held me as Zainal took one terrific swipe, and the next thing I knew I was being held by four men and we were in the back of the fifteen hundredweight.

'He's come to, Tuan.'

Through a haze of pain, I saw the OCPD turn round from the front seat.

'Thank God for that. You'll soon be home, Karim.'

We had had more than our share of luck it seemed. Two terrorists killed and no casualties ourselves, bar me. Both the broken down vehicle and the fifteen hundredweight coming up behind had heard the shooting and the latter had sped to our aid. It was not long before we drew up at the hospital and the Indian dresser was pushing up my sleeve.

A prick, and heavenly oblivion.

That explains why I was at home for a long stay. The splinter had not done any vital damage, but it had earned me some sick leave.

My father had written while I was in hospital and asked if they should arrange my wedding for my next leave and I had replied 'Yes.' It was all right living in the bachelor barracks and eating in the canteen, but I missed my family, and it would be a better life having Rokiah with me.

The preparations for the wedding appeared to have been going on for some weeks before I arrived home. Carpenters were busy in Che Fatimah's house, putting up partitions to provide a separate bedroom and extending the verandah to accommodate the many guests.

It was always the same couple of carpenters who did this job and they knew exactly how much space to leave for the ceremonial bed that went the rounds from one house to another – we usually sleep on mats, which are rolled away during the day-time, but of course this was a special occasion and no wedding would have been complete without the presence of the well-known bed.

I was supposed not to see Rokiah during this time, but we didn't take too much notice of these formalities. She was excited at the thought of leaving the kampong and pestered me for hours on end with questions about station life and what it would be like where we were going. Of course I couldn't tell her, because I had no idea where we would be posted when my leave was up.

The day came when we sat to have our nails hennaed, the contract was signed, and only those parts of the ceremony to be witnessed by the guests remained.

I had been carried to Che Fatimah's house on the shoulders of my bachelor friends and now Rokiah, my bride, and I were seated in state for the long and exhausting bersanding ceremony – the dais and ornate chairs were passed from house to house too, by the way.

I had only had a fleeting glimpse of Rokiah before we were led to our thrones, but I would not have known who it was under so much finery. She was dressed from head to toe in heavy, stiff, purple cloth, interwoven with gold and silver thread, and carried a head-dress of gold filigree, jewels and flowers. Her hands, with their stained fingertips, were hidden under a wealth of rings and bangles, and ears and throat were similarly adorned.

Poor Rokiah. I could not look at her, not even out of the corner of my eye, but I knew she must be wilting. The heat, made worse by the heavy curtains behind, above and to our sides, was suffocating.

When we had discussed adat, our customs, at the Depot, one of the other drivers had once called our marriage ceremony barbarous and I had disagreed with him. After all, there were no difficult rites to perform, no tests of endurance, as I believe they have in some countries. But now I was not so sure. Sitting absolutely motionless for hour upon hour, spread fingers on knees and eyes staring straight ahead, was bad enough for the groom, but for the bride, under her weighty head-dress – no wonder they sometimes fainted and had to be carried out. In the more emancipated communities, the bersanding was being cut to a mere token half-hour or so, but we were still old-fashioned in Pasir Perak and must sit while the guests assembled, chatted, stared at us and tried to make us smile, and then sat down to eat a long and leisurely feast. This could last for hours and usually did.

It seemed an eternity before the guests were being handed the coloured eggs and paper flowers, symbols of fertility, and we were being escorted to our marriage bed.

The bed was decked throughout with yellow silk – colour of royalty – and yellow hangings covered the rough wooden partitions and yellow curtains screened the only window.

I looked at Rokiah, shorn now of her heavy outer garments, as she sat, dazed, on the edge of the bed. Her hair was wet through with perspiration and her skin under its tan was pale with fatigue. Outside, the guests laughed and joked and my bachelor friends shook their tambourines and made ribald jests. How many marriages were consummated on the first night, I wondered, under these conditions?

I loosened Rokiah's tightly coiled hair, then taking her hand, I pushed her gently back on to the yellow pillows and lay down beside her, waiting for the din to cease.

We remained with Che Fatimah until my leave was up, and then I made my way to the district headquarters for a medical check and to find out where I was to be posted.

'Kuala Jelang,' I told Rokiah when I got back. 'The sergeant showed me on the map; it's on the west coast, almost exactly opposite us here.'

I showed her the steamer tickets I had been issued with for the journey and her eyes lit up, for Rokiah loves the sea. We felt sad at leaving Che Fatimah, alone now but for her younger sister, but once we were on board it was difficult to remain downhearted for long.

A stiff breeze made the waves race and the small ship rocked as we headed for the open sea. We were travelling 'deck' and everywhere there were huddles of moaning, sea-sick men and women, spread out on their sleeping-mats and groaning as though their last moments had come.

Not so Rokiah. She stood, laughing into the wind, at the ship's side, her hair coming adrift and clothes whipping against her. She hardly stopped to eat or sleep during the ten days it took us to reach our destination. Dashing ashore the minute the vessel tied up in each port and when at sea plaguing the sailors with endless questions, to say nothing of wanting to dive overboard for a swim each time the ship slowed down. Everything was new, everything exciting. The state capital had impressed her, for she had never been farther than our own district headquarters since she was a baby, but Singapore reduced her to awe-inspired silence.

This was the old Rokiah, best friend of my childhood, and my heart rejoiced that Fate had given her to me for my wife.

Kuala Jelang was quite a large station, District Headquarters, with a European OCPD, two Malay inspectors and a Sikh sergeant-major. There were also several European police lieutenants and numerous other NCOs it seemed, but I was told that I need only worry about those four.

Rokiah became modest and shy again in the presence of so many older married couples and was wont to hide her hands. from which the stain had not yet worn off, whenever she could. I did not have time to worry about these things, because I had to concentrate on learning to drive an unfamiliar vehicle, five tons of it. But I knew that she was homesick. She longed for a beach on which she could walk and swim and get away on her own – she was unused to barrack life.

We were on the coast, but it was all mangrove swamp and river mud. Quite different from the beautiful beaches and fast-running surf to which we were accustomed. But soon there was a different kind of sickness for her to think about, because, although I didn't know it at the time, Rokiah was already carrying our first child.

BOOK III

IN WHICH THE RIVER FLOWS DOWN TO THE SEA

Kuala Jelang

102. THE STREAMS CONVERGE

'So you're the new driver?' It was a statement rather than a question, but Philip had to say something to the young man standing rigidly before him.

'Tuan.'

'Have you driven a GMT before?'

'Not since I left the Depot, Tuan.'

'It hasn't arrived yet, but it should be here within the week. Perhaps the driver who brings it down can take you out in it a few times to get your hand in.'

'Tuan.'

It would be a change driving a vehicle so much larger than a jeep, Karim thought, and went to report to the MT corporal.

Philip watched Karim's retreating back and thought how things had both improved and deteriorated since his own arrival in the district, fourteen months before. On his personal credit side, his Malay was now pretty fluent and he had already passed the first of the prescribed exams ; as far as the station was concerned, they were up to strength bar one inspector, they had the army to call upon – and they never had to call the Gurkhas twice – and now, at last, they were to have an armoured vehicle.

It was the thought of the GMT that brought his thoughts back to the debit side of the page. Seventeen PCs killed – all but three of them in ambushes – and one police lieutenant, the rough-mouthed Moriarty.

Moriarty's death had been a useless tragedy and one that might have been avoided. Suspecting that there were bandits on his estate one night, he had gone out, on his own, to investigate. Why the bloody hell didn't he take some SCs, Philip thought with irritation, certainly not for the first time, or call on us for help. But no, he had to go it alone. And gone he had, with a magazine full in the stomach. Philip had only just dispatched the small parcel containing his George Medal to his mother in Ireland. He was too honest to pretend, even to himself, that he had ever liked the man, but nevertheless, what a bloody waste.

He was still musing on this theme, while he opened the mail, when he heard a car arrive and the guard presenting arms. Oh God, he thought, the CPO's arrived. He grabbed his cap and was at the main entrance by the time the senior officer alighted from his staff car.

'Well, Philip, how goes it? I haven't been down here for months.'

'All right, thank you, sir.'

Grandpa Wales settled into the proferred chair and for the first time Philip thought he looked not only old, but sick.

The Emergency was telling on everyone. Work, work, and more work. Dashing out at a moment's notice, eating and sleeping when one could, always on the alert, never being able to relax. Their social life consisted of dinner-parties in each others' houses and an occasional film at the club, but there was little real relaxation. When the planters and their wives came in they enjoyed themselves, but there was always the thought of the journey home along dark, narrow, lonely roads, eyes glued to the headlamps' beams, hand on the door handle or a gun. Never being able to move in freedom, always escorted. It had become second nature to appreciate the potential hazards of every inch of the road ahead – to such an extent that one planter, on leave, had accelerated and shouted 'Ambush' coming out of Tunbridge Wells! They joked about it, but the menace was always there. For Philip, such dinner dates were an added strain; he fretted if he was away from the station for long and Sally complained that they were always interrupted anyway. She had been stranded on so many estates when he had been called out during the evening, that she had taken to keeping an overnight bag in the car.

'Time you had some local leave, Philip.'

Philip raised his tired eyes to the tired old face before him and smiled. 'I imagine the same goes for you, sir.'

There was no hope of leave and both knew it.

'Let's have your problems then. First?'

'Still the squatters. Pasir Hitam's more or less under control; at least they're guarded and wired in. But we're no further ahead with resettling the Ulu Pandanus crowd and that's where the real trouble lies.'

In fact, Wotherspoon's land had been accepted for the resettlement scheme and plans for wiring and building had been drawn up, but, when members of the Resettlement Committee had come down from Berembang, and James and Philip had thought everything fixed, they had been told there would not be a Resettlement Officer available for another six months. It was frustrating, but only one of the thorns in the police flesh.

The biggest thorn was Wotherspoon himself. He did everything he could to sabotage the police, never dealing with either Philip or the OCPS direct, nor even the CPO, but sneaking up to Kuala Lumpur and going through the back door at HQ level. And when it came to accusations, the planters massed behind him in a solid block. Detestable old man, Philip thought, and yet he felt sorry for him as well. He suspected the other planters – most of whom he got on pretty well with – did not care for him either but, as in most professions, they were not prepared to brook criticism of one of their kind from an outsider.

While the CPO was talking, Philip glanced at the slip of paper, the priorities listed by King, which still remained under a paper weight on his desk. Squatters were still a problem. The timber *kongsis* had been regrouped – he could have become a rich man on the bribes offered by the *towkays* to leave them alone – and poor Donald Thom was confined to his nurseries and the forest edge. The estate defences were under control; some planters co-operating wholeheartedly, and others, like Wotherspoon, a permanent pill. He smiled at the last item on the list, army – lack of, and crossed off the last two words.

'Now for my good news,' Philip looked up at the change of voice. 'I'm sending you another police lieutenant, besides the replacement for Moriarty. A rather staid, elderly type, a bit old for jungle-bashing – you can use him as your assistant if you like.'

'Empire-building, sir?'

'Not really. I shouldn't think you've had much time off during this past year, have you?'

Philip thought. He could not remember when he had last had a day off. His home had become a place where he could dash in for a quick snack and occasionally sleep, Sally his anchorage. It was true that his operational burden had been eased considerably since the arrival of the Gurkhas and Ahmat had become his right-hand man, but a little extra help would not come amiss. He replied, 'No, I haven't. Thank you, sir.'

It was only when they were in the CPO's car, on their way up to the house for lunch, that the old man asked, 'Now what's all this I hear about some Tamil intimidating your wife?'

Now how in Hades could the old man know about that? Jogindar Singh, of course. How strong are wartime ties, Philip reflected, not for the first time. However well he might get to know his OCPS, there would never be the affinity that existed between the sergeant-major and the CPO.

'I wanted to investigate it, but Sally wasn't keen. Still, I did get Lee to make a few inquiries. He'd been one of the district office clerks.'

'Her father was on the Indian Immigration Committee many years ago, you know, the body responsible for bringing the first Tamil and Telegu labour to this country. It could be something to do with that. The originals were untouchables who found a far better life here than in India, but now it's the fashion to decry the previous generation and so many of their children are spouting a lot of nonsense about freedom and chains. It's a pity, because on the whole the Tamils are such a good crowd.'

'She thought it must be something like that. We were going to call him in for questioning, but he seems to have disappeared. Left the district, I hope.'

As far as the rest of the district was concerned, life went on. Emergency or not, personal problems, passions, worries and hates could not be placed in any 'pending' file. Some were busy, some bored, but on all the lives of others impinged.

For James, the Emergency was one long slog and if he did not have the operational commitments of Philip and the police, he was equally overworked, hampered and frustrated on the administrative side.

The Weatherbys took little part in any but duty social functions. Helen would have liked to have had more contact with the outside world and was quite prepared to entertain, but James remained aloof and became so blunt that she was always afraid of what he might say. Only the Morrisons remained real friends, and James actually sought their company.

'Go and ask Sally if she has enough for four,' he would say, 'and we'll provide the booze.' Or, 'What about seeing if Sally and Philip can come and have pot luck to-night?'

'If I were the jealous member of the family, you know I'd be seriously worried about you!' Helen remarked to her friend on one of these occasions.

And indeed Sally did seem to possess the ability to draw James out and make him laugh.

'Thank God I never had to serve under you,' she would often say to him, 'you must have been an absolute bastard!'

James would grin. 'I was – particularly to the WAAF!'

On rare occasions Stan would join them, but then James shut up like the proverbial clam, a surly one at that, and Sally took to inviting him only when the Weatherbys were not going to be present.

Donald had gone on leave and, with the intention that he should return to the same station, had not been replaced. Stan now had the bungalow to himself and Mike Harrington had moved his belongings from the Morrisons' house to his.

Stan had reverted to the habits of his happy days in Johore. He worked hard and spent his evenings studying, reading or occasionally going down to the club. Having mastered Malay, he was now intent on Hakka and enjoyed trying it out whenever he could. The Chinese laughed at him, but they had taken him to their hearts.

Jogindar Singh stood like the rock of Gibraltar, with the tides of the Emergency and police comings and goings washing around him. His wife was pregnant again and he had begun to seek solace elsewhere.

There were one or two young bachelor PCs on whom Jogindar had his eye, but the one who attracted him most was the new driver of the GMT. Karim had fallen into the sergeant-major's web by borrowing money from him shortly after his arrival and Jogindar had intimated that there were other ways to pay his debts. But Karim was terrified and had shied away so violently that Jogindar had laid off, laughing into his beard and increasing the rate of interest at the same time.

Karim had now completely mastered the idiosyncrasies of the GMT and even Philip, who normally had very little good to say for the average police driver, admitted grudgingly that he was pretty good.

The vehicle had arrived one morning, lumbering down the road like some gigantic, prehistoric monster, and all the townsfolk had turned out to stare. And not only the town. Sally had watched from the verandah with Ja'afar, who could say nothing but 'Wah!'

Every off-duty man had followed the OCPD out of the police station to view the monster, and Karim had been the first after Philip to go inside. The driver from Contingent Headquarters had spent half a day refreshing his memory, turning this way and that, going uphill and down. It had been pleasant to be the focal point of attention and he had smiled proudly at Rokiah, standing outside their barrack-room, watching him.

Rokiah too had settled down to barrack life and, if she still had thoughts of home, she kept them to herself.

Omar had mended well. He followed Philip around with soft, adoring, spaniel eyes, and fingered the scar on his chest and his corporal's chevrons with more pride than he had ever fingered his sergeant-major's crown.

He had been accepted. No one asked him for an explanation of his actions in Singapore – if indeed they were interested – no one shunned him.

Jogindar Singh, despite their difference in present rank, began to treat him as an equal and it was not long before Omar mentioned something that had long been on his mind.

'It is indeed strange, Dato, that I should serve under you in the same rank as I served under your father when he was a sergeant-major.' Jogindar looked perplexed. 'Yes, Dato. You would not remember me, and I would not recognise you now, but I was there that day when your father was executed. I saw you walk out to face the Japanese officer. It was a brave act; one that I never could have performed.'

'You were stationed at Mering?' Jogindar asked.

They soon knew each other's histories well and the young Sikh and the elderly Malay not only treated each other with a new respect in their jobs, but became off-duty friends.

Jogindar did not, in fact, look young. Many in the police station would have been amazed if they had known his true age. With his full figure and strong beard, he looked well beyond his years. Only Omar had known him as a boy of nineteen.

Had he but known it, Omar had done some good. Sally, who had pined for so long, had ceased to fret. Omar's sad story had touched her so much that she had felt ashamed of herself and turned her energy to helping other people's babies instead.

A clinic for police families had recently been opened and here, once a week, Sally, with the help of a young nurse on loan from the hospital and occasionally Stan himself, reigned supreme. It was not long before Philip declared that she knew far more about the goings-on amongst the rank and file than he did himself. Sally just smiled, but she knew it was true. Many of the men, as well as their wives, finding her a sympathetic listener, and hoping that what they said would get back to her husband, poured out their problems to her. What they did not know was that she sifted everything that she heard very carefully and only passed on those items which she thought Philip ought to hear.

Ramakrishnan had disappeared. Sally was glad, but both Jogindar and Chee Min were piqued; the former because he felt he had lost face and the latter because he had been thwarted. It was only after the last incident on the padang, which had been witnessed by the OCPD, that he had felt able to come into the open and take some action, but it seemed that Krishnan had done him out of it. And for Chee Min there were other matters weighing on his mind.

Rose had consented to become his wife and now, without the help of his family, he had to arrange everything himself.

It was a pity that he and the Malay inspector had never become friends, for Ahmat too had marriage very much upon his mind and they had far more in common than they knew.

103. AHMAT TAKES A WIFE

Ahmat's wedding was indeed the ordeal he had prophesied.

It was a back-to-front wedding in every sense. Che Puan Sharifa was acting as the bride's mother instead of the bridegroom's, which would have been less incongruous had she already known her future daughter-in-law, and had she approved.

Not that everything was not absolutely correct. Far be it from Ahmat's mother to upset custom by one jot. When Azizah arrived, she treated her with the utmost courtesy and even the chill could be put down to her immense dignity.

Poor Azizah. Ahmat's heart went out to his sophisticated, urban bride when she alighted from the station taxi and was led to his mother's house. She could not have looked more out of place in this rural setting, swaying across the grass in her tight sarong and high-heeled shoes, the sunlight shining down on her lustrous hair. The girls of Daun Chempaka covered their heads when they went out, or at least wore a token selendang thrown casually across their shoulders, but Azizah's head was bare.

Ahmat was too far away to see his mother's expression, but he could imagine it – there would be no expression at all, just a porcelain glaze. But he was not too far away to see that Azizah wore more make-up than usual. He winced. Was she doing it in deliberate defiance of his mother? he wondered.

Uncle Jalil, who stood with him at the entrance to the coffee-shop, barely suppressed a whistle.

'I don't blame you, boy, for not being interested in your cousin Maimounah when that one was around! She's a silly girl anyway,' he dismissed his daughter with a wave of the hand, 'nearly drove me mad, giggling all the time.'

Maimounah had since married; honour was saved and his uncle could afford to be magnanimous, but Ahmat was nonetheless grateful for the easy way in which he had accepted facts.

All the regalia, which had not been used since the wedding of his elder sister a year before the war, had been brought out. Puan Sharifa would not have it said that she considered Azizah second-rate and no trouble was spared.

Ahmat could not criticise his mother, but he was still smarting from her final action the night before.

When their meal was over, she had brought out her jewellery box and laid each item carefully on the table, making two piles. One she had said would be for Ahmat's sisters, in due course; the other would be for his bride, now.

'She will have trumpery stuff no doubt,' she said, 'but only real jewels are worn in this family. I shall instruct her properly before the ceremonies begin.'

Ahmat had thanked her and watched as each item was carefully put away and the lid of the box closed.

Then his mother had put her hands up to her own ears, where the gold filigree pendants had hung for as long as he could remember.

'Nah!' she said, pulling them off and laying them before him on the table. 'She's having you, all I have, she'd better have these as well. And these.' She pulled the rings from her fingers and unfastened a brooch from her kebaya. 'Nah! Take them!'

Ahmat had protested. He could not bear to see the empty holes in his mother's ears, and the kebaya gaping open to show her withered breasts.

'Take them,' she said again and left the room, returning a minute later with her kebaya held together by a large safety pin.

It was the final humiliation.

Somehow Ahmat survived the ceremonies, hardly aware of the girl at his side.

He was relieved to see his mother appearing dressed in her finery and wearing jewellery which he recognised as coming from his sisters' share. He should have known better. Whatever faults she might have, the last thing Puan Sharifa would have done would have been to cause a scene.

He did not speak to Azizah until it was all over and they were aboard the northbound train. He had pleaded the Emergency as an excuse to leave immediately after the bersanding, saying that he had to be on duty the following day.

This was true. He had fixed it before leaving Kuala Jelang. He had gone through what had to be gone through, but he could not have stood the ceremonial putting to bed. Not with his mother looking on.

Thank God for the CTs, he thought, as he stretched out on his sleeper bunk, fully dressed.

In the bunk below Azizah lay, wide-eyed and far from sleep. She was grateful to Mat for sparing her the last ordeal, but she knew already that she was going to miss her urban surroundings.

They arrived at Kuala Lumpur in the early morning, quickly collected her belongings from the left luggage office, where she had deposited them a week before, and boarded the next train north.

They spent that night in Kemuning Rest House, unable to share a room owing to the number of guests. Ahmat was not sorry; he looked forward to spending the first night with his wife under their own roof.

At the police station a tea party had been laid on for them, he knew, to welcome him back with his bride. The OCPD's wife had defied Malay custom and refused to attend herself unless Azizah was there as well.

'I will not come to a party, the only woman among all you men, if the guest of honour can't be there. Really, some of these kampong traditions are too archaic for words – this is

1951,' she had said, and Ahmat realised that his mother was not the only woman who could dig her heels in. And so it had been arranged. Secretly, he was grateful to Sally, although he had pretended to glower at the time. He told Azizah while they were on the last lap of their journey by bus.

Tables had been laid out on the police station padang and Philip and Sally went forward to meet the bridal pair.

It was all rather embarrassing, Ahmat thought, but he enjoyed the admiring looks that were being bestowed upon his wife. A momentary shaft of passion shot through him, as he looked at the sweet cakes and orange crush, at the thought that she was his; the givers of the glances could but admire from a distance, she was his to possess.

'Better put you two women together,' Philip had said, while they were waiting for the newly-weds to arrive. 'We can't impose our customs too much.'

Sally did her best to draw Azizah into conversation, but it was hard going and very much a case of question and answer, the latter usually monosyllabic. She was grateful for the presence of Chee Min on her other side.

'Your turn next,' she said. 'When is it to be?'

'Next month. I have to wait until I'm twenty-one.'

'Gosh!' Sally exclaimed, 'so young and thinking of getting married already. Heavens!'

She, in fact, had been only nineteen and Philip twenty-three when they were married, but one tends to forget these things.

'Will you come to the wedding, Ma'am?'

'Of course. Where will it be?'

'At Kemuning, I think – that's the nearest church – but I haven't spoken to the priest yet.'

'Of course we'd love to come – now that my husband has an assistant, I can afford to make these promises, unless something drastic happens. Let us know if there's anything we can do to help.'

At that moment Philip stood up and a great banging of spoons against teacups brought everyone's attention to him.

How his Malay has improved, Sally thought, as she listened to his speech. I would never have thought it possible a year ago.

The tea-party over, Ahmat led Azizah to their house.

He looked happily at it as the new paint caught the last

rays of the setting sun and the crimson hibiscus flamed.

The house was raised some four feet from the ground. They climbed the steps and kicked off their shoes at the top. Azizah was already across the narrow verandah and about to enter the front door when Ahmat called to her to stop.

'Azizah, wait.' He looked around quickly, but they appeared to be unobserved. He picked her up. 'This is a Western custom; it's supposed to bring good luck.'

Once across the threshold he put her down, but held her close.

'There will be many Western customs for us, Azizah,' he said. 'I do not want you only as a piece of furniture, to cook my meals and bear my children. I want you to be my companion in all things, wholly my wife.'

She said nothing, but released herself and looked around.

'Wait,' Mat said again.

The light was fading, but he had already placed matches beside the lamp. He drew the curtains and lit up. Immediately the room sprang to life. He grinned at her triumphantly; this scene had been rehearsed several times, but without the principal actress.

'How do you like it?' he asked.

It was on the tip of his tongue to tell her that Sally had helped him choose the curtains and cushion covers, but he thought better of it. In fact, he had already painted the house when he had plucked up courage to ask her advice in decorating it. They had been shopping together and then he had had the material made up. It had been fun and all the time he had had this moment in mind.

'Not bad,' she said, 'a bit dull.'

Then she burst into tears.

No one could know what mixed emotions were going through Azizah's head.

An orphan, who could hardly remember her mother and had never even known who her father was, she had never known any home except the room in the Malay Reserve of Kuala Lumpur where she and two other dancers had lodged.

Suddenly she had been parted from all that was familiar; thrown into a kind of life of which she knew nothing. She had had to put up with the icy courtesy of a mother-in-law by whom she knew she was despised; been the focus of attention amongst a crowd of strangers, and now she was alone with this man.

At that moment she would have given anything to be waiting on stage at the Bintang Kilat amusement park.

And yet she was being given a home – something she had never had before. She was wanted, loved, respected, and all by this man whom she thought she had known, but now seemed as strange as the rest.

It was all too much for her.

She sobbed and sobbed, leaving poor Ahmat quite nonplussed, trying to calm her down. A light was weaving across the compound in the direction of the house; unless he succeeded, he was in for an embarrassing few minutes.

'Don't cry any more, Azizah, please,' he begged, looking over her shoulder and through the open door, 'a boy from the canteen will be here in a moment.'

At last she stopped and wiped her eyes. 'I'm sorry, Mat,' she said, 'it's just – '

'I know,' he interrupted. If the wedding had been an ordeal for him, what must it have been for her?

He led her into the tiny kitchen and lit another lamp.

'I haven't bought any pots and pans yet; I thought you'd rather choose your own, so I ordered a meal to be sent over for us from the canteen to-night.'

He rejoiced in her look of pleasure as she fingered a rose-patterned cup.

'These are pretty.' She took down one plate after another and looked at each in turn. 'Did you buy these for me?'

His heart gave a great leap and he would have put his arms round her again if he had not heard the boy at the door. The china too was Sally's choice, but no need to tell Azizah that. She was smiling up at him with her large, adoring eyes, and he would have bought the world for her had he been able to.

'Masok,' he called to the timid knock and watched the boy lay the contents of his tray on the table. He must tip the canteen cook to-morrow, he thought, he had done well.

As soon as the boy had gone, Ahmat pulled a chair out for his wife as he had seen European men do.

'Come,' he said, 'sit down. I'm famished.'

They ate in silence for a while.

'We may have to follow our own customs in public,' he said at length, 'but when we're alone we'll be on equal terms. No waiting on me, you understand? We eat together.'

Azizah only smiled. She was overwhelmed and had not realised until she began to eat how hungry she was.

'You know, Azizah, there are many Western customs for which I do not care; many that to us seem coarse and ill-bred, but there are also many that I admire. I have often been up in the OCPD's house and there the Mem is so free and easy – she is her husband's equal in every way, and yet he still treats her with the courtesy that she deserves. We will be like that when we are on our own. By the way, what did you think of the Mem?'

'All right.'

'You didn't say much to her.'

'I have never spoken to a European woman before.'

Perhaps it was the first warning of the great gulf between them, but Mat paid it no heed, only thinking that she still had much to learn and that he would be her teacher.

He stretched and yawned. The OCPD had said he would not be expected on duty for another couple of days, for which he was thankful. To-morrow they would buy those items still lacking in the house – but that was to-morrow.

'Azizah,' he asked, 'shall we go to bed?'

'What did you think of her?' Philip asked.

'She's the most beautiful thing I've ever seen; I only hope she isn't as dumb as she appears though.'

'Perhaps she was only shy.'

'I hope so. I'm so fond of Mat, I'd hate to see him hurt.'

'Me too. Oh well, they should be well away by now. I hope he finds he's the first.' And so saying, Philip lifted his glass, mentally wishing his inspector and friend all the best, and doubting that he had it.

'Do you think he is?'

'I doubt it.'

But as a matter of fact Mat was.

'Oh Azizah, my darling, my love.' He nuzzled into her neck as the first streaks of dawn were drawn across the sky.

He thought his heart would burst. It was all he had ever hoped for. She had been so expert – the second time as though learning by instinct as they went along.

'Azizah.'

She turned towards him then and smiled. He pulled her head on to his chest, stroking the shining hair and admiring the smooth, pale skin. So peerless, so beautiful, so – he ran out of words and sighed instead.

'Azizah. My wife – at last.'

104. JAMES MAKES A DECISION

It was about this time that James received a letter. The writing was unfamiliar and yet vaguely remembered, as though from someone he had known long ago. There was no address on the back.

He turned to the last page and the signature first. Good God, it wasn't possible. Norman Parkes. He hadn't given him a thought for years. It couldn't be. But it was.

'I hear that you've ditched both the service and the tart,' the letter began. Good old Norman; never one to mince his words.

What was most surprising was that Norman had bought himself a farm – James looked at the address: Mittagong, New South Wales. He laughed out loud to think of the urbane Norman wallowing in cow dung, or whatever it was one was supposed to wallow in on a farm.

He read on. 'I am looking for someone to share my venture and it occurred to me that if this colonial service lark is not long term, you might be interested.'

Now how the hell had Norman traced him? He looked at the envelope again. Air Commodore J. M. Weatherby, DSO, DFC care of the Colonial Office, London. Old Norman really was out of date. Then he looked at the postmark. Penny-pinching bunch, he thought, they would forward it by surface mail. He would most probably have given him up by now and found someone else.

He returned to the letter itself. There was a lot more, mostly details about the farm itself and the amount of capital required.

Me farm? James thought; then thought again. His family had never farmed, but they had always lived in the heart of a farming country; it would not really be such an alien life. He had been thinking more and more recently of asking for a transfer to a less humid territory when his tour was up. But he did not have to stay on in the colonial service at all; he was not yet committed. At the end of the first three years, either he or government could terminate his service; once confirmed it could not be so easily accomplished, unless he were invalided out. Now would be the time to go – if he wanted to.

He picked up the telephone. 'Helen,' he began, 'you'll never guess – oh hell, it's no use over the phone; I'll tell you when I come up.'

For once he did not stay late at the office, but hurried home on the stroke of five.

He waved the letter at Helen but did not give it to her to read. He was still a little sensitive and he'd never told her much about Elsie. The most talented tart in East Anglia, Norman had called her, and been proved right – no man liked to be taken for the ride that he had been.

'An old friend of mine, Norman Parkes, has asked me to go part shares in a farm in Australia. You've never met him – long before your time. He wasn't particularly enamoured with my first wife and, of course, he thinks I'm a lone wolf now. Don't know if he'd have asked me if he knew I had a family in tow.'

'But I have met him,' Helen said quietly, 'on the ship from Capetown. He was one of the ones who warned me off you – I was under the impression that, on the contrary, he was rather pro your wife.'

It was so long ago and she had won in the end, but the hurt and frustration that she had felt at the time reached out over the years.

'Good God. I'd forgotten that. Good old Norman; I expect he was just protecting me. See for yourself.'

He did show her the letter then, tossing it over in a too-casual manner, which did not deceive her for one moment. She smiled as she read.

'What do you think, honey? Would you like to farm?'

'I honestly don't know,' she said slowly, 'and, as you say, the offer might not stand with me and the kids having to be taken into account.'

'I know what you're thinking – that I'm becoming a rolling stone. It's not that, Helen. I like this job well enough; I have had every intention of making it my career, but I don't think I can stand this climate for ever. Australia would be dry.'

'Why don't you write and see if he would still want you, with us as well? Then you can decide.'

That will give us time to hash it out, she thought, disappointed that James should want to change his job again so soon. But it was true about the climate; try as he might, he could not always keep his ulcerated stump away from her view and he had refused to go to Stan to see if anything could be done.

He walked over to the desk and started at once.

'I am married again,' he wrote, 'with two kids – the ATS beauty from the boat – '

He stopped and looked at his wife. She was beautiful still, but her face was becoming lined and the brightness of her hair fading – little wonder that grey streaks were on the increase, it must be hell for her half the time, living with him. She can't have had the happiness she must have expected – and it was his fault, always his fault. He rose quietly, so as not to disturb her, and went to stand behind her.

He stooped to kiss the top of her bent head. 'Do you know, woman, that I love you more than anything else in the world?'

Helen put down her sewing and smiled a sad little smile. When she lifted her eyes to his and spoke, her voice was husky.

'Yes,' she said, 'I believe you do.'

To their surprise, a reply came by return of post.

'Delighted to hear you're happily married at last,' Norman wrote. 'We would have to build a house for you anyway and, taking the best sites, the homesteads would be nearly a mile apart, so our domestic arrangements need not overlap. As a matter of fact, I'm thinking of getting married myself.' And, farther down the page, 'Perhaps your Helen could cope with the bookwork, if you can find someone to look after the kids.'

'What do you think, darling? Even if we don't go, I think I should have to apply for a transfer to another colony – somewhere with a better climate than this.' Before Helen had time to reply, he played his trump card. 'It would mean not being separated from the kids when they reach school age.'

It was the only thing she had against the colonial service as a job; the knowledge that sooner or later the children would have to go home to boarding-school. She dreaded the inevitable separation and he knew it – he dreaded it himself. The fact that he had brought out this apparently casual remark so pat, showed that he must have been thinking out arguments to win her over in advance. Perhaps it would be a good thing, branching out on something quite different from government or service life, and perhaps James would be easier to live with if his health improved.

'When would you have to decide?' she asked at length.

'I'm not sure; I'll have to find out. I should be due for leave any time after the New Year. I presume I would have to give notice during the next two or three months.'

'I don't see how I could cope with the bookwork side though – although I'd like to have an interest in the place other than being just a wife. Angela could, I suppose, start school next year, but John is only three still. I could hardly leave him and I imagine it would mean working in the office.'

'Darling, I've just had the most wonderful – no, the most *bonzer* idea – how about asking old Nannie to come out? She's on her own now; she'd love it.'

Both James's parents had died during the past year and Nannie was indeed on her own. By the time both children had reached school age, she would be getting too old to cope anyway and, if his memory was correct, she had a married sister in Australia somewhere. It really could work out.

'How about it, Helen?'

She had not heard him enthuse so for years.

'All right, darling,' she said, 'if Nannie will come, let's go. We'll make her reply the deciding factor.'

105. A NUPTIAL MASS FOR VINCENT LEE

'How much longer is this going to last?'

'Catholic weddings always take ages. It's only the mixed ones where they whisk the heretics out in a hurry in case they pollute the sacred surroundings!'

The very sophisticated Chinese lady sitting in front of them turned her head slightly in its tall, tight collar and smiled.

Ever since they had driven over to Kemuning for the wedding of Rose and Vincent Lee Chee Min, Sally had wondered who the small woman in the elegant cheongsam could be.

The church was pathetically empty. Mrs. Cheng sat in the front pew of the left-hand side, with a very few Chinese scattered behind her, and the bridegroom's side was worse. When Sally and Philip had arrived only the one woman sat in the front pew and a couple of detectives some way behind. They sat in the second row and wished they could have been farther back.

There was no music, and only a scraping of feet as the few guests rose announced the arrival of the bride.

'She looks perfectly sweet,' Sally remarked.

In her white, Western-style wedding dress, hired, no doubt, from some professional photographer, Rose did look pretty as, smiling nervously, she came down the aisle on her father's arm.

But the surprise came when the best man, who must have been standing behind a pillar, emerged.

'Philip, do look – it's Stan.'

'Good God! Now wherever did Chee Min get to know him?' Philip was beginning to think his detective-sergeant was something of a dark horse.

Then the service began and went on and on and on, and Philip grew bored. He kept looking at his watch until Sally nudged him and shook her head.

'I had no idea it was going to take such hours. I don't like leaving the district for so long.'

'Oh Philip, don't fash! Ahmat's there and you have Cameron now.'

Her remark and the thought of Cameron made him smile and gave him something to think about. The nuptial mass droned on and he sank into a pleasant doze. Cameron was the police lieutenant he had been promised as his assistant, who had arrived a couple of weeks before. He was small, grey and clear of eye and the minute Philip had heard his soft Highland voice, he had accepted him.

Cameron did not hold with what he termed 'larking about in the jungle,' which he considered a job for soldiers. He was a policeman through and through. Philip was still a soldier and it had not taken him more than a couple of days to find out just how ignorant he was! Running a district in the Emergency with his army background was fine, but what would happen when he had to tackle the other side of police work – dealing with crime? Cameron had asked. The Circuit Magistrate visited at regular intervals to hear all cases in the district and he had insisted that Philip should prosecute at the next session.

'It's no use being a soldier, sir; you'll have to pass your law exams before you can be confirmed,' he said. 'I'll teach you as we go along.'

Philip was learning.

A shaft of sunlight piercing a stained-glass window caught his glance and quite suddenly he was overcome with a feeling of immense gratitude to what he called his team.

I have some splendid chaps around me, he thought, how lucky I am with my subordinates. There were one or two police lieutenants whom he would rather not have had, and his second inspector, Zukifli, was pretty useless, but the others – Ahmat and Chee Min, more than mere subordinates, more than just reliable workers; they were friends, people on whom he could count. The sturdy rocks, Cameron and Jogindar; even the old corporal who never left his side, Omar, and Karim, the first decent driver he'd come across in the police, who now drove his jeep when he was not on duty with the GMT.

Perhaps, after all, I should be giving thanks, he thought, instead of fretting about the waste of time. He bowed his head and his wife looked at him in amazement.

'Philip, do you feel all right?'

At that moment, and before he had had time to answer, their attention was arrested by a well-dressed Chinese girl, followed by a young man in a thick, dark suit, who slid into the pew in front of them. She grimaced at the lone occupant and pecked her on the cheek.

'Sorry we're late, Mum.' There was no mistaking the Australian twang.

'Oh Rosalie, I thought you'd never come.'

At last the service was at an end and the bridal pair moved solemnly towards the aisle.

'Hey, Mum, Vin's got himself a doll,' the girl in front remarked, not bothering to lower her voice, 'a living doll!'

At the sound of her voice, Chee Min's head shot up and an expression of such radiant happiness lit his face that Sally felt tears coming into her eyes.

'How ridiculous,' she laughed at herself. 'It's true though, people do cry at weddings.' And looking around, 'I say, Philip, do you realise that, bar Stan, we're the only Europeans here? How awful! I do think that at least the SB type might have come – after all, Kemuning is Circle Headquarters, it isn't as if they had to travel to get here.'

'Both he and the OPCS declined to come to the church, but said they'd be at the reception. Clever bastards!'

'*I* think it's plain bad manners,' she remarked primly.

The reception was held in Kemuning's' only hotel, a crumby place, but the best available. We did better with the mayor's house, Sally was thinking, even if it was a far cry from the traditional white wedding.

Chee Min had borrowed Philip's sword to cut the cake and, by the difficulty he was having, it looked as though he should have borrowed an axe. He had just about given up the battle when an agitated little Chinese, wearing a tall chef's cap, dashed in and indicated that they were trying to cut the wrong tier. Only the bottom layer was actually cake, he pointed out, and showed everybody, as he removed the second and third tiers, that they were only cardboard.

Sally began to giggle. The Chinese were taking it very solemnly, congratulating the cook on his ingenuity, and Philip threw his wife a cross glance as she turned to look out of the window. But the girl called Rosalie caught her eye as she turned and walked over to where she stood, trying to control herself.

'It is comic, isn't it?' she remarked. 'I take it you're Sally.'

Sally at once looked put out and Philip smirked in turn. For all her apparently easy-going ways, she could be on her dignity, as he well knew. Nevertheless, he came to her rescue.

'And you can only be Chee Min's sister,' he said.

'Yeah. We call him Vincent. I'm Rosalie Tan and that's my husband and Mum over there.'

'Chee Min – I mean Vincent – didn't tell us you'd be here. I'm so glad that you are.'

'We sneaked over behind Dad's back, I'm afraid. Mum's supposed to be staying with me in KL, but she came straight here, it's nearer. What do *you* think of this match, Sal?'

Philip had to turn away that time to hide his smile; he could almost feel her wince. But when she spoke her voice was natural enough.

'I honestly don't know. He's very keen on her and she sounds bright. She's certainly a very pretty girl. I hope it works out; I'd like them to be happy.'

'Aw, it'll be okay. Vin's too stubborn – just like Dad. If he'd waited, Dad would have come round in time. Anyway, he's lost his allowance so he'll have to live on his pay now,' she grimaced across the room at her brother, who smiled back; 'that'll teach him!'

'What a relief to kick off my shoes.'

Sally threw them on to the back seat and stretched her toes. It was a relief to be driving home too.

'I hope Chee Min's done the right thing,' Philip remarked, 'you can see his family are upper crust.'

'Doesn't mean a thing,' Sally said tartly. 'Half the rich Chinese here were coolies one generation back. I doubt if their blood is any bluer than the Chengs'.'
'On your dignity still?'
'Not at all. I thought both his mother and sister were extremely nice. Although I must admit, Australian familiarity does take one back a bit – I'm no longer used to it.'
'Tell me, Sal,' he mimicked, 'what did you call your officers' wives behind their back, when you were in the ranks?'
'Our immediate officers didn't have wives – they were women!' She put out her tongue in a gesture that twenty years earlier would have been accompanied by a 'So there.'
'Well? What did you call them?'
'Some we were quite polite about,' she grinned, remembering, 'we had a couple of beauties though – Lezzy Lizzy and Bugger Blight!'
'What charming girls you must have been!'
'We were.'

With the police clinic going full swing, Sally got to know the other ranks' wives far better than she would have done otherwise. And when the clinic session was over each week, she would make a point of calling on Rose Lee, Azizah or Suvindar Kaur.
It did not take her long to come to the conclusion that Chee Min had done well for himself and she became very fond of Rose. Not so Azizah though; try as she would, she could make no headway there.
'I had so hoped to bring her and Rose together,' she complained to Philip. 'Two new brides should have so much in common, especially as in their cases neither was acceptable to the husband's family. But I'm afraid it's hopeless; they're poles apart.'
'Give it up,' Philip advised. 'I've not succeeded with the husbands either. Here am I, doing my best to instil team spirit and yet I know that if I don't tell them both something, the one I haven't spoken to will never find out. Don't Asians ever tell each other anything?'
'I don't think they do, unless they're asked.'
'Well, I find it one of their most infuriating traits.'
Sally shrugged her shoulders; she was used to it from childhood.
One morning, as she was leaving the clinic, Rose called to her from where she was sitting on her verandah, sewing.

'That's pretty,' Sally remarked, picking up the embroidered baby coat, then looked at Rose with interest. 'Not already?'

Rose went into peals of mirth, showing an attractive dimple on either side of her mouth. 'No, Mem, not yet. But one day I shall have a son. I embroider for pleasure. In the evening I sew while Vincent studies. He wants so much to have money enough to buy a car, so I am making him stay in and save. I have persuaded him to buy a motor cycle instead.'

'Good for you.' Sally picked up the tiny jacket again. 'It's beautifully done. That's a convent education for you. I'm sure you could make some money with embroidery like that – not baby clothes, but tablecloths and mats and things.' She was thinking; she could ask around the planters' wives. She would certainly buy something herself, and Helen would. 'Oh, here's your husband coming home. I hadn't realised it was so late.'

'Hello, ma'am.'

'Hello, Vincent. I've just been trying to persuade Rose to have a go at embroidering for money.'

'Say, Rosie, that's a great idea. Hadn't appreciated my allowance till Dad stopped it!'

'According to your sister, it was your own fault!'

'Aw, Rosalie. Still, Dad'll come round one of these days. Especially when we give him a grandson, eh, Rose?'

Once again Rose subsided into a fit of giggles, hand before mouth.

'I must go,' Sally said. 'My husband will be waiting for his lunch.'

'He's still in the office, ma'am.'

'She's nice,' Rose said to Sally's retreating back. 'Just like the European ladies who taught at the convent.'

'Yeah, she's all right. Phil's all right too.'

'Oh, Vincent, you are so familiar,' Rose reproached in her high, staccato tones.

'Who cares? As Snowy White says, sticks and stones may break my bones – that won't' do him any harm. Got any grub fixed?'

106. RAMAKRISHNAN'S NEW JOB

Ramakrishnan had not left the district.

After the humiliating scene on the padang when he had

been shaken like a rat in the jaws of a terrier by that proud and treacherous Sikh, he had lain low and sulked.

It had been bad enough getting the sack – an action which he still considered unfair. After all, was it not his duty to point out to the District Office staff that they were being exploited by the white pigs? Was it not his duty to advise them to ignore government rules and regulations and strike for better wages and less working hours?

That old fool Balasingham had complained. He knew it. A white man's toady if ever there was one. He spat.

It was Maniam, the police CC, who had mentioned that the manager of Bukit Merah Estate was looking for a clerk. But that had been several weeks ago. He had made no friends in Kuala Jelang, there was no one to whom he could turn, no one who was prepared to help. Only one Tamil family had offered him lodging until such time as he could find work, but even they were only doing it for the money he brought in; they would not be sorry to see him go. He knew it.

The only thing he could do was to go to Bukit Merah and find out for himself.

Having made this decision, he took to hanging around the store where most of the estates purchased their supplies. It was a bad road to Bukit Merah, he knew, no vehicles other than estate lorries and the police went along it unless they had to. An estate lorry was therefore his only means of reaching it.

In due course a lorry arrived and Krishnan hitched a ride.

Old Wotherspoon looked at him quizzically. 'How did you know I needed a clerk?' he asked.

Instinctively Krishnan knew better than to say he had heard it from a police clerk. Instead he said, 'I heard it in the store.'

'Why do you want the job?'

'I am after leaving government service, sir, which I could not stand, wishing to revert to former status of estate clerk.'

'Oh?' Wotherspoon's eyebrows rose, 'so you've been an estate clerk before, have you? Which estate?'

Krishnan thought quickly. If he said Tanah Kuning he was trapped. It didn't matter; there were so many estates with similar names.

'Tanah Puteh,' he lied. 'It is in South Johore.'

'Never heard of it.' Which was hardly surprising.

He looked Krishnan keenly up and down, until the latter

began to feel uncomfortable.

'Before I say whether there is a job or not,' he said at length, 'I want you to understand one thing. What goes on on this estate is the business of this estate only and concerns no one outside it. Do you get me?'

The quick brain of Ramakrishnan worked at the double. So the grapevine rumours were true. It was to his advantage.

'You can be trusting me, sir. My mouth is sealed like veritable clam.'

'All right. When can you start?'

'Sir, I am here.'

Krishnan was as good as his word. He kept his mouth shut, but his eyes were everywhere.

The work was simple, but there was one big difference between his work on this estate and that of Tanah Kuning. Here he kept two sets of books. The list of labourers on the payroll was nearly double the number who were actually paid. Similarly with rations; and the indent for office equipment bore no relation to that actually used.

He had been working for less than a month when he had occasion to return to the office one evening. All estate lights were put on and off by a master switch in the manager's bungalow, so he was not surprised to see the lights blazing out from the uncurtained office windows.

He had already started to open the door when he heard the sound of a clacking typewriter and paused.

The sight that met his eyes, as he peeped through the inch-wide crack, caused his hair to stand on end.

A uniformed man sat with his back to the door, typing a stencil on his, Krishnan's typewriter. There was no mistaking the uniform – Krishnan shivered – the pentagonal cloth cap was set firmly on the man's head, and one leg which stuck out from the side of the desk was bound with the type of puttee that only the Chinese wore.

Krishnan began to back and slowly close the door, but as he moved a hand shot out and grabbed his wrist, forcing him inside.

He knew better than to make a sound. He stood, silent, his eyes rolling madly with fright as he observed the second man, who had been watching him but whom he had not seen.

The man sitting at the desk made some remark in Chinese, but the typing never ceased and he did not turn round.

The second man released his grip on Krishnan, but moved to stand with his back against the door. He swung a pistol loosely in his hand.

'Are you the new clerk?'

Krishnan only nodded. He was incapable of speech.

'You have not seen us here to-night. Understand?'

He nodded again.

'We come here often to write our news bulletins. You will never see us.'

This time Krishnan found his tongue.

'But I am your friend,' he said. Then, seeing that the man was unimpressed, 'As far back as 1945 I am trying to join most glorious guerillas in jungle hills.'

The man at the typewriter swung round.

'Which company?' he asked, 'and where?'

'I am not after knowing which company,' Krishnan began to whine. He knew he could not fool with these hard-faced, ruthless men. 'It was in Rembang, Negri-side.'

Why had he said that? He could have bitten off his tongue. Suppose one of them had been at that camp? Suppose one of them had heard him accused of being a Japanese collaborator? Suppose . . . ? But neither of the men looked in the least interested. They spoke together briefly in their own dialect.

Then they looked at him, very straight. 'We shall see whether you are our friend or not,' the man by the door said in Malay. 'Good night.'

He opened the door and pushed Ramakrishnan through it. It was quickly and silently closed again.

Krishnan stood in the blackness, trembling, feeling that there were eyes all about him and wishing he was not wearing his habitual white trousers and shirt.

He had quite forgotten what it was that he had gone to fetch.

107. KUALA JELANG IS HOME

Donald had made a bad mistake. Thinking that he was cured, he had paid sentimental visits to all his wartime haunts. But he was not cured.

The camp in Surrey was still there, used by the TA for their weekly parades. It had not altered much. He walked past the building that had once housed the headquarters of the Canadian Red Cross and had dinner in the small restaurant a stone's throw away that had been one of his favourites. He went up to Scotland and he went to Holland.

And all the time he was alone.

How alone he had not realised before. He made no attempt to seek out old friends and acquaintances, just visited the places where he had known them and looked about.

It was absolutely fatal.

He stood in Piccadilly Circus and gazed at Eros, jostled and pushed by the unheeding crowd. He had been jostled and pushed before – and picked up. It was here that Sally said she remembered him toppling over and she had supported him. That was his friend. Yeah, those were his real friends: Sally and Phil, Stan, James and Helen. He thought with equal affection of his forest rangers, his typist and the clerks, even Salmah.

'Yeah,' he said out loud, 'that's where I belong. Not in this goddam, phoney hub of civilisation.'

I'll think about it over lunch, he thought, weigh the pros and cons.

He ate and thought and put down several beers and by two o'clock he was at the Crown Agents, requesting them to book his passage home.

'Home?' inquired the disinterested clerk.

'Yeah, home,' he had worked himself into a fine, belligerent mood. He spelt it out, 'H-o-m-e. Kuala Jelang, Perangor, Malaya, South-East Asia. Got it?' Then in a more reasonable tone, 'I'm not due back for a couple of months, but I want to be home for Christmas. Okay?'

'As you wish,' the clerk shrugged, 'we're only agents. What address? We'll let you know when we have a booking.'

'I'll be back to-morrow. Save time.' He ignored the raised eyebrow. 'Come on, man, be a pal, you can do it if you want to. Use the phone.'

He went back to his hotel with a lighter heart and settled down to write to Stan.

Strangely enough Stan was pleased. It was not that he was lonely or that he missed Don, but he would be pleased to have him back nevertheless.

'Looks as though you'll have to move back to the Morrisons',' he told Mike Harrington. Not that Mike spent much time there, only the occasional night or two.

'I doubt if it'll be necessary,' he replied. 'I haven't mentioned it, because it's only rumour so far, but I've heard on the grapevine that they may be sending a British company here. We're due for a rest and with any luck we may be relieving the battalion presently in Hong Kong.'

'We'll be sorry to see you go. Does Philip know?'

'Not yet – and neither do the Gurks. Keep it under your hat.'

Stan nodded. Indiscretion had never been one of his vices. 'Let's go down to the club and have a drink. I have a couple of new phrases that I want to try out on my Chinese friends.'

Mike groaned. 'Count me out. Anyway, I have to be off at crack.'

Stan had taken to spending more and more of his free time at the local club. He no longer needed an interpreter when dealing with most of his Chinese patients and frequently told Chee Min that he would be the first to pass his Hakka exams.

'Just as you like,' he said to Mike. 'I won't be late.'

Salmah was waiting for him just inside his bedroom door. She could understand a fair amount of English when she wanted to.

'You going out?' She pouted. 'Always out with Chinese friend.'

'What about it?'

'One day I kill her.'

'Well, you'll find yourself confronting several men! Good night.'

Salmah was becoming a bit of a bore and he often wished that he had never taken her on. Possessiveness was something which had made him avoid marriage – a possesive mistress was too much. He slammed the car door with irritation, forgot it was in gear, choked, and stalled.

'God damn the bloody woman!' he muttered as he restarted the engine. 'Why doesn't Mike have a fling? Take her off my hands now and then?' At that moment he noticed Salmah's shadow advancing along the verandah. He smirked, sat watching for a moment, then said aloud, as he drove off, 'Perhaps he will, perhaps he will.'

The rumour was true. Everyone was sorry to see the Gurkhas go, and the police more than anyone. It was sad seeing the large khaki tents coming down, not to be replaced.

Sally and Helen watched from the verandah of the OCPD's house as the little brown men scurried to and fro, removing every trace of their sojourn there.

A tremendous farewell party had been thrown the night before in the police canteen, and for once the laudatory speeches had been sincere.

Their replacements belonged to an English county regiment and their company commander had decided not to split his men, but to have them all in the one camp at Sungei Belimbing.

'It's his command,' Philip said to Cameron, as they watched the Gurkhas pack, 'but I shall miss not having the army here.'

In fact, they were to miss more than the tents and the presence of the men who had slept in them. Both the new company commander and his second-in-command had quarters at Headquarters and naturally hurried home whenever they could.

'Can't see this new mob ever fitting into the district like the Gurks,' James remarked. He had come to join Philip in saying a last farewell.

The last truck left the police station, full of grinning, smooth-faced little toughs, followed by Mike in his jeep. Both men sighed and, on the hillside above, their wives sighed too. From the door of the hospital office Stan waved as they passed, and turned to watch as the last vehicle sped on its way to a well-earned rest and the bright lights of Hong Kong.

Soon everyone was back at work, but a sad, empty feeling of anti-climax had set in.

108. THE PRICE OF PEACE

'Helen, we're in luck – she's going to come.' James read out the letter from Nannie over the phone.

So now all that remained was to write to Norman and tell him all was set. He put down the receiver and stretched back in his chair, smiling with satisfaction. He had proved to himself that he did not have to stay in a rut; the air force was well out of his system now; he'd mastered another job. In many ways he'd be sorry to leave. There were some good chaps in the colonial service and he had enjoyed his work on the whole. Still, the thought of a dry climate and feeling well for a change was something to look forward to.

He pushed a heap of files to one side and wrote his letter advising the powers that be that he did not wish to be confirmed; then he rang for his clerk.

'Please type it out yourself,' he asked, 'I would not wish the staff to feel that I did not like it here. It's just this,' he indicated his arm and his eye, 'and Bala, would you send round to the shop and see if they have any champagne – two bottles, please – and have it put in my car?'

Balasingham picked up the letter without comment. 'Yes, sir. The OCPD is just arriving, sir.'

'Good. Just the man I want to see.'

He would ask them to supper and the four would celebrate, drink a toast to his and Helen's future.

But Philip was not in a celebrating mood.

'We've got to get a move on with shifting those squatters,' he said without preamble, not giving James a chance to mention his news. 'Has Wotherspoon agreed to the government price yet?'

'He's just hedging,' James admitted, 'although, to be honest, I've had so many other items on my mind, I'd rather shelved it until there was definite news of the Resettlement Officer.'

'We want to have the place cleared and built upon before he arrives,' Philip was terse. 'Take a look at these.'

He threw four photographs on to the desk. Chee Min had taken them the day before and the subject was gruesome.

Five men lay face down, wrists and ankles bound. Each body was horribly mutilated, and even in the black and white prints bruises and bloodstains were clear. Fingers, ears, one hand and two feet could be seen lying separately on the ground.

'Not a pretty sight, are they?'

'Who were they?'

'Residents of Ulu Pandanus who wouldn't, or couldn't, pay their dues.'

James said nothing more, but lifting the telephone receiver asked the operator for Bukit Merah Estate.

After some time a voice told him that the manager was sick.

'Did you tell him it was the DO calling?' he asked the voice. 'Please tell him it's a matter of some urgency.'

There was a long pause before the voice came back. The manager was too sick to speak.

James put the receiver down and looked across at Philip. 'What now?'

'I don't believe he's sick. Stan was there yesterday, dealing with an accidentally wounded SC who couldn't be brought in. Let's ask him.'

James put out his hand to the phone again.

'Do you have Philip with you?' Stan's voice was cautious.

'Yes.'

'In my opinion, the whole trouble is that Wotherspoon's terribly anti-police. He feels that, with a Resettlement Area on his doorstep, there'll be too many of them around – I'm sure that's why he's farting around.'

'Well, why did he make the original offer then?'

'God alone knows.'

James covered the mouthpiece with his hand and repeated the gist to his visitor, who, he could see, was becoming very cross. Then into it, 'Thank you, Stan.'

'He's the only bloody manager who does absolutely nothing for his SCs and goes out of his way to sabotage me. He even wrote a complaint to the CPO, because the SCs had been playing badminton in their off-duty time and had made a mess of the grass. Can you credit it? If there's any more nonsense we'll have to requisition the land, that's all.'

'We can't do that.'

'Why not? Two Gurkhas killed near Ulu Pandanus only last month and now these.' He tapped the photographs. 'Give me one good reason why not.'

'Well, we can, if we *have* to – it's just that I don't like doing things that way.'

'Balls!'

The two men glared at each other across the desk, then Philip turned to go.

James sat down and put his head in his hands. He did not want to ride roughshod over an old man, but he knew he could not put it off any longer. When the Resettlement Committee had gone over the area it had been taken for granted that the land was theirs, and then, quite suddenly, Wotherspoon had jibbed at the government price. It was a fair price; what had happened to make him change his mind?

'Philip,' he called in a quiet voice. The latter turned just as he reached the door. 'I'll go and see him to-morrow. Try and find out what's going on. We may have to requisition, but I'd prefer not if it can be avoided. I think it would be better if you don't come. I'll go alone.'

'Good. I'll give you a police escort.'

He strode out and, as the door swung wildly on its hinges, Balasingham went in.

'Sorry, sir. No champagne in shop.'

James sighed; he'd forgotten all about his request. 'Perhaps it's just as well.'

The DO made little progress with Wotherspoon. The manager invited him to lunch, plied him with drink and talked about every subject under the sun except land. No mention was made of his sickness of the previous day.

By sheer determination, James succeeded finally in turning the conversation round to the Emergency.

Wotherspoon began to whine. The police, he said, were bleeding him white. Didn't they realise the cost of lighting and wire? The labour needed to erect the defences they demanded and the cost of maintenance?

James pointed out gently that other estates had complied.

'Why don't they leave me alone?' The old man moaned in a high-pitched, plaintive voice. 'Why don't they leave me alone?'

'Who?'

Wotherspoon's head jerked up. 'Everybody,' he snarled; 'the whole bloody lot.'

James had done his best to think kindly of the elderly planter; had alienated his fellow-government servants to do so. Now he knew that the police were right. And yet he still felt sorry for him. The old man was so clearly frightened; perhaps he was being intimidated, threatened with the loss of his life or property.

'If you have anything to be uneasy about – after all, this is rather a remote estate – why don't you tell the police? You could seek their protection.' It was a shot in the dark.

The old man's eyes blazed.

'I wouldn't touch them with a barge-pole.' His mouth curled in scorn and he spat on the floor. 'That's what I think of them. That.' He spat again.

James controlled himself with difficulty. He would never have credited the old man with such a gesture.

'We shall have to have that land, Mr Wotherspoon,' he said coldly. 'I'd be grateful if you would finalise the sale now, without further delay.'

'It's out of my hands.' He was looking both triumphant

and crafty now. 'It's up to Head Office to make up their minds. Look, I'll show you the file.'

He called into the outer office and Ramakrishnan contrived to slip the file on to his desk without being seen – he knew James had only one eye.

It was true that Wotherspoon had written to say he felt unable to complete the sale without confirmation by his principals. James passed the letter back. Playing for time, he thought; I should like to know why.

'I shall be glad if you will write to your Head Office, advising them that the land is needed urgently and that we can brook no further delay.'

'Oh, they'll answer soon enough. No hurry. Will you stay to tea?'

James ignored the invitation.

'You do understand, don't you, that under the Emergency Regulations, we have the power to requisition land?'

'You can't do that.'

They were the exact words that he himself had used.

'On the contrary, Mr Wotherspoon, we can.' He got up to go then. 'Please let me have your answer as soon as possible. Thank you for an excellent lunch. Good afternoon.'

There was no reply.

All the way back to Kuala Jelang the problem went round and round in James's mind. It was Wotherspoon who had initiated the sale. Why?

Perhaps, he mused, he did it because, to begin with, he *wanted* to have the police near at hand. The bandits – if indeed he *was* in touch with them – would undoubtedly have found out and maybe they had ordered him to cancel it, or else. Maybe.

It must be grim to be as scared as that. Involuntarily his sympathy went back again to the old man.

'There is someone wishing to see you.'

Ramakrishnan turned to face the labourer who had entered the office on soundless bare feet. His nerves were bad these days. Always the expected hand on the shoulder, the shot in the night.

'Tell him to come in, then.'

'No,' the man looked unhappy, 'he is waiting for you over there.'

Krishnan joined him at the window and the man pointed

to the edge of the rubber. The late afternoon shadows made it difficult to see through the trees. But he knew someone was there. He said nothing to the labourer and went out.

As he had expected, it was the man who had been using his typewriter a couple of months before. He had heard it clacking away many times since then, but had kept away.

He felt sick and his legs were quaking, but by the time he confronted the man, he had succeeded in mustering a bright smile.

'You are sending for yours truly to benefit from my services?' he asked with a small bow.

'The District Officer was here to-day. Why?'

'He was taking luncheon in manager's house and discussing matters of land during afternoon time.'

'What land?' The man took Krishnan by the shoulder and shook him. 'Details.'

Krishnan's eyes rolled frantically. Luckily he had heard the conversation. He repeated it word for word.

'Your information had better be correct.'

The man turned away without another word.

Krishnan could still feel where the fingers had dug into his flesh. He rubbed himself thoughtfully and made his way cautiously back to the office.

The bandits had appeared within a couple of hours of the DO leaving. That meant they must have spies around. Labourers who reported every move, no doubt. Krishnan tried to remember if he had ever said anything detrimental about the terrorists to the tapper who had summoned him; he was a man to whom he had spoken once or twice. He was sure he had not, but he must be careful. They were ruthless men. Perhaps it would be wise to volunteer a little information of his own accord now and then, instead of waiting to be called. Yes, that was a good plan. It should not be difficult. He would see what items of interest he could pick up.

Wotherspoon had finished his solitary evening meal and was still sitting at the dinner-table, reading a book, when the bandits arrived.

It was not the first time, but they still never failed to take him by surprise. He hardened his jaw and waited. He knew what they had come about.

But they were in no hurry.

One man picked up a banana from the table, peeled it

and stuffed it, whole, into his mouth. Wotherspoon watched, fascinated, like a rabbit cornered by a stoat. The other man took a long swig from a bottle of brandy on the sideboard, then walked round, hands in pockets, looking at the pictures on the walls. A third man guarded the door. A fourth would be on the open verandah behind him, he knew.

For several minutes not a word was spoken.

'What did he want?' came at last from the man scrutinising the prints.

Wotherspoon knew better than to hedge. 'He came about the land,' he said.

'What did you tell him?'

'That it was out of my hands. That I could do nothing before I had Head Office's reply. After he had gone, I rang Head Office and asked a friend of mine to make sure the letter was delayed – I made a personal excuse.'

'That was stupid of you. The telephone operator might repeat the conversation.'

'I doubt it. We spoke in French.'

'You expect us to believe that?'

Wotherspoon was tired, but it was the price he paid for peace. He sighed.

'All Englishmen learn French at school,' he said.

The man walked over to the table then and, picking up the bowl of fruit that was the centrepiece, held it at arm's length whilst looking the manager straight in the eye. Then, quite deliberately, he dropped it.

The impact of the china bowl on the tiled floor caused it to break into smithereens. The harder fruit rolled across the tiles, but a slice of ripe papaya splashed and spattered as it hit the hard surface with a most sickening sound. The bandit ground what remained beneath his rubber boot.

'That also can happen to men's bodies,' he said, and his companions laughed.

For many minutes after the terrorists had gone, Wotherspoon remained motionless, apparently reading his book, but he did not turn a page.

He should retire, he told himself, he was well past retiring age. But why the hell should he retire? He had no home; he'd torn his roots out of English soil some thirty years before. *This* was his home, the life he loved. Why the bloody hell should he retire? It was all the fault of the police. Officious young men. First King and now this creature Morrison. Just as bad. Young enough to be his sons. Less than half his age. That had been the trouble in the first place – that bouncy young man, typical product of a grammar school, he supposed, had had the cheek to order him, yes, *order* him, to do this and that. And this one was worse. Wire here, lights there, kubus somewhere else. The SCs had to be molly-coddled, nursed. He wasn't going to put up with that and so he had refused to co-operate on principle.

And then had come the terrorists. Not uniformed men; well dressed, smooth. He was not on the side of the government, so he must be on theirs. They had spouted a lot of Communist propaganda, straight from Peking, and he had told them politely that he wasn't interested.

The murder of the Kangani was the next step and the realisation that most of the labour had been intimidated to such an extent that they were helping the bandits whether they liked it or not.

Then they had come again. The same men, but this time they were wearing uniform.

All they asked was a little co-operation, they said, a little rice, the occasional use of a typewriter. He need not see. All he need do was ignore them and he would be left in peace.

The temptation was too great and he had agreed.

That had been the first stage, then came the requests – requests? Don't be such a bloody fool, he told himself. Demands. Demands for more rice, more tinned food, office equipment, clothing, medicines.

When he thought he would no longer be under observation, he got up and poured himself a large tot. He swallowed three sleeping pills and turned out the light.

'Forgive me, Sally, for bursting in like this.' It was James, coming through the back way, torch in hand.

'That's all right. It's early yet, not ten o'clock.'

He smiled and squeezed her arm. 'Do you think I might have just five minutes with Philip, on my own?'

'Of course.'

James knew, or suspected, that Philip had no secrets from his wife, but he could not bring himself to admit to being wrong with a third person present.

'Philip, I'm sorry. I only got back from Bukit Merah at six o'clock and I've been thinking about it ever since. You were right.'

'I'll get you a drink.'

When they were both sitting down, he repeated the conversation of the afternoon.

'I think I was pretty blunt,' he said, 'let's give him until the end of the month, then we'll take it up with the DWEC if necessary.'

109. DOMESTIC STRIFE

Ahmat was having a bad time.

Azizah could hardly be bothered to conceal her boredom and, after a while, made no effort at all.

What really infuriated him was that she would not try to amuse herself or even keep herself occupied. The food that was thrown at him, on plates none too clean, was almost inedible. He had eaten far better as a bachelor in the canteen.

'Why don't you ask one of the other wives to teach you how to cook?' he asked, but Azizah only shrugged her shoulders and left the room. It was always the same. He had given up trying.

The house, the little house that he had taken so much trouble to beautify for her, was a mess. Dust accumulated, nothing was ever put away. Glass rings appeared on the furniture which he had polished so carefully, stains on the floor and cushion covers, and chips in cups and plates.

The greatest disappointment of all, though, was her complete lack of interest in his work.

That night they had lain in the Lake Gardens, talking about the future, all Azizah's comments had been constructive and intelligent. They had given him false hope. He had tried telling her where he was going, what he was doing and repeating the more amusing items of station gossip, but she paid no attention, often walking away while he was still speaking.

Religiously, he took her to every film at the club, but on one occasion, when he had been leaving on an operation at first light on the Monday morning, he had cried off, saying that he would be too tired. The scene that followed was the first of many and something that he came to dread.

He had returned in the afternoon to find her sitting on the verandah, staring into space – her usual attitude these days. The house had not been touched and the saucepan that she had thrown at him the night before was on the floor where it had fallen, its contents hardened and caked on the wall behind.

He looked at her with disgust.

'It's time you grew up,' he scolded, 'I'll give you anything I can, but it's up to you at least to feed me and keep my home in some semblance of order.'

She still sat, clothes rumpled and hair awry, and he saw the tears welling up in her eyes.

At once he was cross with himself, regretting his words.

'Azizah, please don't cry. I only meant . . . '

She turned her huge, great eyes on him then, the tears slowly trickling down her cheeks, and held up her arms to him in a gesture of appeal.

He was tired and hot, but he led her to their bed and she had pulled him down.

'You've no more duty to-day, Mat,' she pleaded. 'Stay with me.'

He had stayed, and after they had finished making love he cleaned up the house and took her into the town for a meal. But he was worried.

There was only the one thing that he could not complain about – Azizah in bed. Whatever the day had been like, however awful the food and slovenly-looking the house, whatever scene there had been or reception he had received, when he sank into her perfumed, smooth embrace, he was lost.

But lost only until the daylight came.

Since the arrival of Cameron, he had been going out with the OCPD more and more and this Azizah seemed to resent.

'You give him more time than me,' she pouted, 'you never used to be away so much.'

'But, Azizah, be reasonable. He's my boss. I'm only doing my job. His wife is left alone too – I'm sure she isn't always complaining.'

'Who cares about her? She has servants, she doesn't have to cook or clean the house. What does she do all day?'

'And what do *you* do. You can't cook and you won't learn. The house is filthy and you no longer keep yourself as you did – you're becoming a slut.'

A bottle of orange crush had narrowly missed his ear, breaking on the wall behind and saturating a chair in a fizzing orange cascade.

Ahmat jumped up, temper aroused.

'Look what you've done. It'll stain,' he cried. It was still his beloved house. 'Fetch a cloth and some water, quick.'

Azizah did not move. 'Do as you're told.'

'You can't order me about. I'm not one of your PCs,' she screamed at him.

Mat took the dripping cover to the sink and did his best, but it was a woman's job. His hands were clumsy and he made, if possible, a worse mess. Frustration welled up in him like a cork and he flung the sticky cloth to the floor and strode out.

Azizah was already weeping, the usual routine, but this time his patience was exhausted. He went off to the canteen for a meal and, ignoring her open arms on his return, slept on a mat in the living-room. He had very nearly had enough.

In the morning she was contrite and when he returned at midday she had a passable meal waiting. She did not apologise and nor did he, but they were at peace with each other. Perhaps it is the turning point, he hoped; perhaps at last she has settled down, seen sense.

That evening the house was clean and she greeted him in a newly-pressed sarong and kebaya and freshly-done hair. A jasmine blossom was pinned a little above her ear and he smelt the scent as soon as he entered the house. This was the Azizah that he used to know.

He hurried under the shower and changed; white slacks, white shirt and police tie.

She noticed the tie at once. 'Oh Mat,' she said, 'I'm glad you haven't forgotten there's a film show at the club tonight.'

'Of course I hadn't. I'm dressed up to escort my beautiful wife.'

Azizah preened. 'I thought we might eat out first.'

It was near the end of the month. Mat frowned.

'I'm afraid my pay won't stretch to always eating out. I'm sorry, Azizah, I haven't enough this month; we'll have to eat at home.'

Immediately her face assumed sulky lines and it was at that moment that he saw the one bare cushion, standing out starkly from the rest.

'What happened to the cushion cover?' he asked. 'Wouldn't the stain come out?'

'I don't know.' She shrugged and adjusted the flower in her hair. 'I threw it away.'

'Threw it away?' He could hardly believe his ears. His family had never been poor, but there had never been any waste either. 'Why?'

She shrugged again and he had to stifle an impulse to hit her.

'I don't care for them much anyway.'

'When I think of all the trouble I took and the help from the Mem,' Mat flared, 'it makes my blood boil. What do you want? Would you have preferred to end your days as a raddled prostitute on the ronggeng stage? That's what you would have become.' She raised her arm to hit him, but he caught her wrist in mid air. 'Where did you throw it? Fetch it back. I'm sick and tired of all this waste.'

For answer Azizah hissed at him, 'What do you mean by help from the Mem?'

'She spent a lot of time helping me choose things, in getting the house spick and span – and all for you. She was prepared to be your friend. I believe she still is.'

'Stuck-up bitch. I don't want her for a friend.'

She seized the nearest cushion and ripped the cover off, then, picking up a pair of scissors from the table in front of her and looking her husband straight in the eye, she proceeded to cut it systematically into shreds.

For a moment Ahmat was so astounded that he could not stop her, and by the time he came to his senses she was in the kitchen.

'Did she choose these too?'

She held up one of the rose-patterned plates. One glance at his face was enough. The plate crashed to the floor, then another and another.

He was through the kitchen door in one stride and Azizah began to scream.

Jogindar Singh walked outside his quarters nearby and smiled to himself.

The crashing crockery had been heard all over the compound and heads were popping out of every barrack-room.

Serves him right, Jogindar thought – and he was not the only one – for being so soft. He should have dealt firmly with her from the start.

There was not a person in the whole of the barracks who did not hope that Ahmat was beating his wife. But they would have been disappointed. After a few minutes the screaming stopped and Ahmat walked down his front steps. Heads retreated and doors quickly closed.

'One meal needed for Inche Mat,' called the canteen boy to the cook.

The motley crowd surged in and out of and around the club and soon the weekly film show was ready to begin.

Philip had wanted to speak to Mat and had been sure, so he thought, of finding him there. But the lights were already being dowsed and he had not turned up. Before complete darkness descended, he walked over to where Rose and Chee Min were sitting.

'Where's Inche Mat?' he asked. 'He never misses a film.'

Both faces went as blank as only Chinese faces can and Chee Min's eyes were quite opaque.

'Having a little wife trouble, I believe, sir,' he said. He could not help sounding a mite smug.

Philip snorted. Was Ahmat really under the impression that no one knew? He must be.

'Again?'

At that moment something was hurled through one of the side windows and bounced on a shoulder. Chee Min was facing that way.

'Hand-grenade!' he yelled. But the warning was superfluous; the Emergency had been on long enough for everyone present to know quite well what it was.

Bodies hurtled through windows and doors and more people were crushed and injured in the ensuing stampede than by the explosion which followed.

It seemed to James that every woman in the building must have screamed. He jumped on to a chair in front of the screen and shouted, 'Stay put. Give the doctor some space.'

But if anyone heard him they took no notice. Only the police and a couple of planters remained calm, trying to prevent worse tragedy.

Stan was already examining the wounded and soon the ambulance arrived. 'Help me,' he called to Sally, as he lifted a young woman from the floor and passed Helen her child. 'I don't know what damage there is, but try and keep her still.' He left her with the writhing woman, but was soon back with a syringe. Once she was out they lifted her on to a stretcher, then he straightened up. A gruesome pile lay to the side, but the last of the injured was being carried out 'Well, that's the last. It'll be a full ward to-night.' Then he followed the ambulance.

James, Helen and Sally looked at each other and at the mess.

Besides the actual damage caused by the grenade, chairs had been overturned and smashed, empty bottles rolled in every direction and a mass of broken glass and peanuts littered the floor.

'It could have been worse,' James said. 'Only three dead. Bloody lucky Lee saw it bounce.'

Chee Min had gone off with Philip to give chase, although the culprit would almost certainly have disappeared amongst the milling throng outside. Rose stood nearby, white-faced and looking very young.

'This is Mrs Lee,' Sally said. 'I think I'll take her home.'

'Take Helen too,' James suggested. 'I'll stay here and supervise some clearing up.'

The three women left him and climbed into the Morrisons' car. Perhaps it would have made Azizah happy to know they had not seen the film.

110. A RED SQUARE IN THE WINDOW

Having once made up his mind to co-operate with the terrorists, Ramakrishnan lost no time.

On the first occasion that he saw the tapper who had summoned him to the presence of the bandit that day, he beckoned him over and told him that he wanted to meet the same man again.

It was not until the following afternoon that the labourer told him the man was in the same place and to hurry, they did not like to be kept waiting. There was something insolent and familiar in the man's manner that Krishnan did not like.

There were two men waiting in the rubber, both in uniform.

'Well?' asked the one whom Krishnan already knew. 'Why have you sought us out?'

'Master, I have been giving matter much urgent thought and am coming to conclusion that I can render much valuable aid to Communist cause.'

'Such as?'

'I am listening to all telephone conversations in office. I can tell you when arrangements are being made for police or other running dogs to visit estate. You will know then when to set ambushes on road.'

The bandits appeared to ignore him and spoke together in Chinese for a good ten minutes.

Then, 'Why do you do this?'

'Master, I have always been holding most deadly hatred of

white pigs and most especially the police I am not liking at all. Only a few months ago, one bearded Bengali policeman shook me in most humiliating manner in public place, causing much loss of face and honour both.'

Again they spoke together.

'We haven't enough men free to man an ambush position the whole time, only on certain days. We would require the information in advance. Here, take this.' It was a small red square of cloth. 'Stick it in your office window when you have information to impart; then come and wait here.'

'But the manager might– '

'The manager . . . ' Both men laughed scornfully.

It was then that Krishnan made the mistake of showing off.

'I have been clerk in District Office, remember,' he said. 'I am knowing that District Officer keeps engagement pad on desk, telling of all visits and items of importance for following month. I have seen him writing in it often.'

At that some interest was shown.

'Do all government officers keep such a pad?'

'Oh, most verily,' Krishnan stated, without having the faintest idea, 'it is of a certainty.'

The terrorists spoke together again, then, with a sign of dismissal, they walked away.

It was a fortnight before Krishnan stuck the red square in the window and went off to the plantation edge to wait. He was well pleased with himself.

'I have news of informations most advanced,' he announced proudly. 'To-day I am hearing invitement of doctor by manager to come and stay. At Hari Raya he is coming, two months over from now.' He beamed. 'Ambush positions can be arranged in most plentiful time.'

The bandits were not impressed.

'No point in ambushing the doctor, he travels unarmed,' they said. 'You had better do better than that.'

Crestfallen, Krishnan watched them saunter away. He thought he had done very well.

Wotherspoon had asked Stan to come and spend a few days with him on impulse. Nice chap, he thought, and he had said that he had never spent more than a few hours on a rubber estate.

'Come for Hari Raya,' the planter had suggested. 'My

Javanese labour usually put on quite a show.'

That was bait, of course; most of his labour was Tamil, but he did have a few Javanese and he might persuade them to dance a bit.

He would have to square his khaki-clad friends, of course, but that should not be difficult, if they could be persuaded to listen to sense. It would look more normal, he would point out, if he were to have a guest to stay. If friends were kept away from the estate, people would become suspicious.

Not that he had many friends. He had always been a lone wolf, seldom mingling with the crowd.

But he was lonely sometimes. He admitted that. Yes, it would be pleasant to have European company for a few days.

He wandered out of his office and up the drive to his bungalow. It was a good house; he had supervised the building himself before the war and he had been one of the lucky ones; very little stuff had been touched.

He had been happy enough until this confounded Emergency broke out. If he had wanted company he could always go down to the club, or to Kemuning, even to Berambang or Kuala Lumpur; he was very much his own boss. His so-called Head Office were really only agents; they left him alone. But he had not sought company often; he was content with his pictures and his books and his garden. His hobby for many years had been trying to raise rare plants. He had taken immense pleasure in growing flowers and trees that, according to all the experts, could not be grown in the Malayan climate.

He walked round the garden once before going inside.

The mango tree was in full foliage; he looked up at it with pride – it had come over from the Philippines some twenty years before and produced the most delicious fruit.

Then his eyes narrowed. Those damned SCs. They were throwing sticks up into the tree, trying to knock down the still green fruit.

'Stop that,' he yelled. 'Get out of my garden, damn you. Stick to your own quarters; I won't have you here.'

By the time he reached the house his whole body was shaking with fury.

They had come, ruining his grounds and taking away his privacy. A bush had to be cut down because it would give access over the wire, a flower-bed was trampled on, marked as being a good place for a light. Well, the bush had not been cut down, nor had the wire gone up – it was there in rolls still, in the store, but it had not gone up. Nor had the light. He had lived amongst Asians long enough to know that, if you hedge long enough, people turn their attention elsewhere – or so he hoped.

All he asked was to be left alone. To plant what he liked where he liked and to have his privacy undisturbed.

His attitude might cost lives, he had been told. Well, so what? No one worried about *his* life. He had had the SCs thrust upon him; he didn't want them, hadn't asked for them. They were a confounded nuisance. Let them ambush all the government wallahs who came up his road. Who cared? Wish they'd kill that bloody OCPD, and the police lieutenant who kept snooping round the SCs. Well, one *had* been killed fairly recently and not so far away at that. Served him right.

He had a good mind to forbid government servants from entering the estate. Put up a barricade – get the bandits to do it for him. Why not?

That Pole was government. He had a good mind to cancel his invitation. Well, he'd see. He'd think about it.

111. A SEASON OF FESTIVALS: CHRISTMAS AND NEW YEAR

Donald arrived back from leave in good time and announced that the seasonal festivities could now begin!

Sally took a lot of trouble with their Christmas dinner that year. The previous year it had been the Weatherbys' do, this year it was their turn. Ja'afar had done his best to persuade her to make it a big party; to ask as many of the planters and their wives as the house would hold, but she was determined to keep it small and have only what she called 'the hill.' Don and Stan they might meet again, but even if they were posted back to the same district after leave, which was unlikely, they would not see the Weatherbys again, unless they too should end up in Australia.

'I congratulate you on achieving an oasis of civilisation in the wilderness,' Stan said, as he bowed over Sally's hand.

You're still very smooth, she thought, but in fact he meant it. He and Donald stood admiring the table, waiting for the Weatherbys to arrive. The silver and glass had been polished that day and gleamed softly in the pale candlelight. Pink and white Honolulu creeper cascaded out of a central bowl to mingle with tinsel and touch the lace table-mats.

Truth to tell, Sally herself was pleased with the effect, but apprehensive. 'If only we're allowed to enjoy the evening in peace,' she said wistfully. 'We've never yet been left alone on Christmas Day.'

Later she was to say, 'Well, at least they let us reach the coffee stage this year.'

The turkey and plum pudding had been well washed down and they were just making room amongst the debris of nuts and spent crackers for their coffee cups when the telephone rang.

Philip got up. 'Right,' he said, after the voice at the other end had crackled for a time, 'I'll come now.'

'I knew it was too good to last.' Sally tried not to sound plaintive but was unsuccessful. She had started to get up, but Philip motioned her to sit down again.

'I don't want to break up the party,' he said, 'and there's no great rush; it'll take a few minutes to root out the ferry-man.'

He went into the bedroom, followed by Ja'afar with a hissing pressure lamp.

'I hate those things,' Helen remarked, 'but there's no denying that they do give a good light.'

No one could think of anything else to say and Sally suggested that they should take their coffee and liqueurs over to the more comfortable chairs. Philip joined them in a moment, sitting to gulp down his coffee while he laced his jungle boots.

'Rather a garbled message,' he told them. 'Two Europeans reported killed on the other side of the river. I can't think who they can be. There's only one estate there and the manager's on leave. There should be only one police lieutenant in the area – I'll have to go and find out.'

'But couldn't the army – ' Sally began. But he shook his head.

'Both the company commander and his two i/c are spending Christmas with their families. There must be a duty officer, but it's quicker to go myself.'

'Well, I do think – '

'I used to come home to you when I was in the army,' Philip interrupted, and Sally looked squashed.

He picked up his beret and torch, pecked his wife on the cheek, and ran down the steps.

'Well, if that isn't the most tolerant guy,' Don remarked.

'He sure settled your hash, Sal!'

Sally made an effort to laugh. 'I do try not to mind, but it's reached the state where, if the phone doesn't ring for a couple of hours, I begin to think there's something wrong! Half the time it's false alarms, but of course the time he doesn't go it won't be – I can see his point really. You know, one evening, about this time last year, a rather panicky planter rang up to say he was surrounded; that his wire was being charged. Philip and Mike both turned out with every available man, only to find it was a herd of cows!'

The night drew on; they were all tired. Carols from the radio had long since ceased. Sally persuaded Helen and James to go home; she knew that Helen had a children's party on her hands the following day.

Stan and Don had already said that they intended staying.

James actually kissed Sally on the cheek and everyone let out such a whoop of surprise that the tension was broken at last. Conversation between the three became easier and it was not long afterwards that lights were seen on the river.

The sound of the ferry chugging across was quite clear in the still night and soon an engine started up below and a jeep drove off in the direction of the pier.

'Shouldn't be long now –' before Sally had finished her sentence the phone rang. It was Philip.

'I'm back, Sally. Two soldiers, I''m afraid. If Stan's still there, would you ask him if he'd come down?'

Sally and Don watched from the verandah as the jeep and troop-carrier drew up. Then she turned away and sat down.

'I'm sorry, Don. I can't bear to watch. I'm too afraid that one day it might be Philip's body being lifted from that van.'

Donald gave her a sympathetic look, but he was too engrossed with what was going on down below to pay her much attention. Two blanket-covered forms were being carried from the troop-carrier and into the police station, followed by Philip and Stan. Soon a number of men had clustered round and he could see no more. Perhaps it *was* rather sickening.

'May I take the liberty, Sal?'

Without waiting for her reply, he crossed to where the decanters stood on the sideboard and poured them both a healthy tot of Scotch.

'Drink up,' he said. 'Perdition to the Communists.' He finished his at a gulp.

Sally had still only sipped her drink when the other two men returned.

'Two BORs,' Philip told them. 'Apparently they were trying to capture the Christmas spirit in one of the coffee-shops, when a couple of masked men walked in and shot them at point blank range. God alone knows what they were doing so far from the army camp – they didn't appear to have any transport – unless they were going to pay a Christmas call on Stubbs, the police lieutenant who's stationed nearby. Anyway, if the bill the towkay presented me with is correct, they must have been roaring fu' – they can't have known what hit them. I wanted Stan to dig the bullets out to find out what weapon was used.'

'Weren't there any witnesses?'

'Hordes. But none of them will admit to having seen a thing. It's the usual story.'

'And only the other day,' Sally said quietly, 'I was saying what a gay time we had to look forward to – Christmas, New Year, Chinese New Year and Hari Raya, all within a couple of months. Let's hope we don't have a repeat performance each time.'

Luckily Sally's fears were unfounded. At least the Christmas tragedy was not repeated at New Year.

'It only seems to happen when people come to our house,' she remarked as they walked up the Weatherbys' drive. 'It's almost an excuse not to entertain.'

They had reached the steps and she paused to look back. It was a brilliant moonlit night and the sound of the sea could be heard faintly, as the tide flowed into the tangle of mangroves below them. In the other world, a few yards away, voices could be heard coming from the verandah, and Helen's remark that the Morrisons were late floated out to them.

'Come on,' Philip tugged at her hand, 'we're always the last to arrive.'

As they neared the top of the steps, a concerted yell halted them and Donald and Stan advanced towards them.

'Do you see what I see?' Donald was grinning like a Cheshire cat. Philip was wearing the kilt. 'Doesn't this remind you of another Hogmanay?'

With one leap they were upon him, but he was ready for them. 'Duck,' he ordered Sally, and moving forward with outstretched arms, he met them as they charged and banged their heads together.

The Christmas decorations were still up. 'Observe tradition,' Philip cried, 'you're under the mistletoe!'

The three onlookers guffawed.

'I'd never have guessed it of old Don,' Helen laughed. 'He's certainly been in incredible form ever since he came back from leave.'

It was true. Donald had burst on the district like a firework. 'He's almost becoming the professional life and soul of the party,' Stan had been heard to remark, somewhat gloomily.

'Hi, Jim! Hi, Phil! What's cookin', Doc?' had been his greeting at the small welcome-back party that had been arranged for him at the club on his return. And that had been his tone ever since. It was not altogether surprising, therefore, that he should be the one to remind them when midnight was almost due. And James had hardly popped the cork before Don was grabbing hands and starting up with 'Auld Lang Syne'.

'Happy New Year. Happy New Year.'

When everyone had drunk and their glasses were refilled, he called out, 'Now everyone, our own private toasts, our hopes for the coming year.'

The Weatherbys drank to their new life in Australia; the Morrisons to their leave. Don drank to Kuala Jelang and Stan, after being prodded, raised his glass with a whimsical expression and drank to 'Heaven – or hell.'

Still holding his glass high and looking through the champagne as he watched the others, Stan stood aloof. They seemed to be gradually fading out, as actors fade into the wings. He had a fleeting impression that he was above a stage, where each person spoke a part. He looked down on them and saw their mime, but he could not hear their voices any more.

'Stan. Stan, are you all right?'

He saw the top of a brown head below his glass and felt Sally's hand on his arm.

He lowered his glass then and their eyes met. He saw the sadness in hers.

'Stan,' she whispered, 'I do believe – for a moment – we shared the same thought.'

He smiled then and kissed her upturned face.

'Happy New Year, my dear,' he said.

112. CHINESE NEW YEAR

Broomph-broooom! It was Saturday afternoon. Chee Min rode up to the police station on his new motor bike and stopped with a flourish.

Omar, who was on duty in the Charge Room, walked outside to see who had arrived and exclaimed in admiration.

'Wah!'

Chee Min beamed proudly. He had saved for this, he and Rose – it was partly what she had earned from her embroidery that had paid for the bike. He had been going backwards and forwards to the cycle shop for weeks, trying to make up his mind between a Norton and a BSA, and here it was, a Norton, *his* Norton, 500 cc.

Omar ran his hands lovingly over the powerful machine and nodded his approval.

Karim walked over from the MT yard and admired it from several yards' distance. Now that, he thought, is something I would like to have. Perhaps, one day. Rokiah would enjoy it too. Speed. The whistling of the wind as it whipped past one's ears. Wah!

Ahmat looked out of his office window to see what was going on, and his lip curled in disdain. *Nouveau riche*, he thought, just what one would expect. He closed the window and went back to his work.

Jogindar Singh watched from the main door of the police station. Now, if I had a little money to spare, he thought, I'd buy the odd acre of land, or maybe a few more cows. Strange how we all hanker after different things – luckily. The machine did not interest him at all.

All this time, Rose had been standing by the main gate, but Chee Min was so busy explaining the finer points of the bike to its admirers that he had not noticed her until she moved towards him.

'Isn't she a beaut?' he called. And then, 'Hey, Rosie what's this?'

Rose sometimes wore European clothes and sometimes a *samfoo*, but she was dressed quite differently now and in something he had never seen her in before. A red and white gingham smock topped a straight white skirt – maternity clothes?

'Rose!'

The clothes had been given to her by Sally, who had kept them hopefully all this time. And then, one day not long before, when Stan had been examining a police baby in the clinic, she had remarked that she still hoped to have one herself one day.

He had been very stern.

'You'll be extremely selfish if you do,' he had said. And, to Sally's surprise, 'Philip told me exactly what the obstetrician said. It's not an uncommon deformity that you have, but you'll never produce a live child and there's a good chance of you popping off yourself. Think of Philip instead of yourself for a change.'

She had been cross with him at the time and indignant at his accusation of selfishness, but when finally she admitted the truth to herself, she knew that he was right.

Hence the clothes. As soon as Rose had mentioned that she thought she was pregnant, Sally had passed all her maternity clothes on to her.

'Rose! Rose?'

Rose giggled, blushed and turned away. It would be months before she showed, but she wanted to wear the smock, just to give Vincent a surprise.

'Crikey! What a Chinese New Year present. Come and look at her, Rosie.'

Rose climbed on to the pillion seat and soon they were off, up the hill and through the town and back again. A new set of admirers awaited them and a cross face at the window put hands over ears.

Chee Min mentally cocked a snook at Ahmat, working late. It was a good world all right; who wanted to be cooped up in a stuffy office on a day like this?

He grabbed Rose's hand. 'Let's go and tell old Stan.'

'Oh, Vincent, you must *not* be so familiar!'

'Why not?'

Brooomph, roomph-rmph!

'Well, Rose, do I see what I think I see?'

'Oh, Doctor, not for ages yet.'

Chee Min was a little bit peeved that Stan had noticed Rose before the bike. But not for long. Rose frowned and tried to indicate the machine with her eyes. Stan twigged.

'Good heavens, Vincent, what a magnificent machine. A Norton, eh? Something I always wanted but never had.' Which was quite untrue.

They went into technical details then and Rose wandered away into the garden, picking up frangipani blossoms from the grass.

'That sergeant of yours is a blooming menace,' James complained. 'Damned nearly ran me down.'

'The novelty will wear off in a few days, then you'll be safe again!'

'I thought he came from such a wealthy family; couldn't he afford something a little more sedate?'

'It's his own private revolution,' Philip explained. 'Thumbing his nose at his old man and saying, "I'll marry whom I like, thank you." He's got a lot of guts, Chee Min.'

'Well, I wish they'd come out in some other guise!'

'It was last Chinese New Year that I had that row with Dad,' Chee Min remarked. 'Do you think we should try and make it up? Just appear and say, "*Kong hee fatt choy,*" and see what his reaction is?'

Rose shook her head. 'I'll give him a grandson first, a real living *ang pow*. None of your brothers or sisters have had children yet, have they?' Chee Min shook his head in turn. 'Well, then, we have a good chance. Let's let things work themselves out.'

'Dear Rose, you are so prudent and so wise,' he said. 'I must write and tell Mum though.'

113. NOTHING IS SIMPLE

Before Ramakrishnan had reason to stick the red square in the window again, the terrorists sent for him.

'This diary, this engagement pad that you spoke of. You said all government officers keep such pads?'

Krishnan sensed a trap, but he could not, dare not, deny what he had already told them. He merely nodded.

'Then the OCPD must have one.'

'Oh, of a certainty, Masters.'

'Get it for us.'

Krishnan gasped. The clammy sweat sprang out on the

palms of his hands and his eyes rolled.

'That is not possible. I am thinking that police station routine is not being understood. Always there is someone on duty, day and night. It is not like other government departments, which maintain office hours pure and simple. Always the police station is awake.'

'We know that.' The speaker regarded him with scorn. 'You were a government clerk, weren't you?'

'Yes, Master.'

'So you must know the police clerks.'

'I am knowing them only slightly, Master.'

'What are their names?'

'Maniam I am knowing, Master. Names of secondary clerks I am not knowing.'

'Maniam will get this pad for you.'

'But Master, I am only working for short time as government clerk of most junior capacity. Maniam is chief clerk, man. I am hardly knowing him, Master.'

The three uniformed men stood silently regarding the little Tamil, as he wagged his head, rolled his eyes and fidgeted generally. They were very still.

'You will get it,' the leader said and, as usual, turned and walked away without another word.

All night Krishnan tossed and turned in despair. It was true that the District Officer did keep an engagement pad, but what he wrote on it Krishnan had no idea.

Why had he pretended to know more than he did? Oh, truly I am being hoisted with own petard, he groaned; for foolishness I am taking much to beat.

How could he gain access to the OCPD's office to find out if indeed he did keep such a pad? Maniam had never even spoken to him, except in a general way when he had visited the District Office. He had no friends in Kuala Jelang to help in such a venture, let alone the police clerk.

Eyes seemed to be watching him from behind every tree and bush. Voices whispered and he lived in constant fear of the dreaded summons.

After three days he could bear it no longer. He would ring up Maniam, pretending the manager of some mythical estate wanted to see the OCPD. He would ask him to make a note of the time and date on the OCPD's engagement pad and see what the answer would be.

As soon as he had thought of this brilliant plan, Krishnan began to bounce. If such a pad did exist, then he would have to think again but, for the time being, he could always tell the bandits that the OCPD had stopped writing his engagements down.

Oh, it was easy. Why had he been such a fool? To be afraid of three men not much larger than himself. They were only men.

The idea had come to him in the middle of the night, and as soon as the office opened the following day, he put through a call to Kuala Jelang Police Station.

Ten minutes later he was leaning back in his chair, laughing to himself and sweating with relief. He went over to the window to affix the red square.

'Maniam is on leave for two weeks,' Ramakrishnan informed his listeners, 'and then two more days. He will not be returning until the end of the Hari Raya holiday.'

He faced them triumphantly this time, hands thrust into trouser pockets and a smile upon his face. But his cockiness was short-lived.

'Liar!' He felt the blood spurt as the man standing opposite leaned forward and struck him across the mouth.

'Oh, most honestly, Masters, I am not lying. Verily I am not. It is easily found out that it is only the truth I am telling. Only one half-hour ago I am ringing police station and being informed that Chief Clerk Maniam is on leave two weeks and two days precisely.'

'You will go to the police station then yourself.'

'I cannot.'

The police! Oh, what had he done? To go to the police station would mean certain disaster for him. In a flash his mind sped back over the past years; outwitting the police at every turn, only to fall into their hands now.

'You will go with the next lorry that goes into town.'

'To the police station I cannot go, Masters.'

'A lorry goes down on the last day of every month, as you well know. You will be on it at the end of this month.'

'Oh, Masters.' Krishnan fell on his knees, hands clasped in an attitude half of pain and half of supplication.

He received a kick in the jaw for his pains.

This time the bandits did not melt silently away – they were laughing as they tramped through the rubber.

About a week had passed when both manager and clerk

looked up on hearing a tap on the office window.

Outside stood one of the terrorists, his face as impassive as stone.

Krishnan's heart began to turn somersaults. Oh my goodness gracious, he thought, they have come for me.

'The audacity,' Wotherspoon muttered, half under his breath. To come to the office in broad daylight, and in uniform too. 'Better open the window,' he said to the clerk.

Krishnan did as he was told.

The terrorist smiled. 'Just to remind you not to forget,' he said. 'The police.'

He walked casually away, leaving Wotherspoon red with fury and Krishnan grey with fright.

The man had spoken to Krishnan, but Wotherspoon had not known that. To him, it was a warning about the land. Such boldness could only mean one thing – he was entirely at their mercy and had to play their game.

Without a word he left the office, got into his Land-Rover and drove off to Kuala Jelang.

'Aren't you coming to our Hari Raya party, Stan?' Sally asked. 'The police always have a tremendous binge – kenduri, ronggeng girls, the lot. It's fun.'

'No. I'm going to Bukit Merah Estate for the holiday and part of my local leave.'

'Old Wotherspoon's estate? Oh Stan, you traitor!' she cried. 'He's terribly anti-police.'

'But I am nothing to do with the police, my dear,' he said, with the cynical smirk that took her straight back to the war. She was infuriated. 'I've always wanted to know what it's like living on a remote rubber estate during the Emergency, and this is my chance to find out.'

What he did not add was that he had dreaded the thought of spending the holiday in the bungalow alone with Don. His good spirits had been short-lived and he was back to his maudlin state, only worse than ever; drinking himself to death, as Stan had already told him on several occasions. He was becoming so argumentative and belligerent after only a few drinks that Stan was doing his best to keep out of his way.

These thoughts were going through his head as he stood and smiled at Sally. But she had the last word anyway.

'Better take Salmah with you for protection then,' she said. 'By all accounts he's very odd!'

Philip had been listening with one ear to the conversation between his wife and Stan and was amused by Sally's pique.

'Just because he was a boy-friend ten years ago,' he said, when they were walking up to the house for lunch, 'gives you no proprietary claim. Besides, I don't think you're the only one.'

'That Malay girl? I know all about her - practically knocked me out with a corn cob that evening I had supper with them!'

'No, not Salmah. Helen.'

'Helen? Don't be ridiculous. Honestly, Philip, you do imagine things.'

'Do I? I wonder. I don't believe she's nearly as chilly as she appears.'

'But how could she possibly have known Stan?'

'How could you?'

'That's different. We were in the same service.'

'So was James.'

'Well, anyway, I think you're talking rot.'

'Why is she so careful to avoid him then?'

'I don't think she is.'

'Oh no? You watch.'

If Helen had heard this conversation she would have had fifty fits.

James had been so much easier of late; ever since their Australian plans had been settled. But she was still on edge whenever Stan was around, terrified that one of them would make some thoughtless reference to the past which, if heard by James, might start an avalanche.

In fact, she would have loved to have had a chat with Stan about old times, but as it was she never had a chance even to explain fully the reason for her pretence. Once, when Angela had had a fever and he had come up to the house to see her during working hours, she had begun, but, within five minutes of his arrival, James was there too. Why? Because he was worried about his daughter, or because he had seen the doctor's car turn up towards their house? She never knew and gave up trying to catch Stan on his own after that.

But Stan's interests were purely in the present. He enjoyed Sally's company, although he found her irritating at times, and Helen was altogether too aloof. Besides, he not only liked at least one of their husbands, but had to work with them. He was not going to stir up any hornets' nests. The Weatherbys would be on leave in six weeks' time and the Morrisons a few months after that.

Helen would be sorry to go, but James could not get away fast enough. It was always the same with him; once a decision had been made he had to get on with it; it was hopeless hanging around.

Norman had organised a caravan for them – a trailer he called it – large enough to accommodate the whole family while their house was being built. There had been a letter that morning, telling them that the last details had been fixed. Next week would be the holiday; if he could clear up his outstanding work before then, James thought, he and Helen could spend a few days putting their heads together over passages, getting their clothes sorted out, and sucnlike. Nannie would be arriving within the month.

He had just put Norman's letter away and was getting down to some routine work when the telephone rang. It was Helen.

'Mr Wotherspoon's here,' she said. 'He wants to see you urgently, but not in your office. Can you come up?'

James stifled an oath. 'I suppose I'll have to. Tell him he'll have to wait a little while.'

It was always the same. It seemed inevitable that good news should be countered with bad.

He rang Philip to tell him and to ask if he had any idea what it might be about. He did not. 'I'll let you know what ensues,' James said.

Wotherspoon was clearly in a state.

'I can't sell,' his voice rose to a high-pitched note, 'I won't.'

'I think you'd better have a drink,' James said, and poured him a stiff brandy and ginger-ale.

It disappeared in a couple of gulps, but it was no use. Nothing would calm him down. His eyes were shifty and his hands shook. He told a long-winded and completely incoherent story about the reasons why Head Office would not permit him to sell.

James wished he had a tape-recorder, but he had asked Helen to listen from behind the bedroom door.

Wotherspoon did not stay long.

'I've given you my reasons,' he said, 'and they're final.' And then, rather pathetically, 'I don't know where we go from here.'

Helen's shorthand was rusty, but she had taken sufficient notes for them to go over the conversation again. Little of it made sense. James jotted down the gist and went down to the police station.

'It's quite incomprehensible,' Philip remarked after he had read it through. 'What did you tell him?'

'That the matter would now rest with DWEC. There's a meeting to-morrow, don't forget.'

'I hadn't. Good.'

After much discussion, the members of DWEC came to the unanimous conclusion that they had given Wotherspoon more than sufficient leeway; the land should be requisitioned.

But the matter did not rest there. It was not that simple.

Only a very few days after the meeting, the Special Branch officer from Circle Headquarters, Bill Young, was on the blower to Philip.

'I've got the minutes of your last DWEC meeting here,' he said. 'Hold everything. Tell the DO not to go ahead. I can't tell you anything more over the phone. I'm coming down. If I may, I'll spend the night with you.'

'Don't force Wotherspoon's hand just yet,' they were told. 'It might result in open killing – probably of him – and the bandits going to ground. I'm as sure as you that they're there, although that typewriter is still the only proof we have, and he might wriggle out of that – a good defence lawyer would get him out of it at any rate.'

'Do you mean he'd be taken to court?' James felt sick.

'Not if it can be avoided – he's one of us, after all, regrettably – but I want to have a snoop round that estate myself and perhaps post a few men there. Later, we might be able to mount a raid – a lot will depend on what information we can glean and whether the CTs are living in the labour lines or in a camp in the vicinity. In any event, we'll get the old boy removed from the state.'

'You police are very harsh.'

'There haven't been any DOs killed to date.'

James raised his hand in a gesture of resignation. 'I give up,' he said, and he sounded very tired. 'Heaven alone knows I've done my best for Wotherspoon, but one can't go on farting against thunder for ever.'

'I would suggest, James,' Philip said, that you and I go

and see him together and argue it out. Not by arrangement though; take him by surprise. And it must be soon.'

'I'm absolutely snowed under until the holiday.'

'So am I. Let's make it the first day after, then.'

'All right. But let's give him the benefit of the doubt just once more, for the last time,' pleaded James, going back on his resolution. 'There might be something on that land, timber or something, that his Head Office don't wish to lose. Let's have a better look at the land itself before we tackle him. I'd like to take Don along.'

'Why not? I shall certainly take Ahmat and Chee Min.'

114. HARI RAYA PUASA

The thud and thump of the mosque drum reverberated through the small town and the Malay police streamed out of the station compound, dressed in their best, to answer the call to prayer.

It was Hari Raya Puasa, the end of the fasting month of Ramadan, or Puasa. Police on active service were given a special dispensation, but many of them were strong-minded and, particularly the older men, still held their fast throughout the daylight hours, obeying the rhythmic command of the drum as the sun rose and set.

Sally looked on with a feeling of relief. Puasa was always a trying time, even for those who did not fast. Tempers were high for the first few days and Ja'afar was quite unapproachable. As their throats and stomachs grew accustomed to the new routine they gradually settled down, but she hated asking anyone to cook or pour out a drink, knowing that they could touch nothing themselves.

Ja'afar himself was quite philosophic, invariably apologising for his bouts of ill-humour at the outset and laughing when he saw his employers surreptitiously sneaking food and drink from the refrigerator.

From where they stood on their verandah, high on the hill, the men leaving the station looked like so many butterflies winging their way across the green grass. Purple, royal blue, maroon, and bottle-green sarongs, many worked with gold or silver thread, were girt about marching hips. Arms and legs swung in silks of pink and blue, salmon and mauve, white, green or grey; every colour except the royal yellow.

Black velvet songkoks topped almost every head, with here and there a contrasting deep blue, green or crimson.

'Selamat Hari Raya, Tuan. Selamat Hari Raya, Mem.'

They turned to see Ja'afar and Siti, looking quite gorgeous, on their way out.

'Selamat Hari Raya.'

Ja'afar was dressed in pale blue silk and gold embroidered purple. His open leather sandals clacked on the steep stone steps, and Siti, in a flowing, flowered baju kurong, floated behind, her head and shoulders encased in a film of delicate gauze.

'Glad we stayed here?' Philip asked, and put an arm about Sally's shoulders. 'Glad that you were able to take them on?'

She smiled and snuggled into his arm. Of all the festivals, Hari Raya was the one she liked the best.

'It's always a salutary jolt for me,' she said. 'It's only when the servants are off for a few days that I appreciate how much work they do!'

Better tidy the house up now, she thought. Ahmat and Azizah and Zukifli and the most recently arrived inspector, Ismail, would be coming up later on, followed by the Malay NCOs and their wives. Bottles of Coca-Cola, sarsaparilla and orange crush were already nestling in tin baths of ice and the small eats had been prepared.

The sun shone out of a cloudless sky and a gentle breeze stirred the leaves of the rain trees. Fragile pink blossoms shivered and shook, but sprang to meet the sunlight. It was a happy day.

But for Ramakrishnan it was not a happy day. It had been bad enough knowing that Maniam would be back in a few days and that the end of the month was drawing near. But that was not all.

He had been got out of bed by a labourer early that morning, telling him that he was wanted.

No need to ask by whom.

He had dressed hurriedly, shivering in the dawn damp, and gone at once to the usual meeting-place under the rubber trees.

This time there were four men and Krishnan felt sick as he approached them.

'Why did you not go to Kuala Jelang with the lorry yesterday?'

Krishnan hedged. 'But, Masters, you said the end of the

month, and it was not the lorry, but the Land-Rover, that went.'

They looked at him with distaste.

'I did not know it was going,' he pleaded. He knew better now than to go on his knees to them. 'It was not scheduled to go.'

'You told us yourself that the doctor would be coming to stay. You told us more than two months ago.'

'But how am I for knowing that manager would send estate Land-Rover for him? I am expecting doctor to arrive by own car.'

There was a terrible, pregnant silence, while the terrorists looked at Krishnan and Krishnan looked at the trees.

'We are supported by all the labour on this estate,' the leader said at last. 'Do you know why they co-operate?'

'Of course, because they are hating white pigs like I, and are forever looking forward to times of democracy when colonialism is at an end.'

One of the younger bandits laughed.

'When we first came to this estate, more than three years ago,' the leader went on, 'the labour were not co-operative. So we took the kangani and hacked him to death – just where you are standing now.'

Involuntarily Krishnan took a step back and looked at the ground and the young bandit laughed again.

'He died very slowly. We took a piece at a time, until his cries had attracted all the labour force. They stood around; they saw him die.'

There was another silence while all five men stood still and Krishnan felt the vomit rise in his throat. He swallowed, but no words would come out.

'And that is what will happen to you, if you do not do as you are told. If you are not on the next vehicle to leave this estate, you will die – here. And do not think, my friend, that you can escape us. We can get you as easily in Kuala Jelang, or anywhere else, as here. You will return by that same lorry and in your possession will be the OCPD's engagement pad, or it will be the worse for you. Go.'

Krishnan turned. His legs were shaking so much that his knees knocked and his head felt unsteady on his neck. Before he had left the shelter of the rubber, the terrorists called him back.

'Hacking can be a slow death,' the leader said. 'I can hear the screams of that kangani now. Yes, he took a long time to die. There was much blood and many parts of him falling out. I remember it well. You will do well to remember it too, my friend. We make no idle threats.'

One thing they did not do was make idle threats; there was plenty of proof of that. Krishnan crawled back into his bed, pulling the blanket over his head, and wept.

Suddenly, the thought of a police cell seemed a haven. The more he thought about it, the more he preferred the idea of arrest to the fate the bandits would mete out.

He would write a letter to Post Office Box 5000, the police PO Box where informers, who wished to remain anonymous, could post their information. There would be a raid then, no doubt – but what would happen to him? Suppose the raid were unsuccessful? Any terrorists left alive would know at whose door the blame lay.

Krishnan shivered under the scarlet blanket. No, there was only one thing that he could do. Go to the police, give his information in person and demand their protection. After all, he was a citizen; he had the right to protection, hadn't he? If only he did not have to wait. In his present state of mind he was afraid that the bandits might even be able to read his thoughts. He did not get up all day, but lay there under the blanket, stiff and straight, keeping his head covered and jumping at every sound.

Wotherspoon, too, was on edge. Ever since he had returned from the DO's house, he had expected the telephone to ring.

But there was a simple way of dealing with that. The phone in his house was on a ledge behind a potted palm, out of sight. He simply left the receiver off the hook. It was annoying having asked that doctor to stay, but unless he wanted to use the phone – and he was unlikely to do so without asking first – he need not know.

The Javanese wouldn't play ball. What was there to dance about? they asked. Labour was becoming more and more difficult these days. Bolshie. They knew that if they got the sack there were always jobs going on other estates. That was the trouble. A little unemployment would not do the country any harm.

Ever since the invitation to the doctor had been issued, he had wanted to withdraw it, but could do so without arousing suspicion. So here he was, an inquisitive type, always wandering around. Wotherspoon didn't like it. Those ruddy

Communists were becoming so bold, they were as likely to walk in on him as not, guest or no guest. Perhaps when the Pole realised how boring life on an estate could be, he would return. That was his only hope. He had tried to sound surprised when Stan told him the receiver was off the hook and had put it back until the doctor was out of sight, but he would have to take care. Must make sure the one in his office was off too; the house phone was only an extension of the same line.

'Come into the garden,' he called to Stan. 'I have some interesting shrubs that I'd like you to see.'

In Kuala Jelang itself the holiday proceeded without mishap. Friends and relatives visited, prayers were said, a good deal of aimless wandering went on and far too much was eaten.

For the police, who were mainly Muslims, and mostly far away from home, the biggest event was without doubt the party on the last night of the festival.

A platform, some three feet from the ground, had been erected, large enough to accommodate four ronggeng girls and a three-piece band. Hours were spent plaiting palm fronds and forming intricate paper flowers with which to decorate it. Poles were stuck up at intervals round the parade-ground, on which were tacked tins holding candles, and the police station itself, the canteen and the part where the onlookers would be sitting, were festooned with coloured lights.

'It all seems so much work for just one night,' Sally murmured, but she enjoyed it as much as the men.

Certainly more than one man. If it were possible to kill by telepathy, Sally would have fallen dead at that very moment.

'I suppose *she* will be there,' Azizah remarked sulkily.

'If you mean the Mem, yes.'

'And the wife of the DO?'

'Yes.'

Ahmat had done his best to make the holiday a success. He had taken Azizah out on every day and for once the terrorists had done nothing to mar the few days off. Open-air film shows had taken place on the padang every night. They had gone to these, eaten at the only Muslim restaurant and played tombola at the club.

He had never changed his mind about the equal part that his wife should play in their private lives, but he was too disciplined and came from too old a family to do anything which went against custom in his public life. Hence he had vetoed the kenduri and the dancing that would follow that evening. The European women were expected to be there, but Malay women simply did not attend such functions with their men. Times, no doubt, would change, but at the moment it was not done.

It was no use Azizah sulking and stamping her foot and breaking his favourite glass; nothing would change his mind.

No one seeing Ahmat on the night of the final Hari Raya party would have guessed that all was not well with him.

Dignified and handsome in their inspectors' evening dress of black satin with black and silver embroidered sarongs, he, Zukifli and Ismail dominated the feast.

Tables had been set on the grass and Philip sat at the head with an inspector on either side. Sally and James sat on Ahmat's right and Helen and Don on Zukifli's left; it was all very correct.

'Couldn't Azizah join us?' Sally had asked before the meal began. It would take but a moment to set another place and fetch a chair.

Ahmat frowned. 'Our customs are different from yours, Mem,' he said. No doubt but that it was a polite rebuke, but she remained deliberately unperturbed.

'Oh, I know,' she said impatiently, 'but times are changing. This is 1952. You often see Malay wives with their husbands in the "Dog" in KL now.'

'Not my wife. Excuse me, Mem, I have to go and see about the band.'

'That's put you in your place,' James chuckled as Ahmat left. 'I'm all for keeping women in their place -- enough of this emancipation nonsense!'

'I'm very fond of Mat,' Sally mused, 'but he can be a bit stuffy at times. It must be difficult for his wife.' Bitch as she is, she thought, but did not say so aloud.

Eventually the meal was over, the debris cleared away and the band was mounting the dancing dais followed by the four ronggeng girls.

Ahmat tried not to look in the direction of his house. He had moved a chair on to the verandah, taken Azizah a plate of curry and a bottle of orange crush and now had a painful bruise where the bottle had hit his head.

The first tune began and there were cries of, 'OCPD,

OCPD, Tuan Morrison to dance,' from the assembled crowd.

Ahmat pleaded a strained ankle and Philip was tactful enough not to comment. He and Zukifli took the floor.

'Trust him to choose the prettiest girl,' Sally remarked as Ahmat rejoined them. He smiled faintly; it was a sore point.

Soon the first stint was over and others were urged on to the platform. James refused. He was always conscious of his defects when in the public eye; he hated it. Don got up with the young inspector and was joined by Jogindar Singh and the Malay CID sergeant. One after another, everyone took their turn.

'I think we should go now,' Philip whispered across to Sally. 'The girls are only hired until midnight. They'll have a better party once we're no longer in the way.'

'Come and have a glass or cup of something with us,' Helen suggested. 'You'll never get any sleep in your house. Ronggeng girls or not, I should think that party'll go on all night.'

'Not for long then,' Philip said, looking at James, 'we have a heavy day ahead of us to-morrow. Back to the grindstone.'

115. TO BUKIT MERAH ESTATE

Rokiah had been taken into hospital at the beginning of Hari Raya and Karim had spent the whole holiday by her bed-side.

Most police wives were delivered in barracks, but at the outset the midwife had reported that it would not be an easy birth. She had been in labour for more than thirty hours already and now they had moved her out of the labour ward and back into her ordinary hospital bed.

The bed had been screened, but Rokiah asked that the screens should be removed. 'I don't want to be alone when you go back on duty,' she said to Karim, 'it is better when I can see the other women.'

Now the holiday was over and they were at the start of another working day.

'It is a Caesarean section that she is needing,' Mr Ponniah, the chief dresser, explained to Karim, 'but Doctor is not here. He is telling me to ring him at Bukit Merah Estate if any emergency should occur, but all yesterday I am trying, and again this morning early, but nobody answers. What to do? Telephone operator says the line is in order, but maybe receiver has been left off instrument. If by ten o'clock I cannot get through, I am ringing doctor at Kemuning for advice.'

Karim's face fell and Rokiah, seeing his consternation, smiled and put out her hand.

'Don't worry. I am young and strong, only too narrow. You wouldn't want a wide woman, would you?'

'There, my son,' kind Mr Ponniah laid his hand on Karim's shoulder, 'what your wife says is true.'

'I have to go out to-day,' Karim was miserably unhappy at the thought of having to leave Rokiah, but it never occurred to him to ask for time off, 'I am on duty.'

'I am hoping perhaps that police have ways of reaching Bukit Merah Estate,' Mr Ponniah said. 'Radio, walkie-talkie, or suchlike. I will write a note and you see if OCPD can help.'

He went into his office and Karim stood, dumb with misery, looking down at the girl who had been his childhood love.

Rokiah of the coconut palms and the pounding surf; of racing out to sea and collecting turtle eggs. Other men's wives might die in childbirth, but not his, not Rokiah.

'Rokiah," he whispered at last, 'when the dresser returns, I will have to go. Don't be scared; Mr Ponniah is a good man, he will look after you and I will fetch the doctor for you somehow.'

But the elderly Tamil was already back.

'Go, boy,' he said. 'You can do no good here. If Doctor is unable to be found, I shall ring for Kemuning ambulance – ours is broken down – but by hook or crook we shall save your wife, if not baby also.'

Karim left the hospital with tears in his eyes, cramming the letter into his breast pocket as he went. In less than half an hour he would be sitting beside the OCPD; he would ask him if he could help.

Stan had seen the receiver left off the hook and quietly replaced it, saying nothing. He had done the same thing a second time, but after the third he mentioned it to Wotherspoon. He expressed surprise, but Stan was sure it was feigned and later, when he had been alone in the bungalow for a short time, he had lifted the receiver and tried to ring the hospital. The line was useless; clearly the instrument in the office was receiving similar treatment and there was little that he could do about that. It was the same this morning.

He had been on the estate for four days now and there were things going on that he neither liked nor understood. If only he could get hold of a vehicle, he would return to Kuala Jelang and take the remainder of his leave some other time.

In fact, this jaunt had been a bit of a dead loss. He had hoped to wander around and see the various aspects of estate life, but he was not given a chance. Every time he asked Wotherspoon if he could see this or that, some excuse was made as to why it was not convenient.

He had watched the tappers bringing in their latex to be weighed, and that was about all that he had seen. Having observed the same proceeding several times, he grew bored and went through a door into a nearby shed to see what went on inside. Immediately the manager materialised, from what appeared to be thin air, and barred his way.

Stan was irritated. 'It's only a store, isn't it?' he asked.

'Yes, but . . .' and he had been carefully led away.

Wotherspoon had given him free run of his extensive library, but as Stan had tried to point out, reading was not his reason for wanting to visit an estate; he could sit on his arse and do that in his own bungalow. Then there was the matter of the telephone.

It was all rather frustrating.

Ahmat had had a dreadful night. Azizah cursed and screamed and this morning they had had the worst scene to date.

Much as he hated to admit it, it looked as though his mother had been right after all. And yet? He thought back to the night at the Bintang Kilat when he had first seen his wife – in similar circumstances he would no doubt become infatuated all over again.

He felt a fool, drinking his morning coffee in the canteen, with men all around him who must have witnessed the humiliating scene. Impossible not to have done. Azizah's shrill voice must have been heard in the town. And the things she had said. Ahmat went hot under his collar at the thought of them. Language which no well-bred Malay girl could possibly be expected to know, let alone use. And the final insults and curses. 'I'll prepare the yellow rice,' she had screamed. The yellow rice that was for special occasions, the celebration meal on high days and holidays. For any wife to gloat, to threaten, as she had done; it was unspeakable.

He looked up at the canteen clock. Nine o'clock, the OPCD had said he wanted to leave. He was glad he was going out to-day. Allahumma! He could not have stayed in the police station this morning; he was humiliated enough as it was.

Jogindar Singh stood at the main door of the police station, picking his teeth.

It was always a difficult day, the first working day after a holiday. Everyone was lethargic and he himself did not feel like urging for once. Watching Omar cleaning the Bren gun on the GMT, he almost envied him. He would like to be going out to-day. One became stale, never moving out of such an enclosed area and he was in no mood for sitting at a desk.

Suvindar had thought that her first pains might be coming on. There was nothing he could do; best to keep out of her way until the time came. Even then, according to the midwife, husbands were nothing but a nuisance.

He spat out the toothpick and straightened up as he saw the OCPD coming down the steps.

'Good morning, Sahib.' He gave his most crashing salute.

'Good morning, Dato.'

Philip went straight through the Charge Room to his office. Jogindar Singh is getting fat, he thought.

'Ten-to-nine and I've done everything I can before we leave,' Philip told Cameron an hour later. 'Don't know when I'll get back, but you know where we'll be. I just want to have a look at the vehicle before we start.'

He picked up a file and left the office.

'Atten – *shun!*' The whole of the Charge Room sprang up with a resounding crash. Jogindar looked smug, he felt better, he liked to get a good noise out of them.

'Better have one more man for escort, Dato,' Philip said, and then, as though reading his thoughts, 'If you want a bit of fresh air for a change you can come yourself if you like.'

The sergeant-major needed no urging. His white smile split the heavy black beard.

'Thank you, Sahib.'

'Come as you are. No need to change; we're not going on a foot patrol.'

'Sahib. I'll just go and tell my wife.'

He handed over to the sergeant and proceeded to his quarters at the double.

Suvindar was still in the same state. 'Might be to-day,' she said, 'to-morrow, or the next. Who can tell? Better that you go out.'

'Ranjit,' her husband called, 'look after your mother, son. If you think she needs help, you are to run at once for Puron Kaur. You understand?'

'Yes, Father.'

Ranjit was growing into a tall, thin lad, all eyes and legs and topknot. His steel bangle looked too big for his bony wrist. He is a good boy, Jogindar thought; already he has a sense of responsibility.

'Good morning, Karim. You a father yet?'

'Not yet, Tuan.'

'Everyone here?'

Philip peered into the back of the truck. Ahmat stood silent, looking out to sea; Omar was fondly polishing his Bren gun; Chee Min was waiting for the OCPD to move, so that he could climb inside; Jogindar was coming at the double across the parade-ground, hand held out to take his Sten gun from the PC waiting with it at the main entrance. Philip smiled.

'All set,' he told Karim, and climbed into the passenger seat.

'Tuan.' Karim shut the door and walked round to his own side.

'First stop District Office to pick up the DO, the Forest Checking Station to pick up the FO, Pokok Api Police Station, then Bukit Merah Estate.'

'Bukit Merah Estate, Tuan?' Philip turned in surprise at the driver's relieved tone. *'Nasib baik,'* Karim murmured, half to himself. 'Oh, Tuan, fate is kind.'

Then out it all came; his fears for his wife, the note for the doctor, the unanswered telephone.

'Good heavens, man,' Philip said, 'I don't want to take you away from your wife. You'd better turn back. We'll get another driver; it's only just after nine.'

'No, Tuan,' Karim shook his head resolutely, 'I'd rather go. Mr Ponniah said I could do nothing. I hope perhaps the doctor will come back with us. The road to Bukit Merah is a difficult one and – forgive my lack of modesty, Tuan – but I drive this vehicle better than anyone else."

'You do indeed. Come along then, the sooner we see the

doctor the better. I'll speak to him, but I'm sure he will need no persuading to return with us.'

As Karim started up, thoughts on both his wife and his job, it occurred to him suddenly that the heavy GMT was like one of his own giant Trengganu turtles. Just as slow, just as lumbering. It will be good to go home on leave, one day, he thought, he and Rokiah and the child. Then he swallowed and frowned; he must concentrate on the turtle of the present, not tempt providence by thinking of the future.

When they reached the District Office, Philip left the front cabin and climbed into the back.

'You'd better go in front, Dato,' he said to Jogindar Singh. 'You're the best-dressed person here. Good for public morale to see a smart policeman sitting in front!'

Chee Min and Omar laughed, because of course no one could see inside the vehicle anyway, and even Ahmat managed a sickly grin. Philip was in high spirits. He was glad things had finally come to a head; he wanted to get this resettlement area organised without further delay.

''Morning, James.' The DO was given a hand in.

'Good morning, all.' And aside to Philip, 'I'm not looking forward to this jaunt.'

'Oh, I don't know. It's a glorious day and I could do with the odd jolt – that curry is still lying heavy on my stomach from last night.'

'I thought you'd danced it off; you were active enough, heaven alone knows.'

Philip laughed. 'Malays aren't so different from Jocks,' he remarked. 'I never believe it does any harm to play the fool at the right time.'

'I envy you the ability.'

James was stating the truth. He had watched Philip clowning the evening before and wished that he could do the same. He used to be on such good terms with his crew; somewhere along the line he seemed to have lost contact with his fellow-beings.

They were at the Forest Checking Station.

Donald climbed in and the pleasantries of the day were exchanged again.

Karim did not bless the OCPD. Now he was going to have the big Sikh laughing at him all the way out and back. He was terrified of the sergeant-major.

But Jogindar's mind at that moment was on his wife; then he remembered Karim's.

'How is your wife?' he asked. 'Given birth yet, or is she still having trouble?'

'Still having trouble, Dato.'

Jogindar Singh approved of Rokiah. A natural, kampong girl, who didn't paint her face or wear clothes so tight that nothing was left to the imagination.

'Don't worry, lad, she's a healthy girl. She'll give you a fine son soon.'

'I rather hope she has a daughter,' Karim replied. 'I've always liked girls.'

Jogindar gave a great belly laugh and poor Karim felt his face burn.

'What's up?' James asked, as the truck began to slow down. They were at Pokok Api Police Station. He looked out and saw a European and a Tamil standing some distance away. 'I say, isn't that your Special Branch chap?'

'Yes.' Philip was waving to the waiting pair.

'I didn't know they were coming to-day. Why are we picking them up here?'

'I didn't want them to be seen leaving with us from the town. They're going to have a look round.'

The GMT stopped and Bill Young and the Indian climbed aboard. He was introduced to Donald Thom and, in turn, introduced, 'Detective-Corporal Pillai, who is accompanying me.'

'Good,' said Philip.

Soon they were on the winding road to the estate, which made further conversation impossible.

More than one person was listening to the rumble of the heavy vehicle as it approached the office buildings of Bukit Merah Estate.

Stan, standing on the upper verandah of the manager's bungalow, watched with interest as the monster heaved into sight and wondered what was up.

Ramakrishnan listened and hoped. Only the army or police could be coming in anything as heavy as that.

Krishnan was at his wits' end. His nails were bitten down to the quicks and he was sure his hair was turning grey. When the black, armoured vehicle appeared, he burst from the office door like a rocket going off. The police. He was saved. He would demand protection – *now*.

Men were vaulting from the back. Krishnan recognised the OCPD and went running straight to him.

'Sir, sir, oh, most esteemed sir! I have news of great import. Informations most vital to impart. I have composed letter lucid and true to PO Box 5000, but no chance to post. Oh, sir, I need protection; Communist terrorists are all around!'

Before Philip could take in what the excited little man was babbling, Jogindar Singh was at his side.

'That, Sahib, is the man who insulted the Memsahib. He is the one she would not let me arrest.'

'It is true, sir, it is true. It is I who wrote the letters to your lady wife; I who intimidated her on the telephone; I . . .'

Chee Min had drawn near. He recognised the Tamil as the man he had seen upset the table in the coffee-shop. So that was it.

Krishnan saw him too. His eyes rolled and his head wagged vigorously.

'Most honourable sir, I am understanding that you have come here to arrest me. Most bountiful lord, I am confessing, giving myself up to your lordship's mercy. Not only did I intimidate your lady wife. It is true that I collaborated with the Japanese. It is true also that I blackmailed Mr Ramasamy and that I am Mr S. Kandiah – you have no doubt taken fingerprints from car –'

'Hey, steady on,' Philip patted his shoulder, trying to calm him down. 'I don't know how many crimes you're confessing to, but this is neither the time nor the place. You had better come back to the police station with us.'

Krishnan fell on his knees for the second time in a matter of weeks. He felt that he would not be kicked this time.

'Oh, sir, lord, your Excellency, my gratitude is bounding unlimited.'

'For God's sake, get up, man,' Philip said.

'Oh, sir, I am in durance most vile. If I am staying in estate office I shall not be alive to accompany you. Please, oh kind sir, may I be climbing into truck forthwith?'

Philip was completely taken aback. His thoughts had been more on Stan and Karim's wife than anything else. He looked with distaste at the grovelling little man.

'Get into the front then,' he said. 'I don't know when we shall be going back.' And to Jogindar Singh, 'Better keep an eye on him, Dato.'

Karim had left the truck and made a beeline for the doctor, who was walking across the grass from the manager's house.

'Tuan, I am so relieved that you are here. There was no answer to the telephone.' He handed him the dresser's letter.

Stan read it in silence. He did not need any persuading to return with them to Kuala Jelang. In fact, he viewed the arrival of the GMT as a godsend and Ponniah's letter the perfect excuse to get away without offending Wotherspoon. He didn't much care for what he had read though. Ponniah was not given to exaggeration and if his fears were correct, the girl stood little chance. But no point in upsetting the husband now.

'I'll come,' he said. 'We'll do our best for your wife – you had better drive well and make sure you get me there, though!'

Karim smiled. He removed his beret and wiped over face and head with an enormous handkerchief. The doctor was already walking back in the direction of the bungalow, no doubt to pack his kit. He would soon be with Rokiah. What a relief!

At that moment Wotherspoon appeared on the scene from behind the office buildings. He had been told by the kangani that the police had arrived and had already worked himself into what he considered to be a fit state in which to greet them.

'How dare you enter my estate without permission,' he roared.

No one saw fit to comment. They let him rant on for a couple of minutes, then James stepped forward.

'We have decided that, before the matter of your land is taken through the final stages in DWEC, we should discuss it fully with everyone interested present.'

The manager ignored him.

'I saw my clerk climbing into your truck,' he said to Philip. 'You have arrested him. Why?'

'He asked to come of his own free will.'

At that Wotherspoon's eyes widened and he had to fight down a moment of rising panic. So Ramakrishnan had turned informer; no doubt of that. Well, if it came to the clerk's word against his, he would just deny everything. What was there to deny? The terrorist's face at the window. But he had got straight into his Land-Rover and driven off to Kuala Jelang, hadn't he? Plenty of witnesses to that. He had tried to inform the police, but there had been no one there. Then why hadn't he told the DO? No, that wouldn't wash. Better to deny even having seen the terrorist.

He looked at the ring of faces. It was difficult to gauge whether they were hostile or not. He'd bluff it out as best he could.

Bill Young was introduced. On hearing that he too was police, Wotherspoon declined to shake hands.

'As you have insisted on invading my privacy,' he said coldly, 'you had better come into the office.'

The four Europeans followed the manager. Ahmat went off to question the SCs and Chee Min to see the Chinese house-servants. Corporal Pillai had melted away as soon as the truck had stopped.

Everything was still. Jogindar and Omar kept up a desultory conversation and Karim stood by the front of his vehicle. Krishnan huddled inside, grateful for the protection both of the armour plating and the armed men about him.

More than half an hour passed. Then Karim saw the doctor emerge from the house with Chee Min; the sergeant was carrying his bag. Karim ran across the lawn to take it from him and he and Omar heaved it over the back of the GMT and stowed it inside.

'I hear that your wife's time is due as well,' Stan said to Jogindar Singh. 'My God, you're a prolific lot – three of you here with pregnant wives. It's obvious the OCPD doesn't give you enough work to do!'

They all laughed. Stan had become a favourite with the police.

He walked over to peer in at the office window.

'I don't think they'll be long now,' he told the waiting men. 'They seem to be putting their papers away.'

A scraping of chairs soon confirmed his prediction and the door of the office opened.

It had not been a particularly successful meeting, but at least no one could say that Wotherspoon did not know exactly where he stood. The land would be used – whether he sold it or it was requisitioned was up to him.

'I think I'll stay on the estate for a day or two,' Bill Young announced. 'You don't have to put me up, sir, I can doss down with the SCs.'

Wotherspoon was furious but he kept his temper under

control. 'Never let it be said,' he remarked icily, 'that I denied anyone the hospitality of my house. You can have the doctor's room; I see he intends to leave.'

'Yes,' said Stan. 'I'm sorry to go so soon, but the driver here has a very sick wife and the hospital have asked me to return. I am glad I was able to come. Thank you so much.'

The manager waved away his thanks and stood watching while Omar and Jogindar opened the heavy back doors of the truck.

Just as the last man climbed in, Ahmat appeared and quietly went over the top.

'I think I've picked up quite a lot,' he said to Philip.

'I'm not sorry to be leaving this estate,' Stan remarked to no one in particular. 'Place gave me the creeps. Sally was right, I should have stayed in Kuala Jelang for your Hari Raya party.'

Karim pushed home the heavy gear and they started off along the downward slope. Shouldn't take us long getting back, he thought. It was noon; they should be home by two o'clock. It was good to know the doctor was on board, that in a couple of hours he would be with his wife.

His throat was parched. How foolish; he had rushed off to the hospital as soon as it was light, missing his customary coffee and cake. He should have had a drink while they were on the estate. Now he would have to wait. He swallowed, trying to coax the saliva into his mouth.

James was relieved. Not that anything had changed; it was just that he had felt some personal responsibility for Wotherspoon before – although there was no reason why he should – and now, having thrashed it out with nearly everyone concerned present, the air seemed to have been cleared. Let things take their course now; he had done his best.

On the whole it had been a satisfactory holiday. All their arrangements were worked out and Helen would have typed the necessary letters while he was out. Now they could start packing and soon, very soon now, Nannie would arrive and then they would be on their way.

Fancy old Norman Parkes turning up after all these years. He, certainly, had never been included in James's plans for the future. Well, one never knew.

Ahmat looked sullen. He had no wish to return home. Of

course, he could divorce Azizah if he wished – but did he? Perhaps he should ask for a posting – the OCPD would understand and, anyway, he would be going on leave himself in six months' time; Kuala Jelang would change. Perhaps if they were in a larger place she might settle down. Somewhere where there was more to occupy her. Perhaps. But he wondered how it would be when he got back that afternoon, after the morning's disgraceful, humiliating scene.

'I'll prepare the yellow rice,' she had yelled. How *could* she? How could she be so cruel? 'Yellow rice, yellow rice,' went the wheels of the truck, 'I'll prepare the yellow rice, yellow rice, yellow rice.'

Wonder why people don't go in for timber more, Donald was wondering. There were some magnificent trees out there and he had already proved in his research work that there were many more species that would grow well here.

So much emphasis on rubber. Seemed like putting too many eggs in one basket, particularly with the threat of synthetics always just around the corner.

Jesus, I wish I hadn't had so much to drink last night, he thought; this motion is beginning to make me feel sick.

Omar kept his eyes on the jungle most of the time, but every so often he would turn and look at the OCPD with an expression almost of love.

With all the sadness of the past behind him, he was truly happy these days. His story was known to everyone in the police station now, but no one sneered at him any more; he was accepted. It was true, as he had said so often of late, that his corporal's stripes meant more to him now than his sergeant-major's crown had ever done. He would miss the Tuan when he went on leave. Oh well, why think about that – there were still a few more months.

The feeling of security that he had enjoyed whilst sitting in the stationary truck was beginning to desert Ramakrishnan.

He had no idea how the terrorists were deployed, or how many of them were actually living on the estate. They had said they needed advance information to stage an ambush in case there were insufficient men around. *In case* – that meant that sufficient men *might* be there.

Everyone in the vicinity of the estate office had seen the

police arrive. The truck had stood for nearly an hour. Plenty of time for them to get organised.

Suddenly Krishnan began to shake. They had scorned his advice about the doctor because he would be unarmed. But what a target this would make. Eight men in the back of the truck and seven of them carried arms. He glanced at Karim. Even the driver had a pistol. Eight weapons at a minimum; uniforms, dead police. Could they resist this prize?

Suppose there *were* sufficient men at hand? Suppose they should choose to set an ambush for to-day? With him on board. If they had seen the truck at all, the chances were that they had also seen him in it – might even have seen him voluntarily going up to the OCPD.

'Is this the fastest you can go?' he asked.

Chee Min had not been able to glean much. There were no Chinese labourers on the estate; only the house-servants. And they were loyal. Hailams, who had worked for Wotherspoon for years. If they knew anything they were keeping it to themselves. They were genuinely fond of the old man, and within five minutes of questioning Chee Min had realised that he would get nowhere.

Oh well, who cared? That was a slap-up do last night. Hand it to Ahmat, he knew how to organise. Pity his wife was such a bitch. He was sorry when he had refused Sally's suggestion that she should join them, because then he might have brought Rose along as well. As it was, etiquette demanded that she stay put. Not that she minded, she had said, she was feeling sick. Poor Rose. Still, with the clinic and Stan at hand, she'd be well cared for when the time came.

His thoughts switched to his motor bike. Wow! What a beaut! Never thought he'd be so enthusiastic about anything less than a car. Just goes to show.

Jogindar Singh was feeling out of condition. His shorts were tight round his stomach and the webbing belt ate into his waist. Time I had a bit more exercise, he thought; sitting in an office all day, I'm becoming overweight. Suvindar was a good cook too. The journey out had been comfortable enough, sitting in the front, but standing at the back, with no protection against the midday sun, was far from comfortable.

Fancy having to give up his seat for a Tamil clerk. Like most northern Indians, Jogindar held his southern brethren in contempt. The Mem should not have hindered me, he thought, I should have dealt with him that day of the parade
He wondered how his wife was getting on.

Stan was experiencing the same feeling that had come over him on New Year's Eve – or rather the beginning of New Year's Day.

He looked down on the truck as though he were floating above it and saw the occupants, like so many ants, each busy with their own thoughts. Fading away, fading out, all of them, even him.

He looked at each of them in turn. The kindly, wrinkled face of Omar; the dissipated face of Donald Thom. James, hot and sweating, the glass eye standing out bleakly against his sunken cheek. The happy face of Vincent; the shamed, unhappy face of Ahmat, and the hot and bulging face of the sergeant-major – that would teach him to eat less! The clear, tanned face of Philip – his first love's second love. And in the front, Wotherspoon's shifty clerk and the slim Malay youth, Karim, husband of the girl whom he very much doubted he would be able to save.

The thought of the girl in labour pulled him sharply back to earth. But even he, the doctor, was not indispensable – if the dresser has any initiative, he thought, he will have got the ambulance over from Kemuning by now. He could trust Ponniah; she was in good hands.

And so, he thought, there is no reason why I should not fade away as well.

Philip was thinking back to Chee Min's wedding; how he had said a prayer of gratitude for the men with whom he served. Omar, Karim, Jogindar Singh, Chee Min and Ahmat – it was Ahmat's doleful face that was giving him these thoughts. Poor bugger, he thought, what awaits him when he gets home? If it had been anyone with less pride it would not have been so bad. But Ahmat, with his serenity and grace – to have that foul-mouthed wench screaming at him in front of the whole station. The bitch. Something would have to be done about her, but what? Perhaps he should talk it over with the OCPS or CPO. Poor devil, it seemed certain at the moment that if one thing did not put paid to his career, another would.

There was something different about the road. Some alteration since this morning. Nonsense, he told himself, it's the shadows, a different angle of light. The trouble was that, ever since the CPO had told him that it would suit the leave roster if he were to go on leave after only two and a half years instead of three, he had been getting jumpy. Nevertheless, leave or not, this was a hell of a road. Incredible that there had never been an ambush on it. The jungle rose steeply on their left as the road unwound downhill. Below them was a ravine, covered with trees and bushes, but as steep as the other side. He peered down. He could not see the bottom, only the tops of the lower trees, many splotched with a vivid orange creeper.

Never an ambush? He thought he had caught a glimpse of something on the road, but at the next bend it wasn't there Nor at the next. Must have been a trick of the light.

At the third bend he saw it again. So did everybody else. Christ, was it a log? Not worth taking a chance. He raised his hand to bang on the driver's cabin and was about to shout the order to debus when he saw that it was only a rotten bough.

The sweat sprang out on his temples like heavy dew and he wiped it away with relief, conscious that the other occupants of the truck were all doing the same thing. He grinned wryly, half to himself, and looked up on hearing Stan's laugh.

'People change,' the doctor remarked. 'Ten years ago I'd have been on my knees by now. Scared bloody stiff!'

He couldn't look less scared, Philip thought, ashamed of his own clammy palms. It had been a bad moment.

They were on a more even stretch of road, with the trees growing farther from the verge and the sun beating full upon them. Momentarily relaxed, the sound of voices rose above the engine, but Philip listened with only half an ear. He knew the road too well to be complacent. Little chance of an ambush for a mile or two, but then they would begin to climb again, there would be more hairpin bends and overhanging foliage. He took stock of their fire power.

Omar was on the Bren, Ahmat and Jogindar had Stens. He had a carbine; so had Don. James had a service revolver strapped to his belt – but count him out, he thought; he was finding it hard enough to remain upright with his one arm on the side of the swaying, jolting vehicle, let alone fire with it. Chee Min was pulling an automatic from his pocket – perhaps he was having similar thoughts – he and Ahmat had pistols too ; also Karim.

Conversation, spasmodic as it had been, soon died. Each was busy with his own thoughts. The heat was intense and those who knew the road began to look forward to the shade to come, despite the danger the closer-growing trees would present.

Karim ran his tongue over the roof of his dry mouth as he changed down to negotiate the first of the hairpin bends. This was the worst part of the journey, almost a pass. Easy enough in a jeep, but driving the GMT for any length of time was always a strain. He should have had a drink when he could have done. Never mind, once on the straight he'd be able to put his foot down.

They were over the ridge and just beginning to descend when Karim saw the log. Placed strategically on the far side of one of the sharpest bends, they came upon it too suddenly to take evasive action. Instinctively he braked.

What the hell's he slowing down for? Philip's head jerked up. 'Keep going, Karim, don't stop,' he shouted.

At the same time James yelled, 'Who threw that stone?'

The object hit the side of the vehicle and bounced off.

'Hand-grenade.' As Philip spoke he opened fire at a movement in the undergrowth. He could see at a glance that it would be impossible to debus; with a steep wooded bank above them and a sheer drop to the ravine below, they could only jump on to the road itself. They would be sitting ducks anyway; better to stay where they were. Their only hope was that the weight of the vehicle would dislodge or surmount the obstacle – he could not see the log – and to make the most of their fire power. There was no turning back.

Ahmat pointed and fired almost simultaneously. 'There, Tuan.'

Philip followed his aim ; both he and Donald fired at once. Omar rattled away, but he was firing blind, although he had a better chance of aiming than anyone else, with his weapon mounted on the cabin roof.

Jogindar Singh grinned as he fired. He had always been pretty useless on the range, but he doubted if it would matter now.

Philip dropped his empty carbine – no time to change the magazine – and drew his pistol. At that moment there was a cry of anguish from above. 'Seems we've got one,' he yelled. They all floundered as the truck hit the log, the impact sending a shudder through the heavy metal body. 'Don't stop, Karim. Whatever you do, don't stop. Oh Christ, this bloody thing's jammed.'

James tossed over his revolver and Philip let the useless automatic drop. As he took aim, a tremendous burst came from the bank above them. The vehicle lurched and began to go slowly over the side.

116. WHEN WIVES WAIT

'I couldn't stay at home.' Helen came quietly through the back door of the OCPD's bungalow, glancing at the two places still laid on the dining-room table as she passed. 'Sorry if I made you jump – one gets into the habit of creeping about at this time of the afternoon, when the children have just gone to sleep.'

'Do you feel like that too?' Sally asked. 'I don't know why I'm so jumpy; it's not yet two o'clock and Philip said he might not be back until three. Have you had lunch?'

'Yes. I had mine with the children. Are you going to have yours?'

'I don't think I want any. I was about to make a cup of coffee though – would you like some?'

'Please, I would.'

Helen followed her out to the old-fashioned kitchen, placed well behind the house. Loud snores emanated from the servants' quarters nearby.

'One thing I've learned from them,' Sally gestured with her head in the direction of the snores, as she emptied half a bottle of kerosene over the wood, 'is how to light a fire. And to think I spent a whole war trying to learn!'

Helen looked on, aghast.

'Stand back,' Sally ordered, and tossed a lighted match on to the wood. Once the explosion had subsided she placed a large tin kettle on the roaring flames.

'I must admit that the one vestige of so-called civilisation that I do long for,' her friend remarked, 'is electricity. And with you around it's positively dangerous to be without it!'

'Oh well, we all have to die some time.'

The moment she made the thoughtless remark, Sally regretted it. Neither of them said anything more until the kettle had boiled and they were carrrying their cups back to the verandah.

'I never really understood that quaint military term "suspended animation",' Helen said, 'but I'm sure this must be it. There's a terrible scent of destiny in the air.'

'Stan knew it at New Year's Eve – did you see his eyes? Dilated like a cat's – or perhaps I was just looking through the champagne.' She paused and Helen knew that her eyes saw farther than the point on which they were fixed, the rain tree with its dancing blooms. 'One day, not very long before we came here, one of my cats died. I was utterly miserable, because animals are no less precious than humans to me, and Philip had taken me away from the house. There was a tin mine not far from our quarter, and we sat on the hillside and watched the little men far below at work; ants, digging up the tin, day after day of heavy, sweated labour – and for what? To eke out a poverty-stricken existence, always too many children and seldom enough to eat, to die in the end. It is not the finality of death that is so shattering, I think, as the irretrievability. The unfairness. Why, I cried, did my little cat have to go? There must be cats down in that mine to whom death would be a happy release, and yet it was my cat, young still, much loved, a rescued stray with a happy life before her. She was gentle and sweet-natured; she'd never done anyone any harm. Why should she be the one to be taken? It was the same during the war – you must remember – why should a young man with everything before him be killed when others, possibly unhappy men with domestic burdens and troubled minds, be allowed to live? And all of a sudden, feeling bereft and alone – although Philip was beside me – I was no longer there, but away and above, looking down on the mineworkers and Philip and I watching them; looking down on myself. And I could imagine God, looking down too, and putting a finger on one man, one animal – you and you. Why should Fate decree that one life should be saved and another destroyed? And then I knew that it was no use fighting; that we have to accept God's will – as old Omar has accepted it – and resign ourselves to being the playthings of Fate.' Her eyes left the rain tree and turned to rest on her friend, giving her a sad little smile. 'Stan felt all that on New Year's Eve – I know, I felt it too.'

'It's a strange thing,' Helen mused, after they had been silent for a moment or two, 'how a knot of people can be drawn together on a small station like this and, whether we like it or not, we all become part of one another's lives. You and James might have met before; so might Philip and I. You and Stan had met.' She paused to take a deep drink and put her coffee cup down. 'I knew him before too, you know.'

Sally's interest immediately perked up.

'Philip thought so,' she said. 'I told him he was talking rot.'

'Philip? How on earth could *he* have known?'

'He didn't. Only guessed. He said it was something about the way you looked at him.'

'Oh God.' Helen's hand went to her throat in an uncharacteristically dramatic gesture. 'I only hope we can get away before James finds out.' She paused again and went slightly pink. 'You must think me an awful fool, Sally, but James is so terribly jealous – for no reason – it's just something in his nature that he can't help. We had a dreadful row before we were married over Stan – James had never met him. only knew he was a Pole – but he suspected it was him the day he arrived here. It's been a nagging worry ever since.'

Sally felt an involuntary stab of jealousy, because she knew instinctively that Helen and Stan had been lovers when she and Stan had not. She was so flabbergasted that she could not think what to say. So she said nothing and walked over to the verandah rail to watch as the sentry in the police station below marched forward to strike the hour. The length of bent railway sleeper was suspended from the eaves of the main building and the hammer lay on a ledge behind it. She watched every detail as the man transferred his rifle to his other shoulder, took the mallet from its shelf and struck the metal crescent twice. The sound of the strokes reached the listeners on the hilltop a fraction of a second after the PC's arm had swung back each time.

'Two o'clock,' Sally said, unnecessarily. 'Another cup?'

Hardly had she poured the coffee and sat down when a hoarse cry rose from the police station. Both women jumped to their feet and saw the sentry move towards the sleeper once again, this time at the double.

Clang, clang, clang, clang, clang, clang, clang, clang! The man had dropped his rifle and was beating the metal with all his might.

'Oh Christ! The general alarm!'

Men came running from every corner of the compound, those on standby in uniform and the rest in varying stages of dress and undress.

Before the sentry had finished sounding the alarm all the police vehicles were beginning to line up in front of the main gate, waiting with engines running. Cameron stepped into the road and stopped a PWD lorry; after a moment's talk the driver turned round and fell into line. Next a civilian Land-Rover was commandeered, but the driver jumped out and ran away; a police driver took his place and that too joined the queue.

The servants now came rushing in as well.

'Is it an ambush, Mem? Has the Tuan been ambushed?' they cried.

'Yes. It is an ambush.'

'Oh Sally, don't *say* that. You don't know. It might be a fire or something. It doesn't have to be an ambush.'

'Yes,' repeated Sally, and her voice was very quiet, 'it is an ambush. I knew before Philip left the house this morning. Ja'afar, go down and see what you can find out – but don't get in anybody's way.'

'Yes, Mem.' The old man sprinted down the steps and a minute later they saw him speaking to the driver of one of the stationary vehicles.

The men were pouring out of the Charge Room now, some still carrying shirts and boots, but each with a weapon in his hand, and began scrambling into the waiting transport.

'Couldn't we ring up now?' Helen asked.

Sally shook her head. 'Not until the flap is over.'

She noticed the eight white knuckles of Helen's hands clenched on the railing, then saw her own. Sixteen points of tension. I'll count twenty, she said to herself, before I make a move. But she did not have to. As Zukifli jumped into the front seat of the leading vehicle and the convoy moved off, the telephone rang.

Helen watched as Sally listened to the crackling voice on the other end for what seemed an eternity, then, 'Thank you,' Sally said in a quiet voice. 'Please let me know when you have some news. Good-bye.'

She turned to her friend. 'That was Cameron. Apparently the Special Branch chap, Bill Young, stayed behind – I knew that Philip was picking him up somewhere *en route* – a man from one of the outlying divisions came in to report that he had heard shooting; it was about half an hour after they had left the estate. It's taken him all this time to get through. Bill is trying to investigate, with a party of SCs from the estate, but, as usual, the only available transport has gone u/s. It doesn't *have* to be them, but Cameron is pretty certain it is. And so am I.'

The only unusual activity in the police compound now was small groups of wives talking together outside the barracks, during what would normally have been their sleeping-time.

Suddenly, a long drawn-out, keening wail rose from the compound and two women dashed into the station inspector's quarters. It was followed shortly by a high-pitched, hysterical scream, as Azizah raced into the middle of the grass, brandishing a cooking-pot over her head. The immediate cause of her actions was not apparent, but women started running towards her from all sides. It was not possible at that distance to distinguish between the many voices, but clearly above them floated the words 'yellow rice' and 'he's dying, he's dead.'

Azizah went into a kind of drunken dance, flinging the pot in the air and catching it; laughing and screeching all the time. The women had stopped at a safe distance and formed a ring about her. The scene seemed set for a lynching, or a trial for witchcraft.

'I think I had better go and sort this out,' said Sally, and strode out of the house and down the steps. In a way it was a blessing to have something to do.

Nodding to the sentry in passing, she marched straight past the police station and through the milling throng of women, who gave way as they saw her approach. What had been in her mind when she left the house had been forgotten; without further thought she went straight up to Azizah and hit her a stinging blow across the left cheek, then with the back of her hand across the right.

There was a stunned silence throughout the compound. Azizah dropped the cooking-pot and gaped open-mouthed at the woman who had dared to hit her.

Neither said a word and Sally turned on her heel and walked away. One of the women plucked at her sleeve as she passed and pointed to the OCPS's quarters. From where Helen watched, she saw Sally pause and say something to the woman, then continue on her way. Azizah had walked slowly back to her own house, leaving the cooking-pot lying on the grass, and the crowd had begun to melt away. It had had the desired effect, but Helen had shuddered when Sally raised her arm, and Siti, standing beside her, had murmured,

'No, Mem, don't hit her,' and given a start when the hand met its target.

Helen saw the elderly police lieutenant leave the OCPD's office to intercept Sally; saw them speak for a moment, then he put an arm across her shoulders for an instant and they walked back to the police station together. Again they paused and soon Sally's footsteps were heard upon the steps.

Helen could not hear the words, but Cameron had said, 'Thank you, Mrs Morrison. I'd have shut that woman up myself if ye hadna' come along.' And, 'I'll let ye know the moment there's news of the boss.'

'Ought you to have done that?' she asked, as Sally re-entered the house.

'No, I ought not.' She slumped into the nearest chair, head in hands, and Helen wondered whether to go over to her or not. It was only a moment, however, before she regained her composure and, smiling at Siti, she said, 'The sergeant-major's wife has had another son; you predicted right – as usual.'

To Helen she said, 'You and I are not the only wives. That woman was mouthing the foulest obscenities about poor Mat, interspersed with shrieks of joy because she is so sure that he is dead. She's a bit off her rocker, I think, but I couldn't let it pass. There is Suvindar Kaur and Rokiah – the driver's wife, who has been taken to Kemuning, although old Ponniah doesn't think she'll survive the journey – and Rose Lee; we're not the only ones.'

'No,' Helen admitted. 'You were quite right; I shouldn't have questioned it.'

Sally picked up her cup of coffee; it was stone cold.

'Be a dear and make us some more,' she said to Siti, then walked across the room to fetch the box of cigarettes. 'I'd given up smoking, but there *are* times . . .'

Helen nodded.

As Sally held the match for her friend, their eyes met over the tiny flame, each seeking comfort and assurance from the other; each determined to mask despair.

Then they sat down in silence to wait.

EPILOGUE

Abdul Karim died with the first burst. Beside him Ramakrishnan screamed as he saw the blood-spattered body slump over the wheel and felt the heavy vehicle leave the road.

Stanislaus Olshewski smiled as he looked straight into the muzzle of a Bren gun, mounted on the bank at exactly the right height to mow down the occupants of the truck and camouflaged with branches and twigs. He took one of the first bullets straight between the eyes and continued to smile in death.

Omar bent over the doctor's body and never straightened up again. His head split open like a ripe fruit and spilt its contents over James Weatherby, who looked up with a start and, as he did so, clutched his stomach, tightly closing his eyes in pain.

The vehicle slid gently over the side of the precipice and, equally slowly, began to turn. For a fleeting second, those occupants who were still alive, had a horrifying view of the rock-strewn slope towards which they were now hurtling.

Philip Morrison and Vincent Lee Chee Min hung on to one side of the truck and each other, as it somersaulted, righted itself and careered down the hillside again.

On the opposite side Sharif Ahmat too hung on with both hands.

During the first roll Donald Thom was hurled out as though he were a rag doll and hit the slope a split second before the armoured truck arrived on top of him. His neck was broken and although he remained alive long enough to see Jogindar Singh flung out at the next turn, his eyes soon glazed over and within a matter of seconds he was dead.

The truck came to a slithering halt and, with a final jolt, spewed most of its remaining passengers on to the ground, before rolling on to its side.

Only Ahmat was thrown completely clear. Philip lay with his legs trapped under several tons of metal; Chee Min crouched close beside him and, from inside the cabin, Ramakrishnan screamed with fear and frustration as he tried, unsuccessfully, to open the jammed door.

Except for those high-pitched screams, everything was silent. Above them the road appeared deserted and around them not a twig moved.

'Shut up, you little bastard,' yelled Philip, 'or I'll come and slit your throat.'

The screams stopped abruptly and gave way to a low whining mumble.

Jogindar lay with his head against the bole of a tree. His turban had saved it from being bashed in, but his back was broken and he knew that he would never move again. He had inherited his father's spirit though, and even in such straights he was amused by the OCPD's threat, when his legs were pinned firmly under the GMT and his hands appeared to be useless, bloody stumps. He smiled, his teeth showing bright white in his full black beard.

Philip lay silent and still, taking stock of the situation. He himself was useless; he must have put out his hands to protect his face and hit something on the way out. Either his wrists were broken, or very badly sprained. His legs were only visible from above the knees. As yet he could feel no pain, but he dreaded to think what lay under that heavy mass of iron. To his left Chee Min squatted on his heels, holding one arm with the other and rocking backwards and forwards, obviously in pain.

Jogindar continued to smile and rolled his eyes, but there was something unnatural about his position.

'Can you move, Dato?' Philip called.

Jogindar lifted his arms and let them fall. He tried but could not shake his head.

'It must be my spine, Sahib,' he replied. 'Only my arms can move.'

At that moment James crawled from the vehicle, looking dazed and with blood pouring from a gash across his temples.

'Grenade hit me in the stomach,' he explained. 'Must have been a dud, but it creased me; and I couldn't move before.'

He got to his feet and tested his limbs, while the others watched. He looked a dreadful sight, but much of the blood on him was Omar's.

James in turn looked at Philip and his mind at once flew back to a tail gunner, legs trapped, scrabbling in the flames. 'Thank God it didn't catch fire,' he murmured.

'Can you stand, Chee Min?' Philip asked. The sooner the able-bodied amongst them went for help the better.

'Bastards got me in the arm.'

The DO went to him and rolled up the sleeve of his shirt. The elbow was shattered; a bloody mess and Chee Min stifled a scream with his other hand as he touched it.

James was wearing a scarf tucked into his shirt; he pulled it off. 'If someone can tie this, it'll do as a sling.'

'I have a field dressing,' Ahmat said. He appeared to be the only one uninjured.

'Mat, you must go for help,' Philip said. 'If you can get to the main road, there's a Chinese kedai there that has a telephone. We'll need a stretcher for the sergeant-major.'

But Ahmat shook his head. 'No, Tuan. I won't leave you. The DO and Sergeant Lee can get there just as fast.'

'I'm giving you an order, Mat.' Philip knew that there was little hope for anyone who was left behind; better that everyone who could should go. 'See if you can fix Sergeant Lee's arm, then off you go. No delays.'

Ahmat tried to stand up, but one leg straight away collapsed under him. He gave a low moan of pain and sat down. Rolling up a leg of his jungle green trousers, he exposed a perfect compound fracture, the tip of bone gleaming white against the brown skin. Both Philip and Chee Min gasped and Ahmat himself went a sickly, greenish grey.

'You see, Tuan? Tuan Allah has taken it out of my hands. I have no choice but to stay.'

As he finished speaking, their attention was attracted by a sound from the road above. Philip held up his hand for silence.

'The only thing to do is to lie still and keep quiet. If they think we're all dead they may go away.' His voice was little more than a whisper.

'Loot.' The one word was spoken by Chee Min. 'They may take their time, but eventually they will come for our watches and our guns.'

Philip himself did not hold out much hope. He too knew that they would come to examine the bodies, strip them of their uniforms and take whatever there was to take. How they would kill whoever they found alive did not bear thinking about. Hacking to death with parangs was the most common method, but, not long after his arrival in the district, a police lieutenant and his men had been thrown on to their jeep and burned alive and Chee Min's brother-in-law had had a six-inch nail driven into his head. He shuddered involuntarily and quickly looked round to see if anyone had noticed. He of all people must not show fear. James stared up at the road; Jogindar and Ahmat both lay with their eyes closed and Chee Min was praying in a quiet voice, telling his beads by heart.

A cracking branch caused Philip's ears to strain and Ahmat's and Jogindar's eyes to fly wide open. Chee Min stopped his prayer. James continued to stare, unmoving.

There were several minutes of silence, then again the undeniable sounds of movement in the undergrowth.

From the cabin of the truck Ramakrishnan let out a wail. 'Oh Tuan, sir, please to shoot me! Shoot me quickly! Please, sir! I will be suffering most terrible death at hands of Communist terrorists. I would be better deserving death from the hands of you, whom I have betrayed also.'

And then, in fits and starts, spasms and long strings of words, sometimes moaned and sometimes screamed, out came the whole sordid story. All five listeners understood English well enough to get the portent. All were silent.

Again from the truck came the high-pitched, pleading wail. 'Have mercy on me, kind sir! Please to kill me, sir! Do not leave me for the bandits.'

'I would willingly kill you,' growled Jogindar Singh, 'if I could move. But it is justice that the terrorists should look after you.'

Krishnan moaned and the sergeant-major gave a maniacal laugh.

'Quiet, all of you,' commanded Philip, and listened.

The noises in the undergrowth had started again. Cautious, but getting nearer. Still, it was a long climb down and they did not know what reception lay at the bottom. He knew that they would not waste ammunition in finding out.

'Come one step further and we open fire,' he roared in Malay.

All sounds ceased immediately and after a few minutes voices were to be heard, low but audible.

'What are they saying, Chee Min?' Philip asked in a whisper.

'They are arguing, sir.' Then they all kept quiet while he listened.

The talk went on interminably and Philip succeeded in placing three different voices. They argued for nearly twenty minutes and could then be heard retracing their steps.

Jogindar Singh let out a most blood-curdling laugh and there were distinct sounds of hurrying at the top of the ravine.

'There were three men,' Chee Min told them. 'One wanted to throw a couple of hand-grenades down, but the others warned him of their strict orders that grenades and ammo must be conserved. Much of the talk was impressing on him that all three would be punished for his act. One of them wanted to come down and finish us off with his bayonet, but the other two were more cautious – they did not know what our fire power consisted of, nor how many of us were left alive. They knew that only one was dead. They have gone back to the estate for reinforcements, but they will be back later on.'

Donald Thom's body was the only one lying out in the open for the bandits to see. Those of Omar and Stan had, for some unknown reason, remained huddled at the bottom of the truck and Karim was still wedged behind the steering-wheel. There was no reason for them to know that only half the original number were still alive.

'Now is the time for you two to go,' Philip said. 'Your quickest route will be to follow the river – the road is all hairpin bends from here to the main road. You should hit Tukul Puteh Estate, but if you don't, you'll come out by the bridge and the Chinese shop-house is not far from it. Get through to the police station and Cameron will do the rest. Now. For heaven's sake get cracking while the going's good. Good luck.'

James bent to grip Philip's shoulder, his face working, but no words would come out. He touched the hands of Ahmat, and Jogindar and Chee Min did likewise.

'Good luck, good luck, good luck.'

The place seemed unutterably lonely when the two men had gone. Pushing their way slowly through the undergrowth, James limping and Chee Min hanging on to his arm, they could be heard for a long time after they had disappeared from view.

Philip calculated. It would take the CTs the best part of an hour to reach the estate – unless they met a party on the way – and then they would have to tell their story. He knew from experience that the leader would not believe one man straight away. Each would have to recount his version, then there would be question and answer, verification of facts; that should take at least another half-hour. Getting their numbers together would not take long, provided they were not otherwise employed, then the trek back. They should have at the least two, at the most three, hours. If anyone had heard the shooting and reported it without delay – and if it could be heard on the estate Bill Young was sure to act so, help *could* arrive by then. James and Chee Min would not be able to move fast; it was a long way on foot to the main road – the time would be much the same. There was nothing they could do but wait and hope. He told them what he had been thinking.

'Anyone any arms?' he asked.

It appeared that all weapons but his had been lost in the descent. He had taken the revolver from James and stuffed it in his shirt as the truck began to fall. It was still there, cold against his skin.

'Mat,' he called, 'if you can get over to me, the DO's revolver is inside my shirt. I only remember firing once, there should still be five rounds.' He paused then, not wanting to sound melodramatic, but nevertheless to face facts. 'None of our religions tolerate the taking of human life, neither murder nor suicide, but knowing what the terrorists will do to us if help does not arrive in time, helpless as we are, I believe that God will understand and forgive.'

Ahmat dragged himself over to the OCPD, inch by painful inch, pausing several times on the way. At least he reached him and drew the revolver from his shirt.

'Look at me,' Philip said quietly, attempting unsuccessfully to grip his shoulder with one of his bloodied hands. 'This is the most difficult task that any man can be asked to perform. Normally it would fall to me, but now you are the only one who can carry it out. Understand that this is only as a last resort. With luck help may arrive in time, but if it doesn't and we hear the bandits coming down the slope, you must act at once. The Tamil first, then the sergeant-major, myself, and then yourself. If you hesitate before shooting any man, think quickly what his fate may be if you don't.'

Ahmat had nodded several times during the exhortation and a succession of expressions had flitted across his face, but he had seemed unable to speak. Philip gave him time to think and was relieved to see his eyes harden and his jaw set.

'I will do it,' he answered, 'if I have to, but I pray that it will not be necessary.'

'I only remember firing once, but you had better count the rounds.'

Ahmat broke the revolver and jerked his head in the direction of the cabin. 'Surely you are not going to waste a round on that little tick,' he said, and Jogindar gave a great guffaw.

At that Krishnan burst into a new stream of lamentations.

'Shut up,' roared Philip, 'or we *will* leave you to the mercy of the terrorists. Not one more word.'

There was immediate silence.

If Ahmat had known that, besides his other crimes, Krishnan had also been responsible for the death of his friend, Dick Richardson, he would no doubt have refused point blank. But he had been ordered to shoot the Tamil and, if it came to it, he would.

Jogindar had actually seen Philip fire twice and he thought he had heard the DO fire as well, before passing the weapon over to the OCPD. He could not be sure of that, but he was sure that there could not be five rounds left in the chamber. He also knew that the bandits would be back – and sooner, he thought, than the OCPD had said. He tried once more to move his legs and head, without success. Even if help did arrive – which he thought most unlikely in the time – would life still be worth living? He had visited India often enough as a youth to know what cripples were. It would be the end of active service, the end of the police for him. And of what use would he be to his family? Nothing but a burden; if he lived at all.

Carefully, so as not to attract attention, he felt in the folds of his turban and extracted a razor blade, new and greasy sharp. He had kept the blade there, against emergencies, for many years, but never before had had cause to use it. While Ramakrishnan whined and the OCPD scolded, he drew the blade deeply across each wrist, then, burying it in the soil beside him, he folded his hands over his stomach so that the source of the blood should not be seen. He lay there quietly, the fingers of one hand gently caressing his steel bangle and thinking of his father.

'Sahib,' he called after a while, and forcing a smile, 'Sahib, no need to keep a bullet for me – I must have been hit in the belly without realising it before.'

A great dark patch was already spreading across his chest and abdomen, staining the khaki cloth. It was clear that he would not last long.

'Good-bye, old man. May you be as brave in the next world as you have been in this.'

In common with the rest of the police station, Philip always thought of Jogindar as old, though in fact he was younger than himself.

'There are three rounds,' Ahmat said abruptly. He had been holding the broken revolver in his hand all this time. He now clicked it shut and shoved it inside his own shirt.

Philip tried not to look at his watch too obviously although there was little point in subterfuge at this stage. They still had at least an hour to go. He thought of James and Chee Min and wondered what progress they had made. He was glad that James had not been killed – it would have been so unfair, only a few weeks away from a new life. If the journey took them long enough, he could pick up a little Australiana from Chee Min in advance! Better not to think about his own future; of Sally. He resisted the temptation to glance at his watch again and looked at his companions instead.

Jogindar Singh appeared to have fallen asleep; he had in fact been dead for half an hour. Ahmat lay on his back with his eyes wide open, staring up at the sky.

'What are you thinking about, Mat?' he asked after a while.

Ahmat slowly turned his head and surprised Philip with his peaceful smile.

'I was thinking of the day I met my wife. I was being very, eh, debonair – is that the right word?'

'Could be.'

'I don't usually drink much. but I'd had a few beers I suppose; at any rate I felt very bold – I wanted to show off. I had never danced in public before, but when one of my pals dared me to go on the floor, I went up with a great flourish to face Azizah, who was to become my wife. Did you know she had been a ronggeng girl?' He didn't wait for Philip's reply. 'I thought she was the most beautiful woman I had ever seen – I still do.'

His voice faded out and when Philip turned to look at him he saw that there were tears in his eyes. He said nothing and in a little while Ahmat frowned and spoke again.

'After this morning I do not believe that Tuan Allah means me to see her again.'

'Nonsense,' said Philip briskly. 'It will be all right. By this time she will be feeling sorry for all the things she said – you wait and see.'

'Where did you first see your wife, sir?' Ahmat asked, deliberately changing the subject. He in turn saw Philip's eyes go soft, and smiled.

'She was floating down from the sky in the moonlight,' Philip said softly. It was a different world; difficult to believe now that it had ever existed.

'The Mem – floating?'

Philip actually laughed. The incredulous tone of Ahmat's voice had quite taken his mind off the present for a fleeting moment.

'She's not all that heavy,' he said, 'and besides, she was at the end of a parachute.'

'A parachute? Wah!'

Before there was time for further explanation, the sound of movement on the road above drew their attention. So they were back sooner than expected. Must have been better organised than he had thought.

Philip counted ten. If it were the police they would call out, but there had been no sound of a vehicle approaching.

They were not left in doubt for long.

'Red devils, running dogs,' a high voice floated down from the road, 'we are coming. Muslim pigs. And you Indians – we shall defecate on your sacred cows when you are dead.'

'Ahmat, now. But don't hurry, take time to aim – you can't afford to miss.'

Ahmat dragged himself off while the voice from above continued its empty insults.

But it was not the voice that had caused Philip to act. The crashing in the undergrowth of many feet announced the departure of the terrorists from the top. It was impossible to estimate the number accurately, but the sound of violent movement was covering such an area that there could not be less than ten. He reckoned considerably more.

Ramakrishnan sat frozen with terror, his eyes rolling and his face grey. He did not move as Ahmat leaned through opposite window and fired at point blank range.

Crawling back to where Philip lay trapped, he reached out to Jogindar to make sure that he was not still alive. It needed but a touch and, relieved, he crawled on.

Ahmat's mouth formed a hideous grimace as he felt tears prick his eyes and he tried to control them. He looked at the OCPD; the terrorists were still a little way off, if only they could fight it out. But he, who had seen the guerillas at work during the war, knew better than anyone what the odds were.

'Don't waste time, Mat,' Philip's lips barely moved. 'You must not forget yourself.'

'Please, Tuan, turn your head; I cannot shoot when I can see your face.'

Philip smiled and turned his head.

Ahmat gave a great choking sob, as he pulled the trigger for the last time.

'Take that, you filthy, murdering swine,' he shouted, hurling the empty weapon in the direction of the oncoming men. Then, closing his eyes, he lay back to wait for them to come.

Long after the last alien sound had ceased, when the dust had settled and the leaves stopped their quivering, the insects resumed their song.

Below them, the beetle lay on its side, stripped clean; its armour dull and lifeless, untouched by the rays of the setting sun.

Deep in the ravine, already swathed in the shades of night, the Styx-like, yellow river roared, crashing its way towards the sea. And in the distance, disinterested in the foibles of humankind, the blue, eternal mountains slept on.

GLOSSARY

Adat custom
Adohi! Oh dear! Alas!
Allahumma! Oh! God!
Alor place
Amok furious attack, while temporarily insane
Ang pow present, traditionally red packet containing money (Chinese)
Api fire
Atap palm thatch

Baju garment
Baju kurong long loose shirt, worn over sarong
Bakau type of mangrove
Barang things, stuff, 'clobber'
Batu stone, mile
Belachan strong prawn paste, eaten with curry
Belimbing a small fruit
Belukar secondary jungle
Bersanding 'sitting in state' part of Malay marriage ceremony
Betel small nutlike fruit, chewed like tobacco
Bintang star
Bukit hill

Changkol type of hoe
Che Mr, Mrs or Miss; used for women more often than men

Chempaka a sweet-smelling, flowering tree
Cheongsam sheathlike Chinese dress

Datin female of Dato
Dato grandfather, title (courtesy title for senior NCOs)
Daun leaf
Deepavali Hindu 'festival of lights'
Degil stubborn
Durian a large, strong-smelling fruit

Fukien southern Chinese race and dialect

Gunong mountain

Haj pilgrimage to Mecca
Haji man who has made the pilgrimage to Mecca, title
Hajjah female of Haji
Hakka southern Chinese race and dialect
Haram forbidden by Muslim law
Hari Raya Puasa holiday following the Muslim fasting month
Hijau green
Hitam black
Hokkien southern Chinese race and dialect

Inche Mr (courtesy title for police inspectors)

Jaga to watch, night watchman
Jakun aboriginal tribe from southern Malaya
Jambu guava
Joget modern Malay dance

Kampong village
Kangani overseer on rubber estate (Tamil)
Kaum Ibu womenfolk ; in this case the women's section of a political party
Kebaya tight-fitting Malay blouse
Kedai shop
Keling, or *Kling* Malay for Tamils or Telegus (now considered derogatory)
Kelong a large fish trap
Kempeitai secret police, 'gestapo' (Japanese)
Kenduri feast
Keris long Malay dagger with wavy blade

Kilat shining, lightening
Kolek type of canoe
Kong Hee Fatt Choy Happy New Year (Chinese)
Kongsi communal business or association, usually Chinese
Kuala river mouth
Kubu fort
Kuning yellow

Langsat a small fruit, sweet white flesh with thin brown skin
Lima five

Mak Mother
Mangosteen a smallish round white fruit with thick purple skin
Maraiee Japanese name for Malaya
Mas gold
Masok to enter, 'Come in'
Mata-mata policeman (literally: eyes)
Mee ribbon-like noodles (Chinese)
Merah red
Min Yuen plain clothes terrorists, food and money collectors (Chinese)

Nah! Take that!
Nasib fate
Nasib baik good fortune, thank God for that!
Negri country, state

Orang utan large ape (literally: jungle person)

Padang field at centre of most Malayan towns, 'village green'
Padi rice, in growing state
Pak Father
Palong trough, scaffolding used in tin mining
Pandanus type of palm, much used for weaving mats
Papaya a large melon type, marrow-shaped fruit
Parang long-bladed, all-purpose knife, both domestic and a weapon
Pasir sand
Penghulu headman, minor chief
Perak silver
Pokok tree
Pontianak ghost of a woman who died in childbirth (Malay folklore)

Puan courtesy title, extra polite form of Mrs or Miss
Puasa Muslim fasting month, Ramadan
Puteh white

Rambutan a small fruit with hairy red skin
Ramvong a Siamese dance
Rei bow (Japanese)
Rimau tiger
Ronggeng a Malay dance

Sakai generic term for aborigines
Sambal side dishes with curry
Samfoo pyjama-type suit worn by Chinese women (Chinese)
Sampan general term for small boats
Sarong sheath, skirt-type garment worn by Malays of both sexes
Satay mutton or beef cooked on a skewer, similar to kebabs
Selamat Hari Raya Happy Hari Raya (literally: Peaceful Holiday)
Selamat jalan bon voyage (literally: peace on your going)
Selamat tinggal good-bye (literally: peace on your staying)
Sembilan nine
Selendang scarf worn round the head or shoulders by Malay women
Sharif man claiming descent from the Prophet Muhammad
Sharifa female of Sharif
Songkok velvet cap worn by Malay men, usually black
Sungei river
Syonan Japanese name for Singapore

Tahan hold on, bear up
Tanah earth, land
Tanjong cape, headland
Taukeh, or *Towkay* Chinese merchant
Tiga suku three-quarters, slang term for someone 'not all there'
Timbusu a tall, flowering tree
Toddy palm wine, mostly drunk by Tamils
Tukul hammer
Tuan Sir, or Mr in extra polite address

Ulu back of beyond, interior

Wah! exclamation of amazement or surprise
Wayang theatre, show